A BITTER WIND

BOOKS BY THE AUTHOR

Billy Boyle
The First Wave
Blood Alone
Evil for Evil
Rag and Bone
A Mortal Terror
Death's Door
A Blind Goddess
The Rest Is Silence
The White Ghost
Blue Madonna
The Devouring
Solemn Graves
When Hell Struck Twelve
The Red Horse
Road of Bones
From the Shadows
Proud Sorrows
The Phantom Patrol
A Bitter Wind

The Refusal Camp: Stories

On Desperate Ground
Souvenir
Shard
Freegift

A BITTER WIND

A Billy Boyle World War II Mystery

James R. Benn

SOHO CRIME

Published by
Soho Press, Inc.
227 W 17th Street
New York, NY 10011
www.sohopress.com

Copyright © 2025 by James R. Benn

All rights reserved.

This is a work of fiction. Names, characters, places, and incidents either are the product of the author's imagination or are used fictitiously, and any resemblance to actual persons, living or dead, businesses, companies, events, or locales is entirely coincidental.

Library of Congress Cataloging-in-Publication Data

Names: Benn, James R., author.
Title: A bitter wind / James R. Benn.
Description: New York, NY : Soho Crime, 2025. | Series: Billy Boyle World War II mystery ; 20
Identifiers: LCCN 2025003393

ISBN 978-1-64129-646-5
eISBN 978-1-64129-647-2

Subjects: LCSH: Boyle, Billy (Fictitious character)—Fiction. | World War, 1939-1945—Fiction. | LCGFT: Detective and mystery fiction. | Historical fiction. | Novels.
Classification: LCC PS3602.E6644 B58 2025 | DDC 813/.6—dc23/eng/20250204
LC record available at https://lccn.loc.gov/2025003393

Printed in the United States of America

10 9 8 7 6 5 4 3 2 1

EU Responsible Person (for authorities only)
eucomply OÜ
Pärnu mnt 139b-14
11317 Tallinn, Estonia
hello@eucompliancepartner.com
www.eucompliancepartner.com

Dedicated to
Wesley Grace Countiss and Adalynn James Ross

Our two newest great-grandchildren—cousins born five days apart, August 2024.

Every child begins the world again.
—Henry David Thoreau

There's an east wind coming all the same, such a wind as never blew on England yet. It will be cold and bitter, Watson, and a good many of us may wither before its blast. But it's God's own wind none the less and a cleaner, better stronger land will lie in the sunshine when the storm has cleared.

—Arthur Conan Doyle, *His Last Bow*

A BITTER WIND

CHAPTER ONE

Christmas Day, 1944

THE BODY WAS still warm.

Warm, but no pulse, I realized, as I felt his neck right below the jawline. He could have been here three minutes or three hours, but what really concerned me was how much time I had left on this narrow ledge. I was hundreds of feet atop a dazzling white cliff, the frigid English Channel launching waves against the rocks below.

I grasped his collar with one hand and pulled as I struggled to keep a foothold in the crumbling chalk. I dug in my heel, but all that did was send a cascade of pebbles and dirt sliding down the incline before they tumbled over the edge beyond the dead man's feet. I reached out with my free hand to grasp a tuft of grass sprouting from the white chalk, but it came away and threw me off-balance. I tried to dig my fingers into the soil, but nothing offered a solid grip. I felt the body move. Was this guy still alive?

No. The body was deadweight, and I was holding on to it as it slipped away. I was fighting gravity, and it was a losing battle. Small stones clattered below each time I pulled him toward me. The only thing between us and a hard fall was a few strands of rusting barbed wire.

"Billy!" Diana shouted from above. I risked a glance over my shoulder and saw her greatcoat flung my way. "Grab it!"

The sleeve hem was a foot from my hand. Diana gripped one

sleeve with both hands. She was lying prone, so I didn't have to worry I'd drag her over the edge. I pressed my body hard against the sloping ground and stretched out my arm. The greatcoat was almost in reach. I pulled the body closer, my arm quivering against the weight.

"Let him go!" Diana shouted. It was good advice, but I knew I wouldn't take it. Couldn't take it, not with the sticky feel of blood on my hand where I had him by the collar. This wasn't just a random fall. Someone had knocked this Yank on the head and shoved him over.

It was murder. And that was something I couldn't let go.

I tried again. I jammed my toes into the crumbling grit and dragged the body a few inches more up the incline as I strained to reach the coat, my muscles taut from the effort.

I grasped the sleeve, clutching the wool serge in the palm of my hand. It gave a little, not much, as Diana held tight against the weight of two bodies. I knew she couldn't pull me, but if I could get up onto the coat, our weight might be spread out enough to keep the ground from falling out from under us.

I took a deep breath and let go, trying for a few inches higher. It worked. I got my shoulder onto the wool serge, the coarse, solid fabric reassuring. I was sweating even as the cold winds blew up the cliff face, and my heart pounded from the exertion. I took a moment to rest. As soon as I relaxed, I felt the body slip. I had a good grip on his collar, but the slack corpse was letting gravity have its way, and his arms were about to slip out of the leather flight jacket. I didn't have long before that was all I'd take to the top.

"Come on," I said to my dead friend through gritted teeth. I did my best to bunch up his collar and hold everything in place as I lunged forward and landed a good grip on the open greatcoat, right in the armhole.

"You okay up there?" I gasped out to Diana.

"Yes! You're getting closer."

I made another move. I wrenched the body onto the coat and grabbed for the greatcoat collar, feeling the brass buttons dig into my palms. This would work. The avalanche of stones subsided as I pressed my cheek against the rough wool and sucked in air. It was less than a yard to the top, and this last bit was firm. That's what had fooled me going down: the first two steps were solid, then things started giving way.

I risked letting go of the coat and took the body by the arm and pulled him higher. I maneuvered his head above mine before I had to hold on to the coat again and stabilize things.

"I can almost reach him," Diana said. "But I'd have to let go of my coat."

"Hang on," I grunted. I moved the body up again, using both hands for a few seconds. Now the corpse blocked my view of Diana, but we were getting closer. "Let go, just for a second."

"All right," Diana said. "Now."

I felt the slack as she let go, but the coat stayed put. She grabbed the body with one hand while I hoisted it up. I pushed, she pulled, and in seconds the dead man's head and shoulders were safely on flat ground.

Without that added burden, I was able to get up onto my knees and crawl the last few feet as Diana dragged the corpse onto the path.

"My god, that was hard," Diana said. She knelt next to me as I drew in deep lungfuls of air. She grasped my hand and rolled back my sleeve. "You're bleeding. Are you hurt?"

"It's his," I said, and nodded toward the body. "From the back of his head."

"This wasn't an accident, then," Diana said as she continued to check my wrist to be certain I wasn't injured. Satisfied, she pulled my sleeve back into place and worked at cleaning the blood off her fingers with a handkerchief.

"Not unless he whacked himself on the head as he jumped down the cliff," I said. "We need to get the police here."

"There's a constable in Capel-le-Ferne," Diana said, and jammed the handkerchief in her trench coat pocket. "He can call in an inspector from Folkestone and watch the body until he gets here."

"One of us has to stay," I said as my eyes rested on the lifeless form I'd dragged up the cliff.

"That would be you, Billy," Diana said, and looked around. "You need to catch your breath, and I know where to find the constable. Watch out, the killer could still be about."

"That's good advice," I said. "Be careful yourself."

I smiled and Diana took off down the path at a trot. The jeep was only a half mile away, but I worried that the killer was just as close. I stood up and brushed the dirt off my trousers and Ike jacket. I put on the Mackinaw coat I'd thrown off before I climbed down, grateful for the warmth.

Even so, I shivered as I looked down at the body. A major in the Army Air Force, evidenced by the insignia on his leather flight jacket. I straightened his limbs and tried to give him what dignity I could. I fetched his service cap and placed it under his arm.

It was the cap that had first caught our attention. Diana and I had been strolling along, arm in arm, while enjoying the view of the White Cliffs of Dover along the curving shoreline. She'd recently been posted to RAF Hawkinge, an air base outside of Folkestone, and was lucky enough to get a half day off at Christmas. I'd come down from London and met her at the gate, since I didn't have permission to enter the base. Lots of hush-hush stuff going on there, and I didn't have the need to know. I didn't care either, as long as we had time to spend together.

It was a rare sunny winter's day, with cold wind blowing in from the Channel. That wind had sent the service cap floating up and swirling on a gust before it dropped at our feet. That took us a couple of steps off the path to where we peered down the crumbling chalk cliff face. We thought the guy had taken a tumble too close to the edge. He'd landed on a narrow ledge above barbed wire coils that had probably been strung during the invasion scares early in the war. He was close enough to the edge that we thought he was in danger of rolling off if he came to and tried to get up. That's what sent me down what looked like a stable path. True enough for the first two steps, but then the loose, chalky soil gave way, and I skidded like Max West sliding into second at Braves Field back in Boston.

I was lucky the pilot halted my momentum. Deadweight came in handy sometimes.

I studied the guy. About my age and height, maybe a touch shorter. Slim, with a firm jaw now gone slack and hazel eyes fixed on the sky. Brown hair, recently cut. I pushed his lower jaw shut and closed his eyelids. It was as much for me as for him. The stunned look of death is never a pretty sight, and it wasn't a look I wanted haunting me while I waited alone on this windswept path.

The gleaming cliffs had less appeal than they'd had when we started this stroll, and I found myself thinking like a cop. Which is what my job in civilian life had been. Still was, sort of. I looked around at what now was a crime scene. No bloody blunt instrument lying around. No blood spatters that I could see, and not a single indication of a struggle. The only marks on the ground were from Diana and me dragging the body.

I looked at his hands. No bruised knuckles or defensive wounds. He'd been hit low on the back of his head, slightly to the right. A complete surprise. I took a few steps back and imagined walking with the major. A half step back and I take out my weapon—a lead pipe, a sap, or even a solid rock. One hard whack and he's over the edge. Did the killer count on the fall finishing the job? Did he hightail it out of here without even looking?

No. The urge to look over the cliff's edge would have been impossible to resist. What did the assailant think when he saw his victim only a few yards away? Was he too frightened to descend? Possibly. Or too smart, maybe.

Who's to say it was a man, anyway? Many women are capable of striking such a blow. Especially those like Diana, trained by the Special Operations Executive. But any woman angry enough could crack a skull from behind. Whatever the weapon was, it was likely tossed over the edge to be washed clean by the crashing waves.

I knelt by the body even as I told myself to back off and leave it to the local constabulary. This wasn't Boston. And I was here on leave, visiting my girlfriend after a grueling investigation in France that involved way too many German tanks. But idle hands and all that, and in a moment, I found myself checking for identification. Nothing in the outer pockets. I unzipped the flight jacket and reached inside, rewarded with the crinkle of paper. I withdrew two sheets, folded into quarters.

The wind flapped the papers as I opened them. I held them tight, which left smudged traces of the dead man's blood. But that wasn't the problem.

The problem was the word RESTRICTED at the top of each page. The words "Jackal" and "Jostle" were tossed around like someone knew what they meant. I sure didn't, and I had no idea what the maze of wiring diagrams were for.

But what I did know was that this information was worth killing for.

CHAPTER TWO

I WALKED UP and down the path to stay warm, keeping the body in sight as I wondered what was holding Diana up. Her pace usually left me gasping, so I knew it hadn't taken her long to get to the jeep. Maybe the constable was out investigating whatever small-time crime folks got up to around here. The village of Capel-le-Ferne wasn't exactly teeming with villains and thieves, although the Royal Air Force base at Hawkinge, a mile north, meant that the local pubs would do a brisk business. Which meant the occasional fistfight, especially if any Yank flyboys came calling.

"Is that what happened to you, pal?"

I didn't expect an answer. I didn't even have a name for the guy so I could ask him nicely. His field scarf was neatly knotted and tucked into his dark brown wool shirt. Even after being murdered and dragged up a cliff, he still looked like the kind of man who took care of himself. His fingernails were clean and trimmed. Shoes buffed to a sparkle. He had a few gray hairs sprouting around his temples. Maybe he was older than most pilots, or perhaps air combat had aged him. Crow's-feet spread from the outer corner of each eye, an occupational hazard from squinting into the sun to spot Kraut fighters. As curious as I was, I didn't want to disturb the crime scene, or him, by rummaging around and pulling out his dog tags.

Besides, it wasn't my case. I was just here to visit my girl before I headed back to France and whatever job my boss at SHAEF had lined up for me. I'd handled plenty of stiffs back when I was a cop in Boston before the war, and to stumble over a murder victim would've cinched it as my investigation. But I was wearing khaki, not blue, so I figured I'd spend my time providing the constable a statement, then give Diana a kiss goodbye at the heavily guarded gate to RAF Hawkinge, and be on my way.

It was another nice stroll while it lasted.

I spotted Diana walking with a constable as they rounded a bend a hundred yards away. A man in plain clothes trailed the two. I recognized the stooped walk of a flat-footed detective from my old beat back in Boston. His shabby overcoat flapped in the breeze, and he clutched his brown fedora in one hand. The bobby's helmet wasn't going anywhere, but that hat could've flown across the Channel and gotten to France before I did.

Diana strode with a grim determination that I knew well. She wasn't happy about something, but then again, it wasn't the happiest of occasions. As the two cops drew closer, they didn't look too cheery either.

"Detective Sergeant Henry Ruxton, Kent County Constabulary," the plainclothes guy said. He stepped in front of Diana and flashed his warrant card without much care for the narrowness of the path. "You are Captain William Boyle?"

"I am. Watch how close you get to the edge, Detective," I said. I expected him to look down at the cliff or at the body, but he held his gaze full on me, even as he took a step back. He was tall and lanky, with a jutting jaw and narrow, dark eyes that drifted to my hands, where flakes of dried blood were caked around my fingernails.

"Don't you worry, Captain, I'm a careful man," he said as he turned to the constable. As he did, he stared deliberately at Diana's hands, which also bore traces of dried blood, then flicked a look my way. "This is Constable Thomas Sallow. Miss Seaton arrived at the Capel-le-Ferne station just as I did."

"*Captain* Seaton," Diana said. "As I mentioned."

"Of course," Ruxton said. "I'm used to the WAAFs running around here in their blue uniforms, but I don't see many of your sort. Nurses or something, isn't it?"

"First Aid Nursing Yeomanry," Diana said. "As I have also already mentioned. I've recently been assigned to RAF Hawkinge."

Diana's uniform was brown khaki, like the regular British Army kit. But her beret held a red patch with the FANY insignia affixed. It was a cross within a circle, and to those who paid attention to such things, it was a mark of the undercover work many FANY women did with the Special Operations Executive. Dangerous work in occupied Europe.

"Yes, yes, you drive trucks, that sort of thing," Ruxton declared. Diana rolled her eyes, evidently deciding it was no use setting things straight, to the extent she could, anyway. "You both have blood on your hands, don't you?"

"As does the body, Detective," I said. I pointed to the matted blood partially visible at the back of his head. "Although I'm sure you noticed."

"Captain Seaton said you pulled him up the cliff," Constable Sallow said as he stepped close to the edge and peered down. At least he respected the three pips on Diana's epaulets. Sallow was on the short side and had a few years and pounds on Ruxton. He wore a mustache flecked with white and a serious expression at odds with his boss's blather.

"Yes," I said. "We thought he might be unconscious. He was close to the barbed wire and could have fallen off the edge if he came to. It was only when I started to drag him by the collar that

I noticed the blood." I held up my hands, the rusty red on full display. Sallow waved his hand at me and I dropped them.

"Clear tracks, Detective Sergeant," Sallow said, observing the path I'd taken. He pointed as Ruxton looked on, standing a few steps back from the edge. Was Ruxton afraid of heights?

"It's just as I told you, Detective," Diana said. She gave him the essentials of what had happened, her exasperation evident even as she tried to keep it factual.

"We'll have to satisfy ourselves on that account, won't we?" Ruxton snapped. "Who's to say one of you didn't pitch him over?"

"And then climb down to bring him back up?" I said.

"And after that, report the murder to the police?" Diana added.

Sallow stepped in and saved Ruxton from having to respond. "Sir, we should think about a search of the path."

"Certainly," Ruxton said, probably glad of the change of subject. "Now, Captain Boyle, has anyone come by from either direction?"

"No one," I said. "I didn't see a soul the whole time we were here."

"What about you, Captain Seaton?" Constable Sallow asked.

"Nobody," Diana said. "When I ran back to where we left the jeep by the road, I saw no sign of anyone. The body was warm when Billy brought it up, so it could have been two minutes or two hours since the killer struck."

"And it's still warm," I said as I knelt and felt the dead man's hand. The wrist was flaccid. "No stiffening."

"You are an expert on dead bodies as well, Captain Seaton?" Ruxton said. "I wonder what it is you do at Hawkinge."

"The extent of my familiarity with death and my duties with the RAF are not for you to know, Detective," Diana said.

"We shall see about that," Ruxton said. "And you, Captain Boyle? Are you a medical expert with your talk of stiffening?"

"No," I said. I stood and faced Ruxton. "But I am a former homicide detective with the Boston Police Department."

"Well, at least you are forthcoming," Ruxton said as he cast a suspicious eye toward Diana. "Still, keep your hands from the body, please."

"Perhaps I should remain here with the lady, Detective Sergeant," Sallow said. "You and the gentleman can check the path to the east since we've already covered the other direction. Never know what a nervous killer may have dropped."

"You have someone coming for the body?" I asked the constable.

"I left a message for the coroner, but no telling how long he'll be," Constable Sallow said. "So, we may as well have a look around. I will search the immediate area within sight of the body while you work the pathway. Will that do, Detective Sergeant?"

"Very well. Keep your eyes open for anything unusual," Ruxton said, then beckoned me to follow. I looked at Diana and gave her a helpless shrug. A brisk walk followed by tea and cakes had been our plan, but it looked like we'd end our day at the police station. Romantic.

"Not many people take to the path this time of year," Ruxton said as we walked the rocky trail. "Most are indoors with their families on Christmas."

"I wanted to see the White Cliffs of Dover," I said. "It seemed like a perfect day for it." Ahead of us, the path curved and revealed the cliffs drenched in winter sunlight, gleaming even as the wind blew the Channel waters hard and gray. On one side was a sharp drop, on the other a tall embankment of chalk and tufted grasses. Another hiker might have seen the killer making their escape, but from the road, not so far away, all was hidden.

"I meant it would be a good place for murder," Ruxton said. "If the body had rolled any farther, it might not have been discovered. Not soon, anyway." He stopped and took a hesitant step close to the edge. Here, there was no ledge to break a fall. A body might bounce off the cliff face going down, but it wouldn't stop until it hit the rocky shore.

"Maybe the killer wasn't from around here," I said as we continued on the rising path.

"Why do you think that?" Ruxton said as he kept to the inside of the path. He made a show of eyeing the grasses for a clue.

"As you said, anywhere else along here the body would have gone straight down. That small ledge must be known to the locals. Why strike the blow there?"

"Fair point," Ruxton said with a nod as he held on to his hat. "Unless our man dropped something heavy, this damned wind would have taken it away."

"True," I said, and craned my neck to look over the edge. "But I'm thinking about the murder weapon, tossed off the cliff." I squinted and tried to spot anything suspicious on the rocks below. A long shot, I knew.

"But why wait?" Ruxton asked. "Why not throw it as soon as the deed was done?"

"Because maybe it wasn't planned," I said. "The killer reacts to something and whacks the guy. They're horrified at what they've done and just keep going, running along this path. Suddenly they realize they're still holding the weapon and toss it over."

"It could have happened that way, Captain Boyle, I'll grant you," Ruxton said. "The killer would have needed a weapon at hand. These chalk-and-limestone rocks are too soft to do the trick, I should think."

I stopped and loosened a rock from the side of the path. It fit in the palm of my hand, light and insubstantial. But it had a sharp edge, and I wouldn't want it slammed into my head.

"It might do, if struck with sufficient force," I said. I rubbed my thumb against it, and it came away with chalky dust. "If a rock was used, the coroner ought to find traces in the wound."

"You had a good deal of homicide experience in Boston, Captain?"

"Sure," I said. "And we had our share of stiffs tossed in the water too. Makes finding the scene of the crime harder when the tide takes them."

I was talking a good line, but the truth was I'd been a detective for only a few weeks when my draft notice had come through. However, I'd walked the beat plenty, all around Boston, and even worked with my dad and uncle who were actual homicide detectives. They're the reason I advanced quickly through the ranks since the Boston PD was sort of a family business for the Boyles. But Ruxton didn't need to hear my family saga. All I wanted was to give him some pointers and get the hell off this cliff.

"We have our fair share of crime in our part of Kent, but not a lot in the way of murder," Ruxton said, as if he were admitting some sort of failure on his part. "A lot of people were evacuated from the coastline during the invasion scares, and they're only now making their way back. The Royal Air Force handles any crimes committed by their people, which amount mainly to drunkenness and black-market violations. Nothing like this."

"Listen, I can see why you were suspicious of Diana and me," I said, nearly feeling sorry for the guy. "I would have been too."

"I still may be, Captain," Ruxton said. "Who else is there to be suspicious of?"

He had a point. We trudged on, stopping to catch our breath as we crested a hill with a clear view of the undulating path ahead. It was empty of hikers and villains.

"Enough of this. We're not going to find a witness or a suspect here," Ruxton said. "Let's get back and see if the damned coroner has shown up. Then we'll take your statements at the station."

"Captain Seaton will need to make a telephone call to the base," I said. "If it takes too long."

"It will take as long as I decide it should, Captain," Ruxton said as he picked up the pace on the downhill side. "But if nothing untoward pops up, you should be on your way before nightfall. Fair enough, wouldn't you say?"

"Quite fair, Detective Sergeant," I said in my most agreeable tone. After all, folded up in my jacket pocket were two extremely untoward and slightly bloodstained sheets of paper marked RESTRICTED.

Which is how I intended to keep them.

CHAPTER THREE

THE CORONER WAS examining the body when we returned. Wincing, he rose from the ground and motioned to the two auxiliary constables who stood by with a stretcher. The wind blew the coroner's thick white hair in every direction, and he wobbled a bit as he struggled to keep his balance.

"Doctor Yates, what can you tell me?" Ruxton asked when we were close enough.

"Struck from behind and killed, which any child could see," the doctor said. "I'll tell you more later after I warm my bones. I feel as cold as this poor lad."

"Any idea when he died?" Ruxton asked.

"Rigor is just setting in," Doctor Yates said. "Three hours is a guess, good as any. I'll see you in my office and you can go through his possessions."

Ruxton instructed the two constables to search the beach below the cliff when they were done carting the body away. One mentioned the tide was coming in, which resulted in Ruxton saying they'd better get a move on, then. Given his manner, I doubted he was the local bobbies' favorite detective.

"We saw nothing along the path," Ruxton said to Constable Sallow. "Did you spot anything around here?"

"Something, sir, yes," Sallow said. He held a small slip of paper, the wind flapping it against his fingers. Diana stood behind him and shot me a warning glance, a nearly imperceptible shake of the head. "A train ticket. It was caught in the grasses at the top of the embankment."

I looked over Ruxton's shoulder as he studied the ticket. It was for the Southern Railway,

Eynsford to Folkestone via Tonbridge and back again. I didn't see anything suspicious about it, but I kept my mouth shut and waited for Diana to take the lead.

"Anyone could have dropped it," Ruxton said. He squinted as he took the ticket from Sallow. "Could have been days ago."

"It's hardly weathered, sir. I was thinking the assailant might have had it in the same pocket as his weapon, and it flew out when he pulled it," Sallow said. "We're lucky it got caught up in the thick grass." Not a bad theory, but I stood stone-faced, just as Diana did.

"Perhaps, Constable," Ruxton said. "Foolish spot for a train ticket, wouldn't you say? Everyone knows a waistcoat pocket is the proper place to keep your ticket safe. The thing could have blown in from anywhere, but I congratulate you on your excellent eyesight." He handed the ticket back to Sallow, who, lacking a waistcoat, placed it in his tunic pocket and buttoned it up tight.

"Thank you, sir," Sallow said in a perfectly neutral tone of voice.

"Could have been the victim's as well, perhaps," Ruxton said as he jammed his hat on his head. "Once we know his name, I'm sure the Americans can tell us if he was stationed near Eynsford. Probably an air base up there."

"Of course, Detective Sergeant," Sallow said with only a hint of forlorn obedience. Ruxton turned on his heel and followed the coroner's sad parade. Sallow gestured for us to follow as he took up the rear. Whether he was doing so to keep his distance from the detective sergeant or to keep us from escaping was anybody's guess.

"What's the story?" I muttered to Diana as we trailed Ruxton.

"Don't encourage them about the ticket. I'll explain later," she said. I looked at her, but she was giving nothing else away. I resisted patting my pocket where the two sheets of paper sat, just to make sure they were still there. I don't know what Ruxton would make of it if he discovered I had them. It was pretty much a motive for murder, although that begged the question, why did the killer leave them? Whatever was bothering Diana was probably nothing when compared to finding restricted information on the body of a murdered Yank.

I hoped.

This wasn't the time to chat about our competing secrets, so I dropped back a step to gab with Constable Sallow and reinforce the fact that we were simply helpful witnesses who didn't have much time to sit around the station.

"Do you get to work with Detective Sergeant Ruxton often, Constable?" I asked.

"Do you find pointing out the shortcomings of a superior officer is helpful in your army, Captain?" Sallow said.

"Seldom," I said. "Perhaps never. Sorry, just professional curiosity."

"In your professional opinion, what do you think went on here?"

"It was unexpected, I think. It probably happened an hour or so before we arrived, given that the assailant was long gone when we got to the scene. It could have been done with a rock, which means the murder weapon will never be found," I said. "That's about it."

"You may be right," Sallow said. He nodded as he thought it through. "My money is on premeditation. That was a solid blow, according to the doc. Lead pipe or a cosh, something that could be hidden in a coat pocket. That's why the killer didn't worry about him getting hung up on that ledge. He was dead already."

"And with the tide coming in, it'd be hard to find whatever the weapon was on the rocks below," I said.

"Well, if it were premeditated, I'd wager the weapon was taken away and disposed of elsewhere. Why leave it right where the police are bound to look for it? We'll make a show of it, but I'm interested in looking around the Folkestone train station, even if the detective sergeant thinks little of the idea."

"No need for him to know, right?"

"Unless I find something, then he'll know quick enough," Sallow said as the car park came into view. "Now let's get to the station, and I'll put the kettle on while you and the lady write your statements. Then you'll be on your way."

"Sounds fair," I said. I knew his comment about the train station would not sit well with Diana. Why, I had not a clue, but I figured she had a solid reason, so I tried to distract Sallow. "But maybe you should search for a vehicle first. The victim had to have been driven here, right?"

"Yes, of course," Sallow said. "Obviously none of us saw as much as a bicycle here, but you Yanks don't do a lot of pedaling, do you? Jeeps and staff cars are more to your liking, aren't they?"

"True enough," I said. "So, there must be one of those around somewhere. Maybe in the village."

"Perhaps," Sallow said. He stopped to give Diana a look. "Captain Seaton suggested much the same on the way in. Detective Sergeant Ruxton didn't comment one way or the other, but I agree, the lay-by on either side should be checked. Although his shoes didn't look like he'd been out for a ramble, did they?"

I agreed they hadn't. While Sallow had his wits about him, Ruxton seemed to have misplaced those few he'd been granted.

Ruxton was waiting by the police car, a Wolseley sedan. Constable Sallow passed his boss by and opened the rear door for Diana, as a proper gentleman would. Ruxton muttered something as he opened his own door, and Sallow raised an eyebrow in my direction. I was beginning to warm to the constable.

"This shouldn't take long," Ruxton said as Sallow started the engine. "You'll be back at your base in no time, Captain Boyle. Where is that, exactly?"

"The Trianon Palace, in Versailles, outside of Paris," I said. "I'm assigned to the Supreme Headquarters, Allied Expeditionary Force. SHAEF."

"In a palace, you say? You must be desperate to get there. The Dover coast in winter can't compete with Paris," Ruxton said. He turned to face Diana from the front passenger seat. "And you, Captain Seaton, you'll be back to making tea for the lads, or whatever it is you do at the RAF base. Vital work, I'm sure."

He turned away and instructed Sallow to return to the shoreline once he'd dropped us off and to retrieve the constables before the tide washed them away. Constable Sallow suggested a check of the other lay-bys, which Ruxton grudgingly agreed to. He was obviously a man who didn't like hearing a good idea suggested by someone else. I wasn't up on the nuances of British police ranks, but Ruxton had a few too many gray hairs and worry lines to still be a detective sergeant. Maybe he irritated his superiors as much as he did everyone else.

Diana glared at the back of Ruxton's skull, her mouth set in a hard line. She wasn't one to put up with guff from anyone, much less the Kent County Constabulary's village idiot. But she held back, which told me there was something else at work here. Something that involved whatever an SOE agent's duties might be at RAF Hawkinge.

I had the feeling I wasn't going to be flying to Paris anytime soon.

CHAPTER FOUR

I SAT ACROSS from Ruxton in a small, cold room. The brickwork was flaking, and the wooden floor was warped and scuffed. One table, two chairs, and a drafty window. It was as welcoming as the detective sergeant himself. He wrote out my statement, going over each sentence carefully as he searched for the inconsistency that would catch me out as the killer and solve the case.

In his mind, at least.

I glanced at my watch. He'd taken nearly an hour with Diana, and now, thankfully, we were nearly done.

"You stayed with the body while you waited for Captain Seaton to return, is that right?" Ruxton asked, pen poised above paper. I nodded, again. "And you didn't disturb anything?"

"I'm sure I disturbed a good deal dragging him up the cliffside," I said. "But once we had him on the path, all I did was study the body." I could feel the lie crinkle in my pocket as I twisted in the hard-backed chair.

"What did your studies tell you, then?" Ruxton asked. He lowered his pen hand and listened, perhaps for an insight he could pass off as his own.

"The man was well turned out. Careful of his appearance. Shoes spit shined. No dirt on his cuffs, which suggests he hadn't walked far," I said.

"A man who pays attention to his clothing can also enjoy a stroll," Ruxton said.

"Sure," I said. "But he wasn't wearing gloves or a scarf. It was cold up there. I'd left my gloves in the jeep, and I wished I'd had them."

"All this means what?" Ruxton asked, then appeared to give it a thought. "That he'd been dropped off?"

"Could be. At the same place we parked. Maybe someone drove him, and they went along the path together. Or it was just a meeting place. After the deed was done, the killer ran back to their car and drove off before Diana and I arrived."

"Perhaps," Ruxton said. He slid the statement across the table to me. "Read it and sign if it is satisfactory."

I read. It was a decent account, but I took my time, thinking about giving Ruxton more to chew on. Like how the killer could have come from the opposite direction, assaulted the major and whomever he was walking with. That would have sent his companion hightailing it for the car, frightened they'd be next.

Until more was known about the dead man, any number of scenarios were possible. So there was no sense overloading Ruxton with possibilities. It took imagination to conjure up all the myriad ways this murder could have occurred, and brains to discard the theories that didn't hold water. Both were in short supply with Henry Ruxton.

"Here you go," I said. I signed the statement and kept my speculations to myself. Ruxton gathered his papers, and I stood to leave as a knock sounded at the door. It was Sallow, who announced that the constables searching the beach had come up with nothing, as had the man checking the lay-bys for parked vehicles.

"Very well," Ruxton said. "Have the men go door to door along the Old Dover Road. Perhaps someone saw our Yank on his way to the cliffs from Capel-le-Ferne. You can tell Miss Seaton she may leave with Captain Boyle. Their statements are in order."

"Yes, sir," Sallow said. "I figured as much. Captain Seaton has telephoned her air base. Seems there's some sort of flap on."

"There's a perfectly good telephone box on the street, Constable," Ruxton said. "We are here to enforce the law, not to provide conveniences for the public." He brushed by Sallow as he left the room and stalked down the hall. I followed and found Diana at a desk, telephone in hand.

"Folkestone 1130, please," Diana said to the operator.

"See here," Ruxton said, his eyes wide in disbelief. "One telephone call is quite enough."

"One moment," Diana said to Ruxton, holding up a finger as if to still an unruly child. She returned her attention to the other end of the line. "Lieutenant Walters? This is Captain Seaton. Has Squadron Officer Conan Doyle contacted you? Yes? Very good. Thank you."

"If that is all, *Miss* Seaton, I'll ask you to step away from the desk and keep that line clear," Ruxton said.

"By all means, Detective Sergeant," Diana said, going so far as to grace Ruxton with a smile. "You will want that line clear, I assure you."

"Our business here is done," Ruxton said as a look of confusion crept across his face. "Constable Sallow will show you out."

"No," Diana said. "I shall remain. As will Captain Boyle."

"For what purpose?" Ruxton asked, his voice rising in annoyance. The telephone rang and effectively cut him off. Sallow answered and within seconds his jaw went slack.

"It's for you, Detective Sergeant," Sallow said in a whisper. "It's the chief constable. Sir Percy himself." He thrust out the telephone to Ruxton, eager to be rid of it.

"Chief Constable Sillitoe," Ruxton said, and straightened

himself into attention. For the next minute he listened and cast glances at Diana and me, while I wondered why I was staying and what exactly was happening. Ruxton ended the conversation by staring at the receiver in his hand, the chief constable, evidently, having abruptly ended the call.

"Please hang up, Detective Sergeant," Diana said. "We need to keep the line free for another call. Did Sir Percy make everything clear?"

"He did," Ruxton uttered with a mild tremor.

"Perhaps Constable Sallow should know," she said. "This is his patch, after all."

"I was about to do just that, thank you. Constable, Sir Percy informed me that the Kent County Constabulary shall cooperate fully with Captain Seaton and her superior officer regarding this case, which is now under the jurisdiction of the Royal Air Force. Is that clear?" Ruxton made it sound as if the chief constable had called to take him into his confidence, not issue orders.

"Understood," Sallow said. He looked confused, and I'm sure I did too. Who was next in line to ring the station? Winston Churchill?

"I thought we were going for tea," I said to Diana. "What's happening?" Before she could answer, the telephone jangled. Constable Sallow looked to Diana, who nodded her permission for him to answer. Ruxton shoved his hands in his pockets and frowned, clearly torn between stomping out and staying to see what happened next.

"They're asking for you, Captain Boyle," Sallow said. He handed the receiver to me. I took it, raised an eyebrow in Diana's direction, and was rewarded with the briefest of smiles.

"Captain Boyle," I announced.

"You just can't stay out of trouble, can you, Billy? In the slammer already?"

"Big Mike?" was all I could gasp out. First Sergeant Mike Miecznikowski was part of SHAEF's Office of Special Investigations. So was I.

"I've got a message from Sam," Big Mike said. His voice crackled over the line. Never one to cater to the niceties of the military's chain of command, Big Mike was referring to Colonel Samuel Harding, who ran the Office of Special Investigations for General Eisenhower. "He's in a briefing, but the lowdown is you've been detailed to assist the Royal Air Force. The request came from high up. Air Marshal Arthur Harris, no less. Seems like there's been a murder near the air base where Diana's stationed. An RAF intelligence officer is being sent to you now. Say hello to Diana for me if you see her."

"Oh, I'll say something to her, don't worry. Anything else?"

"Sam said to holler if you need help, play nice with the Brits, and not take too long," Big Mike said. "He wants you back at SHAEF pronto."

"You've been busy," I said to Diana as I replaced the receiver. "Is the lieutenant you called the intelligence officer they're sending here?"

"No. Lieutenant Jack Walters is with the RAF Regiment," Diana said. "He's arranging transportation." The RAF Regiment had the job of guarding airfields and ensuring base security.

"I wonder why the RAF wants a FANY and a Yank to investigate," I said. The words weren't out of my mouth before I tumbled to it.

"Maybe they need an outsider or two to see things clearly," Sallow said, beating me to the punch. "Or someone to blame."

"That's enough, Constable," Ruxton said, his stern voice conveying his anger. "You'll provide what assistance is required, keep me informed, and refrain from casting suspicion upon the RAF." With that, he pulled on his coat and stomped out, satisfied with his defense of the Royal Air Force.

"You may have a point, Constable Sallow," I said as soon as the door slammed shut. "Diana, can you fill us in?"

"Constable, do you understand you'll be working with the RAF on this case, and that it is not necessary to share details with Kent County Constabulary?" Diana asked.

"Sir Percy was speaking loudly enough for me to make that much out," Sallow said. "I've no problem working with your intelligence chap, or either of you for that matter."

"Excellent," Diana said. "You were right about the train ticket. Eynsford is the station nearest RAF Kingsdown, where my superior officer's main headquarters is located. A good deal of secret work goes on there, and we need to know why our victim traveled from there to meet his death here."

"Or why the killer traveled from Eynsford," Sallow said. "I'd guess I don't need to know what kind of secret work it is, but that you'd like to know who got off the train from that direction in Folkestone this morning."

"Right on both counts, Constable," Diana said. "I appreciate your willingness to help."

"Well, it's the most excitement we've had since the buzz bombs stopped dropping," Sallow said. "And it gets me out from under his lordship, if you don't mind me saying."

Sirens wailed outside, keeping us from commenting on Sallow's assessment of Ruxton. I went to the window and saw four motorcycles leading an RAF staff car. The automobile skidded to a stop by the front door with the motorcycles arraying themselves around it.

"Lieutenant Walters does love his motorcycles," Diana said. "Frankly this was for show, in case we needed to reinforce things with the detective sergeant."

"Hardly necessary, Captain," Sallow said. "But a nice show all the same. The village will know what's what, that's certain."

Car doors slammed as the motorcycle engines revved, then

quieted. A lieutenant opened the door to the station and stood aside. Diana straightened up, and Sallow and I did the same. In strode a dark-haired woman in the blue uniform of the RAF's Women's Auxiliary Air Force. She was taller and a few years older than Diana, with a striking face that at this moment looked hardened with worry.

"This is Squadron Officer Conan Doyle," Diana said. She made the introductions and explained that Detective Sergeant Ruxton had instructed the constable to assist us.

"Good. We shall need all the help we can get," the squadron officer said. "If the victim is whom I fear it is, this is a serious situation. What do you have to report?"

I felt the paper in my pocket.

"I think the situation may be even more serious than you think," I said.

CHAPTER FIVE

"Before we get into details, perhaps Constable Sallow should alert the coroner that we shall be paying him a visit," Diana said. "He can let Doctor Yates know how things stand."

"I'll do that," Sallow said. "Then I can stop at the Folkestone train station."

"You found a ticket, I understand," Squadron Officer Conan Doyle said. "May I see it?" Sallow produced the ticket and handed it to Diana.

"The return is valid for today only," Diana said as she turned the ticket over and showed it to Squadron Officer Doyle.

"Ah, yes, so the owner, if it's not our dead man, will have to purchase a new one-way ticket," Sallow said. "I know a couple of fellows who work there, and it would be good to talk to them while things are fresh in their minds, meaning before they stop at the pub for a few pints after work."

"Excellent," the squadron officer said. "Your assistance should be invaluable with the locals. It's getting late, so you'd best go now. Lieutenant Walters can provide an escort if you wish."

"No, thank you, ma'am," Sallow said. He appeared a bit flustered. "That would be a tad showy for folks around here. I'd never live it down."

"No worries, Constable," Walters said. He clapped Sallow on the shoulder as they left the room. "I'll simply follow you, sirens silent. That way I'll know where to take the squadron officer." I suspected Walters was removing himself and Sallow from the room, sensing I was about to take us even deeper into the top secret stuff.

"Now, Captain Boyle, tell me what you meant," Doyle said, taking a seat at Sallow's desk. She motioned for us to sit and looked straight at Diana, who shrugged, signaling that she had no idea what I was talking about.

"I told the police I hadn't disturbed the body," I said. "But I did check the guy's pockets. I found two sheets of paper with the word RESTRICTED at the top. I figured they might be too sensitive for the local cops, so I grabbed them. Diana and I haven't had a moment alone for me to tell her."

I withdrew the papers and laid them out on the desk, smoothing the crumpled edges. The bloodstains had dried, but the words "Jackal" and "Jostle" were legible. Arrows pointed to two devices. One the size of an oil drum with cables and electronics snaking out of the top. That was Jostle. Jackal looked more like a large rectangular radio with dials and gauges connected with thick black cables.

"This was on the body?" Squadron Officer Conan Doyle said. She drew the sheets closer to her, as if to shield them from prying eyes. I confirmed it was. "The body of a US Army Air Force major. Brown hair, slim, well turned out?"

"That's the guy."

"Captain Seaton had not met Frederick Brockman, but I had, in my official capacity," the squadron officer said. She paused, drumming her fingernails on the desktop, staring at the drawings.

"I'm afraid I have no idea what your official capacity is, ma'am," I said. I knew that officers in our Women's Army Corps were addressed that way instead of being called sir, and I figured it was the same with the Brits.

"Do you have any idea about Captain Seaton's work with us?" she asked.

"None, other than the base is so hush-hush I couldn't get in," I said. "Even though I'm with SHAEF."

"Captain Boyle and I are both used to keeping secrets," Diana said.

"I know," the squadron officer said. "But we must pause a moment before going any further. Captain Boyle, you may know by now that a request for your assistance went through channels today. And quite rapidly. I want you to understand that you shall be working under my direction, and that Captain Seaton will be my direct representative in this matter. Is there anything that will prevent you from carrying out your duties?"

"Nothing, ma'am," I said. I wasn't sure if she meant taking orders from a dame, working with my girl, or being temporarily assigned to the British. I'd been taking orders from people in uniforms all my adult life, so I saw no reason to bellyache about this arrangement, lady RAF officer and all. Hey, I could ignore Squadron Officer Conan Doyle's orders just as well as I could Colonel Harding's. Diana and I had worked together in occupied Europe, so a murder investigation with her along the Dover coast had to be easy in comparison. Had to be.

"Very well. Diana spoke highly of you, but I like to be certain of things. I've had orders written up, which should assist you if anyone questions your role," Conan Doyle said in a businesslike manner as she handed me an envelope embossed with the RAF crest.

I took out the paper, which stated I'd been seconded to the Royal Air Force at the request of Air Marshal Arthur Harris with the approval of General Walter Bedell Smith, SHAEF's chief of staff. It was funny to have my name on the same page as such senior brass, and I had to suppress a grin as I read on. It closed out by confirming I would report to Squadron Officer

J. C. Doyle, who in all matters pertaining to the investigation would be represented by Captain Diana Seaton of the Special Operations Executive. Which basically meant I'd be working for Diana. Interesting.

I finished, scanning the signature line, where the squadron officer's full name was spelled out. Jean Conan Doyle.

What? Suddenly it hit me.

"Conan Doyle?" I asked. "Any relation to . . . ?"

"Sir Arthur was my father, Captain Boyle," she said, her voice flat and her eyes fixed on the papers in front of her. She gave off an air of weariness at explaining her connection and accepting the usual praise with sufficient enthusiasm. Finally, she folded the papers, tucked them away, and looked me straight in the eye. "So it seems we are bound by our more famous relatives, are we not?"

"We are," I said. "I'll try not to pepper you with questions about Sherlock Holmes. But I am a great fan of your father's work."

"And I will refrain from asking you about your uncle," she said. "I happen to be a great fan of General Eisenhower, but I will not presume upon our working relationship for gossip and personal tidbits, however interesting."

"You never mentioned anything," I said to Diana, who I could see was on the verge of laughter. She knew my fascination with the stories of Arthur Conan Doyle.

"Top secret, Billy," she said. "And I only told Jean about your uncle this morning. It seemed appropriate for her to know."

"Indeed," Conan Doyle said. "I like to know the lineage of people I shanghai. Prevents my stepping on the wrong toes. I did the same when Diana was brought in. I know her father, Sir Richard, from certain government circles. He vouched for her. As for you, Captain Boyle, your Colonel Harding spoke very highly of your detective skills. Seemed like a decent fellow."

"He's a good man," I said. "As is Uncle Ike."

I gave an abbreviated version of my relationship with the supreme commander. How he was related on my mother's side of the family and was actually a distant cousin whom I'd always called uncle. I left out the part about how my family had called in political favors—from a Boston Irish family named Kennedy—to get me appointed to Uncle Ike's staff in Washington, DC, back when he was an unknown colonel. The idea was for me to sit out the war in safety, given that the Boyle clan was anti-British and pro–Irish independence. My dad had lost his oldest brother in the trenches of the First World War, and he'd decided this second war to preserve the British Empire didn't need another Boyle lad buried in France. Great notion, but the army had other ideas for Dwight David Eisenhower. When they shipped him off to high command in Europe, I tagged along. Uncle Ike thought it was swell to have his own personal detective to tackle low crimes in high places. I'd seen more of this war than many, and I knew I was lucky to be alive. That's one reason why I didn't mind this assignment. There were two others.

First, I'd be in England with Diana, where no one named Fritz was trying to kill me with bombs and bullets. I'd be warm and safe enough, as long as I didn't screw up taking orders from said Captain Diana Seaton.

Second, I wanted to know how Major Brockman had ended up dead along the Dover cliffs. After dragging his body up the slope, I found it hard to simply walk away from what happened next. Top secret or just an everyday murder, I wanted to see it through. The curse of being a homicide detective.

"Now that we've discussed our family histories, isn't it time someone told me what this restricted and top secret stuff is all about?" I said. "Why is RAF Hawkinge buttoned up tighter than a vicar's collar?"

CHAPTER SIX

"SECURITY IS CRITICAL to what we do," Conan Doyle said. "We are part of the RAF's wireless intercept service. The Y Service, as it's come to be called. Our headquarters is at RAF Kingsdown, south of London, which is why the train ticket aroused Diana's suspicions. But much of our work is done here, where we are closer to the radio signals we need to intercept. Better atmospherics."

"What does an American pilot have to do with wireless interception?" I asked.

"That concerns another aspect of our work," Conan Doyle said. "It will save time if I show you tomorrow at the base. For right now, do you understand the basics of wireless interception?"

"Listening in to German frequencies," I said. "From the little I know, it requires a knowledge of Morse code, the enemy's language, and the network of frequencies they broadcast on."

"Close enough," Conan Doyle said. "Our people are trained in Morse code and become wireless telegraphy operators. The next step is plain-language intercepts for the radio telegraphy operators. Then the work moves into the intricacies of obtaining line bearings for use in direction-finding units, which is vital for guiding our bombers into Germany."

"Diana, what's your role?" I asked. I knew she spoke French as well as perfect Italian, but German wasn't one of her languages.

I caught Squadron Officer Conan Doyle's nod in Diana's direction, giving her permission to answer.

"My stated assignment is to monitor communications from Mussolini's government in northern Italy," she said. After the Italian Grand Council had ousted Benito Mussolini as the leader of fascist Italy, he'd been rescued by the Germans and set up in the town of Salò on Lake Garda. He ran a bit of northern Italy and had enough armed troops to be dangerous. But basically, the Nazis called the shots. It was officially the Italian Social Republic, but everyone referred to it as the republic of Salò, after its location. Sort of like Vichy France had been.

"Do they have anything worth listening to?" I asked.

"The Italian Social Republic, as they call it, has very little power," Diana said. "But they do receive instructions from the Germans, and often pass those on to their formations in uncoded language. They also maintain communications with Hungary, the German puppet state in Croatia, and commercial concerns in Switzerland."

"We often pick up information from careless talk," Conan Doyle said. "Except from the transmissions to Switzerland. They're careful when it comes to their Swiss bank accounts."

"The Swiss have low standards when it comes to bank customers," I said. No standards at all, really, if they could make a dime or two. "Diana, you described this as your stated assignment. So what's the real deal?" Diana looked to Conan Doyle, an unspoken question passing between them.

"We've had some concerns about other areas of our work," Conan Doyle answered. "I asked the Air Ministry for a new staff member well versed in Italian and intelligent enough to assess our security. Undercover work of a sort, you see. Somehow that got to Sir Richard, and he telephoned me the same day. I took his suggestion with a grain of salt, accounting for fatherly pride. But when I checked in with Vera Atkins, she spoke quite highly of Diana. She referred to you as well, Captain Boyle, in a not entirely unsatisfactory manner."

Vera Atkins headed the SOE's French Section. We got along okay, and she was fiercely loyal to the women who worked for her. Those who survived and those who died. Diana had nearly joined the latter group during a recent mission, and I wondered if Vera had given her this post to keep her from another run-in with the Gestapo. The same went for Sir Richard, who knew what strings to pull when it came to navigating the various British intelligence services. We'd both been concerned about what the SOE might dream up next for Diana, and working at an RAF base seemed a safe bet.

Except for a murderer on the loose.

"Okay, I get the playbook," I said. "What security breaches is Diana looking into?"

"Missing documents, for the most part," Conan Doyle said.

"Wiring diagrams, similar to what you found on the body," Diana said. "Along with a few pieces of hardware. It may all just add up to things getting lost or misplaced. I haven't found anything suspicious, not yet. But I've only been at it a few days. So obviously, this killing and what you found on the body are worrisome."

"All right. I look forward to learning what Jostle and Jackal are all about, but right now we should get over to Doctor Yates and see what he's come up with," I said.

"I'm sure by now word of your involvement has spread far and wide," Conan Doyle said as she gathered her papers and stood. "Our position is that you are assisting the local authorities given the victim was American, but we are saying nothing further. When you are finished with the coroner, come see me at the base. Quarters have been arranged for you, Captain Boyle. Good luck."

"Let's go, boss," I said to Diana as we got into the jeep.

"Behave yourself, Billy, or I'll tell Jean you prefer Agatha Christie to her father," she said.

Lieutenant Walters had waited to lead us to the coroner, while the rest of the escort went off with the squadron officer. He started up his BSA M20 motorcycle and we followed. It was cold, even under the canvas top, and getting colder as the sun neared the horizon.

"I'll be good as long as we get some food," I said as we threaded our way through the narrow streets.

"I'm hungry as well," Diana answered. "I just hope I still am after the autopsy."

Lieutenant Walters led us down a side road, past a post office, and pulled over in front of the doctor's surgery. It was a small two-story house of solid brick with a sign pointing to a side door. Walters said he'd make sure the guards at the gate knew to expect me and roared off on his motorcycle. We were close to the Channel and the chill wind whipped against our coats, the tang of salt spray in the air.

I knocked at the door and entered. The waiting room was empty, but the door to the right was partly open. Doctor Yates, dressed in a lab coat that once was white, stepped halfway into the room and beckoned us to enter.

"Sallow told me to expect you both," Yates said. "If either of you are queasy around the dead, you may wait out here."

"Not necessary, Doctor," I said as we followed him into the small room that served as a temporary morgue. I was relieved to see a sheet covering Brockman. There was no sign of internal organs having been pulled out or his last meal set out in a bowl.

"Thank you for attending to this so quickly, Doctor Yates," Diana said. I could tell she liked that he'd addressed both of us with his warning and made no remarks about delicate female constitutions.

"Slow day for sickness makes a good day for the dead," Yates said as we gathered around the table. "His clothing and effects are on the counter behind you."

"Let's start with what you found," I said. "Anything unusual?"

"There are no wounds or marks upon the body other than the one at the base of his skull," Yates said. He pulled the sheet back and revealed Brockman's head and shoulders. "Which was sufficient to kill him, and quickly, at that."

The doctor turned Brockman's head to show where he'd been struck. Low and behind the right ear. Bone jutted out from torn and heavily bruised skin.

"Was death instantaneous?" Diana asked. She leaned in to study the wound, then straightened up, shaking her head.

"Unconsciousness, certainly," Yates said. "Death would have followed within minutes. He suffered a severe basilar skull fracture. The force of impact drove bone fragments into his brain, disturbing the vital functioning of the midbrain and the brain stem."

"Someone knew right where to hit him, then?" I asked.

"Perhaps. Or it may have had more to do with being struck from behind," the doctor said. "His assailant might have wished to stun him, but swinging a heavy object from behind, if they were of roughly equal stature, would cause the blow to land there. A right-handed fellow, I'd venture to guess."

"Not a woman?" Diana asked.

"It would be unusual, but not impossible," Yates granted her. "A blow struck in anger might suffice, given the weight of the object."

"Any notion as to what kind of object?" I asked.

"Nothing very specific. Possibly blunt and rounded. There is no cut to the skin to suggest an edged weapon. I did find something in the wound, though," Yates said as he reached for a slip of paper. It held a smear of blood and a fleck of a yellowish substance. "Grease. It's likely the murder weapon had a trace of grease on it."

"It's not blackened," I said. "Recently applied, maybe?"

"I'll leave that to you, Captain," Yates said. "All I can do is report what I've found. There was also a bit of that grease under his thumbnail. Right hand."

Diana lifted the hand and we both squinted at the specks under Brockman's fingernail.

"You took a sample?" Diana asked.

"Of course," the doctor said. "It will all be in my report."

"I can see it matches the sample you took from the wound, Doctor. Brockman must have handled the weapon before it was used on him," I said.

"That is one interpretation," Yates said. He pulled the sheet back over Brockman's face. "Or he could have encountered a different object with grease on it earlier in the day."

"Both the victim and the killer could have done that," Diana offered. "And transferred grease onto the weapon."

"Ah, Captain Seaton, you understand how a coroner thinks," Yates said with a smile. "We are often called upon to conjecture when all we can do is state the facts in front of us. There is evidence of grease in two locations upon the corpse. That is certain. How they came to be there? That is not certain, and it is up to those with detecting skills to discover."

"I've heard this speech before, back in Boston," I said. "And right you are."

"Constable Sallow said you were a policeman before the war, so I thought the coroner's lament would make you feel at home. Go through his belongings while I clean up, why don't you?" Yates said.

There really wasn't much. Dog tags that gave his serial number, hometown, religion, and blood type. Lansing, Michigan. Jewish. O-positive. An army-issue watch. A thin billfold with some pound notes and the stub of a theater ticket. A lot of guys didn't carry much in the way of a civilian wallet. Personal items weren't supposed to go on missions, and leaving a stuffed wallet behind was an invitation to pilfering. Maybe we'd find something more personal in his footlocker.

"No train ticket, Billy," Diana said, after turning out all the pockets.

"Let's hope Sallow came up with something at the train station," I said. "We don't even know where Major Brockman was stationed, do we?"

"No. I asked Jean, and she told me to go ahead and see what we could find out and that she'll tell us tomorrow," Diana said.

"Is she always so secretive?" I asked.

"It's a way of life in the intelligence service, isn't it? You learn to keep things close until they must be shared," she said.

"Like Major Brockman and his top secret diagrams? He kept them close to his chest and look what happened to him."

We left the shrouded body behind. As we stepped outside, we faced the setting sun and harsh winds rising from the cliffs. The sky was streaked with color, and I wondered if Brockman had seen the sunset last night. His last, not that he ever could have known.

What do we ever know about the future? All I knew right then was how Diana's hand felt in mine. Warm with life.

CHAPTER SEVEN

AS WE DROVE up Dover Hill Road, we spotted a pub with a grand view of the Channel and decided it was as good a place as any to eat. The Valiant Sailor overlooked a gun emplacement on the cliffs, where cannons still guarded the approaches to southeastern England. Calais, across the water in France, was only thirty miles distant. At the start of the war, the threat of invasion hung over Britain, especially along this vulnerable coastline. The Germans used their big guns to shell the area, forcing the evacuation of thousands from their homes. As Ruxton said, people were only now making their way back, those whose homes hadn't been destroyed.

We picked up our pints of ale at the bar and made our way through the locals, RAF personnel, and a few army types engaged in a darts match.

"Cheers," I said as soon as we settled at a table near the fireplace. We clinked glasses and drank, the ale refreshing and cool. Diana smacked her lips, and we laughed at the unladylike noise. It was nice to be doing something, anything, normal after this day's events.

"Dead bodies aside, how's the new posting?" I asked Diana.

"It's interesting," she said as she set down her glass. "Jean is smart as a whip, and it's fascinating to work with the other girls."

"They all speak German?" I asked, my voice a whisper.

"Not here," Diana said. "Nothing about what we do is spoken about outside the base. You'll get the tour tomorrow and it all will be explained. But I can say it's a bit strange coming in with this rank. The others are mostly sergeants, so they were a bit standoffish at first."

"It's better now?"

"Much. I told them to chalk it up to military incompetence," Diana said. "They all understood that well enough after years in uniform. Then I let it drop that I was engaged and I wouldn't be competition for them when it came to all the handsome pilots hanging about."

"Engaged?"

"Oh, Billy, you should see your face!" Diana covered her mouth to smother a laugh. "Sorry. It was just a story. I overheard one of them saying I'd have my pick of Yank officers, so I commented an hour later on my daring and handsome fiancé. He's a fighter pilot. How am I ever going to explain you? A jilted suitor, perhaps?"

"You are enjoying this way too much," I said. "I hope it at least worked."

"Like a charm. We're businesslike on duty, but afterward we're on a first-name basis," Diana said. "I even gave up my assigned bunk so one of the girls could move in with a friend after Sergeant Miller left us. That endeared me to the remaining holdouts, even though it left me with the coldest room in the barracks."

"Sounds like someone got transferred out," I said, then took a drink. "Or did she marry a fighter pilot?"

"Very droll, Billy. No, from the gossip I heard, she was caught in the men's barracks. According to the girls, it was only the first time she was caught. Her punishment was exile to a small listening post in a windmill on a bluff east of here. Beautiful view, but isolated, with few distractions for fun-loving types."

"Bad news for her. But you're an officer," I said. "Don't you have privileges?"

"Only for my fiancé, dearest," Diana said. She shot me a wink as our rabbit pies were brought to the table. I felt as finely fricasseed as the hare before me swimming in gravy, onions, and carrots.

I AWOKE WITH a start in a dark room, a deepening noise drumming in my head. Where was I? I swung out of my bed and rubbed my eyes as the thrumming grew louder.

"Relax, old chap," Jack Walters said from the other side of the room. "It's the Lancs coming back from Hanover. Or what's left of it."

Right. I was at the air base, bunking with Lieutenant Walters. Those were Lancasters, the big British four-engine bombers returning from a raid. I glanced at the luminous dial on my watch. Three fifteen.

"How much longer?" I asked as the first bomber roared overhead.

"A couple of hours," Walters said. "The squadron put up forty for this raid. They'll be coming back in small groups. Don't worry, you get used to it."

I didn't plan to be around long enough to get used to this racket. I smashed the lumpy pillow over my head to drown out the incessant rattling of the glass. It didn't work. I got up and walked to the window, the wooden floor cold beneath my bare feet. The barracks, a long three-story brick building like much of the base architecture, had a view of the main runway. I pushed back the curtain and watched the procession of Lancasters coming in low and slow, lights on, all four Rolls-Royce Merlin engines snarling.

Three Lancs taxied to hangars in the distance. The low, wide, arched roofs were eerily illuminated by dull lights within. A fourth bomber lumbered toward the runway, losing altitude quickly as flames trailed from one engine. A red flare was fired from the aircraft, a signal that there were wounded aboard, and that the plane was badly shot up. One wingtip lowered and the bomber wobbled as the pilot tried to keep his approach straight on the runway.

I gripped the windowsill, hardly able to breathe as the drama played out before me. Ambulances and a fire truck raced along the road, red lights flashing. The bomber hit hard, bounced, then slewed as one of the wheels collapsed, the left wing scraping the runway until the plane finally ground to a halt. Emergency vehicles surrounded it, floodlights illuminating the smoking wreck.

I could see the figures scrambling out of the damaged bomber. A fire truck sprayed water on the flames spreading along the port wing. Two stretchers carried the wounded to waiting ambulances. It was strange watching this drama play out in the distance, knowing the terror and pain both the aircrew and ground crew must've been feeling while I stood in my skivvies, a soft bed within easy reach.

"You don't really get used to it," Walters said. He appeared next to me at the window and stared at the scene outside. "Not ever."

"No, you don't," I said, and closed the curtain. It was probably the same in the air, waiting at the base, at sea, or in a foxhole. You might tell yourself a story about how it all rolls off your back, but the weight of it never leaves you.

I was curious and wanted to know why this squadron had come back in dribs and drabs. Flying in squadron formation was important for maintaining maximum defensive fire, and it seemed odd that the forty aircraft deliberately returned in small groups. But this wasn't the time for curiosity. I went back to the sack and wondered why someone in England had ended Brockman's life when so many Germans were ready and waiting for their chance.

"Two dead, two wounded in that Lanc last night," Walters said as he set his tray on the table. It was early morning in the officers' mess, and he'd asked about the Lancaster crash last night. "One of our kites was shot down over Germany. No parachutes sighted, but that doesn't mean no one got out. Visibility is wretched at night."

"There's always hope," I said, even though I knew the chances of surviving in the flak-filled sky were slight.

"False hope, probably," Walters admitted, pushing his powdered eggs around. I washed down a mouthful of toast with coffee that wasn't bad, considering this was a British mess. "But overall, losses were incredibly light, for once."

"What's the deal with the squadron coming back in penny packets?" I asked. "Doesn't the whole formation return together, as best it can?" I wasn't an expert on bombers, Yank or Brit, but I knew that was unusual.

"Yes, but things are a bit different here," Walters said. "This is 101 Squadron. I'm sure Squadron Officer Conan Doyle has filled you in."

"Things were a bit hectic yesterday," I said.

"I'll only tell you what everyone on base already knows. The rest I'll leave to the boss lady," he said. "These Lancasters are outfitted for radio countermeasures. They jam the frequencies Jerry uses to vector night fighters to our bomber streams. Just like your American chaps do in daylight bombing, the RAF puts up hundreds of aircraft attacking German cities at night."

"So the job of 101 Squadron is to protect the larger formation with radio jamming," I said as I finished off my eggs. "Which means they must be pretty spread out."

"You are a detective, Captain," Walters said. "Well done. That's why they come back in small groups. The squadron is hundreds of miles apart on the return leg."

"Call me Billy, okay? And tell me about the Americans on this base," I said. "You never saw Major Brockman around?"

"Not that I know of. There are two American B-24 bombers over in the hush-hush hangar," Walters said. "It's on the north side of the base, screened by camouflage netting. Huge thing, and one is cautioned not to loiter about."

"I don't see any Yank flyboys in here," I said as I cast my gaze around the room, checking the uniforms at the long tables. RAF blue and British Army khaki were it as far as variety.

"Oh, they have their own mess and quarters," Walters said. "There's a couple of new buildings near their hangar. Easier than driving around the perimeter road."

"They keep to themselves?" I asked.

"No, there's plenty of our chaps who work with them. The RAF has been at radio countermeasures for a while, and I guess we're sharing our knowledge with the latecomers," Walters said. "No offense meant."

"None taken, Jack," I said. I was eager to hear what Lieutenant Walters thought of the Americans and any trouble they might have brought with them. A casual conversation with him might be more enlightening than the official version I was bound to hear later that morning. "What about the pubs in town? Everybody must go in for a few drinks now and then?"

"They do, Billy. But you must understand aircrews. They stick together, officers and men," Jack said. "They fly together, they drink together. And the only time the RAF lads get to go is when there's no night mission on account of the weather. There's no bad blood to speak of."

"None to speak of," I said. "What's left unspoken, Jack?"

"I shouldn't say, Billy."

"Then whisper," I said. "I never heard it from you. But I need any lead, no matter how slim."

"All right," Jack said. He rested his elbows on the table and leaned forward. His eyes darted from side to side, checking to be sure no one was listening. "There's been some trouble over the Jews."

"What Jews?" I said. Surprised, I spoke louder than I'd meant to.

Jack shook his head quickly, then stood and left.

CHAPTER EIGHT

I TURNED UP the collar of my trench coat as I walked to Elham House where the Y Service was headquartered. It looked like it had been there long before the base. Before Wilbur and Orville, for that matter. It was a small country estate. Georgian, if I understood English architecture. A bit worn, but three impressive stories of red brick with a row of dormers on the roof. It looked out of place amid the Nissen huts with their rounded metal roofs and the more recent utilitarian brick and wood structures. But the tall radio mast behind Elham House proclaimed it as central to the business of modern warfare.

I could have driven, but I wanted to get a sense of the place, and the best way to do that was on foot, even if it was only a quarter mile away across this sprawling air base. I began to question my choice as the dark, scudding clouds spat cold rain. I was glad I'd at least worn my combat boots. I ran across a dirt road, dodging heavy trucks as they ground their gears. Everyone was busy, from the drivers to the ground crews pedaling bicycles, their heads down as they raced to hangars to begin servicing the big Lancasters. No American uniforms in sight. Men of the RAF Regiment drove in jeeps around the perimeter road, checking the barbed wire fence. Everything looked normal and routine. Except I knew that, somewhere, it wasn't.

With Elham House only a few yards away, the rain came down in sheets. I realized I was the only Yank dumb enough to be caught out in it. I dashed up the stone steps to the front door and entered, leaving a trail of water behind me.

"You must be Captain Boyle," a Women's Auxiliary Air Force sergeant said as she looked up from a file on her desk. She had dark hair, eyebrows that had been plucked into a thin arc, and puckish lips that threatened to turn up and smile.

"How'd you guess?" I said. I wiped my boots on the rug and hung my soaked trench coat on a peg along with my service cap. I straightened my Ike jacket and gave her a smile, the kind that has been known to charm desk sergeants on two continents.

"You're the only Yank we're expecting, Captain," she said. "Your orders, please?"

I handed over the papers Jean Conan Doyle had given me, which the sergeant read carefully. Then she asked for identification. I forked over my SHAEF ID card, which she studied twice as carefully.

"Very good. Sign here, please," she said, and opened a leather-bound appointment book. "Be sure to note the time and to sign out when you leave."

"You're quite thorough, Sergeant—?" I said.

"Halfpenny. Sergeant Halfpenny, in case you were going to ask for my given name."

"You were made for this job," I said, and wondered if that really could be her first name.

"Take the stairs at the end of the hall. Squadron Officer Conan Doyle is waiting for you," Sergeant Halfpenny said as she rolled her eyes. Then, under her breath, she added, "Has been for some time."

I decided Sergeant wasn't really her first name as I double-timed it upstairs to a long hallway tiled with black-and-white checkered marble. The woodwork was polished, and the brass doorknobs gleamed. Looked like the Y Service was high on the list for fancy digs.

Conan Doyle's name was displayed above the first door on the left. I knocked and entered.

"Ah, Captain Boyle," she said. She looked up from a stack of papers, which she quickly put away in a folder. "You are well rested, I take it?"

"It was a little rough sleeping with the Lancasters coming in, ma'am," I said. I came to a faint semblance of attention as I suddenly realized I didn't know if a squadron officer outranked me or not. "I spent some time with Lieutenant Walters, getting the lay of the land. Then I took a walk in the rain."

"Did you learn anything?"

"That 101 Squadron is operating some kind of radio interference on bombing raids," I said. "And that the Americans pretty much stay to themselves over in the hush-hush hangar."

"Is that what they call it?" Conan Doyle said with a smile as she gestured for me to take a seat in front of her desk. "As for 101 Squadron, that much is common knowledge. Lieutenant Walters didn't say more?"

"No," I said. I settled into the chair and surveyed her office. It sat at the corner of the building and had a view of the distant runway from one window and rolling hills beyond the fence at the other. I figured I'd ask around more obliquely about who the Jews Walters had referred to were. I found it best not to assume things about people's sensibilities. "He clammed up after that."

"Good. We take security very seriously here," Conan Doyle said. "Everyone, from the newest recruits to the highest rank, is constantly reminded about the need for secrecy. We need to foster the impression that this is simply an average RAF base. Anyone who breaches security is liable for punishment under the Official Secrets Act."

"Perhaps Brockman was killed to stop him from revealing

who had blabbed about 101 Squadron or the Y Service," I said. "Have you had any violations of the Act?"

"No. I've had to transfer a few individuals for comments made to civilians, usually under the influence of drink, but that was more to set an example," she said.

"Could any of them be harboring a grudge?" I asked.

"I wouldn't doubt it, especially since I had them sent to Burma. Two corporals, three sergeants, and a wing commander, which effectively put a stop to loose lips for all ranks," the squadron officer said. "But that rather eliminates them from suspicion, I'd say."

"That would do it," I said. "Diana told me you were going to fill us in on Major Brockman's status today. It would be a good place to start."

"I already briefed Captain Seaton earlier. She's busy monitoring the Italians at the moment. They're very chatty this morning. As for Major Frederick Brockman, he is with the American 36th Bomb Squadron, Radar Countermeasures. Was, I should say."

"Is that our version of 101 Squadron?" I asked.

"It is somewhat more specialized," Conan Doyle said. She stood and walked to the window, her gaze fixed on the view of the runway. "The Lancasters of 101 Squadron carry a reduced bombload while protecting the bomber stream with electronic jamming, which is done by a single specialist crewman. But your 36th Bomb Squadron carries no bombs, despite the name. Their B-24s are so crammed with equipment there is no room for ordnance. Their primary purpose is to deceive, confuse, and outwit the enemy by advanced scientific means. It is modern electronic warfare, Captain Boyle. A whole new front in the fight against Nazi Germany. One we do not wish them to be aware of."

"I'm not sure I understand," I said. "I barely grasp how radar works."

"I can give you one example," she said as she paced in front of the window. "Jackal, which was described in the papers you discovered, is a high-powered VHF barrage jammer designed to thwart German tank communications. Imagine a panzer division about to attack and, suddenly, all their radios are filled with nothing but static. Lovely notion, don't you think?"

"Yes, especially if you're in a foxhole," I said. "It actually works?"

"Indeed, it does," Conan Doyle said. "And the RAF has a version as well. Jostle, as you might have guessed. Tests have shown it to be even more effective, so we are in the process of replacing your American Jackal with the RAF Jostle."

"It all sounds pretty Flash Gordon to me," I said. "Attacking panzers with electrical rays from the sky? It's hard to believe."

"Good. Let us strive to keep the Germans in a similar state of blissful ignorance, shall we?"

"I'm an expert when it comes to blissful ignorance," I said. "What exactly was Brockman's role?"

"Major Brockman was temporarily assigned to this base to oversee the conversion of two American B-24 bombers to Jostle. He worked in radio manufacturing before the war and was an excellent choice for the project."

"Is everything going well with the new hardware?" I asked.

"Yes, very well," she said. "There were some technical difficulties early on, but they were overcome, and now the work is nearly done. But I need to know if Brockman's killing had anything to do with this project."

"Is the work being checked?" I asked.

"Double- and triple-checked," she said. "So far, the equipment looks to be operational. I'd like to trust the people involved just as much. That's where you and Diana come in. Start asking questions and don't stop until you get answers. If the killing was the result of a personal dispute, I want to know. If it had even the slightest bit to do with our work here, I *must* know. And soon."

"When you say 'our work here,' you mean the Y Service as well as the airborne radio jamming?" I asked. "I don't need details, and I probably wouldn't understand them, but it would help to have the big picture."

"Let's go," Conan Doyle said, glancing at her wristwatch. "I'll show you what we do here at Elham House and by then Diana should be done with her shift."

"Diana mentioned that a Sergeant Miller had been transferred out recently," I said as I rose to follow her. "Did that have anything to do with loose lips?"

"Lipstick, actually. Sally Miller. She was found in the men's barracks. Strictly verboten. Very good at her job, so I exiled her to a lonely listening post down the coast to keep her out of further trouble and to retain her expertise."

"No possible connection to Brockman?" I asked.

"It wasn't the American barracks, so I don't see how it could be," Conan Doyle said. "But ask Sergeant Halfpenny if you wish. They were chums. You undoubtedly encountered her earlier."

"I did. She seemed a bit grim."

"Whichever of my girls is on the duty desk has to put up with self-important men who seem to think they can simply brush by them whenever they wish," Conan Doyle said. "Grim work, dealing with such. I've thought about arming them with Sten guns."

"Yes, ma'am," I said, not wanting to appear any more self-important than I already managed to.

"First stop is Operation Corona," Conan Doyle said. She halted in front of a door with a glass window. Inside, workbenches along each wall held banks of radio transmitters. Only two people were working, a WAAF and an RAF corporal, both reading from a script and speaking into microphones as a platter on a turntable recorded their voices. Even with the door closed, I could hear the loud and angry German words.

"What happens here other than playacting?" I asked.

"A great deal more, although there is a strong element of theater," Conan Doyle said.

She explained that Operation Corona utilized German-speaking WAAF staff to impersonate Luftwaffe air defense personnel. They would initiate radio contact with German pilots and countermand orders, directing night fighters away from the RAF bombers as they entered German airspace.

"Do the Germans use women for their communications?" I asked.

"At first they used men, so we did as well. Then they decided to switch to female operators, but we were ready for them and my WAAFs were on the air that night."

"How did you know they were going to switch?" I said.

"That's why it's called Intelligence, Captain," she said. "Now we've refined the operation so that we impersonate individual German ground controllers. Ghost voices, we call them. Quite effective."

"But what are those two doing with the record?"

"We prerecord overlapping voices and then play them back on the frequencies used by German night fighters. It's known as jumble-voice jamming, which generates great confusion and prevents the real communications from getting through," she said. "We make new recordings every morning for the next night's operation."

"I imagine everyone here speaks perfect German," I said.

"For Corona, it is an absolute requirement. Most of the girls who work here are German Jews who were brought over in the thirties as children. It's their native tongue, which is perfect for our purposes. And theirs. No better revenge, I imagine, than using their language as a weapon against those who do their people such grievous harm."

"I can only imagine," I said as I watched the young woman waving her hands and shouting over the fellow who was plowing through his script in an increasingly loud voice, both delivering their harsh words like machine-gun fire. The war of words never felt so real.

The tour continued as the squadron officer showed me the other rooms on this and the next floor. WAAFs sat hunched over radios, both British HRO shortwave receivers and new American Hallicrafters VHF units, slowly turning dials as they searched frequencies for enemy voices or Morse communications. I saw Diana in one room, her army khaki standing out among ten WAAFs in RAF blue. She had one hand pressed against her headset as she took notes with the other. It appeared to be intense work, and we didn't linger for chitchat.

The last room contained radios salvaged from downed Luftwaffe aircraft. The major advantage of these units was the preset dials with established frequencies for communications with air units, ground control, and command. No hunting through the radio waves required.

"Quite an operation," I said as we took the stairs down to the main lobby.

"It is," Conan Doyle said proudly. "We do our job well, and I expect the same from you and Diana. She should join you shortly. Report back to me this evening on your progress."

"We will. One question before you go," I said as we stopped a few paces away from Sergeant Halfpenny. "Are there services on base for your Jewish personnel?"

"Services?" She looked confused.

"Yes. Like with a rabbi," I said.

"I've never seen a Jewish chaplain, now that you mention it," she said. "I know we've had services conducted on a few occasions by Church of England and Roman Catholic chaplains, but we leave regular services to the churches in town. I have no idea if there is a local synagogue. Why do you ask?"

"Just curious," I said. "About everything."

"Narrow your focus, Captain. We're talking about murder and security, not religious differences," she said.

"After listening to all that German being recorded, I thought about how people might feel about Germans in their midst, even if they are Jews who have been persecuted. Do American- or British-born Jews take offense at their presence? If so, did any of that involve Major Brockman? He was Jewish himself."

"I hope you have something more substantial for me tonight," she said, and ignored the question as she walked away.

"Is that what it's like being a copper?" Sergeant Halfpenny asked. She turned in her chair to face me.

"What do you mean?"

"Asking questions that have naught to do with anything," she said.

"Ah, but you don't know until the questions have been asked and answered," I said. Halfpenny gave a mild, derisive snort and returned to her paperwork.

The sergeant had a point. But I'd wanted to raise the issue of Walters's comment with Squadron Officer Conan Doyle indirectly. Confronting an officer about troubling issues on their base was a sure way to put them on the defensive. Bringing it up in casual conversation might give me a notion if there was anything behind what Walters had said.

Far as I could tell, it was clear that the squadron officer had no inkling of trouble with anti-Jewish sentiment. And that we were expected to come up with something for her by nightfall.

The hunt for solid inklings was on.

CHAPTER NINE

I'D GOTTEN OFF on the wrong foot with Sergeant Halfpenny and decided to start over with her as I waited for Diana.

"Perhaps you can help me, Sergeant," I said as stepped closer.

"With what, Captain?"

"Anything you can tell me about Major Brockman. Did you ever meet him?" I said.

"Why? Do you want to know if he went to church?"

"No, it's got nothing to do with that," I said, then saw her cut loose a smile. "Oh, you're making fun of me."

"Not you, Captain," she said. "I'm making fun of your question. Why did you want to know about rabbis?"

"I'm curious about how German-born Jews get along here," I said. "It must be strange for them."

"Most of the girls came over on the Kindertransport," she said. "Ever hear of it?"

"Yes, but not all the details," I said. "Tell me."

"Back in 1938, the government took in ten thousand Jewish kids from Germany, all under eighteen years old. No parents, just kids. They were placed in homes and farms across Britain, and now a lot of those kids are fighting back. Like the girls here. All the native German speakers we have were Kindertransport. So yes, I'd say it is strange for them. A strange life that's taken a terrible turn. By now, their parents are probably dead."

"Britain saved a lot of lives doing that," I said. "But there's always some who take offense at the presence of Jews in their midst, aren't there?"

"Of course. Was Major Brockman Jewish?"

"Yes," I said, having forgotten my original question. "Did you ever meet him?"

"Once, only for a moment," she said. "I was on duty when he signed out, and we chatted a bit. Nice chap, not a show-off like some Yanks. I hope you find who did him in."

"Hello, Joyce," Diana said as she approached. "I see you've met Billy?"

"I have. Friend of your fiancé, is he?"

"No, I haven't had a chance to meet the lucky man," I said, then turned to Diana. "How is Elmer?"

"Marvelous," Diana said. "He just won the boxing championship on his base. I'm sure he'll be glad to give you a lesson. Shall we go?"

I grabbed my cap and raincoat and then remembered what Sergeant Halfpenny and I had been talking about.

"Who was Brockman here to see?" I asked her. "Squadron Officer Conan Doyle?"

"I don't know, I came on duty as he left. Should be easy enough to find, it was only a fortnight or so ago," she said, and began to flip through the pages of the leather-bound ledger. She ran her finger down the column of entries, and stopped, her eyes wide. "Oh my, that's a surprise."

"What?" Diana asked, looking over her shoulder.

"Sergeant Sally Miller. He was here to see Sally, and she never breathed a word to me!"

■ ■ ■

"WE NEED TO talk to Sally," I said to Diana as we walked to the jeep. "How far up the coast is she?"

"About twenty miles," she said as she sidestepped a puddle. The rain had stopped, but the low, gray clouds looked ready to cut loose again. "St. Margaret's at Cliffe, past Dover at the most southeastern point in Britain. There's a house with a windmill overlooking the Channel, where the Royal Navy operates a small listening post. Sally is under orders not to leave the premises."

"Then she'll be easy to find," I said. I unfastened the canvas side for Diana to step into the jeep. "The question is, do we start with her or talk to the Yanks first?"

"Sally is supposed to stay put," Diana said. "But who knows how long before the American crews leave? The plan is to bring in more B-24s for conversion once these two have been thoroughly tested. I'd say we start with the Yanks while we have them. But we can also question whomever it was Sally met in the men's barracks as well. I do wonder if he's escaped punishment. Jean never mentioned him to me."

"You don't know who it was?"

"No, it happened before I arrived. Other than the location of Sergeant Miller's new posting, I didn't get any details," Diana said. "Perhaps we should see if Jean can answer that question."

"Let's try," I said, and we hurried back to Conan Doyle's office as the rain started. Diana knocked and entered. She said we had a quick question, and Conan Doyle nodded for us to proceed without inviting us to sit.

I began with our discovery that Major Brockman had signed in to see Sergeant Miller just before she was sent packing. I watched Conan Doyle for any trace of reaction to the connection between those two, but she seemed just as surprised as Sally's pal Halfpenny had been.

"Sergeant Miller's transfer happened before I arrived," Diana said to Conan Doyle. "Is there anything you can tell us about the incident that led up to it?"

"It was reported to me that Sally entered the noncommissioned officers' barracks," she said. "When I asked her, she readily admitted it. The regulations are in place to protect all parties and to prevent the barracks from becoming a bordello. I had no choice but to send her away."

"Who did she visit?" I asked.

"Flight Sergeant John Adler. One of the special operators," Conan Doyle said. "A German lad, as most of the SOs are. His original name was Johann. Known as Johnny now."

"What was his punishment, ma'am?" Diana asked.

"Since I was not his commanding officer, it was not left to me," she said.

"Is Sally from Germany as well?" I asked.

"No, but she speaks the language like a native," Conan Doyle said. "Her father worked for a shipping line based in Hamburg, and she grew up there."

"Where can we find Johnny Adler?" I asked. "He may know something about Brockman's interest in Sally."

"In a POW camp somewhere in Germany, unfortunately," Conan Doyle said. "His Lancaster went down a few days after Sally left. They were hit on the return leg. Fortunately, the crew managed to bail out, so we hope they all survived. The Red Cross notifies us when prisoners are processed and assigned to a camp, which can take weeks. Not much help, I'm afraid."

"Well, I guess we're back to questioning the Americans," Diana said. We took to the stairs once again.

"Then we should find Constable Sallow and see if he came up with anything at the train station," I said. "We can drive out to interview Sally tomorrow."

"Let's not forget the constables who went door-to-door along the Old Dover Road," she said as I cranked the wipers to clear the rain from the windshield. "Let's hope we can come up with something. Jean is expecting progress."

"She made that clear," I said. I threaded my way through traffic and told Diana what Walters had said about Jews and asked if she knew of anything brewing.

"No trouble I know of," Diana said. "The girls who were born in Germany told me they overheard a few snide remarks when they first arrived here, about both their religion and their former homeland."

"But nothing overtly threatening?" I asked.

"No. From what they described, it smacked of the infamous English distaste for foreigners. It seemed to pass as soon as people realized they were doing important work at Elham House, work that benefits Great Britain. Even if they don't know what exactly goes on there, they know it must be vital," she said.

"I'm puzzled by the way Walters said it. 'There's been some trouble over the Jews.' That could mean anything from his being bigoted to concern with how Jews are being treated," I said.

"Well, there are those of the Jewish faith throughout the RAF," Diana said. "And 101 Squadron has an extra crewman on each Lancaster. All German-speaking, many of them Jewish refugees like the women at Elham House."

"Interesting. Let's see what dope we can pick up without being obvious. Who's the American commanding officer now?"

"One of the pilots, Lieutenant Peter Harker. I don't have much more dope than that," Diana said, and let loose a sharp laugh at the sound of Yank lingo mixed with her plummy accent. "Oh, that won't do, will it, Billy?"

"You ain't that sorta dame, kid," I said, gangster-style. I

turned onto the wide roadway that led to the massive hangars where Lancasters were being readied for tonight's raid. If the weather allowed. The Lanc's huge one-hundred-foot wingspan dwarfed the ground crew servicing the heavy bombers.

Approaching the American hush-hush hangar, we saw a tractor towing one of the B-24 Liberators out onto the runway. Unlike the Lancaster's dark-green-and-brown camouflage, the B-24's unpainted aluminum frame gleamed, even under the overcast skies. I parked a respectful distance away, and we followed the bomber's slow progress.

"They must be loading Jostle," Diana said, and pointed to an oversize cylindrical steel drum strapped to a forklift awaiting the B-24. Half a dozen men stood around it. They ignored us and kept their eyes fixed on the advancing bomber.

"Is that a ditch they're putting it in?" I said as I spied the outline of planks set around what looked like a grave.

"Yes. It's too tall to load into the bomb bay, so they place it in a ditch and then hoist it into the aircraft. Very carefully, I might add," she said.

Two men jumped into the pit as the forklift lowered the Jostle unit into the ground, guiding it as they attached steel cables. When they were done, the forklift backed up and the tractor pulled the B-24 over the ditch and halted. The bomb bay doors opened with a mechanical whine, and only then did one of the men take notice and walk over to us.

"Lieutenant Harker," he said, tossing off a salute. "Captain, ma'am, how can I help you?" His one-piece herringbone twill mechanic's suit was covered with grease and oil stains, and he pulled a cloth from his pocket to clean his hands. Sandy hair stuck out from under his service cap. He was young enough to still have a few stray freckles splashed across his nose.

"I'm Captain Boyle and this is Captain Seaton," I said. "We're here to ask some questions about Major Brockman."

"I heard someone was coming," he said. "I'll be glad to help. We all will, but I gotta finish this job. You mind waiting?"

"Go ahead, Lieutenant," Diana said. "It's important work."

"Great. I'll have Sparks explain things to you in the meantime," Harker said. He waved one of the men over and told him to give us the rundown.

"I thought all radiomen were called Sparky," I said, alluding to the most common nickname in the army. He wore the same herringbone twill outfit with sergeant's stripes sporting a *T* for Technical, which reflected his specialist duties.

"Well, I am the radio operator," he said. "Sparks is my real name, so I guess it was destiny." He grinned and his dark eyes lit up as he studied Diana for a moment too long. Then his cheeks reddened. He was just a kid. Not that we were that much older, but the few years we had on him had been filled with death, grief, and betrayal. Made you feel old.

"How long you been over here, Sparks?" I asked.

"Four months," he said. "Only nine missions, though. We'll be back at it once the Jostle equipment checks out. Look, they're getting ready to hoist it up."

Sparks beckoned us to come closer as the whirring from a hydraulic winch filled the air. Two men were in the ditch, carefully guiding the unit held by strong cables as it rose. It was larger than a regular steel drum, with gauges, electric components, and conduits arrayed on its top surface. The lid was secured by heavy bolts, and the whole thing looked like it weighed a ton.

"There must be a lot of complex equipment inside," Diana said. "Do you understand how any of it works?"

"A little, Captain. Jostle is a two-point-five-kilowatt jamming transmitter. It's connected to a panoramic receiver that scans radio bands at high speed. When it finds traffic on any band, a blip pops up on a cathode-ray tube. That gives us a fix on the transmission, and once we confirm it's German, we flip a switch, and the jamming signal grabs hold of it and overwhelms the voice chatter. Works for ground and air communications. Pretty remarkable stuff, isn't it?"

"It is," I said as the Jostle contraption disappeared into the bomb bay. "I'm glad you didn't know a lot. We might have been here all day." I winked to show him I was joking. Sort of. I could barely keep up with what he'd said. The cables were tossed down and the doors closed.

"Did Major Brockman instruct you in its use?" Diana asked.

"The major was a great guy," Sparks said. "I can't believe he's dead. Twenty missions and not a scratch, can you believe it? Think you can find out who did it?"

"We're on the case," I said. "Anything you can tell us will help at this point. So, answer the question, please."

"Well, yeah, the major oversaw the whole project. He knew electronics backward and forward. He had some kind of business manufacturing radio parts before the war, I think," Sparks said. He rubbed his chin like people do to stimulate their memory. It left a smudge.

"Yeah," Harker said. He climbed out of the ditch and wiped his hands on an already filthy cloth. "Between the major and Bigsby, we had a regular brain trust here when it came to radar countermeasures."

"Who's Bigsby?" I asked as I eyed Harker's hands and the grime on Sparks's cheek.

"Bigs? He's one of the British ground crew and knows more about electronics than most of us, even Sparks here," Harker said. "He's on loan from 101 Squadron, and Major Brockman worked with him a lot."

"We shall speak to Bigsby, then," Diana said. "But first, tell us if you noticed anything unusual in Major Brockman's behavior in the days leading up to his death. Was he worried about anything or anybody?"

"He was worried about getting Jostle to work," Sparks said. "Maybe a little short-tempered the last coupla days before he died. But nothing out of the ordinary."

"We're under a lot of pressure to get this installation completed," Harker said. "I've been told you have security clearances, so you probably know this machine disrupts tank communications. The brass wants us flying missions, pronto."

"Over Bastogne, would be my guess," I said. The Germans had launched a massive offensive earlier in the month through the quiet Ardennes sector. The town of Bastogne marked an important crossroads, and the standby American GIs had stymied the Kraut advance. But there were still too many panzers knocking at the gate.

"Yeah, that's one of the areas we'll be taking the Beast of Bourbon," Harker said as he pointed to artwork that graced the nose of his bomber. It showed a bottle of Old Crow Kentucky bourbon pouring bombs instead of booze. "You can understand how Major Brockman would be under a lot of stress."

"He was on the prowl early yesterday morning," Sparks said. "He asked me about a few components that had gone missing."

"What kind of components?" Diana asked.

"Oh, an oscillator and some of the gauges you saw," Sparks said. "He told me to clean up the workbench and then do an inventory."

"It's tough with two crews working in this hangar," Harker said.

"Where's the other B-24?" I asked.

"Out on another test flight," Harker said. "They got their Jostle installed before ours, but something's not working. They were flying Christmas morning too. The major was nervous about it. Maybe that's why he went for a walk by himself."

"Have you done the inventory?" I asked Sparks, who looked sheepishly at his pilot.

"No, we haven't had a moment to spare," Harker said. "Things can get hectic real fast, and we swap parts between the two crews as we need to. They gave us plenty of spares, and we've been too busy to keep records. All of us, not just Sparks."

"Yeah, you've been working hard, I can see," I said. I stepped forward and wiped my finger against Sparks's chin. He flinched, startled.

"Captain?" he asked, rubbing his face as if my touch had burned.

"Grease," I said, and rubbed the substance between my fingers. "Sticks to you, doesn't it?"

CHAPTER TEN

"Yes, sir, it does," Harker said, a wary look crossing his face. "That's why we wear these coveralls. Is there a problem?"

"There was for Major Brockman," I said. "There were traces of grease found in the wound on the back of his head. From grease on the murder weapon, which will certainly be on the hands and clothing of whoever hit him."

"Is that how he died, sir?" Sparks asked. "Smashed in the head?"

"Yes. You didn't know?" I said.

"No. We just heard he was killed off base somewhere," Sparks said.

"If you didn't know the details, then it could have been an automobile accident," Diana said. "Why did you say you hoped we caught whoever did it?"

"I just figured he'd been killed, that's all," Sparks said as he took an involuntary half step back. "By someone, I mean, not like being hit by a bus."

"Why?" I asked.

"I dunno, I guess because we don't have a lot of accidental deaths over here," Sparks said. "Sorry, sir."

"Sparks, the guys could use a hand with the electrical connections," Harker said. He crooked a thumb in the direction of the B-24 as it was wheeled back into the hangar. Harker watched him go, then turned his attention toward us. "Sparks is a gunner as well as a radio operator. On our last mission, the other waist gunner took a 20-millimeter explosive shell to the chest. He and Sparks were buddies. You can excuse him for thinking it was a violent death."

"Sure. What was your first reaction, Lieutenant?" I asked.

"As soon as I heard they were sending two captains to investigate, I knew it meant trouble," Harker said. "Especially one from Elham House, ma'am. The house of secrets, they call it."

"We like our secrets well kept, so don't even mention there is such a place, especially off base," Diana said. "Getting back to the point, Lieutenant, did you observe any unusual behavior on the part of Major Brockman or anyone else?"

"No, nothing that wasn't part of our job here," Harker said. "Leading Aircraftman Bigsby probably spent more time with the major, so you can ask him this afternoon. I guess 101 Squadron wanted him back for some job."

"When did you last see Major Brockman?" Diana asked.

"Yesterday morning. We'd had a big Christmas Eve dinner the night before, and the skipper told us we could start a couple of hours late in the morning. I saw him when I went to breakfast. He said he was going off base for a few hours to take a walk. First time I'd seen him take any time off from the job, but hey, it was Christmas. Then he got into his vehicle."

"Did he go off in a jeep?" I asked.

"No. The skipper used a staff car. Ford sedan," Harker said. Now we knew what to look for. An olive-drab four-door with a big white star ought to be plenty easy to find.

"Okay, let's meet the rest of your crew," I said. "Then we'll need to look at the major's office and quarters."

"There's only two others here," Harker said. "The bombardier and the other gunners are back at the base flying missions. We have Sergeant Sparks here for his electronics specialty. And

Sergeant Levinson, the flight engineer. He mans the top turret and is responsible for the engines and overall mechanics. Then there's my copilot Doug Slade, and our navigator, Stan Bailey. Bailey was just assigned to us and only arrived a couple of days ago, so I don't know how much help he'll be."

"We will start with the major's office and leave you to work with your men," Diana said.

Harker led us to a partitioned section at the rear of the hangar. We passed a long workbench strewn with tools, radio sets, and electrical components. I could see why Sparks hadn't gotten around to that inventory. Harker opened the door to Brockman's office and said he'd take us to the major's quarters when we were done.

"Unlocked," I said when Harker was gone. "Clues may be lacking."

"At least we learned something from Harker," Diana said as we entered the office. "Brockman drove himself to the cliffs. The question is, what happened to his vehicle?"

"Maybe it was simply a theft," I said, not really believing it. Diana raised an eyebrow of doubt at the idea.

"Well, at least Major Brockman was neat and organized," she said. She surveyed the nicely aligned stacks of papers and files. "It makes searching easier and tampering noticeable."

She was right. Brockman's office was as squared away as he was. Personnel reports were held in several files on the left side of the desk: Harker's, along with the rest of his crew's. Comments about performance and readiness. Other than a few quibbles here and there, the fitness reports were exemplary. Not surprising, since I expected the 36th Bomb Squadron would be assigned top-notch aircrew given their special jamming role.

Opposite his desk, a typewriter sat on a small table. A three-tiered inbox held carbon paper, two recently typed memos, and their carbon copies. One was to his squadron commander, dated on Christmas Day. Brockman must have typed it in the morning before he left for the cliffs. Not the most cheerful way to start Christmas Day, but war has its demands. The note said that Jostle should be operational in both bombers in three days and then he'd be ready to receive two more. The second was dated the day before, addressed to the supply officer for 101 Squadron, requesting a new Mandrel jammer.

"Diana, what's Mandrel? Brockman wanted a new one," I said.

"It targets German radar," she said with barely a glance up from her search of a four-drawer file cabinet. "It's usually used as the bombers approach enemy territory to broadcast radio noise on known radar bands. Disrupts the Nazi early-warning radar quite nicely."

"I guess we use it too," I said, after I'd read through Brockman's request.

"Oh yes, standard-issue, especially for this squadron," Diana said as she flipped through files.

I tossed the paper back into the tray and moved on to the desk drawers, reminding myself to tell Harker about the memos. The drawers held little more than discarded pencil stubs, paper clips, a few requisition forms, and the kind of dust that ends up in desks everywhere.

"Nothing," I said. "It doesn't look like Brockman spent a lot of time in here. Probably too busy with the aircraft."

"These files are of no help either," Diana said. "Manuals, schematics, reports on enemy radar frequencies, and operating instructions for various radios, British and American. Not to mention blackout procedures from 1940."

"Okay," I said as I stood to survey the office. Not much else other than a few wooden shelves holding boxes of tools and spools of wire. Brockman did what he had to do in here and not much more.

"Did you check the carbon paper?" Diana said. "You never know."

No, you never do. I remembered a clue once being found on carbon paper, but I think that was in a movie. Real life is never that easy, but I pulled out the dark, flimsy sheets to check them. The request for the Mandrel jammer was right on top, a worn, well-used sheet that had seen its final roll around the platen. Even so, I could make out the salutation to the 101 Squadron supply officer. The sheet under that was the memo to Brockman's commanding officer at the 36th, the unit's name clearly visible on the fresh page.

"Wait a minute," I said, and set the sheets down side by side. "Brockman typed this one yesterday, using a new piece of carbon paper. He typed the supply request the day before, using a sheet that was on its last legs."

"Very economical of him," Diana said as she waited for me to make my point.

"This is how they came out of the tray," I said, and placed the well-used sheet on top.

"Oh, I see," she said. "It's in the wrong order. Someone went through the carbon papers to see what the major had typed. Someone who got here before us."

"Which means Brockman took both the original and carbon copy with him, which is why our intruder was reduced to riffling through the carbon paper," I said.

"Or Major Brockman made a simple mistake," Diana said with a sigh. "Out of character, but still possible. This is thin gruel, Billy."

"If we didn't find him with his head bashed in, I'd agree it was just a mistake. But you're right, it's not much," I said. "This must have something to do with what Conan Doyle had you investigating."

"Yes. And the request for a new Mandrel unit is interesting," she said. "I'd like to know if the machine it replaced was broken, stolen, or lost. Clearly no one here is bothering to work on an inventory of missing parts. There's enough pressure on them to get back in the air as it is."

We decided to try Major Brockman's quarters next, then follow up with the rest of Harker's crew. The lieutenant told us where to find Brockman's room and said he'd arrange for his personal effects to be sent to his family.

We drove the short distance to the American barracks and found Brockman's quarters, right where Harker had indicated. It was on the third floor with a view of the hangar and the runway beyond, and it looked just like I'd expected.

"Neat as a pin," Diana said, echoing my thoughts.

The bunk was made the way they'd always insisted back in basic training. I was tempted to bounce a quarter off it for old times' sake. Uniforms were hung carefully, and drawers were full of neatly folded clothes.

A nightstand held a gooseneck lamp and a paperback Western by Zane Grey, one of the Armed Forces Editions. A table and two chairs completed the decor. A copy of *Stars and Stripes* was open on the table, next to stationery and a bottle of Scotch. A musette bag hung from the chair, and Diana went through it as I snooped around for anything of interest. There wasn't much. It looked like Brockman worked hard and long hours, spent little time in his quarters, and less in his office.

"Oh dear," Diana said. She was leafing through letters. "They're from his girlfriend. It's heartbreaking. And his mother as well. Nothing else, just plans that will never be." She put the letters back and laid the musette bag on the table. Personal effects.

"Here," I said, and tossed the paperback novel onto the table. It wasn't much, but perhaps it would hint at some leisure time that Frederick Brockman had enjoyed and bring a smile to his mother's face. The book slid off the musette bag onto the floor. I picked it up, along with the bookmark, which was nothing more than a page from a notepad, folded in half the long way.

"Whoa," I said, reading what Brockman had written. "APT-3 remote power control, H2S radar scope, high-speed scanner, S27 control box, VCR-97 cathode-ray tube, 5FP7 radar display tube, Mandrel high power transmitter."

"Hidden in plain sight," Diana said. "Well done, Major."

"Brockman did his own inventory of missing parts," I said. "Which got him killed."

CHAPTER ELEVEN

WE'D GONE BACK to the hangar and found Harker's crew ready to break for lunch. They weren't happy about being held up, but the chance to sit and gab with Diana seemed to soften the blow. We had a quick talk with Lieutenant Stan Bailey, the navigator who'd only recently arrived. He was new to radar countermeasures as well as to the crew and couldn't offer much of anything. The same with Lieutenant Doug Slade, copilot. He'd been laid up with an ear infection and hadn't been around the crew for a week. We sent them both off to chow and brought Sergeant Levinson into Brockman's office.

"Sergeant Felix Levinson?" Diana asked, her notebook at the ready.

"Technical Sergeant, ma'am. I'm the flight engineer." Levinson leaned back in his chair and sat quietly. Usually people being questioned by investigators are nervous, even those as innocent as babes. But Levinson had a calmness about him, which probably was useful for a guy who had to sit in the top turret and fight off Me 109s while he watched his four big Pratt & Whitney engines for any sign of trouble. He had thick black hair and a fair imitation of a Clark Gable mustache.

"You've got a big job," I said. "How involved are you with these jamming devices?"

"Plenty, Captain. I used to work for Ma Bell back in Jersey,"

Levinson said. "Installing telephones. All that experience with wiring comes in handy, especially getting all the fittings tight. You can't have a loose connection at thirty thousand feet."

"It doesn't look like you could easily open the Jostle container if you did," Diana said.

"No, the thing is pressurized to keep the hardware stable," Levinson said. "It's a beast, weighs about six hundred pounds. But it looks like it'll do the job."

"Are the other devices pressurized? Mandrel, for instance?" Diana asked. I knew where she was going with this. How easy was it to pop open these electronics and steal parts?

"No, Mandrel is not as sophisticated as Jostle. Does the job, don't get me wrong," he said. "But all it has to do is bounce back a Kraut radar signal onto itself."

"Ever have to repair Mandrel in flight?" I asked.

"No. Had one shot up, but there was no fixing it. Why? I can't see what that has to do with Major Brockman buying the farm," he said.

"Maybe nothing," Diana said. Levinson's gaze rested on Brockman's desk as if he expected to see him sitting there. "When was the Mandrel destroyed?" Diana asked, smiling to keep Levinson relaxed.

"Oh, about two weeks before we were sent here," he said. "We were given a newer model as a replacement, which came in handy. Works like a charm."

"You have everything you need here? Any equipment shortages, that sort of thing?" I asked.

"We have to do the paperwork dance, you know how the army goes," Levinson said. "And some days you just gotta scrounge as best you can. Now, tell me what this has to do with the skipper."

"We'll let you know when we know more," Diana said. "Now, tell us if you noticed anything odd in the days leading up to his death. Was anything upsetting him?"

"Major Brockman was a stickler for doing things by the book," Levinson said. "Nothing wrong with that, but he did get bothered if we were behind schedule. Or scrounging too much, not to mention gambling. He warned us off gambling with the RAF guys since we're paid more, and it wouldn't be right to take their dough. The major wanted us on our best behavior, on account of us being guests here."

"Are you behind schedule?" I asked.

"Maybe a half day's work. All this going to help you catch whoever killed the major?"

"Too soon to tell, Sergeant Levinson. What's the story with pilferage here? Anybody scrounging their way through your supplies?" I asked.

"We've had a few items go missing," he said with a shrug. "Lost in the shuffle, who knows? We got bigger things to worry about."

"Do you need a new Mandrel unit?" Diana asked.

"Yeah, I think so," Levinson said. "The major had the spare tested last week and it was on the fritz. I don't know if it was repaired or not." We'd have to check that out. Maybe someone had sabotaged the spare and that was how it got onto Brockman's list.

"We've learned that Major Brockman was looking into the theft of parts," Diana said. "Electronic parts. Do you know anything about that?"

"Hey, don't look at me," Levinson said. "I ain't the sticky-fingered type."

"We're only looking for information," I said. "You haven't heard of any vital components going for a walk?"

"Nope. Not that I would. I help out with the wires and cables, but my main focus is on those four engines. I make sure I have everything I need to keep them working, but I don't keep track of the radar countermeasures gear. That was the skipper's domain," he said.

"Understood," Diana said, and raised an eyebrow in my direction. Time for the next topic.

"You have any problems with the British here?" I asked. "Any fights?"

"Nah, not really," Levinson said. "We're all in the radar countermeasures business, so we got a lot in common. Everyone's been helpful, especially Bigs."

"That's Leading Aircraftman Bigsby, right?" Diana asked.

"Yeah. He's just a kid, but he's been fiddling with radios since he was old enough to hold a screwdriver," Levinson said. "Told us he was recruited into the Voluntary Interceptors when he was fourteen."

"What's that?" I asked. I looked to Diana, who gave a quick shrug.

"Amateur radio buffs worked, using their own gear for signals interception," he said. "I never heard of it, but Bigs said it was secret. Sounded pretty smart to me."

"Okay," I said, and tried to steer the conversation back to my question. "Have you seen any prejudice against Jews on base?"

"Sure," Levinson said. "I'm Jewish. You learn to pick up on things quickly. Whispers and muted laughter, people who look away rather than acknowledge your presence. Saves you the trouble of associating with jerks."

"British or American jerks?" Diana asked.

"Both, I guess, but my crew is solid," Levinson said. "Our navigator is new, but he seems okay. I really haven't had any serious guff from the RAF guys."

"What about Major Brockman?" I asked.

"What about him?" Levinson said.

"Did he ever have any problems? You know he was Jewish, don't you?"

"No. We never talked religion. He was an officer and kept to himself anyway. I wouldn't think about chewing the fat with him.

Not like Lieutenant Harker, who's practically one of the guys. Brockman, huh? Whaddya know?"

"So, no one on this base ever gave you a hard time about your religion?" I asked.

"Hell, Captain, I ain't religious. Never even been inside a synagogue. Maybe you ought to talk to some of the Lancaster crews about that sort of thing."

"Why?" I asked. Levinson shifted in his seat and looked around.

"Listen, I know we're supposed to cooperate with you, but I don't think it's my place to tell tales out of school," Levinson said. "Ma'am, if you work at Elham House, you should know what the deal is."

"I'm fairly new here," Diana said. "Perhaps they haven't filled me in yet. It would be helpful if you would."

"I don't think so," Levinson said. "I just heard some gossip, that's all. You want to ask about wires, cables, radios, or engines, I'm your man. Otherwise, I need to get some chow."

"Come on, Levinson," I said. "Give us something to go on. A hint, at least."

"Ask about Jonah," Levinson said. He stood and folded his arms. The gesture said it all. He was done talking.

"That's all, Sergeant," I said. "Thanks for your help."

"Such as it was," Diana said after he'd left. "I should press Jean to see what she knows."

"I asked her if any rabbis had been to the base for Jewish services, just to get a reaction. She didn't take the bait, or maybe she doesn't know of any issues."

"I doubt there's much that goes on here she's not aware of," Diana said. "Perhaps she doesn't think it relevant to our investigation."

"Or it's something that needs covering up," I said. "The less said about bigotry in the RAF, the better."

"There's bigotry everywhere, Billy. But right now, I must get back for my afternoon shift," Diana said as she looked at her wristwatch. "I'll ask Jean directly."

"I'll hunt down Jack Walters and press him to tell more," I said. "Say, didn't you just come off duty?"

"That was the dawn patrol, to listen for early-morning messages," Diana said. "The Italian traffic is light after that and picks up again after lunch. There are two other girls who cover for me, but their Italian accents won't hold up if we need to spoof Mussolini's fascists. And I'm better at Morse code. They sometimes can't keep up."

"Let's see if we can grab some chow before we split up," I said. I didn't need to check my watch to know it was lunchtime. As we stood to leave, the telephone on Brockman's desk rang. I wanted to ignore the jangling and get to the mess hall, but Diana answered it, giving her name. She listened, her eyes widening.

"When? All right, I'll tell him." With that, she hung up the phone.

"What is it?"

"That was Jean. We have another dead body. An RAF sergeant in Hangar 9, and it looks like murder."

CHAPTER TWELVE

"WE NEED HELP," Diana said as I drove her to Elham House before heading to Hangar 9. There wasn't enough time for her to get involved with this corpse before her shift began. "There's too much ground to cover, and I have to monitor the Italian radio traffic twice a day."

"Right," I said as I hit the brakes in front of Elham House. "Now we have more RAF personnel to interview, and we haven't even finished with the Yanks. Not to mention following up with Constable Sallow."

"And we need to talk with Sergeant Sally Miller at the St. Margaret's listening post," Diana said, and stepped out of the jeep. "With the drive, that's half a day at least. It's time to ask Colonel Harding for reinforcements."

"Absolutely. This thing is out of control," I said. "If you have time, maybe call the Dorchester and give Kaz a warning. He won't be happy."

"Who's the last happy person you met, Billy?" Diana said over her shoulder as she ran up the steps. She was gone before I could say that it was me, yesterday, when I thought we were taking a walk and then going for tea.

I spun the steering wheel and, just as rain began to fall again, headed to the long row of hangars bracketing the main runway. This downpour was in earnest. Unless it cleared by sunset, tonight's mission would probably be scrubbed. I slowed as men dashed across the road, seeking cover in Quonset huts and tents before the cold pelting rain soaked them to the skin. The only thing more dismal than this heavy weather was driving through it to see a corpse. Well, maybe getting caught out in it while thinking about tonight's bombing mission.

Diana had a point. We weren't exactly tripping over happy people around here.

I hadn't really expected Kaz to be thrilled about joining this investigation, but I did feel bad about bringing him in. After all, Lieutenant Piotr Kazimierz was my best friend. My partner in SHAEF's Office of Special Investigations, he was possessed of a keen mind and a deadly aim with his Webley revolver. Both had come in handy more than once.

Kaz was with the Polish Armed Forces and wore a British Army uniform with the red POLAND shoulder flash. He'd been studying languages at Oxford when the war broke out, and as it happened, that saved his life. He soon received the news that his entire family had been wiped out when the Nazis executed members of the government, the intelligentsia, officers, aristocrats, and anyone who might resist the brutal occupation of their nation. Not only was Kaz's family very wealthy, but as a member of the Augustus clan, Kaz was a real baron. One of the few Polish barons still alive.

This year had brought Kaz welcome news. He'd discovered that his younger sister, Angelika, had escaped the Nazi killing squads and joined the underground Polish Home Army, working as a courier. The bad news was that she'd been captured and sent to the Ravensbrück concentration camp for women. Diana had been imprisoned there as well, having been arrested while undercover on an SOE mission. They were both finally freed through the auspices of the Swedish Red Cross and brought back to England to recuperate.

Angelika's time at Ravensbrück had taken a terrible toll on her body, and Diana's father, Sir Richard Seaton, had provided a refuge at Seaton Manor in Norfolk while she recovered. Finally, she was well enough for Kaz to bring her to London to stay in the suite of rooms he kept at the Dorchester Hotel. It was the same suite his family had used when they visited him one Christmas season before the war. The rooms held sacred memories, and with the family fortune that his father had transferred to Swiss bank accounts before the invasion of Poland, Kaz was able to keep that suite as his home.

I knew that bringing Angelika there was important to Kaz, especially for the Christmas holiday. The staff at the Dorchester treated Kaz like a member of their family, knowing the losses he'd endured, and I was sure they'd roll out the red carpet for his kid sister.

I spotted Hangar 9 and pulled in out of the lashing rains. Two Lancasters loomed before me, their great hundred-foot wingspans arching across the cavernous space and making the men beneath seem small and immaterial. All except the casualties, who had in death become the center of attention.

As much as I expected Kaz to be sore about being pulled into this, I was sure about one thing. He would take great offense, as I did, at the notion of a criminal murder during wartime. Amid so much death and suffering, murder robbed the victim of at least the chance of survival. We both believed war was evil enough without adding another layer of vileness.

Wind whipped rain against my back as I exited the jeep. The first person I saw was Jack Walters, who was speaking with an RAF noncommissioned officer wearing a red military police armband.

"Captain Boyle," Walters said. "This is Sergeant Fisk, Royal Air Force Police."

"Sergeant," I said. I returned his salute and glanced at the half-dozen men milling around the underbelly of the bomber. "Who are those people and why haven't you secured the crime scene?"

"They're the crew," Fisk said. He turned to look at the small knot of blue uniforms. "Sir."

"And why are you gabbing with Lieutenant Walters instead of stopping them from trampling all over whatever evidence may have been left? A man was killed here, right? Or am I misinformed?"

"I was just telling the sergeant that word has come down from Elham House that you and Captain Seaton are in charge of the investigation," Walters quickly said. "Sergeant Fisk arrived only minutes ago."

"He should have been left to do his job," I said, steamed at their incompetence. "Fisk, get those men away from the body, but don't let them leave. I want a list of their names, pronto. Go!"

"I'm sorry, Captain," Walters said. "Our MPs aren't equipped to deal with this kind of crime. Neither am I, for that matter. I didn't think about keeping the crew away."

"It's too late for that now," I said. I watched Fisk as he herded the men to one side of the hangar. "What do you know about the dead man?"

"Flight Sergeant David Cohen," Walters said. "This was his aircraft. He was the special duty operator. SO for short."

"What were his special duties?" I asked.

"Radio countermeasures," Walters said. "It's what this place is all about. He was one of the German Jews jamming the Jerry frequencies, as I explained to you this morning."

"Was he one of the Jews having troubles here?" I asked as I walked to the Lancaster's undercarriage.

"For being Jewish? I don't know. Perhaps some of the men harbor prejudices against Jews," Walters said. "But it's more complicated than that. The SOs can be resented, but through no fault of their own. They're called Jonahs by most crewmen. It's half a joke, most days."

"Sergeant Levinson mentioned the same," I said as I wondered what the punch line was, my hand held up to stop Walters from going any farther. "Wait here and tell me more later. I need to see the body."

The overhead lamps in the cavernous hangar swung in the blowing wind, sending shadows dancing across the floor. The Lancaster's long bomb bay doors gaped, and I walked around them to view the victim. He lay face down on the ground, inert and limp, outside the hatch on the fuselage.

The flight sergeant wore a blue wool RAF uniform, sergeant's stripes on the sleeve. His service cap lay a few feet away. And by the look of one leg folded awkwardly beneath the other and an oddly twisted arm, it seemed he'd taken a tumble from inside the aircraft onto the hard concrete.

"Anyone have a flashlight?" I said, looking to Fisk and the others. "A torch?"

Fisk brought me one and then scurried back to the airmen. From the way he studiously avoided looking at the body, I figured his police duties were more focused on traffic and fistfights than murder.

I played the light across Cohen's face. One cheekbone pressed hard against the concrete. I lifted his head and saw where his face had struck the ground. Grit and oil were compressed into broken skin. Above one eye sat a dark bruise, probably from his head bouncing as it hit. I checked his hands and found no scrapes, which meant he hadn't tried to break his fall.

It was a dead-man drop for sure.

I stepped across the body, knelt, and shined the light on the back of Cohen's head. His hair was thick and black, and in the dimness, it almost hid the oozing gash above his hairline. But there it was, right at the same angle as the blow that had killed

Major Brockman, low on the back of his head and slightly to the right.

Same killer. Same method. Brockman and Cohen probably never suspected a thing. Looking up into the open bomb bay, I realized how similar the killings were. This wasn't a cliff, but Cohen had still taken a hard fall, flat on his face. It would've finished him off if by some miracle he'd survived the hit.

Hit with what? I stood and scanned the hangar. There were tables and workbenches filled with tools and hardware. Solid wrenches, drills, hammers, and all sorts of parts that would fit easily in the hand. No shortage of makeshift weapons here.

I stood, looking at the men gathered along one wall. Sometimes the killer really does return to the scene of the crime.

"Hands out in the open," I shouted. "Everyone. You too, Lieutenant Walters."

"What's the big idea?" Walters said. He made no move to show his hands.

"Come on, lads," Sergeant Fisk said, addressing the others as he extended his hands, palms up. "Show the captain your hands."

They did, with a few murmurs of reluctance, arranging themselves in a line, which Walters joined even as he rolled his eyes.

"Thank you, Sergeant," I said. I started with him and checked for grease and blood. I moved down the line, doing the same with each man and finding that cleanliness did seem next to godliness on this base.

Until I got to the last man before Walters. He was short, with sandy hair and a trace of freckles splashed across his face. He looked too young for the service, but what really stood out were his hands. A faint sheen of oil and grime showed on his fingers, and his fingernails needed a good scrubbing. His blue coveralls were also stained with a variety of colors. Blood, perhaps?

"Looks like you've been handling tools, Private," I said as I rubbed his fingers and felt the oil along with his rough skin.

"I'm not a private anything," he said, and yanked his hand away. "I'm a mechanic, and it's my job to work with tools, innit?" A ripple of laughter spread through the others.

"Billy, you need to learn the difference between aircrew and ground crew in the RAF," Walters said as he laughed and removed his gloves, offering up his clean, pale hands. "The other chaps are aircrew, and they wisely leave the maintenance work to our highly skilled ground crew."

"Leading Aircraftman Roscoe Bigsby, Captain," the kid said, barely hiding a grin. "And I'm proud to have my hands marked by honest labor. Ain't nothing wrong with that, is there?"

"It was Bigsby who found the body, Captain," Sergeant Fisk said before I could answer and stick my foot further in it.

"That must have been a shock," I said with a nod in the direction of Cohen's corpse.

"Naw, that's no shock," Bigsby said. "It's up to us ground crew to pull the dead out of the aircraft when they come back with casualties. That's grisly stuff, I'll tell you. Cohen looked like he was taking a nap in comparison."

CHAPTER THIRTEEN

SERGEANT FISK HANDED over the list of names and confirmed each man had shown up after Bigsby. Lieutenant Walters had arrived on the scene to find Bigsby kneeling near the body with no blood spatter or weapon in sight. Neither had gone up into the Lancaster, and Fisk hadn't thought to search it. If the killer had been hiding there, it wouldn't have been too difficult to slip out in the confusion. Too late to worry about that now.

I'd searched Cohen's pockets and come up with nothing but a few coins and a nearly empty pack of Player's Navy Cut cigarettes. Hardly crime-busting clues.

I watched as medics put Cohen on a stretcher and loaded him into the ambulance. I didn't know what the protocol was, but I asked Walters to call Doctor Yates and arrange for him to conduct the autopsy here on base. While my gut told me it was the same killing method as the one used on Brockman, I'd feel better if Yates confirmed it.

"I still need to talk to you," I said to Walters as he headed for the telephone at the back of the hangar. "About the trouble the Jewish boys were having. I had no idea you meant the kind of trouble Cohen met up with here."

"I didn't," Walters said. "Nothing like this."

"Later," I said, "I want to talk with Bigsby while things are fresh in his mind. Sort out Yates, will you, then let's meet up at Elham House."

"I'll be there," Walters said as he turned on his heel, the bitterness in his voice leaving me to wonder if the trouble he'd mentioned was with his own prejudices.

"Come on, Bigsby," I said, and motioned to a stack of crates by a low workbench along the side wall. "Have a seat. You're working with the Americans, aren't you? Lieutenant Harker was singing your praises."

"Yeah, he's awright," Bigsby said as he took a seat on a crate facing me. "Sparks knows what he's about. Don't mind lending a hand." Bigsby's eyes darted about, and he moved his makeshift seat a few inches away from mine. He was nervous and tapped one foot to some silent rhythm, like a kid called into the principal's office.

"How long have you been in the service, Bigs?" I leaned back, giving him some more space between us, since it looked like he was expecting the third degree.

"Five months now. Joined up when I was eighteen," Bigsby said. "Aren't you going to ask about Cohen? Why ask about me?"

"Hey, there's nothing to worry about," I said, and held up my hands in mock surrender. "I was just impressed that someone so young was brought in to help Harker and his crew. Especially with something as vital as Jostle. You must really know your stuff."

"I like radios," Bigsby said. He nodded his head as if agreeing with himself. "Always been curious about how it all works."

"Sergeant Levinson said you were part of some civilian program to listen to enemy frequencies," I said. "What was that all about?" Giving Bigsby something else to talk about would allow him to calm down before we started in on the body.

"That was the Voluntary Interceptors. I joined the Radio Society of Great Britain when I was a kid, and they asked for volunteers at the start of the war to listen in on assigned frequencies. They didn't care how old you were, long as you did the job. They'd give you wavelengths to monitor and you'd record any Morse that come over," Bigsby said as he warmed to the topic. "If you got anything, you'd post it first thing for some boffin to decode."

"So, at the start of the war you had your own radio gear?" I asked. "You were so young. Twelve, maybe thirteen?" Thunder rumbled in the distance, and we turned to face the open hangar doors. The windy rain had lessened, but dark clouds had turned the afternoon into night.

"Yeah, I'd built my own, see?" Bigsby said, one eye on the weather. "The government confiscated transmitters so no spies could get their hands on them. But they left us our receivers, which is all you need, right? I liked it well enough," he said. "But, Captain, I shouldn't've gone on about it to Levinson. It's still supposed to be a secret, after all. No need to mention that, right?"

"None. I was just curious. You had to work in secret?"

"Right. Couldn't even tell my mum why I spent hours every night wearing headphones and twisting dials up in the attic. I had to make her promise not to mention my radio to folks. Didn't want the neighbors to think I was a spy, after all. Felt good to do my part, it did."

"How come you didn't get into signals-interception work with the RAF?" I asked.

"I knew radios, but I'm no good with languages or codes. I figure this is the best place for me, making sure these kites fly and their radios work proper. All this jamming stuff is important for the war, ain't it?"

"It's all new to me, Bigs, but it certainly seems so," I said as Lieutenant Walters strode over. "Now, tell me how you found the body."

"Doctor Yates is on his way," Walters said abruptly. "And the mission for tonight is scrubbed. Filthy weather across the Channel as well."

"Very good, Lieutenant Walters," I said, with just enough stress on his rank to suggest he might want to address me more formally given the circumstances. "Dismissed."

He was already half-turned away but stopped himself and managed to look straight at me. "I'll be at Elham House as soon as I know Doctor Yates is through the gate, Captain Boyle."

With that, Walters left, huff and all.

Bigsby let out a laugh, and I asked him what he thought of Lieutenant Walters.

"Thank you, sir, but I don't want to get between officers when they start going fussy at each other. It's smarter to just watch and learn, don't you think?"

"You're wiser than your years, Bigs. So just tell me what happened when you found the body," I said.

"I came in, hung up my mac right there," he said, and pointed to a row of pegs along the wall.

"What time was it?"

"I left the mess hall at 1300 and ran here in the rain. So probably no more than five minutes later. Is that important?"

"I don't know," I said. "It might help to establish the time of death if we know when he was last seen alive."

"Can't vouch for that," Bigsby said. "Didn't keep track of him at the mess hall, just noticed at some point that he wasn't there."

"Okay, so tell me what happened after you hung up your mackintosh," I said.

"Turned around and saw Cohen laid out flat. Thought he'd fallen out of the hatch and knocked himself out."

"Anyone else here?"

"Not a soul. Soon as I saw he was dead, I called old Fisk. Seemed to be the right fellow, not that I was sure. Pulling mangled bodies out of shot-up bombers is one thing, but finding a fellow dead by his own Lanc is another," Bigsby said as he gave a sad shake of his head. "What do you reckon happened?"

"That's what I'm here to find out," I said. "Where was everyone else?"

"The mess hall put on a big feed," Bigsby said. "Christmas dinner leftovers and all that. I got there early on account of how hungry I was. When the lads started up singing Christmas carols again, it just made me miss my mum, so I scarpered back here."

"Anyone else leave?" I asked.

"Hard to say. The lads were moving about the tables, visiting with chums, that sort of thing. A few of the Welsh boys stood up to sing like a proper choir, and all eyes were on them. I'd had enough of hymns by then and left. Can't say I paid attention to who was coming or going."

"Why do you think Cohen was here?" I asked.

"Well, him being a Yid and all, I guess he didn't care much for 'Hark! The Herald Angels Sing.'"

"That's a pretty nasty term, Bigsby. You have a problem with Jews?"

"Oh no, not me, Captain. It's just what they were called in my neighborhood. I never gave it no thought. Hackney ain't the fanciest part of London. Real rough at times. I got along fine with Cohen and the other Jonahs."

"Okay," I said. I knew what it was like to grow up on the tough side of town. "Tell me, why are they called Jonahs?"

"Well, you know they're an extra crewman, right? The special operators. These Lancs are filled with all sorts of electronic hardware. Mandrel, Dina, Airborne Cigar, there's all sorts of code names for the gear they carry. It's the job of the SO to jam radar and signals to the night fighters out to attack the bomber stream."

"I get it. So why the bad-luck nickname?" I asked.

"Because one way for a bomber not to be spotted at night is

to maintain radio silence," Bigsby said. "The SO does the exact opposite. To protect the other aircraft, they light up the airwaves on every bandwidth. That's how they find the frequencies to jam. It's worse than being caught in a spotlight. The Jerries just follow the radio signals and they've got the plane in their sights. They say 101 Squadron has the highest casualty rate in the RAF because of it. Can't really blame the SOs, but some do. Them being German and Jews to boot, it comes natural like."

"They're just doing their job," I said, although I wasn't surprised at the power of superstition when it came to fighting off the fear of death. If I remembered my Bible stories, God wanted Jonah to go to some city to preach against their evildoings. Instead, Jonah set sail in the other direction. God himself then brewed up a wicked storm, and when Jonah admitted it might be his fault, the sailors cast him into the waters. The storm ended and that's when the whale showed up and swallowed the poor guy whole. It wasn't hard to see the parallels.

"And they go down with the rest of the crew if their kite is hit," Bigsby said. "There's no explaining it, not so it makes sense."

"I'd be satisfied if I could just make sense of what Sergeant Cohen was doing here," I said. "He was on a mission last night, so why was he here so early?"

"He might have wanted to check out his hardware. To get ready for the mission tonight, even though the betting was it'd be scrubbed," he said.

"People will bet on anything," I said. "What were the odds?"

"Four to one the Lancs would be grounded," Bigsby said. "I'm no gambler, but your Yanks got into the action quick enough. Anyway, I think the new turret is what drew Cohen here. He'd been asking about it."

"What's that got to do with him?"

"I can show you," Bigsby said, and led me to the rear of the hangar. He flipped a switch and work lights pierced the gloom, illuminating the rear turret of the Lancaster. It wasn't the usual configuration of four machine guns, and the turret itself was larger. "They got rid of the four 7.7-millimeter machine guns and replaced them with two American 13-millimeter Browning heavy machine guns. That's .50 caliber to you Yanks. Better range and stopping power. We just finished installing them this morning when I connected the intercom."

"A better chance at survival for a Jonah and his crew," I said.

"Yeah. Just didn't work out too well for Cohen, did it now?"

"No," I said. I could imagine Sergeant Cohen's eagerness to have more protective firepower, and perhaps his hope to rid himself of the Jonah curse.

"Tell me, Bigs, did you work directly with Major Brockman?"

"Like him and me gettin' our hands dirty together? No, not that way. He was more the supervising type. Kept things on schedule, he did. A bit strict and none too cheery, but he knew his stuff and got the job done. I was right sorry to hear he was done in," Bigs said.

"You know he was Jewish?" I asked.

"What? Like Cohen? Had no idea," Bigsby said.

"Okay, that's all for now, Bigs. Thanks for your help. I'm going to take a look around inside the Lanc."

"Right you are, Captain. Want me to show you where the SO station is?"

"Just tell me where to look," I said. I didn't want anybody clambering around and destroying what evidence might have been left.

"Go right once you're through the hatch. You'll see the radio operator's position on your left over the wing. The SO is tucked away just beyond and lower. No window, and the only view he has is of the radioman's feet. Can't miss it."

Bigsby donned his mac as I grabbed the flashlight I'd left on the workbench. We both stood at the hangar's open doors and watched the dark skies. The rain had eased up, but the wind had increased. Thunder rolled through the black clouds and lightning crackled, a distant bolt flashing a brilliant, bright white.

I considered giving Bigsby a lift to wherever he was headed, but a jeep pulled in before I could speak. Sergeant Levinson was at the wheel.

"Bigs," Harker said. He poked his head out from under the canvas top on the passenger seat. "You all done here? We'll drop you off at the barracks. Hop in."

"Scuttlebutt says Cohen was killed the same as Major Brockman," Levinson said. He awaited a reply.

"It's suspicious," I said. "Either of you know Cohen?"

"Not me," Harker said. "Can't say I ever laid eyes on him."

"I knew who he was," Levinson said, "but I doubt I exchanged more than a couple of sentences with him. The SOs tend to keep to themselves. They have their own section in one of the barracks."

"I'll have a talk with them when I'm done here," I said. I held off on asking Harker if he knew about Brockman's religion. Better to ask when he was alone. "Thanks."

The three drove off, leaving me alone with the crime scene. What I really wanted was a ham sandwich and a hot cup of joe, but I knew I had to check out the aircraft before anyone got in the way. I climbed up the short ladder into the fuselage and was surprised to find myself standing up straight with room to spare. As I went forward, the deck sloped upward. The space narrowed as I crossed the massive wing struts. I played the flashlight over the interior and found the radio operator's station, the transmitter and receiver being easy to spot. Beyond that, a small chamber was crammed with electronics. It was lower in the fuselage, and I saw what Bigs meant. From his seat, the SO was eye level with the radioman's feet. I didn't even try to fit in, but instead shined my light around the equipment, looking for any trace Cohen might have left behind. All I saw were a few screws on the small table beneath the hardware. Above them, a unit with a small radar screen hung unevenly in the rack. Maybe Cohen had come to finish the job as well as to check out the new turret?

There was nothing else to see here, and I slowly worked my way back to the hatch. I used the flashlight to seek out blood spatter or anything unusual. Nothing. I shined the beam around the edge of the hatchway, thinking Cohen might have been struck here and pushed out. Still nothing.

The rear turret. He'd been interested in that. I worked my way back, watching my steps so as not to obliterate any evidence. At the turret, I went over every square inch of the fuselage wall. Then I saw it. On one of the metal frames, a few dots of dark red. Just right for a blow to the head. Not that it helped much, but I knew it had happened here. And that Cohen must have known his assailant since there was no way to stealthily sneak up on him. Climbing the ladder and entering the hatch wasn't exactly quiet.

Or had the killer already been in the bomber? He could have stayed there and slipped out as the place filled up. Bigsby had said he hadn't gone inside the bomber, so it was possible. If the timing was right, the killer might have been trapped.

Whatever happened, Cohen had been struck in the bomber, then had fallen out or been pushed. I didn't know by whom, and I had no idea why. At least Brockman had something on him, a clue that I could follow up. But Cohen was a question mark. A big one.

I went out, stepped down the ladder, and backed up to study the hatch. I tried to envision what had happened. One possibility was that Cohen had been killed by the rear turret and dragged to the door and tossed out. But why not leave him there? It would have taken more time for him to be discovered. So maybe he'd only been stunned and tried to escape. Disoriented, he'd stumbled to the hatch and tumbled out and had been hit again by his assailant. I could have missed the second splatter if he'd fallen on it, or if the killer had whacked him while he lay on the ground. I'd have to ask Doctor Yates about a second wound.

A crack of lightning startled me out of my thoughts. The crash of thunder followed seconds later, and the lights in the hangar flickered. Another bolt struck. The air turned electric white for a split second and then the lights went out.

I heard a footstep. It echoed in the darkness, and I couldn't get a fix on the direction. I switched on the flashlight and sent the beam swinging across the hangar. A shadow danced behind the tail of the bomber, but I couldn't spot anything attached to it. I held back asking if anyone was there, since if someone was, and they were up to no good, they'd hardly answer.

I kept shining the flashlight about as I walked to the jeep, satisfied that I was alone and probably just spooked by the storm. Before I climbed in behind the wheel, I took one more look around and probed the far corners of the hangar with the flashlight before giving up.

At the edge of my vision, I saw a raised hand come at me from behind. I twisted around to ward off the blow. I wasn't quick enough, and I took it on the left shoulder, feeling hard metal and pain. I screamed, angry and hurt, and reached out with my good arm as the assailant darted behind the jeep and vanished into the storm.

It had happened too fast to get a look at whoever it was. All I could see was what neither Brockman nor Cohen had likely seen.

A raised arm, poised to kill.

CHAPTER FOURTEEN

A JEEP PULLED into the hangar, and I unsnapped my holster, grateful for the feel of cold steel, not to mention a working right arm. It was Walters, and I relaxed, then tensed, since I didn't know whom to trust around here.

"What's the matter, Captain?" Walters asked as he braked to a stop next to me. I was in my jeep, rubbing my shoulder. I wondered how big the bruise would be.

"Someone jumped me," I said. "Third time was a charm, at least for me."

"Did you get a look at who it was?" Walters asked. It was a good question, one that would come naturally to either a concerned officer or a failed assailant.

"No, it happened when the lights went out. All I saw was something between a shadow and a blur. Why did you come back here?"

"To see if you were all right. I was supposed to wait for you at Elham House, but you never showed up," Walters said. He sounded a bit miffed. "Power's out across half the base. They had to shut down the electricity to this row of hangars to work on the lines. It should be back soon. I also wanted to tell you Doc Yates is at the base hospital."

"Okay. Good work. You happen to see anyone on foot as you drove here?"

"No. Anyone with sense is indoors. You still want to meet at Elham House?" Walters asked. "With the power off, I should be checking my perimeter patrols."

"That's fine," I said. "I mostly wanted to ask you about this Jonah business, but Bigsby explained it all. Tell me, how serious do you think the anti-Jewish feeling is on base?"

"Ah, Bigs. Smart lad, that one. As for the Jews, I think there is an undercurrent of mistrust, but it's probably as much to do with them being German as Hebrew. One should cancel the other out, but it isn't that simple," he said.

"Because the SOs draw fire by doing their job, you mean?"

"I don't put a lot of stock in that, Billy. I mean, when the pilot flies right into heavy flak, no one blames him when they get hit," Walters said. He was more relaxed now, using my first name as I'd invited him to last night. Apparently, he was over being miffed at being ordered to show his hands.

"But every plane has a pilot," I said. "Only 101 Squadron has SOs on board. Those crews are taking the same chances with flak as everyone else, plus they have the SO jamming like crazy and announcing their presence to the Luftwaffe."

"Fair point. I'll admit it's a potent mix. You've got a nasty brew of fear of dying, distrust of anyone with a German accent, and prejudice against Jews. Might boil over in the right circumstances," Walters said. "But what's that got to do with Cohen, or Brockman, for that matter?"

"Brockman was Jewish, not that he mentioned it to anyone."

"You don't say. Do you think that had anything to do with his murder?"

"I don't know," I said, not for the first time today. "What's your attitude toward Jews, Lieutenant?"

"Me? You don't think I clobbered Cohen, do you?" Walters said.

"I'm not accusing you; I'm only trying to get a sense of how Jewish aircrew fit in on the base. Just humor me, okay?"

"All right. To be honest, I never met a Jew before I joined up. Not that I know of, anyway. I'm from Northamptonshire. We don't even have many Catholics. Guess I thought of Jews as different from us. Overly religious and vaguely exotic, perhaps. But setting aside the SOs with their Germanic accents, they're just regular fellows, far as I can tell. Major Brockman certainly seemed normal. No, I didn't mean it that way. Damn, you know what I trying to say, don't you?"

"I think so," I said. He sounded genuine. I knew plenty of Jewish kids growing up, but it sounded like Walters was late to the party and had just realized the world wasn't all Church of England types.

The lights flickered on, then off, then came back on, bathing the hangar in brightness. Outside, rows of lights rippled to life.

"Looks like they've got power everywhere," Walters said. He stepped outside and shielded his eyes from the rain.

"How much of the base was out?" I asked.

"It was the line that supplied this row and the next, all the way to the American hangar," he said. "Do you still need me for anything, Captain?"

"No, that's it. Thanks for checking in," I said. As Walters drove off, I wondered how many people on this base could have used the cover of darkness to try to finish me off.

Jean Conan Doyle wanted a report by the end of the day. I had time to drive to the base hospital and see if Doctor Yates had come up with anything interesting. At least the autopsy would take my mind off how hungry I was.

I drove to the hospital through blowing wind and light rain. I parked around back, figuring that would be where the morgue was. Hospitals preferred recovered patients to walk out the main door for all the world to see, while the dead were left in the cellar to be taken away with much less scrutiny.

I took the cellar stairs and found Yates in a cold brick-walled room, with only Cohen's corpse for company. The place smelled of disinfectant overlaid with the cloying odor of decomposition. Two other tables were empty except for where Cohen's clothes were laid out. Yates glanced up at me and then adjusted an overhead light for a better look at Cohen's skull.

"Thanks for coming in, Doc," I said. "Sorry to drag you out in this weather."

"Glad to help, Captain," he said. "No worries. The storm's blowing itself across the Channel, and I'll be seeing the tail end of it when I'm done here."

"You heard a weather report?" I asked, and moved closer to the body. There were no other marks or wounds that I could see.

"Don't need to, not after living on the coast for fifty-odd years. I can feel air changing, or at least I did before I came down to pay a visit to Flight Sergeant David Cohen," Doctor Yates said. "Am I to understand you wish a comparison with the wounds sustained by Major Brockman?"

"Yes. I'd like to know if it looks like the same weapon was used," I said. "Far as I could tell, the blow was struck in the same general area."

"First, tell me about how the body was found," Yates said as he checked Cohen's fingernails.

"On the ground by a Lancaster's rear hatch," I said. "Looked to me like he was hit from behind and fell onto the concrete."

"Half right, Captain. You likely thought that these abrasions and grit on his cheek were due to the fall. But look here," Yates said as he moved aside a patch of hair on the back of Cohen's skull. "At first it seems like a wider impact than Major Brockman's wound. But a closer inspection reveals something else. Can you make it out?" He swiveled the light closer, and I studied the point of impact. It looked different from Brockman's. Rounder, in an uneven sort of way.

"Two blows to the head," I said. "The weapon has a rounded edge, and I can see the second impression overlapping the first."

"Exactly," Doctor Yates said. "The first strike would have stunned the flight sergeant, certainly. It might have resulted in death, but not immediately. However, the next undoubtedly killed him in seconds."

"He was inside the bomber," I said as I visualized the scene near the rear turret. "His killer had less room to wind up for the initial blow, so it wasn't as forceful as the one that killed Brockman. Cohen makes it to the doorway, falls, or is thrown out. Then came the second hit."

"Yes, and the bruising on his face was not a result of the fall," Yates said, and pointed to the grit embedded in Cohen's cheek. "It was from being hit in the back of the head while face down on the concrete."

"Any notion as to what the weapon was?" I asked.

"There were traces of oil in the wound," Yates said. "Which doesn't help to identify it, other than to say it came into contact with that substance. The weapon was narrow but heavy, possibly weighted at the end. A tool of some sort. Perhaps fresh from being used on machinery."

"I may have a clue myself," I said, taking off my coat. "Literally. Someone tried to smack me on the head when the lights were out. Fortunately, it wasn't lights out for me, but I did get a good whack on the shoulder." I pulled off my shirt and showed Doc Yates my left shoulder and the reddish bruise.

"Hmm," he said as he poked and prodded. "Does that hurt?"

"Yes, but not as much as the original hit. Does it look like the same weapon? I know it left a helluva mark."

"Nothing appears to be broken. You're lucky you have a well-developed deltoid muscle, which absorbed the blow. And you were clothed. I can't say it was the same weapon, but I am fairly sure such a weapon could have left this mark.

Among others. Sorry to be so imprecise, but that is the nature of my business."

"Thanks, Doc," I said, and buttoned my shirt. "At least now I have a sequence of events. But as for the weapon, this base has no shortage of tools, oils, or machinery, and I'm still in the dark. No defensive wounds on our friend?"

"No," Yates said, "and nothing under the fingernails either. Wish I had more to offer, Captain. It's a shame that this lad didn't have the chance to see if he'd survive the war. Pity."

"As I understand it, the odds here aren't good. Do you know anything about 101 Squadron?" I figured if he didn't know, I could change the subject without giving away military secrets.

"Radar jamming, as far as I can understand," Yates said. He stepped away from the slab and folded his arms. "Was Cohen one of the German refugees? I've heard they are highly valued for their native-language skills. One can easily imagine a number of ways in which they are used."

"But does everyone value their presence?" I asked as I thought about the double blows to Cohen's head.

"Obviously there may be some closed-minded types about," Yates said. "But I've not heard of any violence directed at any of them for being either German or Jewish. We had a football match in town a few months ago, RAF versus the locals. Some of the German lads played and they got along well. I had a chance to chat with a few when I taped up a sprained ankle for one of them. I sensed a certain wariness at first, only natural given what they'd gone through in that unfortunate land of their birth. But soon it was handshakes and slaps on the back all round."

"I've been asking people, and I haven't gotten the sense there was any serious problem with prejudice against them," I said.

"No. The few comments I heard were directed at them being German. That was before people learned who they really were.

Does this have anything to do with the murder of Major Brockman?" he asked.

"It might, but I have nothing to go on other than the fact that Brockman was also Jewish," I said. "Had you noticed his dog tags?"

"No, I was more concerned with the flesh itself and just put his clothing and effects aside," Yates said. "Will someone arrange to have his body picked up? Soon?"

"I'll get in touch with his commanding officer," I said. I wished I had thought of that earlier in the day.

"Is there any reason for you to suspect these killings are based on religion, Captain?" Yates said as he washed his hands energetically.

"No, it simply struck me as an unusual situation. German-born Jews in the RAF performing vital tasks might breed resentment. When clues are lacking, sometimes it helps to turn over a rock and see if anything crawls out."

"Well, we English have been known to view foreigners with a jaundiced eye. But I surmise the common goal of defeating the Nazis has bound us to those who have come here to aid in the fight," Yates said.

"Seems to be the case," I said. "There's nothing I can see, yet, to connect Brockman and Cohen, other than Judaism and their role in radar jamming."

"They must have something else in common," Yates said. "Other than how they were killed. That would be the *why* of the thing, and I'll leave that to you, Captain." Yates drew a sheet over Cohen's body and folded his hands for a moment.

Flight Sergeant David Cohen, dead too soon. His death might have come tomorrow, or it might have come fifty years from tomorrow. If not for the killer's desire to silence him.

CHAPTER FIFTEEN

"You have a party waiting for you in the conference room," Sergeant Halfpenny said as I entered the lobby at Elham House. "Squadron Officer Conan Doyle is waiting for you. Again."

"If I knew there was a party, I would have come here instead of the morgue. It's bound to be cheerier," I said.

"Flight Sergeant Cohen, poor man," Halfpenny said as she signed me in. "We just heard who it was. Everyone's talking about a madman on the loose, or a German spy."

"I doubt it's the work of a spy, but we'll get to the bottom of it. Did you know Cohen?" I asked.

"Yes. He was quite pleasant. We had the SOs here a few times to meet with our German-born WAAFs," she said. "Tea and scones, all very proper, of course. Go on upstairs. The conference room is next to Conan Doyle's office."

I hoofed it up the steps and knocked before entering.

"Kaz!" I said, shocked to see him here already. But also surprised to see his sister, Angelika, deep in conversation with Jean Conan Doyle. "How'd you get here so quickly?"

"I had just purchased an automobile in London," Kaz said. "An Aston Martin prewar two-seater. Just the thing for Angelika to drive when she's ready. I planned on motoring back to Seaton Manor, but when Diana called, I decided to put it through its paces and show Angelika the famous White Cliffs."

"Kaz, we're in the middle of a murder investigation," I said, even as I worked to hold back a grin at his enthusiasm, not to mention at the sight of Angelika. She looked healthier than the last time I'd seen her. She brushed back a lock of her straw-colored hair, tucking it behind her ear as she looked at me with her deep blue eyes.

"Please excuse me, Squadron Officer," Angelika said to Conan Doyle, and stood to greet me. I watched her steady herself, then walk four steps in my direction. It wasn't long ago that she couldn't have made it. After the horrific medical experiments at Ravensbrück, it was only through surgery and excellent nursing care that she'd come this far.

"Billy, I'm so happy to see you," Angelika said, and gave me a kiss on the cheek. "I promise to stay out of the way and not bother Piotr with anything. I will be the church mouse."

"I've been having a delightful conversation with Miss Kazimierz," Conan Doyle said. "It's not often that we are graced with a visitor from the Polish Home Army."

"Thank you," Angelika said. "I'd like to learn more about what you do here, but I should leave you to your work. I can wait downstairs."

"No need for that, Miss Kazimierz," Conan Doyle said. "If you were trusted as a courier in Nazi-occupied Poland, you can be trusted to hear our sad story. Sir Richard Seaton has vouched for you, so you come to us highly recommended. Take a seat, Captain Boyle. Lieutenant Kazimierz already knows the basic situation."

"Yes, we saw Diana for a moment when we arrived, and she explained how you two found the body. Yesterday's body, I mean," Kaz said. Angelika took a chair against the wall. Kaz and I sat across from the squadron officer, who nodded for me to begin.

"I've been to the morgue. Cohen was killed in much the same manner as Major Brockman," I said. "It took two hits for Cohen, but it was a similar weapon. Narrow, weighted at the end, with oil or grease adhered to it."

"No witnesses?" Conan Doyle asked.

"None. Apparently, Cohen left the luncheon early. He was interested in seeing the new rear turret that had just been installed in his Lancaster. The first blow was struck inside the aircraft near the turret. Then he was finished off outside," I said.

"Captain Seaton mentioned you were interested in any incidents of anti-Semitic behavior on base," she said. "While there's been nothing reported to me, there's likely been the occasional snide comment. But nothing that rises to the level of violence, threatened or otherwise."

"Major Brockman and Flight Sergeant Cohen were both Jewish," I said. "Cohen's religion was obviously well known. It was less so with the major, so I can't claim any connection to the murders."

"Cohen must have known and trusted his assailant," Kaz said.

"Yes, but unfortunately there's no evidence of who that was," I said. "Although I do know they're worried. When the lights went out, someone took a swing at me in the hangar. I turned just in time to avoid a crack on the head, but they got away."

"I'm glad you escaped serious injury, Captain," Conan Doyle said. "You have no idea who it was?"

"No. All I saw was a shadow. They clipped my shoulder hard enough to send me reeling," I said. "Then they ran out into the darkness."

"This business about the religion of these two men. Is it relevant as a motive at all?" Conan Doyle asked, her eyes narrowing as she studied me.

"I see no evidence of it," I said. "Nothing as simple as prejudice. But Captain Seaton and I did find evidence in Major Brockman's office that may point to a real motive."

"Good. This second murder has people worried," Conan Doyle said. "We don't need religious animosities making things even worse."

A knock on the door announced Diana's arrival. She entered, breathless, obviously having hurried from her shift. She explained that a WAAF was monitoring the Italian frequencies but was under orders to fetch her if anything vital came up. I quickly brought Diana up to speed on Cohen.

"Have you gotten to the major's list yet?" she asked.

"Just about to. Major Brockman had ordered an inventory of parts, but no one on his crew had gotten around to doing anything," I said.

"They claimed to be quite busy, which does seem to be the case," Diana said. "But evidently the major was concerned about missing hardware."

"We found this in his room," I said, and brandished the list he'd hidden in a book. "APT-3 remote power control, H2S radar scope, high-speed scanner, S27 control box, VCR-97 cathode-ray tube, 5FP7 radar display tube, Mandrel high power transmitter. Sounds like high-end stuff."

"All those items are missing?" Conan Doyle asked, her wide eyes betraying her alarm.

"I'd guess stolen," I said. "Otherwise, why kill the major? And Sergeant Cohen, if he has anything to do with this."

"Flight Sergeant Cohen was one of our special operators," Conan Doyle said. "And those are all valuable components. Each plays a part in radio jamming and interference."

"Which would be of interest to the Germans, of course," Kaz said.

"Quite. It's often a cat-and-mouse game we play," Conan Doyle said. "Any increase in their understanding of our techniques can be catastrophic. Our current casualties are worrisome enough. This is not to be repeated outside this room, but for every hundred men who join Bomber Command, forty-five are killed. We cannot bear the losses to grow higher."

"We still have leads to follow up. Enough to warrant Lieutenant Kazimierz being brought in. I'm sure we'll get to the bottom of it," I said with more conviction than our progress to date warranted.

"There's something else," Diana said. "This afternoon I telephoned Major Brockman's base in Cheddington to notify them of his death and to arrange for his body and personal effects to be picked up. The commanding officer had his clerk take the details. A most helpful young man."

By the glint in her eye, I could tell Diana had discovered something. "The reports?" I asked.

"Yes. When Billy and I searched the major's office, we noticed that the carbon papers of his recent reports were out of order," she said. "We thought someone had merely leafed through them. But it seems one carbon copy was taken. Major Brockman had written up Lieutenant Harker for gambling. The report arrived at Cheddington just this morning."

"Gambling? Between dice and poker, half the GIs in Britain gamble every day," I said. "How serious can it be?"

"Harker was gambling with his crew and other enlisted men," Diana said.

"Bad form for an officer to gamble with his men," Conan Doyle said.

"The army has a fine and a possible three-month imprisonment for gambling with subordinates," I said. "They say it erodes discipline. I always thought it was to prevent an officer from sending a private on a suicide mission after he lost to him at craps."

"It is a bit different with a bomber crew," Kaz pointed out. "Every mission is almost suicide. Still, it is against regulations. Harker must be an inveterate gambler for things have gotten to this point."

"You mean shoving Major Brockman off a cliff?" Diana asked.

"I am not taking it that far. I mean his gambling must be out of control for the charges to have been brought at all. As Billy said, games of chance are endemic in the military. Surely the major would have warned him off at first," Kaz said.

"Add to that the desperation he must have felt to try and steal the report," Conan Doyle said. "Simply rifling through his commanding officer's paperwork is a serious enough offense. He clearly did so to determine what action Major Brockman was taking against him."

"It shows poor judgment at best," I said.

"Even if he isn't our killer, this should be followed up, don't you think?" Conan Doyle said, an eyebrow raised in Diana's direction.

"Yes, ma'am," Diana said, understanding it was an order, no matter how nicely phrased. "Now that Piotr is here, we should discuss divvying up the next steps in our investigation."

We settled on Diana handling the questioning on base, since her time between shifts was limited. She'd tackle Flight Sergeant Cohen's crew and then speak to Americans on Lieutenant Harker's bomber about his gambling. Kaz and I would follow up with Constable Sallow about his contacts at the train station and anything else he'd come up with. Then a drive to Sergeant Sally Miller, exiled to the St. Margaret's at Cliffe listening post, to ask why Major Brockman came specifically to see her at Elham House before she was shipped out.

"I'm curious as to who snitched on Sally Miller," I said to Conan Doyle. "Was it a jealous boyfriend?"

"No. Lieutenant Walters brought it to my attention," she said. "Not a competitor for Sally's affections, as far as I know. And since I trust his judgment, I didn't think to inquire as to his source."

"Kaz and I will ask Sally about that tomorrow," I said. "I don't suppose there's any news about Flight Sergeant Adler's whereabouts? It might help our questioning to bring her news."

"None, sadly," Conan Doyle said. "There is hope, though. I checked and found that Johnny Adler had his religion changed from Jewish to Protestant on his identity tags. So it is less likely the Nazis will shoot him immediately. A wise precaution that several special operators have taken."

"I shall ask about Adler when I question Cohen's crew," Diana said. "Perhaps he mentioned something to them."

"Major Brockman's interest in Sally Miller is curious," Conan Doyle said. "I'd like to know more about that. For now, I shall also order an inquiry into the missing parts to be handled by RAF personnel."

"That would be useful," I said. "I don't know if you're considering Lieutenant Walters for the job, but he's a little too close to the investigation, in my opinion." I guessed Walters might be her choice given his responsibilities for security, but with a murderer running around this base, I wasn't exactly sure of his qualifications. Or motives.

"Jack Walters is with the RAF Regiment," Diana said for Kaz's edification.

"I do hold him in high estimation, but this is your investigation," Conan Doyle said with a nod to both Diana and me. "I will find someone else. Now, we have other matters to attend to, Captain Seaton. And Angelika, of course." With that, the three departed, off to listen in on whatever the Germans were allowing Mussolini and his pals to hear these days.

"Angelika is certainly getting the red-carpet treatment around here," I said. "Where are you and she staying, anyway?"

"Angelika will be rooming with Diana, here at Elham House," Kaz said. "Diana, being a captain, has one of the nicer rooms. I'm sure Angelika will enjoy the experience. Shall we find a decent place to eat in town?"

"Wait a minute," I said. "What's going on? You're up to something, aren't you?"

"What makes you say that?" Kaz said. He clearly enjoyed whatever secret he held up his sleeve.

"The fact that you brought Angelika along, in the first place," I said. "And that Squadron Officer Conan Doyle had already talked to Sir Richard about her. It didn't register at the time, but how and why did that conversation happen so quickly?"

"Because it is my duty to protect Angelika," Kaz said. "From herself, if need be. Now, Capel-le-Ferne must possess one singular dining establishment. Shall we find it?"

CHAPTER SIXTEEN

"I WANT TO hear more about that," I said. "But first, we should check in with Constable Thomas Sallow. He's the local flatfoot working this case and he may have news for us. You can drive us to the station in that swanky new car of yours. Then we'll get some grub."

"You make it sound so appetizing, Billy," Kaz said as he donned his overcoat. As we left Elham House, I realized I hadn't seen an Aston Martin roadster parked out front.

"Where is it?" I asked, and turned my collar up against the cold wind.

"There is a garage around back," Kaz said. "Jean offered a space, which was quite considerate." It was a low three-bay garage with heavy wooden double doors. He opened one and there sat the sleek, low-bodied two-seater, its aerodynamic design making it look like a crouching tiger about to pounce. "Nice, isn't she?"

"Beautiful," I said. The paint job was deep green, waxed to a gleam. The black convertible top looked like it had a chance of keeping the rain out, unlike my jeep. I waited while Kaz pulled out and then shut the doors behind us. The motor purred as we drove to the gate. "I hope we have good weather for our jaunt tomorrow."

"Dry would be good," Kaz said. "She tends to swerve when going into a curve. At high speed, at least."

"Oh, this is gonna be fun," I said as we approached the main gate at a sedate speed. I pulled out my orders and rolled down the window as a guard wearing corporal's stripes and the RAF Regiment patch stepped forward and lifted the gate.

"No need, Captain," he said, and waved us on with one hand. "You only need to show identification when entering."

"Is that standard procedure?" I asked.

"It is. We stop anyone who doesn't look right, but the idea is to focus on who comes in, not who goes out," he said.

"You keep track of names on that side?" I asked, and crooked a thumb in the direction of the opposite lane.

"Aye, we do. Almost always, day and night," the corporal said.

"What do you mean by 'almost'?" I asked.

"Well, Christmas Eve and Christmas morning, up to noon, we didn't bother. Lots of the lads had a bit of leave, so we were right busy. Just waved them through on both sides."

"Who gave that order?" I asked.

"Lieutenant Walters. He's in charge of perimeter security. Said as long as it was our lot coming and going, we didn't need to bother with signing in," he said. "Besides, we weren't expecting the brass to come visiting, not on Christmas. The high and mighty would be warm and snug, enjoying their Christmas goose, that's what the lieutenant said. Anything else, Captain?"

"Nothing, Corporal. Thanks," I said, and rolled up the window. Kaz shifted into first and the little Aston Martin took off like a shot.

"This is the same gentleman you did not wish to be involved in the inventory of missing parts, if I recall," Kaz said. "Are you suspicious of him?"

"Seems to be a nice guy, but I do wonder if he harbors any anti-Jewish feelings. Not that I can figure how religious prejudice plays into either murder," I said.

"Whatever his beliefs, he may have a point about senior officers and their cooked geese."

"Fair enough," I said, and pointed out the left turn that would take us to the police station. "His name just keeps popping up, like now. I roomed with him last night, and I have the feeling it's going to get awkward."

"Oh, I forgot," Kaz said. "Jean has arranged a place for us in the visiting officers' barracks. She had your bags moved. Apparently, it is a step up from your previous accommodations." With that, he downshifted while rounding a turn and ably demonstrated the Aston Martin's tendency to fishtail.

"You and the squadron officer have gotten as thick as thieves pretty quickly, haven't you?"

"She knows Sir Richard, and he has given us his imprimatur," Kaz said. "That explains much of it." The rest of it had to wait as we pulled up to the station. I wasn't sure if Constable Sallow would be there, but a light burning in the window gave me hope. I unfolded myself from the passenger seat and led the way in.

"Ah, you've finally decided to grace us with your presence," Ruxton said. He and Sallow were seated at a table with photographs spread between them. "And you have a new friend today, I see."

"This is Detective Sergeant Henry Ruxton, Kent County Constabulary, and Constable Sallow," I said. "My colleague is Lieutenant Piotr Kazimierz, part of our group at SHAEF. He'll be working the case with me."

"Captain Boyle is sorry he was detained," Kaz said. He stepped forward and gave the two men a little continental bow. "As soon as I arrived, I insisted we consult with the local constabulary. I am sure you must have valuable information to share."

"Well, blow me down, that's kind of you, Lieutenant," Ruxton said as he rose to shake hands with Kaz. "Not at all like the sentiment of others I could mention."

I remained silent as Ruxton and Kaz chatted, knowing my friend was working his magic. He had the quiet charm of a true aristocrat. Without mentioning his status as a baron, he had Ruxton ready to do pretty much whatever he wanted. He'd read the man perfectly without even a hint of warning. Was that how he'd gotten Jean Conan Doyle to be so gracious? My rumbling stomach reminded me we'd be talking about that over dinner, which could come none too soon.

"Constable, did you find anything at the train station?" I asked, ignoring Ruxton. Since he'd left in a huff when we'd been given carte blanche to take over, I didn't see any reason to include him.

"That we did, Captain," Sallow said. "Nothing less than Major Brockman's staff car. Paperwork in the glove box confirmed it was his."

"When did you find it?"

"Yesterday afternoon," Sallow said, and cast a wary glance at Ruxton.

"You didn't think to call the base?" I asked, even though I figured it was Ruxton who'd put the kibosh on that call.

"I instructed the constable to wait," Ruxton said. "If this case was so important, I expected you would return, or at least telephone, to learn the results of our search."

I was about to light into Ruxton and tell him there'd been another murder occupying our time, but Kaz wisely intervened and asked the detective sergeant if he would share his opinion on the investigation to date. While Ruxton puffed himself up to expound on the subject, I quietly spoke with the constable.

"Good work finding the staff car," I said. I leaned against the desk and eyed the photographs of the US Army vehicle.

"Thank you, Captain. I would have called you, but the DS showed up and had his own idea about that," Sallow said in a low voice. "The automobile was parked close to the train station, but not anywhere the ticket takers would have seen it."

"You questioned them, I assume."

"Him. Only one fellow worked the morning shift, it being Christmas and all. He didn't see any Yanks, just a lot of RAF lads making their way to and from Christmas leave. But there was something interesting," Sallow said with a tap on one of the photos. It showed the rear doors open and a smudge on the seat.

"Grease?" I guessed.

"Yes, but not the sort found in the wound. Bicycle grease, I'd reckon, from a chain. Turn the front wheel up and that's right where the chain would rest on the seat," Sallow said.

"I doubt Brockman would park there and then bicycle to the cliffs," I said.

"But someone might have tossed their bike in the back and taken off," Sallow said. We were both thinking along the same lines. "Sadly, the door-to-door turned up nothing. Folks were indoors, focused on their celebrations and Christmas dinner."

"I'll leave you to it, Constable," Ruxton said. He stood to leave, and cut short his monologue with Kaz. "I will inform Sir Percy of our progress in assisting SHAEF."

"Oh, how is Chief Constable Sillitoe?" Kaz asked.

"You know of him?" Ruxton asked.

"Sir Percy is an old friend of the family," Kaz said. "I really should ring him up, it's been ages."

"Well, yes, please be sure to mention our help when you do," Ruxton said, then mumbled something else as he stuck his hat on his head and stomped out of the room.

"The chief constable is a friend of yours?" Sallow asked as he leaned back in his chair and studied Kaz.

"Never met the gentleman, but I did read about him in *The Times*," Kaz said. "He was described as an innovator in law enforcement."

"Ha! You shook the DS to his boots," Sallow said. "Sir Percy isn't a man afraid of new ideas. Radios in motor cars and more women police officers. All that change makes people nervous, if you take my meaning."

"Indeed, I do," Kaz said. "It was evident from the man's demeanor. Now, did I hear correctly? You have Major Brockman's staff car?"

We talked it over for a while and agreed that the killer likely arrived at the cliffs via bicycle and drove the staff car back to the train station. From there it would have been a simple matter to ditch the bike and board a train. The door and steering wheel, probably having been wiped clean, had provided no fingerprints.

"It was cold enough for gloves," Sallow said. "Especially if the killer was out on two wheels. Not much to go on, I'm afraid."

I told Sallow he'd come up with more than we had and filled him in on the murder of Flight Sergeant Cohen. He said he'd heard of the German Jews at the air base but didn't know what their role was. He didn't ask now. I told him to keep the news of the new murder under his hat and that I'd return tomorrow for the staff car.

Kaz asked about restaurants and Sallow recommended the Royal Oak, just down the street, for a decent meal. Kaz and I walked and soon spotted the restaurant with its thick oaken beams and wrought-iron sign. We sat near the fireplace, the glowing coals welcome after the cold night air. There were a few civilians at the bar and a scattering of RAF officers at the tables. It was sedate and charming. I figured the pub where I'd dined with Diana yesterday was a livelier joint right about now, but the quiet was welcome. We ordered the local ale and settled on lamb with roasted potatoes and parsnips, recommended by the waitress. Once the ales arrived, we toasted and drank.

"Now, fill me in," I said as I set down my glass. "What are you cooking up for Angelika?"

"As you know, she has talked about joining the Polish Armed

Forces," Kaz said. "She already has contacted the government-in-exile based in London. I fear that with her experience with the Home Army, they may want to send her back."

"And that she would go," I said.

"Yes. But I believe she has done her bit, as our British friends say. When Diana told us of her posting here, I became interested. It is important work, and perhaps suited to a young woman with Angelika's physical limitations. She is doing well, but I doubt she could outrun the fattest German in Poland."

"I understand," I said. "I feel the same way about Diana being here, even if she was actually brought in to snoop around for Jean Conan Doyle."

"Oh, I did not know that she had her own security concerns," Kaz said. "Interesting. Sir Richard did not mention Diana's dual role."

"He's a man of secrets too. I guess you asked him to mention Angelika to Conan Doyle," I said.

"Of course. She speaks German well and Italian fluently. She's a perfect fit, and there is little running involved with the work at Elham House."

"You're a devious man, Kaz," I said, and raised my glass.

"Not so devious as our murderer," he said as we clinked.

We drank, and I sent up a silent prayer to Saint Michael, the patron saint of police officers and all individuals in dangerous occupations. I asked for his help in closing this case.

Saint Michael had to be a busy man these days, and I hoped he'd spare us a thought.

CHAPTER SEVENTEEN

"Wake up. Wake up!" The voice was muffled and overlaid with a rhythmic pounding. I pried my eyes open, trying to make sense of it all. It was dark in the very comfortable room Kaz and I shared in the visiting officers' quarters, but I could see a glow of light under the door.

"Hang on," I managed, stumbling half-awake across the room.

"Are you all right?" Lieutenant Walters said. He panted as if he'd sprinted up the stairs. Two men behind him stood with their pistols at the ready, flashlights searching the hallway.

"I was sleeping just fine, thanks," I said, and glanced at the luminous dial on my watch. "It's four o'clock in the morning, Walters. What the hell is going on?"

"Someone tried to kill you," he said.

"It was not I," Kaz said. He stood behind me, donning his silk dressing gown.

"You're not making sense, Walters," I said. I turned on a lamp and beckoned him in. "I'm fine, no one tried to kill me."

"Not here, but it's a different story in my quarters. Get dressed and I'll show you," he said. "I'll leave one of my men to drive you and meet you there."

I told him I could drive myself, but he insisted on an escort. I got the sense it would be embarrassing for the guy responsible for security to have a guest murdered on his watch, so I agreed.

Twenty minutes later, Kaz and I were at Walters's barracks where he awaited us in the hall.

"At 0200 hours my men received a call from the motor pool. There had been a breach in the perimeter fence. They sent out a patrol and summoned me, which is standard protocol. We found no breach and no one at the motor pool. But when I returned to my quarters, I found this," Walters said. He opened the door and entered the room.

My bed—the one I had slept in the night before—was a mess. Shattered glass lay on a torn pillow, and the thick smell of alcohol assaulted our nostrils.

"Someone thought you were still sleeping here," Walters said. "I'd shifted my stuff around after they took your duffel but hadn't finished. I left some clothes on the bed and a full bottle of brandy resting on the pillow."

"It was dark, of course," Kaz said, and approached the bed. He shifted the pillow, and shards of glass fell to the floor. A rip marked where a blunt object had unexpectedly hit glass. "The intruder came in, saw a form he mistook for Billy, and struck quickly."

"He got a helluva surprise," I said. "We should be on the lookout for anyone smelling like a distillery. Sorry about the damage, Lieutenant."

"It's nothing," Walters said. "But I don't want a third attempt on your life to succeed. I'll post two of my men to serve as your bodyguard around the clock."

"That won't be necessary, but thanks. Try to keep this under your hat. We don't need rumors flying around the base faster than they already are," I said. "There are no locks on the barracks rooms?"

"No. The feeling is, if you can't trust your brothers-in-arms, who can you trust?" Walters said.

"All but one, it appears," Kaz said as he waved his hand in front of his face. "You need to open a window."

"You'd think we must be getting close to frighten the killer into a stunt like that, but it doesn't really add up, does it?" I said as I blew on the hot cup of joe. We'd driven to the American mess on the theory that if I was going to get my head bashed in, there were statistically fewer candidates among the Yanks at RAF Hawkinge. And stronger coffee.

"From what you've said, there are many here with the means and opportunity to have committed both murders, but to me, motive is lacking. I don't see how this investigation threatens anyone. Sadly," Kaz said, "the attack on you in the hangar might have been merely convenient timing, but this one required planning."

"It could have to do with our trip to the listening post," I said. "Diana and I have talked about visiting Sally Miller for two days. Someone might have overheard us. Sally's exile is probably prime gossip material, and the rumor mill could have spread it far and wide."

"A good theory," Kaz said as he nibbled at a serving of powdered eggs and eyed the yellow concoction warily. "Perhaps we should warn Diana before we leave."

"Walters said he would report the incident to Conan Doyle, but I agree, we should be sure Diana takes it seriously. She could be a target as well." I chewed on my bacon sandwich and watched Kaz as he set down his fork. His forehead wrinkled, and I knew he had something on his mind.

"There is another possibility," he said. "I only bring this up because of your feeling about Lieutenant Walters. We only have his word that the events unfolded as he claims. It's possible he made that telephone call himself. Or, if it was real, he might have used it to conjure up this supposed attack."

"'Supposed' is easy for you to say. Your skull never rested on that pillow."

"True. But if he is involved in the murders and the missing hardware to any extent, it would be the perfect opportunity to cast suspicion elsewhere," Kaz said. He raised an eyebrow in my direction and bit into his toast.

"So he smashes his bottle of brandy and comes running to me," I said. "Then we assume the killer is anyone but him. Not bad. It would be a smart move if he is the killer."

"But motive is entirely lacking," Kaz said. "Perhaps Sally will explain all."

"Here's to Sally," I said, and drained my cup of joe.

We drove to Elham House as the sun cracked the horizon, the pale, rosy light promising good weather. Bombing weather. Inside, Sergeant Halfpenny was at her usual post.

"Sergeant Joyce Halfpenny," I said, and introduced Kaz.

"I've already had the pleasure," Kaz said, offering up a smile. I fully expected him to kiss her hand like in the movies, but he held back.

"How is Angelika doing, Baron?" Halfpenny asked. I guessed Kaz had played the nobility card. He'd made a better impression on the desk sergeant than I had.

"She is quite fascinated by your work here, thank you," Kaz said. "Are you always on duty, Sergeant?"

"I just arrived, actually," she said. "Glad to see you up and about, Captain."

"You heard?"

"The whole base knows by now. People are on edge with a killer about, not that we don't deal with death every day," she said.

"News travels fast," I said. "Was it like that when Sally Miller was sent away?"

"Tongues wagged, I'll give you that. Why do you ask?"

"I wonder if word about our interest in Sally got around," I said.

"I saw how surprised you and Captain Seaton were about Major Brockman coming to see her," Halfpenny said. "Then Squadron Officer Conan Doyle came down to check my register. She wanted to see for herself. Lots of traffic through here, Captain. Anyone could have overheard either conversation."

"But you didn't hear anyone talking about it?" I said.

"No, but I'm not one for gossip as some are," Halfpenny said. "Be sure to say hello to Sally for me, will you? And tell her if we get any news about Johnny I'll be in touch. She's probably worried sick. It's bad enough thinking he's in a POW camp, but if the Jerries discover he's a Jew, and German-born at that, he's sure to earn a bullet."

"Let us hope he is safe and does not reveal that he speaks German," Kaz said. "It is often easy to identify a native speaker by accent and phrasing."

"Johnny's a smart one," Halfpenny said. "He always studied maps of the ground they'd be flying over and went through intelligence reports about escape routes and the like. Some of the lads don't like to think about it, but Johnny said he needed one leg up if both feet hit the ground. A little joke of his. Now excuse me, I need to attend to some things. Be nice to Sally, will you?"

"Of course," I said while Halfpenny busied herself with the pile of incoming mail.

"You're up early," Diana said from the upstairs landing. "Pillow too lumpy?"

"I'm glad you're not consumed by worry," I said as I climbed the stairs. Kaz was right behind me and could barely keep his chuckle to himself. "But I am worried about you."

"Don't be," she said, and slipped a pistol out of the front pocket of her FANY uniform. "My Beretta hardly breaks the line of my coat, but it will do the job."

"It's almost elegant," I said. The Beretta M1935 was a slim

.32 automatic, an Italian sidearm highly prized by scroungers, souvenir hunters, and spies alike.

"Is Angelika with you?" Kaz asked.

"Yes, she's quite safe," Diana said. "When I'm on duty she's with other WAAFs to learn about what they do, at Jean's direction. You don't have to worry. Between my Beretta and Angelika's knife, an attacker wouldn't stand a chance."

"A knife?" I said.

"An SOE-issue gravity knife," Kaz said. "A Christmas present."

"That's a cheery gift," I said. The gravity knife contained a blade within the handle, which at the push of a button could be opened or closed one-handed. Designed mainly for parachutists who needed to quickly cut themselves loose from tangled shroud lines, it was also issued to commandos and agents as a compact and silent weapon.

"She's never without it," Diana said. "Must run. There's a lot of radio traffic from Salò this morning. Quite unusual for our Italian friends to be up so early. Don't let Kaz drive too fast. Ciao!" I was glad to see Diana had taken precautions. But still, I wished for a touch of sympathy after the second attempt on my life, even if I hadn't been anywhere near it.

Kaz took the Aston Martin out of the garage, and I pulled my jeep in, knowing I'd be driving Brockman's staff car back later in the day. Maybe I'd keep it. The army loses stuff all the time, and it would be nice to have real windshield wipers.

Kaz drove slowly through Capel-le-Ferne. He wound through the narrow streets where wisps of fog clung to the cobblestones, waiting for the feeble morning sun to burn them off. Leaving town, we took the Folkestone Road along the coast, where the wind off the Channel took care of what fog remained. Kaz shifted coming out of a turn, no fishtailing this time. With a clear stretch of road ahead, he accelerated, and I did my best to enjoy the ride without glancing at the speedometer.

"Refreshing, isn't it?" Kaz said with a wide grin on his face. "Gives one a sense of freedom from responsibility."

"Along with an appreciation for life," I said.

"Ah yes, it wouldn't do to die today, would it?" he said, and took his foot off the gas. "I am very interested in what Sally Miller can tell us, after all. From Sergeant Halfpenny's description of Johnny Adler, he sounds like the sensible sort."

"What does that tell you?" I said as I caught a glimpse of white chalk cliffs when the road curved.

"That Sally may be the same," he said. "Perhaps she had a very good reason to see Adler in the men's barracks. Beyond the libidinous, that is. Both must have known the penalties. And the fact that Sally was only sent to another posting, no matter how remote, demonstrates the high regard Conan Doyle must have for her work."

"Nothing happened to Adler. Except for having to go on another mission and being shot down," I said. It would be hard to give him any punishment that was worse than doing his own job. "Once we learn more from Sally, I do want to question Walters about snitching on them. Seems petty."

"And Lieutenant Harker about his gambling," Kaz said. "If he has significant debts, it could be a factor."

I mulled that over as we drove through Dover and circled around Dover Castle. The fortress overlooked the Channel where the Dunkirk evacuation and rescue was organized. I looked down at the harbor and realized that this was probably where Diana had come ashore after her destroyer sank out from under her. Ages ago now, but, I knew, still fresh in her mind.

The town itself was in shambles. Most civilians had been evacuated early in the war due to heavy shelling from across the Channel in Pas-de-Calais. It looked like a few had returned, but the streets remained thick with rubble and burnt timber.

Once we cleared Dover, the road along the cliffs opened up

under a cold, crystal-clear sky. A loud drone grew from behind, and I craned my neck to catch sight of big four-engine B-17 bombers streaming toward us as they climbed on their flight path from airfields in Kent and Suffolk. Kaz pulled over on the verge, and we got out to watch the procession that grew larger by the moment. The thrum of the radial engines rapidly rose to a crescendo as the dozens—no, hundreds—of aircraft passed overhead, the bomber stream wide and long as it gained altitude. The morning sun glinted off the gleaming metal, but I knew it wouldn't warm the ten crewmen in each B-17. Where they were going, the cold was beyond cold; a frigid ice blue that was as deadly as flak.

"You're right, Kaz. It wouldn't do to die today."

We drove in silence.

CHAPTER EIGHTEEN

WE NEARED ST. Margaret's at Cliffe, passing a massive gun emplacement where two heavy cannons silently watched over the Channel. A few months ago, they had lobbed shells across the water, but the war had moved far beyond their range. The octagonal windmill was easy to spot, painted white and perched on a slight rise overlooking the cliff. It stood upon a sturdy one-story structure built in the same eight-sided pattern. Smoke curled from the chimney of an attached house, and the whole place looked like a picture postcard.

"Hardly a terrible banishment," Kaz said, and parked the Aston Martin next to a small truck in front of the windmill. "The view is spectacular." I had to agree. I stepped out of the car, and, with the perfect visibility, I could easily see across the Channel to the coast of France, about twenty miles away.

"Can I help you gentlemen?" a Royal Navy officer asked. He'd stepped out of the windmill and shrugged on his wool overcoat. "This is a restricted area."

"We know," I said as I handed over my orders. It would have been simpler to ask Conan Doyle to call ahead and clear us, but I wanted to question Sally before she had time to think about her story. I studied his face as he read, his surprise quickly covered up as he took in the names that granted me the authority to do pretty much as I pleased.

"Lieutenant Commander Stanhope, Captain Boyle," he said as he handed the orders back. "How may I assist you?"

"Lieutenant Kazimierz and I would like to speak with Flight Sergeant Sally Miller," I said. "A quick chat and we'll be out of your hair."

"What is this regarding, may I ask?"

"It is a routine matter, Lieutenant Commander," Kaz said. "We simply need to gather information, which the flight sergeant may be able to assist us with. She is in no trouble herself."

"Those orders tell me it's more than routine, but that's your business, I suppose," he said. "Mine is to make sure our work here is not compromised. Since Squadron Officer Conan Doyle signed your orders, you must be aware how important security is."

"Absolutely," I said. Out of the corner of my eye I caught a glimpse of movement. A sailor wearing a duffle coat and toting a Sten gun appeared from the direction of the house. Stanhope gave a nod and the guy halted before he got any closer.

"Good," Stanhope said with a polite smile. "Sally's work is top-notch, by the way. I'll take you to her."

Stanhope led us inside. He earned disapproving looks from the Wrens in the room, members of the Women's Royal Navy Service, at the blast of cold air from the open door. He muttered an apology that went unheard, as each of the women wore headphones and immediately went back to tuning radio dials or taking notes.

Radios were set up on workbenches around the octagonal perimeter of the room. Six Wrens in their blue double-breasted jackets and skirts were at work, along with a solitary WAAF. She looked up from her radio, her brow wrinkled in confusion.

"Sally, these men would like to speak with you," Stanhope said. "Perhaps you could take them into the house for a cup of tea?"

"Oh no," she said. Worry raced across her face.

"It's not bad news about Johnny," I said, before she could mistake our visit for a condolence call.

"But it is bad news, isn't it?" Sally Miller said. She removed her headphones and sighed. "Whatever it is you want, I suppose tea is in order. Thank you, Lieutenant Commander."

Sally led us out through a back door at the end of a short hallway, sparing the Wrens another blast of cold air. I introduced myself and Kaz and told her we wouldn't take too much of her time.

"Time? I've got plenty of that, Captain Boyle," she said. We entered the kitchen of the adjacent house. It was painted a light blue, and, with the view of sky and water out the tall windows, it was much more pleasant than the crowded radio intercept room. Sally herself was tall and trim, with wavy blond hair and striking blue eyes.

"We understand you were sent here as a punishment," Kaz said as he admired the view.

"Yes. Picturesque, isn't it?" Sally said. She plugged in a brown enamel tea kettle and readied three cups. "I adored the view the first twenty times I saw it. Did you come out here from Hawkinge?"

"Yes. Has anyone else visited you, or been in touch?" I asked.

"You're the first," she said. "Do you have any identification? I find it odd that Squadron Officer Conan Doyle hasn't called to say you were coming. And neither of you are RAF."

I handed over my orders and watched again as they worked their magic. Sally handed them back and raised an eyebrow. "I'm fascinated to hear what comes next," she said as she carried a tray to the table and set out three cups.

"It's not pretty," I said. "Major Brockman was killed on Christmas morning. Murdered."

"Dear God," Sally said. She set down the teapot with a thud. "Who would do such a thing?"

"And why? During our investigation, we found that he came to see you at Elham House, about two weeks ago," I said. "What was his purpose?"

"He wanted to know if Johnny had told me anything," she said. "Flight Sergeant Johnny Adler, I mean, although you probably are aware of that. Major Brockman was concerned about missing documents, the restricted sort."

"Yes," Kaz said, and reached for the teapot. "Allow me. Joyce Halfpenny sends her regards, by the way, and said to tell you that if they receive any news of Johnny, she will be in touch."

"She's a good egg," Sally said. "Thank you."

I waited for the first sip of tea to be drunk and then returned to my questions.

"Why didn't Brockman speak directly to Johnny? Why come to see you?"

"I imagine because Johnny was on his way to bomb Berlin at the time," she said. "The major was in a hurry. He didn't explain himself fully, but I didn't expect him to. I got the distinct impression some important plans had gone missing."

"Radio intercept hardware, that sort of thing?" I asked.

"That's a fair guess," Sally said. "But Brockman didn't confide in me. So I thought I should give Johnny a heads-up when he returned."

"Got it. When was it you visited Johnny in the men's barracks?" I asked. I sipped my tea, the warmth going down easy.

"It was the next day. I'd stopped at Johnny's aircraft first. He sometimes was wound up so tight after a raid that he couldn't settle down. He'd check and recheck his equipment."

"You came across something," Kaz said.

"I did. The entrance hatch was open but there didn't appear to be anyone aboard," she said. "The wind was gusting, and I saw a piece of paper dancing about inside the fuselage. I didn't think much of it until I got closer."

"Did you go inside the aircraft?" I asked.

"No, I simply looked in and hollered for Johnny," she said. "There was no response, then a gust of wind blew the paper right into my face. It had RESTRICTED plastered across the top. My first thought was that Johnny could get in trouble for leaving it, so I stuffed it in my pocket."

"Is that why you went to see him in his barracks?" Kaz asked.

"Yes," Sally said as she let out a heavy sigh. "The more I thought about Major Brockman's interest in Johnny and the fact that the document was left so carelessly, the more I worried. The special operators have their own barracks, and I knew they must have been sound asleep after a night raid, so I went round to see if I could wake him without disturbing the others." Sally drank more tea and looked beyond us at the view she said she'd become so accustomed to. "I took a chance that nobody would spot me and entered the SOs' barracks. Obviously, someone did and told tales out of school. I was only in there for a few minutes, so worse luck for me."

"What was Johnny's reaction?"

"He told me he was working with Major Brockman," Sally said. "He'd noticed that some electronic components had gone missing as well and they were both concerned. He said I should bring the document I found to Brockman, and not tell a soul about it. Johnny wanted one more piece of information but said he was certain he knew who was behind the whole affair."

"I assume he didn't tell you," I said.

"Right. He thought it too dangerous. He gave me a kiss and promised he'd make things right. But that night his Lanc was shot down before he could speak to Brockman. When the major came to see me, I gave him the document. He told me the same thing—to keep mum about it."

"Did you look at the restricted document?" I asked.

"No, I was nervous enough just having it," Sally said. "I was worried someone would turn me in."

I sipped my tea, thinking about Sally's story, while Kaz kept her talking with questions about her duties here. He knew it was vital to keep a witness talking about anything, since each word could bring up a forgotten memory. He asked how she got along with the Wrens. They were friendly and welcoming, and after what happened to Johnny, she was glad of the peace and quiet. As she spoke about St. Margaret's, I wondered if she'd disturbed the killer when he was searching Johnny's Lancaster. Perhaps secret documents had been left on the plane and were about to be pilfered when she showed up and called for him. She was lucky she hadn't gotten whacked herself. I knew that when Lancasters came back from a raid, the ones that had been damaged received immediate attention. If Johnny's was in good shape, it could have sat unattended for hours.

"Are there any devices Johnny mentioned specifically?" I asked. I wondered if Jostle or Jackal had come up in conversation.

"He was quite excited about H2S and told me about it," Sally said. "It's ground-mapping radar designed to pick up areas of water or large buildings in any weather. It's mounted on the underside of the aircraft, and data is fed to a cathode-ray tube at the navigator's position. Good for assessing bomb damage as well as navigation."

"For the navigator's use," Kaz said. "Not the special operator?"

"Right, strictly speaking," Sally said as she glanced at her wristwatch. "But Johnny took special interest in navigation. He wanted to be sure of the ground they were flying over in case he had to hike it. He didn't fancy being captured by the Nazis, not one bit."

"I understand he prepared for the possibility," I said.

"He carried an Enfield revolver stuffed in his jacket pocket, and he always flew with a pair of sturdy civilian shoes tied around his neck," Sally said as she drained the last of her tea. "He said he couldn't get far in heavy fur-lined flying boots, and the one thing he hoped to do was put miles between him and the Germans hunting him as quickly as possible."

"One leg up in case both hit the ground," Kaz said with a smile. "According to Sergeant Halfpenny."

"That was Johnny's favorite line," Sally said. Her eyes lit up at the memory. "He and David—one of the other SOs—were the most serious about evading capture. There was a briefing for aircrew shortly before I left about escape lines into Switzerland and Yugoslavia. Not much friendly territory under their wings, so those were the recommended routes."

"David? Flight Sergeant David Cohen?" Kaz asked. Sally nodded, concern flashing across her face. I broke the news about Cohen.

"I can't believe it. They were best friends," Sally said. Her hand went to her chest. "Maybe Johnny revealed the name of the murderer to him. If anyone was doing something underhanded with H2S, Johnny would take it as a personal affront."

"He may have shared his suspicions, at least," I said. "It was over two weeks between telling you he knew who it was and Cohen's murder. Perhaps David started investigating on his own."

"Who else was Johnny close with?" Kaz asked.

"*Is* close. He's still alive, I have to believe that," Sally said. "Johnny's everyone's friend, but there was no one closer than David. Unlike some of the other crews, Johnny's didn't cut him out. They accepted him and the risks of operating with 101 Squadron."

"But we can't speak with them," I said. "What about anyone else? Lieutenant Walters, maybe?"

"I doubt that," Sally scoffed. "He's a little too snotty, and he's the one who reported me."

"He claims he was tipped off," I said.

"Of course he does," Sally said. A bitter laugh escaped her lips. "You could talk to some of the ground crew. Corporal Fletcher for one. William, I think. And a young lad, Leading Aircraftman

Roscoe Bigsby. The pair of them are responsible for the electronics on several Lancasters. Johnny spoke well of both, but they weren't mates." Sally looked again at the distant view, out over the water and in the direction of enemy lands.

"Thanks for your time, Flight Sergeant," I said as I stood. "Just to be certain, you believe Johnny knows who's responsible for taking the plans and hardware?"

"Yes, absolutely. I can't speak to the killings, but Johnny was certain about the thefts. He'd been worried it could be the work of a German spy. Maybe that's true, or maybe he'd discovered something else," she said. Her eyes brimmed with tears as she continued to stare at the blue sky and cold water. She shrugged, as if the truth of it all was unimportant.

"Thank you—" I began, but she cut me off.

"Do you want to hear the worst-kept secret of St. Margaret's?" Sally said, her voice drifting into a whisper. "It's all right, it's made the rounds here and everyone knows. We still have the decoded transcript."

"Are you sure you should speak of this?" Kaz asked as he stepped to her side. She waved a hand as if swatting away a silly question.

"Back when the Germans held France and there was talk of invasion, Hermann Göring would stand on the cliffs at Cap Blanc-Nez. Just there." She tapped on the windowpane, along the line of the far horizon. "Through his binoculars, he spotted the windmill, white against the sky. He ordered it not to be destroyed, so he could have it moved to his private estate once the Nazis took Britain. Funny, isn't it?"

"How so?" I asked, not finding much amusement in anything concerning the head of the Luftwaffe.

"That Göring spared this lovely place, and now Johnny is in one of his POW camps while here I sit, safe, at the end of the world."

CHAPTER NINETEEN

I COULDN'T GET Sally out of my mind. There were so many ways to be injured in this war. She had kept her hurt well hidden, the only hint of it showing when she'd tapped on the far shore through the glass and held back her tears.

And now we had someone who could identify the killer. I couldn't shake the image of Johnny Adler lugging those civilian shoes on each mission so he could outrun his former countrymen. But Johnny was either in a POW cage or hoofing it to Switzerland. Either way, it didn't help us much.

"We're dead in the water," I said as I rubbed my gloved fingers together. The Aston Martin was a hot little roadster, but that didn't hold true for the car's heater.

"Well, at least we know how Major Brockman came to have that restricted document," Kaz said. "Sally handed it over and he took it to his meeting on the cliffs."

"Perhaps Diana has come up with some evidence," Kaz said as he pulled over by the police station. "She was going to speak with Cohen's crewmen today."

"Evidence? That'd be a nice change," I said. "See you at Elham House."

I retrieved the keys to Brockman's staff car from Constable Sallow and updated him on what we'd learned from Sally.

"Your Johnny sounds like the sort of lad who could make it

to Switzerland," Sallow said. "If he does, you'll know who you're after soon enough."

"And if he ends up in a POW camp, it could be months before we get notice from the Red Cross," I said. "Then we have to figure out a way to ask him who he had in mind. The killer could be long gone by then."

"Where to, that's the question," Sallow said. "If it's anyone on the base, it would mean desertion. It may be the work of a German spy. Who else would have an escape plan?"

"You deserve a promotion, Constable," I said. "You might be on to something."

"No thank you, Captain. That'd mean a transfer to Folkestone, where I'd encounter his nibs every day," Sallow said with a grin, slapping his hand on the arm of his chair. "This suits me well enough."

"Ruxton would probably claim the idea as his own anyway," I said. Sallow pointed a finger at me as if I'd hit the bull's-eye.

Back at Elham House, I found Flight Sergeant Halfpenny at her post and told her we'd passed on her greeting to Sally.

"How did she seem?" Halfpenny asked.

"She likes it there," I said. "It's quiet, which seems to fit her mood. But a bit lonely, I'd guess."

"I wouldn't mind a bit of lonely now and then," she said. "This place is mad today. Go on up. There's a flap on over something, and I was told to send you and the baron upstairs the moment you showed. He's a dashing fellow, isn't he?"

"Kaz? If you're talking about his driving, I agree completely," I said, and tossed a wink in her direction.

I knocked on the door to the conference room and entered. Conan Doyle and Kaz were studying a large, detailed map spread out on the table.

"Come in, Captain," Conan Doyle said, gesturing with a ruler. "I'm waiting for Diana to finish with a transmission. It's been rather hectic here. Our Italian friends are more excitable than usual. But I do want to hear what you learned from Flight Sergeant Miller."

The squadron officer went back to her map, where, using her ruler, she measured distances in southern Germany and Austria down to the Italian border. She was oblivious to our presence, drawn into the details of the map. Wolfsberg in Austria, close to the Yugoslav border, had been circled in red. Kaz looked at me and shrugged, then sat. His eyes followed the course of the lines Conan Doyle sketched on the map.

"I have the preliminary report," Diana announced as she burst into the room. She held up the file she grasped and gave it a shake. She barely spared a nod in my direction. "The names are coming through now and we'll have them shortly."

"Why don't you summarize the situation for the baron and Captain Boyle?" Conan Doyle said as she took the file and began to read.

"Monitoring communications from the republic of Salò yesterday, we picked up mention of escaped POWs," Diana said.

"You said they were extra chatty today," I said.

"Right. The communiqués kept coming in all morning. The Germans have instructed both the Salò Italians and the Croatian fascist government in Yugoslavia to conduct searches for twenty escapees."

"There was a prison break?" Kaz asked.

"No. From what we've pieced together, two days ago a column of trucks was attacked by American fighter planes on a road in Wolfsberg, Austria. Right here," Diana said as she pointed to the red circle. "Close to the Drava River, which is a stone's throw from the Yugoslavian border."

"And that part of Yugoslavia is run by the Croatian Ustaše," Kaz said. "A bloodthirsty group, even by fascist standards."

"Correct," Diana said. "The convoy included three truckloads of POWs being transferred to Stalag 18 in Austria from camps farther east. We confirmed that the American 332nd Fighter Group did conduct ground attacks in that area two days ago in the early-morning hours. Several vehicles were hit, and it appears twenty men did escape in the confusion."

"Good for them," I said. "But where can they go?"

"Switzerland is unlikely," Diana said, and waved her hand across the length of Austria. "Lots of snow and mountainous terrain. But if they head southwest, they'll cross into the Po Valley and the Venetian Plain. Easy going, but they'll have Germans and Mussolini's fascists to deal with."

"Yugoslavia is a possibility," Conan Doyle said. She handed the file back to Diana. "If they can evade the Croatian Ustaše and move south, they might make contact with the Partisan forces."

"Those are the closest friendly troops," Kaz said. "The Italian route is easier terrain, but the forests and hills of Yugoslavia provide better cover."

"I agree," Conan Doyle said. "Captain Seaton, draft a flash message to be sent via teletype to Mediterranean Allied Air Forces command informing them of the escapees and potential routes. Also to MI9, SOE, and OSS. With luck, there may be some way to help these chaps."

MI9 was the British military intelligence unit responsible for aiding escaped POWs and instructing pilots and aircrew in how to evade capture when downed over enemy territory. As for the SOE, Diana's outfit, there was a chance they'd have agents in the vicinity of the escapees' routes. Same for our Office of Strategic Services.

"There are SOE missions in Yugoslavia, I'm certain," Diana said. "Probably the same for the OSS. I'll get the message written immediately. Sorry, Billy, but I haven't had a moment to interview anyone today." With that cheery news, she was out the door.

"Do you think these fellows have a chance?" I asked as I stood and leaned over the map. The Italian route looked inviting. After a hilly start, it opened up along the Tagliamento River, easing into a broad floodplain that led to Venice and points south. The way into Yugoslavia was rougher terrain, with the Croatian city of Zagreb directly on the path. But after that, while the hills and forests would make for rough going, they'd give good cover. That would be my choice, one I was glad I didn't have to make.

"It's been two days," Conan Doyle said. "There's been nothing about their capture, which is good news. There's a chance they could make contact with Italian partisans. The north is crawling with armed bands, some young men seeking to avoid conscription by Mussolini's army or forced labor for the Germans. I imagine the SOE is actively aiding them, but that's not my department. Our job is to intercept the information and pass it on."

"If they went into Yugoslavia and the Ustaše captured them, you may well never hear of their fate," Kaz said.

"While the Croatian fascists are savage, they understand how to obey their masters. The German transmissions make it clear they want the escapees captured and returned. Undoubtedly, they don't like their lackeys to see them fail," Conan Doyle said.

"If they get by Zagreb, they're closer to the Chetnik forces and Tito's Partisan Army," Kaz said. I didn't know much about Yugoslavia, but I was aware that Josip Broz Tito led the Partisans, and that they were giving the Germans a run for their money. Tito's bunch were also Communists, which didn't seem to trouble anyone as long as they kept killing Germans. The Serbian Chetniks supported the former king and didn't like Communism. From what I heard, there were questions about exactly how hard they were fighting the Nazis. The suspicion was they were keeping their powder dry for a postwar showdown with Tito's gang.

"The SOE and your American OSS are both active among those groups," Conan Doyle said. "Although His Majesty's Government now prefers to arm Tito's Partisans' exclusively. Which the Chetniks hate, of course. It's all a bit of a mess down there. But enough of that for now. Tell me how you got on with Sally."

"She told us Johnny Adler knew who was taking the plans and electronics," I said as I sat, my elbow landing next to Rome on the well-creased map. "He told her when she saw him in the men's barracks."

"And he was shot down on his next mission," Conan Doyle said with a sad shake of the head. "Why didn't she say something?"

Kaz explained how Sally had come to find the restricted document in Johnny's Lancaster and her worry about him getting in trouble over it, followed by her passing it on to Brockman.

"I sent her away before we heard Johnny's Lanc had gone down," Conan Doyle said. "If only I'd waited. How is she?"

I said the location suited her and left it at that.

Diana returned with the flash message, which Conan Doyle read and signed. She called in a WAAF to take it to the teletype room just as Angelika entered and handed Diana a file.

"I see you have kept my sister occupied," Kaz said. He smiled at the sight of Angelika. She looked happy, and it seemed like Kaz's plan had a chance of working.

"I'm glad to do whatever I can," Angelika said as she glanced at Diana.

"Two developments, ma'am," Diana said. "The Germans just told all commands in Yugoslavia and northern Italy to expect a detailed list with names and descriptions of the sixteen escapees still at large. Four were recaptured earlier today in Krapina, just north of Zagreb. We'll have the intercept soon."

"What is the second item?" Conan Doyle asked.

"The Ustaše sent a message in Croatian, in the clear," Diana said. "It went out to their subordinate units and local police as well as the Germans, which is probably the reason. While we have no one on staff who speaks Croatian, Angelika is familiar with the language."

"Can you translate this message, dear?" Conan Doyle asked.

"Somewhat," Angelika said. "I know a bit of Serbian, and the two languages are closely related."

"You had a Serbian friend at school, did you not?" Kaz asked.

"Yes. She taught me a few phrases, and I studied the language in hopes of visiting her family one day," Angelika said, her face falling into a frown. "Then came the war."

Angelika took the message from Diana and set it on the table in front of her. Kaz had been a student of languages at Oxford before the war and had at least a nodding acquaintance with most European languages. He could have done the translation, but instead let Angelika have center stage.

"It does refer to prisoners," she said, her finger tracing the lines written on the sheet. "It appears the word is the same in both languages. *Zatvorenici*. They are headed south. *Jug* in Croatian, *jyr* in Serbian. There are no numbers, so we don't know how many, but the prisoners were sighted in Caprag."

"That's south of Zagreb. *Jug*," Diana said, as she traced the line of a road on the map. "Some of them have made it through."

"Oh, wait. This refers to *željeznička* in Caprag. That must be the same as *železnica* in Serbian. Željeznička stanica," Angelika said, tapping her hand on the map. "They were sighted at a train station in Caprag. On board a train, or in a boxcar, perhaps. I can't get much more out of this."

"When were they sighted?" Conan Doyle asked.

"*Zora*," Angelika said, and found the reference. "Dawn. Today."

"If they'd been apprehended, the Croatians would have shouted it from the rooftops," Diana said. "Good work, lads, no matter how many of you there are. You're getting closer."

The rail line split southeast of Caprag. One route went to the Adriatic coast and the other to Belgrade. Along that leg, narrow-gauge lines branched off into mountainous terrain. I doubted any escapees would head into Belgrade if they had a choice. Too many Krauts and associated fascist patrols. But any of those lines that dead-ended in heavily forested small towns would be just the ticket, especially for a few bindle stiffs hiding in a boxcar.

"Ma'am," a WAAF said as she entered and waved a piece of paper. She was breathless and rushed. "Two more men have been captured. We have the intercept of the POW names and descriptions for the remaining fourteen. The names are in alphabetical order. You might want to check the very first one."

"Flight Sergeant John Adler," Conan Doyle said. Her eyes widened in surprise. "Our very own Johnny."

CHAPTER TWENTY

"Johnny Adler knows who the killer is," I said. Diana looked startled.

"Why didn't you say anything?" she asked.

"I was waiting," I said. "I didn't want to interrupt your work, and until we saw Johnny's name on that list, it wasn't exactly urgent."

"Captain Boyle told me briefly, before you came in," Conan Doyle said. "Johnny Adler told Sally he knew who the thief was, but that he wanted one more piece of information before he acted. That very night his Lancaster was shot down."

"Johnny Adler has the answer we've been seeking," I said.

"That would be far more helpful than anything we've discovered so far," Diana said. "If only we could get him out."

"Then we will do everything possible," Conan Doyle said. "Johnny has already done more than his fair share. Here's what we shall do."

The squadron officer reeled off a series of instructions. Angelika would work with Diana to monitor Croatian frequencies to intercept any further news, while Diana focused on the republic of Salò communiqués. Conan Doyle sent out another flash message with an update requesting all possible assistance. This time she included Colonel Harding at SHAEF. Then she called Lieutenant Jack Walters and ordered him to bring in a couple of men who had been part of the MI9 briefing on escape and evasion that Johnny had attended.

Which is how Conan Doyle, Kaz, and I came to be sitting around the table with mugs of tea, talking with Flight Officer Adrian Connell and Sergeant Jock Lewis.

"Gentlemen, we just have a few questions," Conan Doyle said. "You both attended the MI9 briefing along with Johnny Adler. Do you know him?"

"Sure, he's one of the special operators," Lewis said, spooning a healthy amount of sugar into his mug. "Heard his Lanc went down. Johnny was keen on not getting picked up by the Jerries."

"Don't think much of the idea myself, ma'am," Connell said. "I'm a bomb aimer, and if the Germans found out, I wouldn't fancy my chances. They might take it personally."

"The briefing was voluntary, I understand," Conan Doyle said.

"Better that way, ma'am. More time for the lads who show up to ask their questions," Lewis said.

"What sort of questions did Johnny ask?" Kaz said.

"Lots about Switzerland," Lewis said. "How to get across the border, that sort of thing."

"And about Resistance networks in Holland and Denmark," Connell added. "They're often on our route to Berlin and targets in the Ruhr. Wasn't it the Salzburg raid where his Lanc went down?"

"Yes," Conan Doyle said. "Farther south than Bomber Command usually ventures. Did Johnny ask about that area?"

Connell and Lewis looked at each other, neither of them answering.

"You're not in trouble, fellows," I said. "Just fill us in, okay?"

"All right," Connell said, after Lewis gave a nod of approval. "But it's not us that might get in trouble. You see, our commanding officer was at the briefing. The chap from MI9 was smart as a whip. He'd made his own escape in France back in '40, so he knew what he was about."

"If you are worried about getting him in trouble, have no fear," Kaz said. "We only wish to know what Johnny learned."

"Well, Johnny asked about any underground groups in Austria, but the MI9 officer said it was too dangerous to go about speaking German and asking for help," Connell said. "But he said there were people in Yugoslavia who would help downed fliers. Tito's Partisan Army. And that we'd know them by the red star badges on their caps. He told us there was another resistance group, the Chetniks, and to avoid them at all costs."

"I am not surprised to hear that," Conan Doyle said. "It is Great Britain's official policy to support only Tito's group. Why would the briefing officer get in trouble for saying that?"

"It was what he said after the briefing, ma'am," Lewis said. "After our CO left."

"Lewis, Johnny, and I were chatting with the fellow," Connell said. "He told us to forget everything he said about Yugoslavia and find the Chetniks if we wanted to get out. They're strongest in Serbia, the center of the country. He could tell we were keen on evading capture, especially Johnny."

"According to him," Lewis said, "the Chetniks are really helping American fliers. Lots of them go down in Yugoslavia while they're flying to and from bases in Italy. But our government has gone all in with Tito, and no one's supposed to have a good word about the Chetniks. He told us not to mention it came from him, but to do our best to pass the word."

"What did Johnny have to say about that?" Kaz asked.

"That he didn't much like Communists anyway," Lewis said. "Mark my words, if anyone can shake Jerry off his trail and make it home, it's Johnny Adler."

"JOHNNY KNOWS WHERE he's going," I said. I tapped the center of the map. "We need to find out more about this Chetnik operation to get aircrew out. How are they managing to do that? I doubt either Tito's Partisans or the Chetniks have an air force."

"You should ask your Colonel Harding about that," Conan Doyle said. "I'm afraid there is not much I can do to help."

"But this could tell us who the killer is and why they're stealing top secret material," I said. "It's what you wanted me to investigate. And it would help get Johnny and whoever's with him home."

"It is important, yes," Conan Doyle said. "But ask yourself why the MI9 officer had to speak off the record, without a senior officer present."

I sat back and stared at the folded map on the table. I didn't like to beat around the bush, but Conan Doyle was clearly worried, and she didn't want to come right out with it. I looked to Kaz, who often had a calmer approach to things. Plus, he was damn smart, not to mention crafty.

"I believe the Americans have also begun to support Tito exclusively," Kaz said. "But if the Chetniks are actively working on a rescue operation, it would stand to reason that American forces across the Adriatic in Italy would cooperate."

"Yes, it stands to reason," Conan Doyle said, with a slight nod of encouragement. "The American Fifteenth Air Force all fly over Yugoslavia when they leave Italy to hit oil refineries in Romania and elsewhere in southern Europe. Bomber Command, on the other hand, focuses more on Germany itself. Johnny Adler's Salzburg raid put him close to the Yugoslav border, but that is not the norm for the RAF."

"So what problem would the British government have with Yanks working with the Chetniks?" I asked as I tried to see through the foggy layers of suspicion. "Winston Churchill is hardly a bomb-throwing Marxist."

"No, he isn't," Kaz said as he drummed his fingers on the table. "But there are elements within the government who may be quietly pro-Communist. Even the well-educated can be swayed by propaganda and utopian promises."

"Moles. Soviet spies, to be even less polite," I said.

"I make no accusations," Conan Doyle said. "I have no proof, but the tilt toward Tito may have more to do with dismay over the Chetniks' willingness to fight. And right now, anything that sheds a positive light on their activities may not be welcome in certain circles. So, tread carefully, Captain Boyle."

"What can you do about it?" I asked.

"I will walk down to the switchboard and have them connect to Colonel Harding at SHAEF. Then I will go to the canteen for a bite to eat," she said as she rose from her desk. "Feel free to pick up the telephone if it rings."

She was careful to shut the door behind her.

"We must be cautious, Billy," Kaz said. "We are about to enter strange territory."

"So is Johnny," I said. "We might get a paper cut, but he could get his throat cut."

"Do not underestimate the powers we may be up against," Kaz said. "If they wish to stop us, they will do it in a way that leaves no trace. I understand the reluctance of the MI9 officer and of Squadron Officer Conan Doyle to become officially involved."

"You're a British officer yourself, Kaz, and you're involved," I said, beginning to worry a bit myself.

"Indeed. I am a lowly lieutenant in the chain of command," Kaz said. "It would not be difficult for the British government to order me elsewhere or instruct me to act dishonorably. Unlike you."

The telephone rang.

"Hello," I said. It wasn't the most military way to answer a call, but I had a good idea of who it was.

"Boyle? Where's Squadron Officer Conan Doyle?" Colonel

Harding barked. Either it was a really good connection, or I was hearing him shout all the way from Paris. "The message was she had news about the escaped prisoners."

"She asked me to update you, Colonel. I'm here with Kaz and there's been a development," I said.

I went over the last known sighting of the evaders and the interception of the recent message giving names and descriptions. I told him about Johnny Adler being on the list and how critical he was to the investigation.

"You think Adler is one of the POWs who made it into Yugoslavia?" Harding asked. "How can you be sure?"

"Adler attended a briefing given by MI9 on escape and evasion techniques," I said. "The briefing officer said to look for Tito's Partisan forces if they were on the ground in Yugoslavia. But after the session, he took Adler and a couple of other airmen aside and told them not to listen to the official line. He said the Chetniks were actively aiding US and other airmen, and to look for them."

"You're sure Adler has the information you need to catch Major Brockman's killer?" Harding asked.

"Yes, sir. And there's been another murder as well. Adler had his suspicions and was about to come forward, but then his Lancaster went down near Salzburg," I said. "He's resourceful, and we have every reason to believe he can contact the Chetnik forces. Adler is one of 101 Squadron's special operators. A Jewish refugee from Germany, actually, and he's highly motivated to evade capture."

"Okay. Put Lieutenant Kazimierz on," Harding said. I handed the receiver to Kaz and watched him nod as he listened to Harding.

"Yes, Colonel, I understand completely," Kaz said, then he returned the phone to me.

"Boyle, the lieutenant will remain at the base and assist

Captain Seaton with her investigation," Harding said. "I'm sending a C-47 Skytrain to pick you up. Big Mike and I will join you at Villacoublay airfield." That was a few miles from SHAEF headquarters at Versailles.

"Where are we going from there, Colonel?"

"Bari, Italy. Then the next stop for you and Big Mike is Yugoslavia," Harding said. "Let's hope you're right about Sergeant Adler."

"Sir, I could really use Kaz," I said. "The language is going to be a problem."

"Negative," Harding said. "The C-47 will land in an hour. Grab your gear and keep it zipped about your destination."

With that, all I heard was static.

"Looks like you won't be getting an all-expenses-paid trip to enchanting Yugoslavia," I said as I hung up the receiver.

"Belgrade is lovely, or rather it was before the war and in the springtime," Kaz said. "It seems this is to be purely an American operation. The colonel said your air force and OSS units involved in the rescue flights have excluded the British entirely, due to security concerns."

"Conan Doyle knew what she was talking about," I said. "I'm not supposed to mention where I'm off to, so I better find Diana and say goodbye. I've got less than an hour until my flight."

"Diana and I will begin again tomorrow questioning people," Kaz said. "Who knows, we may find the culprit all on our own. Although Diana did find out that Lieutenant Harker's gambling debts were relatively minor, and there were no repercussions other than a letter in his file counseling him on the wisdom of avoiding games of chance with subordinates."

"Not much of a motive for murder there. If you do find anything, give Harding a holler," I said. I shivered involuntarily as I looked at the map with its tight contours marking the hills and ridges of central Yugoslavia. "This place looks really cold."

■ ■ ■

"Take care of my staff car," I said to Diana as she drove me onto the tarmac where the twin-engine C-47 sat waiting.

"Don't worry, Billy," she said, and pulled up to the rear of the port wing. "It's evidence. I'll only release it into your custody when you return. Safely."

"You're probably in more danger here with a killer on the loose," I said. "Be careful."

"One killer," Diana said. "Yugoslavia, on the other hand, is full of Nazis and other assorted cutthroats." Harding had told me not to talk about my destination, but there were no secrets between me and Diana, except perhaps how deeply worried we were about each other. "Tread carefully."

I leaned over and kissed her.

"Hubba-hubba!" shouted one of the C-47 crewmen standing by the open hatch.

"We have an audience," Diana said as a smile spread across her face. "You'd better go. I'll see you soon."

"With Johnny Adler," I said. I wondered how likely that was. I squeezed her hand, got out, and boarded my flight to destination unknown.

CHAPTER TWENTY-ONE

I HAD THE entire C-47 to myself. The four-man crew was busy forward, but in the rear, I had my choice of seating along the hard metal benches. Deluxe travel, army style. It was dark by the time we touched down in France and the C-47 taxied to a hangar and cut the engines. The radio operator told me I could stretch my legs while they loaded supplies.

I exited the rear hatch as a truck backed up and GIs hustled to unload wooden crates.

"Hey, Billy!" Big Mike shouted from inside the hangar. It wasn't the most military address, but that was Big Mike's way, at least around officers who knew his value. Not only was he true to his name, with the broadest shoulders in the European Theater of Operations and a heart to match, but he was an expert scrounger who could talk a supply sergeant out of his own paratroop boots.

"Good to see you, pal," I said as we shook hands. Big Mike and I had both been cops. His precinct was in Detroit, and he was a bluecoat through and through. He still carried his Detroit PD badge to prove it.

"Come inside," he said. "We've got time for sandwiches and coffee while they load up." We went into a room partitioned off in the back. A woodstove gave out a glow of warmth, which was more than I got from Sam Harding.

"Your hunch better be right, Boyle," Colonel Harding said. He sat at a table and flipped through a file as he sipped coffee. I stood at attention and saluted, knowing that as a West Pointer he'd appreciate proper military courtesy.

"Colonel, I have every reason to believe this is our man," I said. I relaxed as Harding returned the salute and gestured for me to sit.

"I figure you must know the details of this rescue business." Harding didn't only head up Ike's Office of Special Investigations. He acted as a SHAEF liaison to organized resistance units in occupied Europe, and the groups in Yugoslavia were among the most numerous.

"Captain, this is top secret information," Harding said as he glanced at his watch.

"Twenty minutes to get the supplies loaded, Sam," Big Mike said, sensing the question before it was asked. He produced a corned beef sandwich wrapped in wax paper along with a thermos of coffee and three mugs from a knapsack.

"Thanks," I said as Big Mike poured. I wrapped my hands around the mug of hot joe. "Colonel, I got the impression from Conan Doyle that this was sensitive stuff, as well as highly classified."

"It is all that and more," Harding said. "We'll work with the 1st Air Crew Rescue Unit, operated by the Office of Strategic Services, supported by the Fifteenth Air Force. You never heard of it and damn few people ever will. They've managed to rescue almost four hundred American airmen from Yugoslavia plus about eighty Allied fliers."

"With the help of the Chetniks, who seem to have fallen out of favor these days," I said.

"Right. The British have completely cut ties with the Chetniks, and our own government is close to doing the same. Supplies and support have been greatly curtailed," Harding said.

"But the Chetniks still risk their lives, not to mention reprisals, to help our boys."

"Which is why Kaz will sit this one out," I said.

"Right again. I didn't want him in a position to receive orders from the Brits that might compromise the mission," Harding said. "I trust Lieutenant Kazimierz would do the right thing, but it would be difficult. For all concerned."

"Understood, Colonel. Besides, Kaz will have enough work to do with Diana at the air base," I said. "We can only hope that word about Adler's escape hasn't spread around. I'd like the killer to think he's gotten away with it."

"You think the second killing is the work of the same man who killed Brockman?" Harding asked.

"Same modus operandi," I said. "The second victim was one of the special operators, so he's linked to the plans Brockman had and the missing parts. Plus, he tried the same thing with me. Twice. But he missed both times."

"Let's keep the airborne radio countermeasures out of the conversation," Harding said. "The Luftwaffe doesn't fully grasp our capabilities, and we need to keep it that way. Don't talk about it in Italy and don't even think about it in Yugoslavia. Glad you're okay."

"Luck of the Irish, Colonel," I said, glad Harding took note of my double brush with death.

"Only an Irishman would call it luck to have two attempts made on his life," Harding said, which spoiled the jolly mood we had established.

I ate my sandwich and washed it down with the now lukewarm coffee. The corned beef was good, but I didn't say anything in case that was top secret too.

"What's with all the gear?" I asked Big Mike once we were outside. GIs had finished loading the last crates into the C-47, and the radio operator and navigator were securing them under canvas webbing. "Are we piggybacking on a supply run?"

"Nope, this is all ours. When Sam told me how supplies to the Chetniks have been cut," Big Mike said, "we decided to bring in some of our own. Boots, K rations, ammo, and medical supplies. It's not much, but at least we won't arrive empty-handed."

"How'd you get all this if Uncle Sam doesn't want to supply the Chetniks?" I asked.

"All it took was a little Detroit charm," Big Mike said. "That and the magic of a SHAEF requisition form."

"Signed by Harding? He could get into hot water for that."

"Nah, it was some other colonel with bad handwriting," Big Mike said. "This stuff is headed to Lyon, at least on paper. Don't mention it to Sam, he'd prefer not to know the details." I kept everything but a smile to myself. Big Mike would've made an excellent crook if blue didn't run in his veins.

We settled in with our gear, sharing the interior of the C-47 with dozens of stacked wooden crates. The navigator went over the flight plan with Harding. It would take about six hours, due to having to dogleg east to avoid Nazi-occupied Italy. Then west across Italy to Bari on the Adriatic coast, where we'd land at dawn. Woolen army blankets helped to soften the bench seats, and as we took off with the engines roaring, I had a hard time remembering that I'd started my day visiting a pleasant windmill at the end of the world. Now here I was, about to travel to a strange and faraway land shrouded in secrets.

I THOUGHT I'D never get to sleep. The C-47 shook, droned, and vibrated as we flew over the Mediterranean. But I was surprised to be jolted awake as the aircraft touched down and rolled along the runway.

"Welcome to Italy," Harding said as he turned to look at the thin sliver of light at the western horizon.

"It's been a while," I said. Almost a year since Rome. And Anzio. I shook off the memories, all of which made me look forward to Yugoslavia. The pilot killed the engines, the silence almost as loud as the Pratt & Whitney power plants themselves.

"Let's find some chow," Big Mike said, never one to dwell on the past when there was a meal to look forward to.

"Thanks for the ride," I said to the navigator, who'd come back to check on the supplies. "Where you boys off to next?"

"Across the Adriatic with you, Captain," he said. "We've been assigned to this outfit."

"Okay. No one said anything, but that's SOP around here," I said.

"Sam picked the crew," Big Mike said. "They know what they're doing, and the radio operator speaks Serbian."

The navigator was Sergeant Jerry Sullivan, known as Sully. He was also the loadmaster, responsible for balancing whatever the aircraft carried. He was thin and wiry, with a thick black mustache and a sharp nose. The radioman, Sergeant Earl Petrović, went by Petro for short. Which he was.

"The skipper's busy writing up an after-flight report," Petro said as we exited the hatch. "He said the port engine was running rough."

"How good is your Serbian, Petro?" I asked.

"I know a few phrases, and I can say *hello, thank you*, and *where's the bathroom*," he said. "Mostly stuff I picked up from my parents. They're from the old country. Now I wish I'd paid more attention."

"If I need the can, I know I can count on you," I said.

We carried our duffels and weapons as we followed Big Mike to search out the smell of bacon and coffee. I glanced at the port engine. I couldn't see what was wrong, not that I knew much about those twelve-hundred-horsepower monsters. I just hoped they checked the starboard one as well, just for luck, before we flew into enemy airspace.

The air of southern Italy had a touch of humidity even with

the early-morning chill. I could smell the salt air of the Adriatic coming in on the wind. Not balmy but not bone-chilling either. We entered a two-story brick building behind the hangar, dropped our gear in the hallway, and made for the mess. Harding was already inside with a cup of coffee in hand, deep in conversation with a US Army captain.

He didn't look like your everyday officer. He was turned out in a class A dress uniform with his wool trousers tucked into paratroop boots, and a leather belt weighed down with a .45 automatic. But it was the nonregulation bushy black beard that stood out.

"Boyle, this is Captain Martin Dilas, head of Air Crew Rescue Unit," Harding said, then introduced Big Mike.

"Welcome to Operation Halyard, fellows," Dilas said. He shook hands with a grip firm enough to crush walnuts. He was stocky and muscled, with dark, piercing eyes. "So, Sarge, I understand you're the one to thank for the supplies."

"What supplies, Captain?" Big Mike said, his blank face a study in innocence.

"Ha! I may have to recruit you," Dilas said. "The OSS appreciates initiative and falsehoods in a good cause. Come on. Get some food and I'll give you the lay of the land."

We took our seats at the end of a long table, with Dilas at the head. I started on my eggs and bacon, then took a gulp of coffee. It was all top-of-the-line grub. I'd always heard the air force fed its men well, and I figured the OSS, being a shadowy outfit, would put on a good feed themselves.

"What gives with the beard, Captain Dilas?" I asked. "You're lucky you're not in General Patton's jurisdiction. He'd have a fit."

"It may not be regulation, but I've been operating in Yugoslavia for the last eight months. Not having to worry about shaving makes things easier behind the lines," he said. "The Chetniks favor beards, so it helps me fit in. The fancy uniform is to make a good impression." Dilas laughed, and I sensed he was a no-nonsense guy who didn't take himself too seriously. A rare combo for any officer.

"How long has the Air Crew Rescue Unit been at work?" I asked, then shoveled another forkful of eggs into my mouth.

"The evacuations started in August," Dilas said. "I was in Serbia organizing arms drops and found airmen who'd been hidden by villagers. We had no idea how many there were. By last count we'd flown out over four hundred of our boys, plus dozens of other Allies."

"Captain Dilas has just been appointed as the new commander of the ACRU," Harding said. "He knows the area and the people, and speaks Serbian."

"I was born there," Dilas said. "Came to the US when I was a little kid."

"You still have relatives in Yugoslavia?" I asked.

"Had. The SS and their Bulgarian allies were hunting Chetniks when they passed through Kriva Reka, the little town where my people lived. They didn't catch any fighters, so they murdered every villager to make up for it. They packed hundreds of people into a church and blew it up. I'd hoped to visit my uncles one day. Now they're all gone, along with their families. Kriva Reka is a graveyard."

"I'm sorry," I said.

"So are a lot of Serbians," Dilas said. "And Croatians, Albanians, you name it. Not that they have facilities to house them, but you don't see many German prisoners taken. Things have gone too far to show much in the way of mercy."

"Does the OSS still support the Chetniks, Captain?" Big Mike asked.

"Hey, call me Marty, okay? I'm OSS, not regular army," Dilas said. His eyes went to Harding, then lit on Harding's West Point class ring. "No offense, Colonel."

"Don't worry about it, *Captain* Dilas," Harding said. By the slight curve of his lips, I realized that was Sam's version of a joke.

"Okay, Marty," Big Mike said, plowing ahead. "What about the Chetniks?"

"There are no more active OSS liaisons in Chetnik territory," Dilas said. "We've been ordered to stand down and cease all supply runs. We're only allowed to go in and get our boys. As soon as we've gotten the last man out, I'm under orders to shut the operation down."

"Because we're not pals with the Chetniks anymore?" Big Mike asked.

"No, it's because the campaign against the oil fields in Romania is over," Dilas said. "Most of our downed fliers were on that route, which is now pushed farther north to targets in Germany. My job is to make sure no one is still in hiding and left behind in Yugoslavia. We've been amazingly successful so far, flying in C-47s without the Krauts catching on. We gotta wrap things up before they do."

"I've informed Captain Dilas that we are searching for an RAF escapee," Harding told us.

"Is he alone?" Dilas asked.

"There may be a dozen men working their way into Serbian territory from the Austrian border, but we are most interested in this British POW. For reasons that cannot be disclosed," Harding said. "We believe he's made it through Zagreb and boarded a train heading southeast."

"I don't need to know the reason," Dilas said, draining his coffee cup. "RAF?"

"Yes. Flight Sergeant John Adler," I said. I left aside his original name and origin.

"What does he know about us?"

"Nothing about Operation Halyard, specifically," I said. "But he's been briefed about escape routes through Yugoslavia."

"Then he's been fed a line of bullshit," Dilas said.

"The MI9 guy did say to look for Tito's Partisans and avoid the Chetniks," I said. "But after the briefing, when the senior officer had left, he told our man and a few others to forget the official line and make contact with the Chetniks. He knew they helped Americans."

"Well, well, an honest Englishman," Dilas said, and leaned back in his chair. "They've been in short supply around here. There's an SOE contingent on base. Watch what you say around them. They're a loose-lipped bunch."

"They're not involved in Halyard at all?" Big Mike asked.

"Oh, they're involved all right," Dilas said. "On which side, that's the question, gentlemen."

"That's a helluva accusation, Captain," Harding said.

"Oh, I didn't mean they were Nazi fascists, Colonel," Dilas said. "Quite the opposite, in fact."

"The Soviets are our allies, Captain," Harding said. "Don't forget that."

"Hard not to," Dilas said as a corporal approached him with a sheet of paper. Dilas scanned it and gave the GI a nod. "We're on for this afternoon. Weather's good and no Germans reported in the Ravna Gora area."

"Good news," Big Mike said.

"Yeah. Except for the Luftwaffe base thirty miles from where we land," Dilas said. "Odds are we'll fool 'em one more time."

CHAPTER TWENTY-TWO

WE HAD ENOUGH time to catch a few winks, shower, and change into fresh fatigues. I crammed extra socks and clothing into a rucksack, along with K rations and ammo, figuring it would be enough to last a couple of days. I hoisted the pack, grabbed my Thompson submachine gun, and headed for the hangar. It was a blue-sky day, with a damp chill in the air and only a light wind, which suited me just fine.

Two C-47s sat outside the hangar, their khaki-green paint jobs dull in the bright sun, which was the general idea. I crossed the tarmac and narrowly avoided a jeep marked with a red cross. It was loaded with wooden crates and pulled up beside one of the transports. I found Harding and Big Mike talking with Captain Dilas, who traced a route on a large wall map.

"It's three hundred miles," Dilas said, tapping the map with a pointer. "Our destination is Pranjani, in central Serbia. Flight time should be ninety minutes."

"What kind of airstrip does Pranjani have?" Harding asked.

"A long stretch of meadow," Dilas said. "The villagers dug out rocks and trees to create it. Hundreds of them worked with pickaxes, shovels, and bare hands. General Mihailović is dedicated to helping our boys."

"General Mihailović is the Chetnik leader, right?" I asked.

"Draža Mihailović is a force of nature," Dilas said. "His people love and respect him."

"Mihailović is an officer of the Royal Yugoslavian Army," Harding said. "He organized a resistance unit when the army was defeated."

"Getting back to this airfield, how come the Germans haven't spotted it? They must be flying close overhead with a Luftwaffe nearby," Big Mike said.

"We see them a lot," Dilas said. "The villagers use the field for grazing cattle when we don't have an operation scheduled. The cows obscure any traces of landings and create a peaceful scene for any Kraut pilots looking down. The farmers even wave at the low-flying aircraft."

Dilas said he'd sent a coded message to his OSS radio operator telling the Chetniks a dozen escapees were making their way from the Zagreb area and to watch for them. There were patrols and observation posts throughout Chetnik-controlled Serbia who watched for threatening German movements. They were also well placed to take in downed fliers and escaped POWs brought in by sympathetic villagers.

"There are twenty-one aircrew waiting to be picked up," Dilas said. "Some are injured. One Skytrain is set up with stretchers and medical supplies. I'll be on that one and you two on the bird that brought you here. It'll be a fast turnaround once we land. We unload your supplies, get the men on board, and wave goodbye."

"I'll be monitoring the OSS frequencies," Harding said. "Keep me updated and let me know if things get dicey. We can pull you out anytime." I didn't mind the sound of that, but I hoped we'd find Johnny before the Fritzes started sniffing around.

"Speaking of dicey, do we get any fighter cover?" Big Mike asked. "These gooney birds will get chewed up if we run into any Messerschmitts."

"Negative," Dilas said. "A fighter escort would attract too much attention. They'll send up a flight of P-51s thirty minutes after we take off, but they'll stay well behind us. They can be called in if needed, but they won't alert the Krauts."

"All set, Marty," a voice rang out from behind us. A medic waved and walked away.

"That's our cue, boys," Dilas said. "Let's get airborne."

Colonel Harding shook hands all around and wished us luck. I thought I caught a wistful look on his face as he glanced up at the sky. Did he wish he was going along with us? He was no stranger to combat, having seen plenty in the first war to end all wars.

"Thanks, Colonel," I said. "Good to know you'll be here."

"Cut the malarkey and get going, Boyle," he replied, which I took to mean *you're welcome*.

I caught up with Dilas and asked, "You taking a medic along? I saw him bring a jeepload of crates to your C-47."

"No, he just brought supplies we might need for the wounded," Dilas said. "In case of emergency."

"Looks like enough for a few major operations," I said.

"Like the Boy Scouts, I believe in being prepared," Dilas said, and gave me a wink. "Although I have a feeling we'll have to leave them behind. Weight limitations and all that."

"I like your style, Marty," I said as we parted ways. I tossed my rucksack through the open hatch of the C-47 and clambered aboard, Big Mike right behind me.

The navigator checked the load, which seemed to have grown by two cases of grenades and one marked *Nobel 808. Plastique*. Always fun to share a ride with high explosives.

"Hope you've got all that secured, Sully," I said. I gave the loadmaster a grin to show I wasn't worried. Which I was.

"Oh, it's fine, Captain," Sully said. "If only I could remember where I put the detonators."

He disappeared forward, then Petro climbed aboard.

"That port engine okay?" I asked Petro.

"Yeah, it was running a little hot, but it checked out," Petro said. "You know anything about this field we're supposed to land in?"

"According to the CO, it's seven hundred yards long, cleared and leveled by the locals," Big Mike said. "Do you know how to say 'nice airfield' in Serbian?"

"*Lep* means nice, but I plan on saving that for the first pretty girl I see," Petro said. "Strap in, we'll be rolling soon." He went forward to the radio compartment while Big Mike and I donned life preservers and settled in.

Dilas's C-47 took off first. It climbed and banked right as we rolled down the runway. Ours followed, rumbling along until the heavy weight seemed to vanish and the plane went wheels up, and we soared into the sky.

I watched the azure Adriatic slip by beneath us, its waters broken by the occasional bow of a craft slicing through the waves. Dilas was ahead of us on the portside, which gave me a chance to watch the port engine and worry if it was running hot again.

Forget about it, I told myself. These guys are pros. There'll be plenty to worry about on the ground once we get there. It was too loud for conversation, so I folded my arms, closed my eyes, and worked at imagining a lep landing.

"Hey, Billy," Big Mike said, yelling into my ear. He pointed out the window. The lead C-47 was farther ahead of us than it had been. Too far. Then I saw it. I elbowed Big Mike and pointed to the engine. A thin line of black trailed from the cowling. Maybe it was oil or smoke or soot, but whatever it was, it looked like trouble.

We were losing altitude, but so was Dilas's aircraft, so maybe it was part of the plan to go in low once we reached the coast. I went forward, past the radio room where Petro was intently twisting dials. In the tiny navigator's compartment, Sully hunched over his charts, compass in hand. I leaned into the cockpit and watched the pilot as he craned his neck to check the port engine.

"Skipper, are we okay?"

"Had to throttle back," the copilot said. "She's running hot again. Should be okay, it'll just take us a little longer." The pilot ignored me, his attention focused on the controls and the engine.

"Why is the other C-47 leaving us behind?" I asked.

"Doesn't make any sense for both of us to slow down," the copilot said. "Don't worry, Captain, we'll get there, long as we don't try to set any speed records."

"Why are we losing altitude?" I asked.

"Standard procedure," he said, his voice hissed in exasperation. "To fly under the German radar, although there's no evidence they have anything in operation along the coast. Please just let us do our job, okay?"

I got the message and backed off. They weren't worried, so why should I be? I filled in Big Mike, who gave me a thumbs-up, drew a blanket over his shoulders, and went to sleep. Or pretended to. I kept my eye on the lead C-47 as it grew smaller. When we left the sea behind and crossed into Yugoslavia, I lost sight of it entirely against the terrain of stone and forest below. For the rest of the trip, the port engine had my full attention, except for when I sent up a few prayers to Saint Christopher, the patron saint of travelers.

He must have had a sideline as the patron of radial piston engines, since ours ran smoothly for the rest of the flight.

"Touchdown in ten," Petro announced, then returned to his radio room. The pine trees grew closer as the plane banked, flaps up. I spotted a field, lightly dusted with snow, along the top of a flat plateau. At the far end sat a C-47, making its turn for takeoff. So far, so good. I heard the whine of the landing gear and hoped the ground wasn't frozen rock-hard, praying for a soft touchdown. I gripped my seat as the treetops became level with the aircraft. Then we dipped and wheels touched earth. We rolled down the short runway, the pilot hit the brakes, and the aircraft shuddered as it slowed. It finally halted about thirty yards short of the trees. The pilot eased back on the throttle and turned the plane to face the runway, feathering the props.

Petro opened the hatch as Sully loosened the canvas that held the supplies. "A little late, but all in one piece," Petro said.

"Never doubted it," I said, and gave him a wink. I started down the steps and saw Dilas approach at a run. He waved his arms to hurry along a group of Chetniks steps behind him.

"Germans!" he shouted.

CHAPTER TWENTY-THREE

"Get those supplies unloaded!" Dilas said. There was no time for questions. Big Mike and I helped Sully and Petro pass crates of supplies to the waiting hands of Chetnik fighters gathered at the door. Before we could finish, the other C-47 revved its engines and took off, making one helluva racket. If the Krauts were close by, they'd hear it easily.

As soon as we got the last crate out, twelve excited airmen started to clamber aboard. Petro wished us luck as we exited and was about to close the hatch when the airmen yelled for him to stop. Each man unlaced his boots and tossed them to the waiting Chetniks. Next came their heavy sheepskin aviator jackets. The Chetniks cheered and the airmen waved. They shouted farewells even as Petro closed the hatch and the Skytrain lumbered down the runway, the prop blast sending us stumbling back.

"Let's go!" Dilas shouted above the drone of the engine as the aircraft picked up speed, rose, and cleared the treetops at the end of the runway. The Chetniks carried the crates, jackets, and boots to three waiting vehicles—rusted and rickety Opel trucks—loaded them up, and drove off. Three fighters stayed with us, big, bearded guys with bandoliers of ammo across their chests, armed with American M1 rifles along with an assortment of pistols and knives, all close at hand. They made Big Mike look mousy.

We followed Dilas away from the landing strip and encountered a group of women with long pine boughs. They hustled to where the C-47s had left tracks in the thin layer of snow and began to work the boughs like brooms to erase the evidence. Behind them, an old man led four cows out into the field to disguise the landing ground as just another winter pasture.

"Okay," Dilas said as he halted once we were under cover. "We just got a report that a German patrol was sighted about six miles distant. We're watching them now. If they head this way, we'll have to stop them. We've got too many men and supplies hidden in this area to let the Krauts snoop around."

"You don't think they heard the engines?" Big Mike asked.

"Probably not, they're to the north with a ridgeline between us. But if they did, they'll send a recon plane to take a look, so that's why we cover our tracks," Dilas said. "I need to look at the situation. I'll turn you two over to my radio operator. You'll be the first to hear if we gotta scatter."

"We'll stick with you, Captain," I said, and looked to Big Mike, who nodded.

"You're our tour guide, Marty," he said.

"Okay, stick close to me and don't do anything stupid," he said, and set off at a trot along a dirt road. Just around the bend we came to a village. Pranjani, I figured. There was one large stucco building and a wooden church with a steep roof. The houses were spread apart, most built with a stone base and wood planks. Outhouses and pens for animals completed the picture.

Dilas entered one of the houses after a short talk with his Chetnik pals, who loped off down the road. Inside it was dark, with small windows that barely let in enough light to see.

"What's happening?" Dilas bellowed up the narrow staircase.

"They've halted and sent out patrols on foot," the Yank said. He wore lieutenant's bars and regular fatigues, nothing as showy as Dilas. "Three half-tracks and a Kübelwagen."

"Not a major push, then, but enough to be trouble if they come this way," Dilas said. "This is Lieutenant Rudy Jankov, radio operator for our team. He speaks Serbian and maintains contact with all the units watching the roads. Rudy, this is Billy and Big Mike."

"No need to ask who's who. You guys staying here?"

"No, they're with me. And you should move out too. Radio Bari and tell them to cancel the next flight until we give the all clear. Then get to the cabin and set up there. Monitor the frequencies but don't give the Krauts enough time to triangulate your position. They might be on to us, or maybe they're just doing a sweep," Dilas said.

"Don't worry, I know the drill," Jankov said. "You two can leave your rucksacks here, Sanja will hide them."

"Who's Sanja?" I asked.

"I am," a young woman said. I hadn't heard her come down the stairs. "This is my house. Welcome. We have many things hidden here, two more are no problem."

"Your English is excellent," I said, and shrugged off the heavy pack.

"I learned in school," Sanja said. "And Rudy teaches me." Her face lit up as she said his name. Sanja had sandy-brown hair pulled back, strong cheekbones, and sparkling blue eyes. She wore dark green trousers stuffed into leather boots, a wool sweater, and a holstered pistol.

"I will teach you more about baseball on the hike to your father's cabin," Rudy said. "We may be gone overnight." He went upstairs to disassemble the radio, and Sanja began to gather food.

"Are the Krauts on the move?" I asked.

"No. They've halted by a bridge where we have an observation post. The Germans are across a valley and our OP is on the other side. If they stay on the road they're on, it will take them away from us. But if they cross the bridge, it will bring them straight to Pranjani. If that happens, we'll have to hit them hard. Follow me," Dilas said, at the sound of a braking truck.

It was one of the Opels that had taken the supplies away, with a Chetnik at the wheel and two others in the open flatbed, a carton of grenades between them. We climbed aboard and watched as Jankov and Sanja left the house. He lugged the SSTR-1 radio gear, and Sanja carried a shoulder bag and a German Mauser. The two of them spoke with the Chetniks who sat with us, and they all laughed. Maybe it was a joke about driving on a bumpy road with a load of grenades, but I laughed anyway, just to be friendly.

"Baseball?" I yelled to Jankov as the truck lurched forward.

"Cardinals!" he responded, which left me with no comeback since St. Louis had won the World Series last year.

"Home run!" Sanja said. She gave a quick laugh and increased her pace, disappearing into the forest with Jankov. The two Chetniks roared with friendly laughter, but I doubted it had anything to do with the World Series.

"Lep," I said, trotting out the one word of Serbian I knew.

"Da," one of them replied. "Nice. Jankov good man. Sanja good."

"You speak English," I said. He shrugged and put his thumb and forefinger together in the universal sign of *just a little*.

"Good man, you. Dobro," he said. His finger pointed at me, then Big Mike. "Nacisti, bad." He patted his rifle, and it wasn't hard to figure out that it was the Nazis who were bad, and we who were good. Now I knew three words of Serbian.

"Dejan," the other fellow said, then patted his friend's shoulder. "Nikola."

I told them my name and learned there was no equivalent of Billy or William in their language. It took a moment to get Big Mike's moniker across, but we finally arrived at Veliki Mihajlo. *Big Mike* in Serbian. My vocabulary was growing.

After a few twists and turns while ducking low-hanging branches, the driver pulled the Opel to the side of the road. We vaulted off and gathered around Dilas. He spoke first with the driver, who grabbed the box of grenades and jogged off into the woods.

"We have a position set up to cover our retreat, if need be," Dilas explained. "And another on our flank. Follow me. Stay low and quiet."

Nikola took the lead, and we went single file along a stony uphill path. At the top of the ridgeline, he halted, waved his arm, and nodded to Dilas. The OSS captain went forward and did the same.

"See there?" he whispered, pointing to our right, where the crest rose slightly. "Four of our boys. A few of them got restless and wanted some action. Their job is to fire a few rounds if the Germans try to flank us, then beat feet for town."

"Where?" I said. Even though it was cool, I took off my steel pot and wiped the sweat from my brow. Then I saw them not twenty yards away, perfectly camouflaged behind a fallen pine. A couple of gloved hands signaled, and I returned the favor, waving my helmet. I hadn't thought much about our guys going stir-crazy, holed up in a barn and waiting weeks or longer for rescue. Grabbing a gun and having a go at the Krauts would sound exciting. They knew the terrors of combat at thirty thousand feet, and I hoped they didn't have to get too close to the down-to-earth variety.

"You've got everything covered," Big Mike said, and snapped off a salute in the direction of the grounded flyboys.

"Yeah, except for the odds," Dilas said, then followed Nikola through a path in the underbrush, nearly invisible amid the brambles and boughs.

A gesture from Dilas to go low told me we were at the observation post. The path sloped down into a dugout behind rocks, which jutted out from the loose soil. A weathered tree trunk lay across them and gave good cover for viewing the valley below for the five-man squad.

A .50 caliber machine gun was set up between the rocks. Probably salvaged from a downed bomber, it was mounted on a tripod that looked like it had been hammered out by an ironsmith. Dilas squatted next to the gunner. He questioned him in Serbian while he viewed the scene below through his binoculars. Behind him, a radioman spoke into his SCR-300 and relayed information from Dilas.

All I could see were two German half-tracks and the command vehicle, about seventy yards out. Soldiers stood around, smoking and gabbing without much thought for security. A good sign. If they knew how close they were to a Chetnik stronghold, they'd be on alert. Voices drifted up, echoing off the valley walls. The chatter of men who didn't realize a heavy machine gun had them in its sights.

"A half-track went around the bend to the left thirty minutes ago," Dilas whispered. "Then a squad climbed up the hill, like they were trying to trap somebody between them."

"Maybe they're tracking some of our escapees," I said.

"Could be. That would explain why this group stayed by the bridge, to keep anyone from crossing." I looked below. The bridge spanned a steep ravine that had a trickle of water flowing at the bottom. The ground was crumbling sandy soil, and it would make for a tough climb.

"There," Dilas said, his glasses trained on the hilltop. He handed me the binoculars. "They have someone."

"A civilian," I said. I focused on the single figure being pushed and prodded by the Krauts. He was bearded, but it wasn't the full, bushy beard of a Chetnik fighter. A farmer, maybe. He wore a loose, long coat that flapped in the wind as he was marched downhill. I handed the binoculars to Dilas. "Poor bastard, whoever he is."

"Italian, by his coat," Dilas said. "When the Italians surrendered, some took to the hills and the Germans hunted them."

"Half-track on the left," Big Mike said. I heard the engine and the clank of treads before it turned the corner.

"The vehicle they sent out earlier," Dilas said, focusing his binoculars. "They've got a prisoner too. How long ago did your chaps break out?"

"Four days," I said. "They were in a POW camp before that, most likely."

"Not one of yours, then," Dilas said. "This one looks too worn and scruffy. I'm still guessing Italian deserters. Tito has a brigade of Italian Communists, but these two look like bums. Probably didn't want to end up doing slave labor for the Krauts."

Nikola said something in a hushed voice and the others relaxed, tension fading as it looked like the Germans had found their quarry. Dilas focused his binoculars, studying the Germans. Each half-track held six men in the open back, with the two captives in the lead vehicle. Engines revved and gears ground as the vehicles began to move.

Toward the bridge.

"Damn," muttered Dilas. He spat out an order to Nikola, who took off. The machine gunner swiveled his weapon and aimed at the first half-track as it approached the bridge. Dilas laid a calming hand on his arm and motioned for everyone to stay low.

The lead half-track moved onto the bridge. It was a single-lane wooden trestle, about one hundred feet long and thirty feet above the ravine. The second half-track crossed onto the bridge.

"You two target the Kübelwagen," Dilas said to me and Big Mike, then returned his gaze to the bridge. The first half-track was almost across.

"Sada!" he shouted as he slapped the gunner on the back.

The .50 spat fire. Tracers slammed into the half-track. Gunners on heavy four-engine bombers used armor-piercing incendiary rounds, and the lightly armored half-track was no match for well-aimed fire at close range.

Smoke and flame blossomed from the engine, and the vehicle swerved within the narrow confines of the wooden bridge. The gunner kept firing until the half-track leapt ahead, veered to the left, and crashed into a stout wooden guardrail.

The noise was horrendous as we fired. Big Mike squeezed off carefully aimed rounds at the Kübelwagen, where the German officer in command sat in relative comfort. He launched out of the door and clawed at his pistol, as two bursts from my tommy gun kicked up spouts of dirt beneath his feet and sent him sprawling. Big Mike hit the driver, a blood-splattered windshield demonstrating his marksmanship.

Between the two vehicles, Germans were cut down as they scrambled to get out of the open half-tracks. Some took cover behind their vehicles, only to be felled by volleys of M1 fire from our right. I figured Nikola had been sent off to bring in the flank guards, who peppered the Krauts with murderous fire.

The gas tank on the second half-track blew, ignited by the incendiary rounds. Yellow-orange flame exploded and engulfed the vehicle, sending burning soldiers over the side of the bridge and into the ravine. Those who lived tried to douse the flames, only to be shot.

Four Germans tried to make a run for it, but the .50 trailed them and tore them to pieces. Another stood up, hands raised, and was hit from two directions. Not many prisoners were taken in this sort of warfare, but in the middle of fierce combat, any attempt to surrender was madness.

Dilas ordered everyone to hold their fire, then threw a grenade onto the bridge. It exploded next to the burning half-track but there was no response. No screams, no return fire.

"Let's check it out," Dilas said.

I stood and heard a thump on the ground behind me. A

German potato masher grenade rolled into the trench. I grabbed it and flipped it out. My gut tightened as I thought about it going off in my hand, but it exploded just over the edge of our firing position.

I sprayed the woods behind us and vaulted up, diving for cover behind a tree and listening for movement. Which was damn hard with my ears ringing from all the shooting and explosions.

"See anything, Billy?" Big Mike asked from behind, his M1 at the ready.

"Nothing. He must've made it over the bridge and worked his way around us," I said. I gave the foliage another burst for good measure. "We ought to search for him."

"Billy, you and Big Mike come with me. I'll send off a couple of my men and the flyboys to hunt for him," Dilas said. "We might find some intel down there."

"That was quick thinking, Billy," Big Mike said. He clapped me on the shoulder. "We owe you."

"If I'd had time to think about it, we all would have been filled with shrapnel," I said. Dejan was wrapping a bandage around the machine gunner's head. There was a fair amount of blood, but his eyes were okay. He'd been the closest to the explosion, so it could have been worse.

Dilas issued orders, and his men began to break down the machine gun. Nikola and another Chetnik went with us to check out the Krauts while Dejan and the rest watched for reinforcements. We took a route through the trees that led us down to the road that the Germans had been headed for. Still no sign of the grenade-wielding attacker. At the bridge, the smoking half-track was slewed across the lane. The driver hung out the door, his uniform singed and bloodied. But even so, the SS collar tab was clear to see.

A faint moan arose from behind the half-track. Nikola

followed the other Chetnik, cautiously approaching the source. A pistol shot put an end to the sound.

"It's a mercy," Dilas said. "We can barely treat our own wounded, and no one wants to save the life of one of these SS bastards."

The mercy of the pistol echoed along the ravine again, but the .50 and the rest of the firepower directed at the unsuspecting SS had wreaked such havoc on human flesh that little life was left to snuff out.

I heard a noise from under the half-track and went flat, my Thompson ready. It was one of the prisoners the Krauts had taken. He held up one trembling hand and muttered in fear.

"Come here," I said, and beckoned with my free hand. He'd evidently been quick to take cover and avoided the heavy fusillade. Nikola pushed the guy from the other side with the butt of his rifle, and he crawled out from under the vehicle.

"His buddy's dead, still in the half-track," Big Mike said. "I'll check out the officer." Nikola went with him as Dilas searched the prisoner, coming up with nothing. He peppered him with questions, his voice ranging from harsh to consoling. At one point he stood and retrieved a canteen from a dead German and gave it to the prisoner, who drank from it greedily.

"This is Tomo," Dilas said. He stood back with his arms akimbo. "He's Croatian with Italian mixed in. He served with the Italian Croatian Legion until Mussolini was toppled. Then his company was sent to reinforce the Tiger Division, a German Croatian unit organized for anti-Partisan operations. He says he never wanted to fight for the fascists but was forcibly drafted. He and several men from his squad deserted and have been living in the hills. He says the Germans hadn't hunted them before, but someone must have betrayed them."

"Doesn't sound like the Krauts were looking for us," I said.

"They seemed focused on hunting deserters. The SS officer

told him if he didn't give them the location of his friends, they'd hang him," Dilas said. "He claims he didn't, but why would he say otherwise."

"Did they ask him about escaped POWs?" I asked. Dilas raised a finger and spoke to Tomo, who watched us with bewildered eyes.

"No," Dilas reported. "Nor about Chetniks. Only deserters."

"That's good," I said. "What are you going to do with him?"

"That's not my call," Dilas said. He eyed Big Mike and Nikola as they returned from their search.

"The Kraut officer had a map," Big Mike said. "There's a village marked in red on the other side of that hill. That must be where they nabbed these two. Then another about two miles farther on."

"There's another bridge off to the west," I said, and traced the possible line of advance. "They might have planned to cross back over the river and approach the village from the rear." The map showed where the road split, one route heading to Pranjani, the other curving back along the river and leading to a bridge behind the targeted village.

"They weren't coming for us," Dilas said. "We could have just let them go."

"We couldn't have known," I said. "There was no choice."

A few words came from Nikola in a low, harsh growl. His eyes narrowed as he studied Tomo, who'd gone from captive to captive again in a matter of moments.

"Can you show him mercy?" I asked. I looked at no one in particular, especially not Tomo. Dilas took me literally and translated for Nikola, who rubbed his beard, and finally nodded his head. He bent down and undid the leather harness from a corpse. It held ammo pouches, a canteen, and a scabbard. He handed it to Tomo, then gave him a Mauser. Finally, he took a bag from his shoulder and gave it to the deserter, showing him the half loaf of black bread and a tin of something undecipherable.

"Idi!" Nikola said as he flicked his hand in the air in a gesture of dismissal. Tomo stood, dumbfounded, and Nikola repeated the word, gently. Tomo awoke to what he was being told. A smile dawned as he backed away.

"Idi!" Nikola repeated, this time with a laugh. Tomo ran and made for the hill that he'd descended in the clutches of the Germans.

Nikola raised his rifle, aimed, and shot Tomo square between the shoulder blades.

CHAPTER TWENTY-FOUR

"Goddamn!" I shouted. "Why? What happened to mercy?" Even though we were surrounded by death, adding this last corpse to the pile was too much for me. I stood in front of Nikola and asked the question again. He shouldered his rifle and remained silent.

"Ask him," I demanded of Dilas. "Ask him that question, damn it!"

"You don't know how things work out here, Captain Boyle," Dilas said. "Things are complicated."

"Ask him."

Dilas obliged with a few sentences in Serbian. Nikola responded, his eyes on mine the entire time.

"He says he did show mercy, even though the Croat did not deserve it," Dilas translated. "He betrayed Yugoslavia when he joined the Italian Croatian Legion and supported the fascist occupiers. Then he betrayed once again and deserted the Tiger Division. He had no honor."

"That may be true, but where is the mercy?" I said as I gestured with my hand to the body sprawled in the roadway.

Dilas continued after Nikola finished speaking. "He gave Tomo bread and a weapon. He gave the man hope, and he died quickly, believing he was free. So many more die with so much less. It was a mercy, but perhaps one you Americans may not comprehend."

Both Dilas and Nikola turned away. Did they feel shame, or were they unable to comprehend my naivete? Dilas was an American, and I wondered if he felt out of place amid this savagery, even though he was only a generation gone from these hills. But then again, I was Irish American, and barely removed from the religious killings and civil war that had scarred my own homeland. Who was I to judge?

"Strange place, ain't it?" Big Mike asked as he surveyed the carnage.

"Yeah. Let's hope we find Johnny soon and leave it in the rearview mirror," I said. Dilas and his men were still checking bodies, gathering food and ammunition. We decided to go up the hill and watch the road for approaching vehicles. I signaled to Dilas, and we hustled to the vantage point and scanned the road in both directions.

"Nothing," Big Mike said. He shielded his eyes as he checked the route the Germans had taken.

"Same this way," I said. I looked down the hillside and along the lane, thinking that if there were any more Krauts in the area, the gunfire would have brought them running. "Nobody."

"Except for the guy who lobbed a grenade your way," Big Mike said. "He's still running around loose."

"Yeah, I hope they catch the sonuvabitch. I don't know how he did it. I was sure no one moved across the bridge once we opened fire," I said.

"Maybe he was already there," Big Mike suggested. "Coming back from scouting out the route."

"Could be. I'll check with the flyboys and see if they found anything." I tilted back my helmet and looked at the terrain beyond the bridge. The thick pines and rocky incline could have easily hidden a single German scout, and I hoped our boys nabbed him before he got too close to Pranjani.

"Will you look at that," Big Mike muttered. He nudged my

arm and shot a look toward the vehicles below. Nikola and Dilas had pulled the bloody body of the other Croatian out of the half-track and outfitted him with German gear, just like Tomo. They dragged him next to the Kübelwagen and dropped him there with a Schmeisser submachine gun draped around his neck. "They're making it look like this was the work of a gang of deserters."

"These are brutal men," I said. "Dilas included."

"We don't know much about their war," Big Mike said. "Maybe these Croatian Italians or whatever they are were ten times as brutal when they had the upper hand. Just because the Krauts are hunting them now doesn't mean they didn't butcher Serbs together last year."

"I think you're beginning to get the hang of the place," I said. "Let's go."

The saying is that the enemy of my enemy is my friend. Around here, the enemy of my enemy is still my enemy if he ever looks cross-eyed at me. As we shuffled downhill, I promised myself a kick in the pants if I ever found myself thinking that way.

"Do you think this bit of stage managing is going to fool the Germans?" I asked Dilas.

"It may confuse them and at least buy time," he said. "If the engines hadn't been all shot up, we could have driven the vehicles farther away and dumped the bodies. But this will have to do."

"Yeah," I said, with a glance back at Tomo, who looked like a rag doll cast aside by a careless child. "It will have to do."

I hoisted a canvas bag of potato mashers over my shoulder and lugged a couple of ammo pouches away from the scene of the ambush. Nikola took enough for two men, and Big Mike carried the food they'd scrounged. We headed up to the observation post, abandoned now that its location would be obvious from all the bullet holes in the German vehicles. At the trench, we met up with two of the airmen who'd been on our flank.

"Any luck tracking that Kraut?" Dilas asked.

"Nothing," one of them said. "We circled back here in case he was going to have another go at you but came up empty. Shakey and Rip went up the road about a half mile to see if they could find him."

"We're going to have to use your spot as our new OP and keep eyes on the ambush site," Dilas said. "Dejan and the radio operator should be there already. I'll send some men from the fallback position to reinforce you, then you can make your way back."

"No problem, Marty," the lieutenant said, then turned his attention to us. "You must be the guys who flew in today. I'm Joe Irwin, former B-24 navigator, currently employed as a ground pounder. This is my copilot, Al Hooper."

"Hoop," the copilot said. We shook hands and I introduced the two of us. "What brings you to beautiful Pranjani? We appreciate the place, but we're not here voluntarily. You OSS reinforcements for Marty?"

"No, we're just here to help," I said. Joe and Hoop took some of the supplies from Big Mike and we began the hike back up the path. "There are POW escapees who may be working their way here, and we don't want them to be left behind." I left it at that, seeing no reason to advertise Johnny's name or how much the Germans would like to get their hands on him again if they learned about his special operator duties.

"You guys been here long?" Big Mike asked to move the conversation in a different direction.

"It's been two months for Joe and me," Hoop said. He held a branch back for the rest of us to pass. "Longer for Shakey. Rip is the newest guy. He blew in a couple of days ago. Kinda hard to keep track of time here. One reason we were glad to volunteer for this job."

"Nice to hit back after hiding in haylofts for weeks on end,"

Joe said. "It's the least we can do for these guys. The Chetniks would give you the shirt off their backs."

"That reminds me," I said. Ahead, Dilas came to the flank position, and we followed, dumping the supplies next to the radio. Dejan searched through the food bag right away. "What's with the guys who left this morning tossing out their boots and jackets? It's going to be a cold flight to Italy."

"It's a tradition," Hoop said. "The Chetniks aren't getting any more supplies, not enough that matter, anyway. So when a planeload takes off, everyone gives away their stuff. I seen guys leave their socks in their boots."

"These people would die to get us back into the fight," Joe said. "*Have* died. I can't understand why the brass is ignoring them."

"I stopped trying to figure out the brass long ago," Dilas said. "You guys stay here and work on camouflage. You'll need to patrol down the path to check the bridge for Krauts." He handed Nikola his binoculars. Then he arranged for a truck to wait at the road for the Yanks once the other two returned.

"What's with Shakey's nickname?" I asked. "Doesn't exactly inspire confidence."

"Flight engineer on a B-17," Hoop said. "He manned the top turret. Said he earned the nickname from getting the shakes so bad he couldn't eat breakfast before a mission. But once he got on board, they went away."

"What about Rip?" Big Mike asked.

"That's his name. Fred Ripper," Joe said. "B-17 pilot and the only survivor from his crew. Doesn't like to talk about it."

"Yeah, I wouldn't either," Big Mike said. "What could you say, anyway?"

We left some of the food and ammo with Hoop and Joe, and they helped themselves to grenades. We followed Dilas and trudged out with Dejan and Nikola, all of us bearing the trophies of war. At the fallback position, we left more supplies and picked up the machine gunner, who deserved a rest after being peppered by that blast.

When we finally piled back into the Opel and drove into Pranjani, the sun was about to set. The sky turned a reddish blue that matched my mood. I hadn't much liked almost being blown up by a grenade, and I didn't appreciate Tomo's execution, no matter how much of a mercy Dilas and Nikola dressed it up as. Come to think of it, I didn't really like killing people either, except that when it came to the SS, someone had to do it.

We drove into Pranjani, where airmen with their collars turned up walked along the road or sat in front of houses and smoked.

"We had a flight scheduled for tomorrow, but I canceled 'cause of the Krauts," Dilas said, hollering out his open window so we could hear from the truck bed. "Now it feels like rain. We're going to have a lot of guys waiting here."

I looked up at the sky, heavy cloud cover moving in from the west. First the Germans threatened to stall the rescue plan, now the weather.

"Kiša," Nikola said, thrusting a thumb skyward, then moving his fingers down like fluttering raindrops.

"*Kiša* is rain," I said. "*Sada* means now. *Nacisti* is Nazis, and *lep* is nice. *Idi* means go," I said. "Five words."

"Dobro," Nikola said. "Good. Veliki Mihajlo, dobro."

Six words. I'd already lost count. I agreed Big Mike was a good guy, and we had a laugh about it, working at putting blood, death, and betrayal behind us.

Dilas let us off at Sanja's house and told us he would send a runner up the hill to tell Rudy and Sanja it was safe to return. He promised to drop by later and let us know the plan for tomorrow once he got the waiting airmen squared away for the night. He said to go into the root cellar behind the house and lift the third floor plank from the right. We found the cellar, a stone foundation built into the earth with an upper level of timber. Inside were casks and barrels arranged across the width of the small structure. We moved a few, grasped the floorboard by the edge, and lifted.

Our rucksacks were underneath, with a bottle labeled SLIVO-VITZ on top. I didn't know what that meant, but by the shape of the bottle and the picture of a cluster of plums, I figured we would toast our first evening in Yugoslavia with the local plum brandy.

And I'd raise my glass to Tomo. That would be a mercy.

CHAPTER TWENTY-FIVE

WE WARMED OUR hands over the kitchen stove after we started the wood fire. The stove was a big, ornate thing, done up in bright blue tiles, built for cooking as well as heating the joint. Big Mike organized chow out of the C rations we'd brought, and before long, Rudy and Sanja returned.

"We got the all clear," Rudy said. He set down his radio gear and wiped his hand across his forehead, damp with sweat. "Sounds like you stopped the Krauts."

"All but one," Big Mike said. "He's running around loose somewhere. Almost took us out."

"He will not try again," Sanja said. She dropped her bag of supplies and investigated the canned rations. "Germans are afraid to be alone in our mountains."

"They're searching for him now," I said. "And Dilas set up a new OP to watch the bridge in case they try again."

"Good," Rudy said. "We'll be stacked up with guys here. Rain and fog expected tomorrow, so that run will probably be canceled too. Right now, I've gotta get the radio set up in the attic and check in."

Rudy headed upstairs. Sanja held up a can, trying to read the contents.

"Spaghetti," she sounded out. "Špageti. Is it good, American spaghetti?"

"Are you hungry?" Big Mike asked. She nodded. "Then it'll probably taste fine."

He opened three cans of meat and spaghetti in tomato sauce and dumped them into a pot. Sanja warmed it over the stove while Big Mike opened packages of bread biscuits. The slivovitz was opened and glasses were arranged on the table. This was a lot better than heating C rations in a foxhole.

"If we had been at my father's cabin longer, we could have hunted boar. Boar is good. I think better than spaghetti in tomato sauce," Sanja said, her nose over the pot as she stirred.

"Does your father hunt boar?" Big Mike asked.

"He did. Before the Germans killed him when they first came. It is a small cabin, only for hunting, you understand. A good hiding place for Rudy and the radio," she said. "We do not have time to hunt the boars now. And we do not want the Germans to hear the gunshots. Or Tito's men. It would be good to have a feast, as we used to." Her eyes set on a picture of a man and a woman standing in front of this house. "But nothing is as it used to be."

It wasn't. Not in this house, or in so many others, near and far, that carried the weight of death, hunger, and fear. Sanja's house was one of the lucky ones, still standing, and with warm food close at hand.

A knock sounded at the door and Dilas let himself in.

"Welcome, Marty," Sanja said. "Do you wish to eat?"

"No, I just wanted to be sure you and Rudy were back okay," he said. "And to see if he received a weather report." Rudy's footsteps sounded on the stairs.

"Just got it," he said as he entered the kitchen. "Light rain and fog forecast through tomorrow afternoon. Bari confirmed no flight tomorrow, too risky."

"Ask for three Skytrains the day after tomorrow. Tell 'em we're standing-room-only here," Dilas instructed.

Rudy pushed up the sleeve of his jacket to check his wristwatch. "I've been told to stand by for a message. I'll get it out right after that. Hey, fellas, give that slivovitz a try, it's the local specialty," he said, and disappeared back upstairs.

"My father used to make his own, but this is almost as good," Sanja said. She poured the clear liquid into the small glasses. "Živeli," she said, and stared directly at me, Dilas, and Big Mike in turn. "Cheers."

Seven words.

Sanja downed her portion and smiled. I took mine and gasped. The taste reminded me of grappa without the finesse. And it had the aroma of almonds, but so did cyanide.

"Wow," Big Mike said, with a smack of the lips. "That's some hooch."

"Billy, every Yank who tastes this stuff for the first time has the same look as you do," Dilas said, and laughed. "Profound shock. Then they learn to love it."

"If I can eat American spaghetti in tomato sauce, you can drink slivovitz," Sanja said, with a fair amount of logic. She poured me another glass, and I was about to give it a go when Rudy came downstairs with a puzzled look on his face.

"Beats me what this is supposed to mean," Rudy said. "Some sort of code, maybe?"

"Let's see," Dilas said. He laid out the small page from Rudy's notebook on the table and scanned the words. "Huh?" He turned the paper for me and Big Mike to read.

FOR PEACHES. SHERLOCK MARYLEBONE. BETWEEN YOU AND SAM.

"Easy to tell who it's for," Big Mike said. "But what does it mean?"

"Enlighten us," Dilas said. "Who's Peaches?"

"That's me. A nickname I received from a London gangster," I said. "I know who Sherlock is too. Squadron Officer Jean Conan Doyle."

"As in Sir Arthur?" Rudy asked.

"His daughter. She's in RAF intelligence," I said, leaving her exact role unstated.

"Okay," Dilas said. "But what's Marylebone? Someplace in London, ain't it?"

"Yeah. It's the district where Sherlock Holmes hangs his hat at 221B Baker Street," I said. "I don't get it."

"You're a big fan, and you've been there, right?" Big Mike said. "Think about the neighborhood. It's gotta mean something."

"Well, I took the tube to the Baker Street station," I said. "There's also a Marylebone station close by. Wait, that one's a train station too! Marylebone train station is the one Holmes would have used."

"Where does that get us?" Dilas asked.

"I'd better not say too much about how we know, but I think it means the POW we're looking for is still on board a train, hopefully headed this way," I said.

"Sam is Colonel Harding?" Dilas guessed.

"Has to be," I said, and explained to Sanja and Rudy. "Colonel Sam Harding is our boss. He probably relayed that message from Bari."

"But what is between you and Sam but water?" Sanja asked. "Not the prisoner you seek."

"No. They obviously didn't want to tip their hand in case anyone intercepted the message, so they didn't spell things out. It's up to us to decipher it," I said.

"You're a captain and Sam's a colonel," Big Mike said. "But Johnny's a sergeant, so where's the sense in that?"

I took another slug of slivovitz, thinking it might shock my mind into awareness. All it did was give me was a cough.

"Rudy, where is the map we looked at?" Sanja said.

"Here," Rudy said. He rummaged around in one of the packs he'd left at the foot of the stairs. "Why?"

"I showed Rudy the routes to the other villages in the area," Sanja said as she smoothed out the folds on the wood tabletop. "And taught him how to pronounce the names like a Serb. He knows the language, but his accent is very American."

"What does this have to do with Sam?" Big Mike asked.

"Do you remember what you called this town?" Sanja asked Rudy. She stabbed her finger at a place northwest of Pranjani.

"I said 'Major'!"

"Yes. But Majur is the name, and we draw it out, making it sound longer. Perhaps they meant the train that goes to Majur," Sanja said, a look of pride on her face.

"But the trains run to plenty of towns," Big Mike said. "I agree the name is close to the rank between Sam and Billy, but it's a long shot."

"Look close at the map," Sanja said. "See, from Zagreb to Majur?" She traced her finger on the hatched line marking the path of the railroad.

"It ends in Majur," I said. "That's it. Johnny made it to Majur."

"It's only seventy miles from here," Dilas said. He looked up from the map. "Either of you fellows know how to ride a horse?"

"I did a stint with the mounted patrol on the Boston Police Department," I said.

"Same here in Detroit," Big Mike said. He reached inside his jacket and produced his Detroit PD badge, the brass as shiny as the day it was pinned on him.

"Didn't know they had horses that big," Dilas said. "Okay, we'll get out word to units in that area to watch for a Brit looking for help. You know if he's alone?"

"He started off with a group of escapees," I said. "But we don't know if they've managed to stick together."

"Rudy, send out the alert," Dilas ordered. "Better radio back to Bari as well. Tell them message received and understood. Anything else?" He raised an eyebrow in my direction.

"Yes. Ask them to confirm quantity. That should be vague enough," I said.

"Sure thing, Captain," Rudy said. He clumped back upstairs while Dilas gave me a hard stare.

"I'd like to know more about your source for this information. It better be solid, or you could be walking into a trap and taking Chetniks with you."

"It's the real deal," I said. "But I can't tell you more. That's how important the source is." It was vital that the Germans and their allies didn't tumble to how easily we listened in on their frequencies, whether it was Johnny and his pals in their Lancs or the WAAFs at RAF Hawkinge. Most people thought of spies when it came to this kind of intelligence, as Dilas probably did. A source was a spy, and I was glad to let him think it was a secret agent somewhere in Germany, as opposed to German refugees and others using their language skills and electronics to bring down the Third Reich.

"Fair enough," Dilas said. "Now all we need is a guide."

"A guide who knows the area, can read a map, speak English, and ride a horse?" Sanja said. "Wherever could you find such a person?"

"Are you certain, Sanja?" Dilas asked.

"Yes. If these men came all this way to save one Englishman, it must be important. Even though the English have left us to the wolves, they still fight the Germans. They burn their cities. So I will help," she said.

"Sanja is an excellent fighter," Dilas said. "It's why I entrusted Rudy to her care. Our radio operator is our lifeline."

"I'll try to survive without her for a few days," Rudy said as he stuck his head into the room. "Response received. 'V for Victory.'" He flashed the V sign and headed back to the attic.

"Two," I said. "It was twenty at first. They were being moved from camps to the east and the column was strafed by Mustangs.

We believe sixteen made it to Zagreb, but two were captured after that. The other twelve could have been taken or are in hiding."

"Well, your chap may know more about them," Dilas said. "Anyone close to our people, we can get out. If there's time."

A knock sounded at the door, several quick raps. Dilas rose, his hand on his pistol. The OSS man was cautious, and that single gesture went a long way in reminding me that we were in enemy territory, no matter how isolated this village was.

"It's Hoop," the airman shouted, his voice loud and frantic. Dilas opened the door.

"What's wrong?" he asked.

"Shakey's dead. The Kraut got him," Hoop said. "He's somewhere close."

CHAPTER TWENTY-SIX

"Slow down and tell me exactly what happened," Dilas said, guiding Hoop to the kitchen table. He poured him a shot of slivovitz and told him to drink.

"We were waiting for Rip and Shakey to meet us at our position," Hoop said after downing the liquor. "We'd heard gunshots off in the distance but couldn't tell which direction they came from. We hoped they'd nailed the Kraut, but instead Rip came up the path with Shakey across his shoulders. He was dead. Rip said the German got the drop on them."

"Where's Rip and Joe now?" Dilas asked.

"I'll tell ya, Rip was pretty torn up about it," Hoop said. "We got Shakey up to the truck and started to drive back. Then Rip told Joe to stop along the road and took off. He said he wanted to get the bastard and cut him off before he stumbled into Pranjani."

"Ripper is out in the forest, now? In the dark?" Dilas said. "He must be crazy."

"He was fighting mad," Hoop said. "We told him to get back in the truck, but he just vanished into the woods."

"He'll be lucky to last the night," Dilas said. "If the Kraut doesn't get him, he might fall off a cliff."

"Or be killed by a wild boar," Sanja added. "There are many now that we hunt less."

"Jesus, what a SNAFU," Dilas muttered. "You and Joe take the body to the basement at town hall, and we'll bury him in the morning."

"Uh, Marty, Joe went off to search for Rip," Hoop said. He clutched his empty glass and avoided Dilas's gaze. "Soon as we got here, he headed back out. He was worried about him."

"Which way did he go?" Sanja asked.

"He didn't want to stay on the road. Too long with all those switchbacks," Hoop said. "So he cut straight across. He figured he'd find a spot to watch the trail in case the Kraut worked his way here."

"He's a navigator, right?" Dilas asked. Hoop nodded. "Then why's he acting like a damned hotshot fighter pilot?"

"He said he knew the woods, Marty. He did a lot of hunting back in Michigan. He'll be all right," Hoop said.

"I doubt they had Germans roaming the woods back in Michigan," Big Mike said. "Not to mention a half-mad Yank gunning for them."

"Listen, Hoop, take Shakey to the town hall. Then get some chow and stay put," Dilas said. "You hear me?"

Hoop said he understood and left. By the hangdog look on his face, he wasn't about to go off sprinting through the night woods.

"Messages sent out," Rudy announced, coming down the stairs. "What was all the ruckus?"

"Just don't stick your head out the door tonight, it might get shot off," Dilas said as he headed to the door. "I gotta go and spread the word about the Kraut and our missing pilot."

As Dilas shut the door behind him, Sanja doled out the grub, and we filled in Rudy on the rampaging Fritz. Big Mike had his fork at the ready when Sanja folded her hands to pray. Rudy followed suit and so did we. She spoke softly, then gestured for us to eat.

"It sounded very nice," I said. "We used to pray before meals at home too. Kind of got out of the habit. What did it mean?"

"The poor shall eat and be satisfied, and those who seek the Lord shall praise him; their hearts shall live forever," Rudy said.

"Exactly," Sanja said with a devilish grin. "We are poor, so we must be satisfied with American spaghetti."

That got a chuckle, and we dug in with all the enthusiasm of those who have been in the cold outdoors all day. The slivovitz helped the pasta and sauce to go down. I had to admit, it was already growing on me.

"You know, it's strange," Rudy said. He set down his fork and sipped the plum brandy. "The SS always travel and fight in packs. I never heard of a lone wolf."

"Maybe he's a sniper sent to infiltrate the area," I said. "He could have hitched a ride with the half-tracks and vamoosed into the woods as soon as they halted."

"Vamoosed?" Sanja asked.

"Left in a hurry," I said.

"I shall remember that word," she said. "But the fascists do not vamoose. They come in great numbers, or they do not come at all."

"Maybe he's on the run," Big Mike said. "Doesn't want to surrender to the Chetniks, so he's looking for someplace safe."

"Someplace safe is down the road he came in on," I said. "If he wanted to cross that ravine, it would have been easy after dark. But instead, he ambushes Rip and Shakey."

"I hope nobody starts firing off rounds tonight," Rudy said. "We'll be shooting at each other most likely."

"I assume there are guards and patrols around the village," I said.

"Sure, and once they hear there's a Kraut on the prowl, they'll be shooting at anything that makes a sound," Rudy said. "Which includes Ripper if he gets cold and wet and wants to give up playing cowboys and Indians."

"Or Joe," Sanja said. "I have talked with him. A nice man. But Lieutenant Ripper does not speak much. I think his soul is weary."

"He's the only survivor of his crew," Big Mike said. "That's got to be tough."

"Tough. Yes. Now tell us, Billy, how did you come by the name Peaches?" Sanja asked me. "You say it was given you by a zločinački?"

"A gangster," Rudy clarified.

"Fellow by the name of Archie Chapman," I said. "He liked his gin as much as he favored his bayonet. They both reminded him of his time in the trenches during the last war."

Big Mike and I entertained Rudy and Sanja with stories of some of our cases, including the theft of sixty-four crates of the US Army's Peaches, Canned, Syrup, Heavy. This bit of black-market skulduggery is what led to our making Archie's acquaintance and me being christened Peaches, a nickname that I expected would follow me until the end of time.

After the slivovitz was lowered to a respectful level, Sanja bolted the door. Rudy stoked the woodstove, and we all went upstairs, weapons in hand, unsure of what the night might bring. At the top of the stairs, a short hall led to a large bedroom on the right. Sanja showed us to a smaller room farther back and told us it used to be her room, but that now with Rudy here, she needed the larger bed in her parents' old room. She was apologetic, and I chalked it up to embarrassment over the sleeping arrangements. Then I opened the door.

"Uh, Billy, where's your bed?" Big Mike said, looking over my shoulder. The bed was small, not exactly a single, but smaller than a double. The good news was that it was piled high with quilts, and it looked like we'd stay warm at least.

"You better sleep on your side," I said. "Your shoulders are way too wide for this thing."

Big Mike sat on the edge and unlaced his boots. "Hey, it's comfortable," he said. "My brother and me shared a bed no bigger than this for years. We did okay. But I'll admit, I wasn't always the Charles Atlas of Detroit."

"Just don't roll over on me," I said, and peered out the single window, which looked over the road. Light from the half-moon cast shadows from the forest as the wind whistled through the pines. I was sure glad I wasn't spending the night out in those woods. It was one thing to hunker down at the observation post with maybe a blanket for comfort, but roam around on your own? No thanks. I almost pitied the Kraut that Ripper was hunting, but not much.

Shedding my boots and web belt, my Thompson close by, I burrowed under the covers and counted myself lucky. Big Mike had wiggled around to give me some room, and my eyelids quickly grew heavy. The talk of Archie Chapman had brought up other cases Big Mike and I had worked on, and a cavalcade of places and people played out in my mind. Some of the people were still alive, as far as I knew. Others were dead. Some, deservedly so.

Not the best mental images for drifting off to sleep, but I was so damned tired it didn't matter. I awoke to the sound of boots on the attic floor as a dull light filtered in through the window.

"Sounds like Rudy's at work," Big Mike said from the edge of the bed. He pulled on his boots and got up with a grunt. "You hogged the blankets, buddy."

"Makes up for you hogging the bed." I threw off the quilts and shuffled to the window. Outside, a gray fog blanketed the village and the woods beyond. We headed downstairs, where Sanja was brewing coffee. A platter of small, round loaves that had just come out of the oven sat on the table. The place smelled like heaven.

"These are lepinja," Sanja told us. "Flatbread filled with sausage. German sausage from tins, but it is still good."

"Smells great," Big Mike said as he sniffed the air.

"They must cool," Sanja said. She set out cups and apologized for the lack of sugar. "But it is real coffee. American coffee is better than American spaghetti, I think." She got no disagreement from us as we sipped the hot, strong brew.

"News from Bari," Rudy announced as he came downstairs. "They confirmed today's flights are off. Tomorrow, weather permitting, they'll bring in three Skytrains, which ought to be enough for everyone we have waiting. But they're nervous about the SS showing up in the area. So after that, they'll wait a day, and then send one more C-47 in the early morning to take out any stragglers. Meaning you two and your wandering POW."

"That doesn't leave us a lot of time," Big Mike said. "Maybe we should ask for another day."

"I figured you'd say that, so I asked," Rudy said. "Got a firm negative. We haven't lost an aircraft yet, and it's my bet the brass are getting nervous after hearing the SS were snooping around. Remember, there's a Luftwaffe air base not far away, as the crow flies, anyway."

"Okay, we just need to find Johnny and get back here in three days," I said. "Easy, right?"

"If the weather cooperates," Rudy said. "I've alerted our units to watch for him, and Sanja knows the area well. Odds are in your favor."

"Any word on our Kraut?" Big Mike asked, his eyes devouring the cooling lepinja.

"Not sighted. Joe turned up at the OP around midnight. Rip had already been there for some chow and moved out again to hunt for him. He was mad about Joe prowling around and getting in his way." Rudy poured a cup of coffee and stared out the small kitchen window. "Doesn't look too bad out there."

"When are the horses coming?" I asked Sanja.

"Soon. We keep them at a farm higher in the hills," she said. "Near my father's cabin. It is best they are hidden. If the Germans see them in our fields when they fly, they might come to take them."

"You know a path off the main roads?" I asked.

"Of course. So do the horses," Sanja said. A smile turned up the corners of her mouth.

"Relax, Billy, you're in good hands," Rudy said.

"I know. I'm just a little worried about the three-day deadline," I said. "As soon as this fog thins, I'd like to get going."

"After we eat lepinja," Big Mike said. Sanja told him soon, and I made my way to the front door. I unbolted it and stepped into the mist. The air was damp and cool and filled with tiny, swirling droplets of moisture. A blur of yellow in the eastern sky promised to burn off the fog, and I hoped for it to kick in before too long. I took a deep breath and let loose a long plume of air as I turned to go inside.

I heard the whirring *crack* of a slug as it passed close to my ear, followed by the distant sound of the shot. I hit the deck and crawled the rest of the way inside as another round thudded into the wooden door. I kicked it shut with my foot. Sanja flew by, vaulting up the stairs. Big Mike was at the window. He peered cautiously from the side, his M1 clutched in his hands.

"Everyone okay?" I shouted, louder than I needed to.

"No, goddamn it," Rudy said. I rolled over to see him sprawled on the floor next to the stairs. Blood oozed through his fingers as they clasped his wounded arm. "He got a piece of me. Somebody better nail that Kraut!"

Shots rang out from the floor above. It was Sanja with her Mauser, working the bolt and sending rounds in the direction of the shooter. Chances were she wouldn't hit him, but he'd damn well keep his head down.

I looked over to Big Mike, who nodded. I scrambled to my feet, threw the door open, and let loose a burst from my Thompson. I aimed straight ahead and darted across the road as Big Mike banged away with his M1. I took cover behind a tree and listened for footsteps, but with all the shooting going on, it wasn't in the cards.

Men emerged from the village, running toward the sound of gunfire. I waved, wanting to be sure they knew I was one of the good guys. As for the bad guy, unless he was the stupidest German in Yugoslavia, he was long gone into the fog-shrouded hills.

Vamoosed.

CHAPTER TWENTY-SEVEN

THERE WAS A lot of hubbub. Chetniks ran around with rifles aimed in every direction, farmers peeked out from behind barns and outhouses, worried airmen asked questions, and an angry Dilas shouted out orders in English and Serbian.

"That was a near miss, Billy," Big Mike said. He carried his M1 at the ready on our way back to the house. "It went right by your ear and winged Rudy's arm."

"He must have fired as I turned around," I said. "Probably got tired of waiting all night and took a pop at the first Yank he saw." Two pops, I reminded myself. The second shot was stopped by the door. I felt the rough edges of the hole. A damn close call.

Inside, Sanja had cut off Rudy's sleeve and was cleaning his wound. He had a long gouge along his right bicep. The bullet had struck the wall behind him, leaving a hole in the plaster.

"Doesn't look too bad," I said. "You have a medic?"

"Yeah. Me. Radio operator and medic. Funny, huh?" Rudy said. "I just need this bandaged tight so it will hold until we get to Bari. Use a lot of sulfa, okay, Sanja?"

"No," she said. "It must be sewn. I am good with a needle." She lit a candle and held a needle in the flame, then threaded it.

I patted Rudy on the shoulder and congratulated him on his Purple Heart. He let out a yelp as Sanja started stitching him up, but he quieted right down. I studied the bullet hole and eyed the slug's likely path. I asked Big Mike to open the door, which he did, one hand holding a lepinja.

"Come on," I said. I drew an imaginary line from the hole, out the entrance, and to the trees beyond the road. Outside, I did the same from where the slug had hit. I sighted along my Thompson with my shoulder against the door and spotted a mound of something deep in the woods.

Dilas emerged from the trees twenty yards down. When he joined us, I explained what I was up to. We went into the trees, and Dilas and Big Mike spread out on either side. In the thinning fog, I saw that the mound was a stack of logs about six feet long and four high.

"This'd be about right," Big Mike said. He faced the house. "A good distance off but still a clear view."

I ran my finger along the topmost log. It had been scraped clean of moss and dirt where a rifle would have lain. Behind the stack, pine needles and leaves had been churned up, revealing fresh dirt underneath.

"Why here?" I said, more to myself than anyone.

"To target our radio operator," Dilas said. "He must have mistook you for Rudy."

"I could see taking out the radio, but Rudy can't be the only guy around who knows Morse," I said.

"Could he have made it up here in time to see them hike in with the radio gear?" Big Mike asked.

"If he knew the lay of the land and had strong legs, sure," Dilas said. "He might have waited until morning to leave so he could escape in the fog."

"Yeah," Dilas said, his hand on his chin. "What worries me is that he's seen an American uniform at all. If he goes back with news that there are Americans in Pranjani, all hell could break loose."

"Maybe we should stop hunting for him and focus on blocking his way back," I said. "Keep him bottled up."

"Good idea," Dilas said. "I'll step up security in the village and send out patrols along the ravine."

"The fog might have kept him from making out the uniform," I said as I tried to think it through. "But he had to have a reason for staking out Sanja's house in particular.

"That's one dedicated bastard," I continued. "We got the drop on those SS at the bridge, but they didn't seem like savvy frontline combat veterans. They acted like security troops who were used to having their way. This guy's different." I walked a few paces into the woods and saw nothing but mist dripping from pine boughs. The only way I could tell he was gone was the fact that I was drawing breath.

"I'll move Rudy to another house, just to be sure," Dilas said. "After I get the horses organized." Dilas and I turned to walk back, but Big Mike was intent on scanning the ground behind the log pile, so we stopped to watch.

"You see something?" I asked.

"No."

I joined him as he scuffed aside ground debris and felt with his hands between the logs. He didn't speak but raised an eyebrow in my direction.

"Damn," I said. With a cop's eye for evidence, Big Mike had spotted what should have been there but wasn't. "Two shots. There should be at least one shell casing here."

"Odds are he would have worked the bolt to chamber another round after he fired the second shot," Big Mike said. "Just to be ready."

"So?" Dilas said with a shrug.

"He policed his shell casings," I said. "That's the mark of an assassin, not a regular soldier."

"If he left them, it would have marked this as his firing position," Dilas said. "Maybe he's planning a return visit."

"Maybe," I said, unconvinced. There was something at work

here I didn't understand. Either a highly skilled German commando was roaming these hills, or it was someone else. Either way, I wanted him stopped before he adjusted his aim a tad and put a bullet in my head. I scoured the ground for any evidence we might have missed. I came up empty. But there had to be something I'd overlooked. Something besides the absence of shell casings. What, I had no idea.

Nothing came to me. I walked back to the house with Big Mike while Dilas corralled wandering Chetniks for patrols. As we entered, Sanja was wrapping a gauze bandage around Rudy's arm.

"Feeling okay?" I asked.

"Yeah. Sanja's got a steady hand and a tight stitch," Rudy said.

"And I will take them out when I return," Sanja said. "You did not find the German?"

"No trace," I said. "Is it common knowledge that Rudy stays here?"

"Every person in the village knows where everyone lives," Sanja said. "Of course they know about Rudy and the radio. Do you think the sniper was after him?"

"It's possible," I said.

"I'm not that important," Rudy said. "Marty knows Morse, he's just slow at it. If a German wanted to take out anyone, it would be him. He's the senior OSS officer."

"The German is still running, I think," Sanja said. "He knows he is being hunted. But right now, I must go over the map with Rudy. He needs to see the path we will take to contact our units in the villages we will pass. Then we should eat. It will be a long ride."

It was good advice, even though my heart was still pounding more than my stomach was growling. Big Mike and I sat in the kitchen while Sanja tended to Rudy in the sitting room. I nibbled at a lepinja. It was soft and chewy, the sausage inside warm. The nibbles turned to full bites, and before I knew it, I was washing the last of it down with coffee.

"That's good," I said, and took another. "I told you about the two attempts on my life in England, right?"

"Yeah. Someone tried to clobber you during a storm and then slashed the bed you'd slept in the night before," Big Mike said. "Whoever did that is pretty far away, Billy."

"I get that. I may be paranoid, but I'm not crazy. What I do know for sure is that those two attempts made sense. There's a murderer on that base, and he was trying to stop me," I said. "Now I'm here in Serbia, and someone is gunning for me."

"In the middle of a war. Hardly surprising."

"But why me? Why did the shooter stake out this house? Why did he risk so much to take that shot?"

"You have a point," Big Mike said. "I'm thinking you could have been a random target. But what I can't figure out is what motivates this guy. His whole unit has just been blown to hell. If he wanted vengeance, it would make sense to observe and then get back with word that Americans are in this village. The Luftwaffe could flatten it in a heartbeat."

"Instead, he's stalking us."

"Stalking you," Big Mike said. "You got enemies in Yugoslavia, maybe?"

"Seems like I do now."

I sipped the last of the coffee, trying to come up with a rational explanation. Maybe I was overthinking things, and we had nothing more than a foolish Fritz taking potshots after curling up behind a woodpile.

I worked to mentally reconstruct the scene. Opened the door and went outside. Trees shrouded in mist. Turned at the crack of a bullet past my head. Dove and kicked the door shut as the second round hit. Rudy held his bleeding arm. Sanja fired from the upstairs bedroom, the loud report from her Mauser alternating with the click-clack of the bolt action. Burst outside with Big Mike and found nothing but confusion.

Which was the state I found myself in when my coffee was gone. I tried to stop thinking about it and went upstairs to grab my rucksack. I was back downstairs when Dilas came in, his face lit with excitement.

"They're bringing the horses, and you're in for a surprise," he said.

"Is Johnny Adler riding one of them?" I asked. Otherwise, I'd had enough of a surprise already.

"No, but you're about to meet General Draža Mihailović himself," Dilas said. He explained that the Chetnik leader had stayed at the farm where the horses were kept and wanted to meet the new Yanks who'd arrived in Pranjani. Dilas had tried to warn him off because of the German, but Mihailović and his men had only laughed. He didn't sound like the kind of general to worry about a single enemy soldier.

We hefted our gear and filed outside to get our mounts and meet the Chetnik leader. Sanja wore her Mauser rifle slung over her shoulder. I blinked, knowing something important was right in front of me.

The bolt.

The shots that came my way were fired quickly, one after the other. Too fast for even a skilled marksman to work the bolt and take aim.

It wasn't a Mauser. It was an American M1 Garand.

CHAPTER TWENTY-EIGHT

NOT ONLY HAD it been a semiautomatic M1, but I doubted it was fired by a German. Why would a Kraut bother to pick up his shell casings? It wasn't unthinkable that the enemy would favor a semiautomatic over the bolt-action Mauser, but only someone on our side would want to remove any evidence of the weapon. The only question left was, Yank or Chetnik?

I didn't have much time to think about that as a half-dozen men on horseback paraded down the street with villagers walking beside them. Chetnik fighters, children, and older folks smiled and chatted with the man in the lead. He wore a green felt cap with the Serbian double-headed eagle coat of arms and wire-rimmed glasses that gave him the air of a renegade professor. His beard was full but neatly trimmed, his mustache twirling up at each end. He was the kind of guy you spot thirty yards out and know you're never going to forget.

"General Mihailović," I said, coming to attention and offering a salute that would have made Sam Harding proud.

"Welcome to Serbia, my American friends," Mihailović said. He returned the salute, dismounted, and made right for Rudy, whose arm was now in a sling. "You were not badly injured, I see."

"No, General, I'm fine. Sanja stitched me right up," Rudy said.

"Good. We need you and your radio. Captain Dilas, my men

will assist you in the hunt for this Nazi," Mihailović said. "He cannot be allowed to escape."

"Thank you, General," Dilas said. "We'll use them to patrol the roads. I'll get started right now and have some men from the village guard you."

"Do not worry about me, Captain," the general said with a smile. "The Germans have yet to find me. I will stay the night and my men are yours while there is light."

Dilas went off to speak with the mounted guard while the villagers held the reins of the three horses brought along for us.

"General, this is First Sergeant Mike Miecznikowski, known as Veliki Mihajlo," I said.

"Well named, my friend," Mihailović said with a grin as he shook hands with Big Mike.

"I'm Captain Billy Boyle," I said, and took the general's offered hand. His grip was firm, and his eyes drilled into mine.

"I understand you both helped defeat the fascists at the ravine," he said. "A good fight, except for the one who got away. No matter, a single German in our mountains is a dead man."

"I'd be happier seeing his dead body, sir."

"As would I, and many more," Mihailović said. "I understand you brought in supplies for my men. This is appreciated. But we need much more. Boots, medicines, and ammunition. First the British abandoned us. Now the Americans are about to. Will this change, do you think?"

"General, it's been my experience that the brass takes care of the thinking and the rest of us are left to make the best of what they've thought up," I said. "I'm glad we could help, but it doesn't repay you and your people for what you've done for our aircrew."

"Watch out, Captain Boyle. You may end up being a diplomat when this war is over. Thank you for your words, but your air force carries the war to the Germans in their homeland. This is good for us. You, our allies, we are obliged to help. Sadly, I think the British have poisoned the American leaders against us. Tito and his Communists now have the upper hand, and I grieve for my nation if they take control. To go from Nazis to Communists is only another form of enslavement," Mihailović said. "Tell your generals that when you return."

"I will, sir," I said. I hoped I'd have a chance to ask Uncle Ike about what was happening to the Chetniks. It sounded like they were getting a raw deal, but then again, maybe Tito had his side of the story to tell.

"Now, you must go," Mihailović said. "The air is clear. I hope you find your men. The last flight will leave soon enough."

"You should be on it," Big Mike said. "Tell the generals in Italy what the story is. So many airmen owe their lives to you."

"Veliki Mihajlo, you have a great heart, I can see that," Mihailović said. He laid a hand on Big Mike's shoulder. "But I will never leave this soil until my people are free. Now go. With Sanja as your guide, I am sure you will have success."

He and Sanja embraced, then the general left. He walked his horse and chatted with a gaggle of kids who'd gathered around him like he was Father Christmas. Dilas had a few words with him before he returned to us. A couple of Chetniks brought our horses close. We stuffed the saddlebags with rations and food, leaving our packs for ammo and medical supplies.

"Here, take my binoculars," Dilas said. "Might come in handy for spotting your POW."

"Thanks," I said, and hung the powerful binoculars around my neck. I motioned for Big Mike to come closer and spoke in a low voice. I told Dilas about my suspicions.

"You're saying one of our people is the shooter? That there's no Kraut?" Dilas said. "That's crazy."

"Billy's got a point," Big Mike said. "Those two shots came in *bang bang*. Just enough time in between to take aim. Working a bolt would've meant more of a delay."

"I know that, goddamn it," Dilas said. "But I can't believe it was one of us. Maybe we got a Kraut smart enough to know an M1 is a better rifle. We've had a few arms drops go south and they've gotta have a fair supply."

"All I can tell you is what makes sense to me," I said. "Keep an eye peeled."

"You too," Dilas said. "And get back in time to make that last flight."

He didn't need to tell me twice. I wanted to come back with Johnny Adler in tow and get to Italy, where I was pretty sure no one wanted me dead. I mounted up. Dilas slapped my horse's flank, and we were off. We rode out of the village, past the town hall where three Chetniks tied their horses to a fence, and joined Mihailović at the entrance.

"Some kind of powwow going on," Big Mike said as two more Chetniks rode into town. These fellows sported relatively clean uniforms, as opposed to the rough garb of the local fighters. We exchanged greetings as I admired their horses, one a light gray, almost white, and the other jet black. A striking pair.

"Probably trying to figure out what to do once we leave them high and dry," I said once we'd passed each other.

"It ain't right," Big Mike said, and settled into a surly silence. We stayed on the main road, which wasn't more than a dirt road barely wide enough for a truck. In about a mile, Sanja led us into the woods on a narrow path that dropped down to the level of a stream. Fallen leaves carpeted the route, and the bare branches of trees arched overhead. Sanja and the horses seemed to know the way, and our mounts were sure-footed on the rocky slope. Serbian mountain horses, Sanja told us. Small and nimble, they possessed thick, muscled necks and stout legs. Even Veliki Mihajlo would not be too heavy a load, she promised.

Sanja rode her chestnut mare gracefully, erect in the saddle even as the trail dipped and turned. Big Mike and I let our bays follow her lead and kept an eye out for any movement in the deep woods. We rode for an hour, hidden among the forested ridgelines. Pretty soon, my posterior reminded me it had been a long time since I'd last ridden.

We halted before a trickle of water that crossed our path, leaving a patch of mud and wet leaves before it flowed into the stream. Sanja sat taller in her saddle, looking carefully at the wet surface.

"No tracks," she said. "No one has come this way. This is good."

We descended farther, the sound of falling water not far ahead. We reached a level surface where flat mossy rocks overlooked churning rapids as the stream grew into a more sizable river. Sanja held up her hand and dismounted. We followed suit, and from the grimace on Big Mike's face, it seemed we were both glad for a break. We stepped onto a wide ledge, where, for the first time this morning, we were out from under the cover of the forest canopy. Here, there was no fog, nothing but wispy clouds floating over the narrow valley below. Smoke curled from farmhouses along the river where a road led to a cluster of homes around a stone bridge. On one side sat an orchard, fruit trees planted in neat rows. On the other, naked fields waited for spring planting.

"Planinica," Sanja said. "We have fighters there. Rudy contacted them to watch for us and for the man you seek."

"How many?" I asked. I scanned the scene below through my binoculars. No one was in sight.

"Ten, I think," Sanja said. "Some live here and keep their weapons hidden until needed. Others guard the radio and watch the roads for Germans. Or Tito's Partisans, or Ustaše. Sometimes they find American fliers, but too often it is the enemy who comes through." She pointed out a rise behind the bridge, which gave a good view of the road where it wound around a hill. "The observation post is up there. They move it every two days to hide their tracks. They may be watching us now."

We waved and ate lepinja. We watched and listened. The scene looked peaceful. Very quiet. I raised the binoculars and scanned the road and the village.

"I can't see a soul," I said. "Where is everybody?" Nobody was out doing chores. No movement. Then I saw it. A body, near the bridge. I found another, sprawled on the ground at the back of a house.

"Look," I said, and handed Sanja the field glasses.

"Bože moj," she murmured. "My god. We must go. Now. They could be watching."

"Who?" Big Mike asked.

"Those who slaughter Serbs," Sanja said. "There are many to choose from. Follow and be quiet."

We mounted and trailed Sanja single file down a path worn flat by centuries of feet, beast and human alike. Set along a rock ledge, it provided no cover for about a hundred yards. Most of the way, there wasn't room to turn around, much less dismount. I should have been nervous, given the drop-off, but I was too busy watching for movement below. If anyone down there had a machine gun aimed at us, a couple of quick bursts would put an end to our search for Johnny Adler.

But no one shot at us, and no one ran to greet us. The path from the ledge emptied onto the dirt road that led through the village, but Sanja took us along the river, giving us cover from anyone hiding in the houses.

It didn't take long to realize no one was hiding. The river meandered and soon revealed an array of bodies on the bank. Baskets of laundry were overturned, the contents coated with mud and blood. Bodies were half in the river, half on shore. Some had been shot at close range. Others had gaping wounds to their throats. Two children slumped together, silent in their final embrace.

"Shouldn't we check for anyone still alive?" Big Mike said as we halted our horses.

"No. There are none left alive. This looks like the work of the Ustaše. They enjoy cutting throats and would not leave a Serb breathing. Come," Sanja said. She kicked her horse's flanks and ascended the bank, stopping between two houses. She dismounted and tied her horse to a fence post, motioning for us to do the same. "I must look for our fighters. If they are not here, they may still be alive."

We followed Sanja as she went into each house. Big Mike stayed on guard outside while I helped her search the small dwellings. Most had just one large room with a bed, a stove, and rough-hewn wooden furniture. Not to mention more bodies. Old men, women, kids. A few men of fighting age.

There were ten houses in the little village, each with its own horrors. Some were blood spattered, with corpses in unimaginable poses, and family belongings scattered. Others were intact, traces of domesticity still evident, like the dying embers of a fire. Plates set out for the midday meal. A child's doll on the bed. Chaos was almost preferrable.

In the last house, a card game had been in progress. Glasses on the table. A hand dealt and in play. The queen of hearts sat waiting to win or be taken.

"We are done," Sanja said, her mouth set in a grim line. "Jovan and Stephan are not here. We will find them." She left, her Mauser clutched in her hands as if she ached to find a way to take her vengeance.

I stood at the table, unable to take my eyes off the red queen. I was unaccountably drawn to it and held the card in my hand as if it had some greater meaning than a dead man's last play. I placed it in my pocket while I tried to put the jumbled thoughts that ran through my mind into some sort of order. They didn't cooperate.

"We can't just leave these bodies like this," Big Mike said as we walked to the horses.

"We must leave them," Sanja said. "There is no time to dig graves, not if you wish to find your friend and return for the last flight out of Pranjani. But it is also important to not disturb the dead. If the Ustaše return and see the bodies have been cared for, they will hunt us. So, we leave everyone as they fell. It is their last duty."

"We don't need the people who did this on our trail, buddy," I said to Big Mike.

"Veliki Mihajlo, I am sorry you had to witness how we make war," Sanja said. "There are many villages like this poor place. Serb, Croat, Albanian, Catholic, Muslim. We all suffer revenge many times over. It is no good, not for anyone, yet we cannot stop ourselves."

"Do you think Jovan and Stephan are alive?" I asked.

"Yes. If no one betrayed them. They know their duty is to protect the radio, so they would have stayed hidden. There was not much two men could have done, but it must have been difficult," she said.

"If they're here, they must have spotted us," Big Mike said. He looked toward the hill at the edge of town. The road forked at its base. One route followed the river and the other headed east. "Where are they?"

"Watching," Sanja said, and led us to the hill. She explained that since the observation post was frequently relocated, there was a hidden meeting place. We walked the horses into the woods and tethered them in a small glen. Sanja whistled, and in a moment, a Chetnik emerged from the trees. He was tall and thin and had the usual bushy beard and cloth cap with the Serbian double-headed eagle. His eyes were vacant, his mouth agape, and he moved with a halting gait, as if his body and mind were ill at ease with each other.

"Stephan," she said. They embraced, and Stephan led us silently uphill. In a few minutes we were on a rocky outcropping, the valley floor spread out beneath us. The houses, the orchards, the bodies. Jovan sat under a pine tree, almost invisible behind the low-hanging branches. He nodded to Sanja, glanced at us with indifference, and returned to his dials and headset. Stephan spoke to Sanja and pointed to the road below with a sweeping gesture, the bitterness evident in his curt, clipped tone. When he was finished, he rubbed his eyes and turned away.

"It was the Ustaše Black Legion," she told us. "They came this morning. Four truckloads. They began to kill immediately."

"Why?" Big Mike asked. "A reprisal?"

"The Black Legion are the most savage Ustaše," she said. "Even the SS is shocked by their butchery. They need no reason to kill Serbs."

"Which direction did they go?" I asked. "After." I felt ashamed to ask, inquiring about our own safety in the wake of this massacre, but we needed to keep moving.

"That way, to the east," Sanja said. "Jovan has news. Two escapees are with our men in Virovac."

"How far?" I asked.

"Six hours, perhaps. We may not make it before dark. In the morning, certainly," she said. "We take the road along the river. Jovan said our men sent out a patrol to meet us."

Stephan spoke hurriedly and pointed to the eastern road. A tiny plume of dust arose in the distance.

"The Black Legion," Sanja said. "We must go."

I trained my binoculars on the road and made out the trucks headed our way. I pivoted to the river road and was relieved to see it clear. Then I scanned the path that we'd taken to the village as we'd come down from the top of the ridge.

A horseman was perched at the overlook, a flash of white fluttering in his hand.

It couldn't be.

I pulled the red queen out of my pocket. Finally, she spoke to me.

I knew exactly who the horseman was.

CHAPTER TWENTY-NINE

"Požuri!" Sanja shouted. I didn't need a translator to understand she wanted us to hurry. We scrambled down the rocky path, burst through the undergrowth, and raced to the horses in the glen. By the time we emerged onto the road, we could hear the trucks rumbling closer. Following Sanja's lead, we went into a canter since the turn was close.

As we reached the fork and went right, I risked a quick glance up to the overlook. The horseman was gone, and I cursed his perfect timing. He'd spotted us and also avoided running smack into the Black Legion. I couldn't focus on more than that as I pressed my calves against the horse's flanks and urged her into a gallop.

Sanja was well ahead of us. She rode hard, her horse's hooves sending clumps of dirt flying. I gripped the reins and leaned forward, resisting the temptation to look over my shoulder again. Maybe I'd hallucinated him because I'd seen the queen of hearts on that table. But it had been a damn vivid hallucination, especially with him astride the light gray horse we'd spotted in Pranjani.

The road curved with the river and narrowed as pines encroached on the path. Sanja leaned into the turn and picked up speed, her body close to the horse, the two of them moving with an animal's grace. I pulled the reins to my right and managed to stay upright even as branches flashed by my face. Engines growled in the distance, and I knew if the Ustaše spotted us, they could floor it and have us in their sights at any moment.

The image of the horseman was burned into my mind, but it was only now, as I gripped the reins and kept my knees tight against my mount's flank, that I saw one detail clearly. The flash of white I'd spotted? It had to be the map Sanja had marked up for Rudy, which detailed our route to Majur. How else could he be on our tail?

Sanja pulled in her reins and slowed her mount. I did the same and checked on Big Mike. Just behind me, he stood tall in the saddle, his feet braced against the stirrups. I didn't see or hear anyone behind us, but I didn't waste a lot of time craning my neck since I was too busy trying to save it. I followed Sanja as she veered off the road onto a narrow path through the conifers. She patted her horse's neck, murmuring encouragements. I gave mine a few rubs and was rewarded with a playful snort. She liked to run, but I didn't want to overtire her. We still had a long way to go.

The trees thinned out until we were on open ground with a ridgeline looming over us. The path ended by a stream, where we halted and let the horses drink from the gently flowing water. Leather creaked as Big Mike looked around and cupped a hand behind his ear.

"Nothing," he said. "Maybe they took the other fork."

"There's something I need to tell you," I said, and withdrew the playing card from my pocket.

"Quiet!" Sanja hissed. "If they did take the other fork, they could be close. That road is behind the ridge. There." She pointed to the rocky outcropping above us.

"Look," I said to Big Mike, my voice low. I held up the red queen.

"Goddamn," he said, his eyes widening. "It can't be."

"Come!" Sanja said. "This is no time for card games. We are in the open. Follow me." She made a clucking sound, and her horse moved off smartly as they worked their way upstream. The banks were rocky and blocked with boulders, so we splashed through the water. I kept an eye on the high ground above us. She was right, this wasn't the time and place to talk about what that card meant. But from the look on Big Mike's face, he knew.

Our mounts picked their way through the clear mountain waters, dislodging rocks that clattered in the streambed. The noise echoed sharply against the stony ridge, and I kept scanning the horizon for Ustaše. The air was cold, and the sun settled low in the western sky, nearly touching the top of the crest to our right. I hoped Sanja had some place in mind for us to spend the night.

On the left, the bank flattened, and Sanja urged her mount out of the streambed and onto dry land. I turned for a last check of the high ground and caught a flicker of movement. Even with the sun in my eyes, I made out three figures, silhouetted against the sky.

Three men. With rifles.

"Go!" I shouted just as shots cracked and bullets zinged off the rocks. Sanja ducked, her head on the horse's mane, and darted into the woods. My horse followed, but Big Mike's reared in terror as a slug ricocheted off a rock not a foot from her hoof. Big Mike held on, but as his mare bolted out of the stream, he tumbled off and hit the ground hard.

"I'm okay," he grunted, and got up. "Go."

There wasn't much for me to do except serve as a second target, so I made for cover as Big Mike ran behind me. At first, the trees were nothing but saplings. They screened us from view but wouldn't be very good at stopping a bullet. I pulled on the reins and waited for Big Mike to catch up. He crashed through the branches, M1 slung over his shoulder, carrying his helmet.

"Are you hurt?" I asked. Branches snapped as bullets flew overhead.

"Only my pride and my backside," he said as he hustled by me. I urged my horse forward, weaving between trees, until we came to a small ravine where Sanja awaited us.

"Where is your horse?" Sanja demanded.

"I don't know," Big Mike said. He looked around, surprised, as if he'd misplaced it accidentally. "She threw me and bolted."

"Vamoosed?" Sanja said. "That is not good."

"She got spooked by a bullet," I said. Seeing Sanja's furrowed eyebrows, I clarified. "Scared."

"She will find us. I hope. Horses smell each other. Now hurry."

Sanja clucked again and headed up the trail. I told Big Mike we'd switch off riding and walking until we got to our destination, then trotted closer to Sanja.

"How far to Virovac?" I asked.

"Farther than I planned," she said. "This is the long way. The Ustaše took the shorter path."

"Why didn't we?"

"It is too rocky for the horses to go fast," she said. "If the Ustaše also took that route, they would have caught us. So we go this way and hope to find the road before dark. Virovac in the morning."

"But if the Ustaše continue on that road, they'll be in Virovac before us," I said.

"Yes," Sanja said. "Would you like to turn back?"

"No, of course not."

"Well then, watch for Veliki Mihajlo's horse," she said. "That would be the most useful thing. Unless you wish to stop and play cards?"

"I'll tell you about that tonight, over some slivovitz," I said. "Where are we staying?"

"We will find a house," Sanja said. "The village where I hoped to stop is not on this road."

"This isn't exactly a road," I said as our horses walked on the path thick with pine needles.

"Look for the horse," she said, and clucked.

Big Mike and I switched, and I hoofed it for a while, which felt good after being in the saddle all day. Shadows were growing longer, but at least we were on a dirt track that looked well used by horses and carts. No Black Legion trucks, thankfully.

The path took us by a field with neat rows of stubble from fall crops. Woodsmoke drifted in along with the sound of a mooing cow, announcing a farmhouse nearby.

"Friendly?" Big Mike asked.

"In this area, people should be, but I cannot be certain," Sanja said. Ahead, a dull yellow light glowed from a window in a one-story farmhouse set back from the road. It had outbuildings attached and a barn in the rear.

We dismounted and led our horses to the house. Sanja called out, alerting the family to our presence. The light was doused and the door swung open. A man holding a shotgun stepped outside. His beard was shot with gray, and his huge hands held the scattergun like it was a toy. It wasn't pointed at anyone, which I took to be a good sign.

Sanja spoke in soothing tones and gestured to us. The farmer gave us a stare. Americans were unexpected, and I could see the wariness in his eyes. But there was interest too. We were something new and different, commodities in short supply on a farm in winter.

He spoke to Sanja, sounding friendly. Then he pointed to the barn and said a few things with a lot of emphasis. As he did, two young girls, around twelve or thirteen, poked their heads outside. Sanja made agreeable sounds and spoke to the girls, greeting them.

"Give them some food," she said, glancing at me. I dug into the sack and produced two Hershey's bars and a pack of

Chesterfields. Sanja took them, gave the smokes to the farmer with a small bow, then handed the chocolate to the girls, who looked to their father for permission. He nodded and spoke to each of them. Now we were all friends.

But not close friends, since he led us to the barn instead of inviting us inside. The younger daughter followed with an oil lamp, holding it high as her father opened the wide wooden door. Inside, a musty, warm smell greeted us, along with a cow blinking her eyes at us from his enclosure.

"There is clean hay in the stalls," Sanja translated. "We may sleep there but we must leave at dawn."

We said thanks again in two languages, and the farmer grinned as he patted his pocket, happy with his Chesterfields. The girl left the lamp, and we unsaddled our horses and led them to their own stalls.

"He asked what happened to our horse. I told him it went lame, and we shot it," Sanja said. "I still hope we will find her in the morning."

"Why did you lie about the horse?" Big Mike asked, removing the bridle from Sanja's mare.

"He had horses, which the Germans took," she said. "It might tempt him to watch for the lost horse and keep it."

"No one else in the farmhouse?" I asked. I set down my saddle in the stall, where the thickly piled hay looked inviting.

"He said his wife is dead and his son is with the Chetniks in Virovac," she said.

"So he's on our side?" Big Mike asked.

"That is what he says, but sometimes people claim whatever will keep them alive," Sanja said. "I told him we were going to Planinica tomorrow in case he talks too much."

"To whom?" I asked. "This is pretty deserted country."

"Our men in Virovac radioed Rudy about a unit of Tito's Partisan Army passing through a few days ago. They could stop and question him," Sanja said. "Better to leave a lie behind than the truth." Words to live by.

While Big Mike took care of the horses, I dug out our C rations. Three cans of franks and beans plus Sterno to heat it up. I scraped a section of dirt floor clean and popped the lids of the flammable jelly.

"We need water for the horses and ourselves," Sanja said, eyeing my preparations. "The little girl told me there is a pump at the back of the house."

Buckets were lined up in an enclosure that served as the tack room, where old bridles, coats, blankets, and riding gear hung on pegs. I dug out a flashlight from my pack and grabbed two buckets, and Big Mike followed suit. Outside, night had fallen. The clouds obscured what little moonlight there was, and I needed the flashlight to find the pump. It was in a ramshackle outbuilding, open on one side. We got the pump going, a creaky, clanging affair that soon gushed streams of frigid water. With the buckets full, we washed our hands and faces as best we could, laughing at the ice-cold sting.

"Could it really be our Anzio killer?" Big Mike asked, his smile wiped away as he drew his hands across his face.

"Let's talk it through when I explain it to Sanja," I said. "It might not make sense if I say it out loud. But it does right now."

A door slammed, and a light flickered from the front of the house.

"Maybe Old MacDonald is coming to tell us to pipe down," Big Mike said. "Let's get back."

We closed the barn door behind us and brought each horse a bucket of water. By the flickering light of the oil lamp, Sanja nosed around in the tack room, scrounging for blankets. She hoisted a coat from the wall, and a wool cap fell from the pocket. She picked it up and suddenly dropped the coat and the blankets.

"I do not think the farmer's son is with the Chetniks," Sanja said. She held out the brimless wool cap, the enameled red star glinting in the light. "This means the Communist Partisans. And the bridles are not all old. Some are well cared for."

"We heard a door open while we were getting water," Big Mike said. "We thought it was the old man, but no one showed."

"The older daughter," I said. "She didn't come with us to the barn."

"She could have run to town, or to another farm where they have a truck or a horse," Big Mike said. "That could've been her coming back, not someone leaving."

"We go. Now," Sanja ordered.

We had no choice. Tito's Partisans may have been on our side, but they wouldn't take kindly to a Chetnik being with us. We grabbed the saddles and gathered our gear. The horses weren't happy leaving their stalls and began to neigh loudly. The cow joined in on the action and snorted and grunted at the excitement. I tried to calm my mare, rubbing her mane while holding the reins tightly.

The barn door swung open. The farmer advanced, his shotgun at the ready. This time it was aimed right at us. He barked at Sanja, and she gave it back to him, but he didn't move. His two daughters stood behind him and stared at us with wide eyes. He waved them back with one arm and quickly returned his grip to the weapon.

"He says he will shoot if we raise our weapons," Sanja said.

"Tell him we're leaving," I said. "And to stand aside. We don't wish to hurt him." Sanja translated in a tone that betrayed the fact that she'd be happy to hurt him right now. He replied in a tone that told me he'd said no, hell no.

The barn went silent. Even the cow stopped his bellowing. I stepped to the side of my horse and threw the reins over the saddle. I figured he wouldn't want to pepper her with buckshot along with me, so it was a safe bet. Besides, I had an idea.

"Slap her rump," I said to Big Mike. "Hard."

I heard a *whack* and the mare bolted and sent the farmer reeling against the wall. The girls screamed and Sanja tried to wrench the shotgun from him. She grabbed it by the stock, but he shoved her back into the other horse, which neighed and stomped her front legs, keeping me from getting close. Sanja and the farmer stumbled in a deadly dance, each trying to get their finger on the trigger. Big Mike stepped in and delivered a sharp hit with the butt of his M1 to the farmer's head. Not a killing blow, but one that brought him to his knees and knocked over the cans of Sterno. As he collapsed, the shotgun slipped from Sanja's grip and went off, both barrels. It hit the lantern and sent burning oil into the hay we'd heaped in the stall and ignited the Sterno.

The girls shrieked even louder as the flames spread. Sanja led her horse out, then darted back in to unlatch the door to the cow's stall. Big Mike tried to kick the burning hay out of the stall, but the oil had spread too far. The fire clawed at the wooden slats separating the animals and ignited the old, dry wood. The farmer was sprawled on his back, moaning as his eyes fluttered open, taking in the destructive fire as it spread through the barn.

Big Mike dragged the guy outside. I tossed the empty shotgun into the flames just in case anyone was thinking about reloading. Smoke billowed from the open door. The younger daughter cried as she held on to the rope around the cow's neck. Old MacDonald babbled as he touched the back of his skull, his hand coming away red.

Sanja spoke to the older girl, her words firm but not angry. The girl nodded and pointed down the road. The fire cast light and flickering shadows against her face, and she looked at her father with what seemed to be disgust. Sanja ended by patting her on the shoulder.

"Her father made her run to the house down the road," she said. "They have a horse and took the news of our presence to the village. That is where her brother is, with the Partisans. She wished only to be left alone and said life will now be much harder. She never wanted her brother to join Tito's army."

"It will be hard, without that barn," Big Mike said. "It's gonna make things tough for us too. It's like a searchlight announcing where we are."

"We have to get a move on," I said, stating the obvious. "The Partisans are probably on their way right now."

"Ana told me of a path around the next farm," Sanja said. "I believe her."

"We have to," I said. "Ustaše behind us, Partisans ahead. We need a shortcut."

Ana spoke to Sanja, her eyes wide as she pointed to the road. Lit by the growing conflagration, Big Mike's horse sauntered down the lane, trailing her reins and whinnying as she made her way to us.

CHAPTER THIRTY

"This way," Sanja said, her voice low. We left the road for a narrow path nearly hidden by undergrowth. Off to our right, the fire lit the dark night sky with a yellow-orange glow. I felt bad for the two girls, knowing what a blow this must've been to their lives. As for the farmer, he probably would've gotten Sanja killed and put an end to our mission, so my sympathies went only so far.

I hadn't been sure about trusting Ana, but the farther we ventured, the more certain I was that she hadn't sent us into a trap. This path was filled with broken branches and narrow ruts, fit more for a farmer's cart than heavy vehicles. Beyond the small trees and brambles, empty fields stretched out on either side. This was a lane for hauling in the harvest, not transporting armed men.

We halted as a distant drumbeat drew closer. Horses, the sound of their hooves passing by on the road we'd just left. At least ten, as far as I could tell. They galloped toward the burning barn. We waited a minute, then set off slowly and quietly, not wanting to alert anyone running late to the party.

The thicket thinned out, and as we left the last whiff of woodsmoke drifting on the wind, we emerged onto a stretch of high ground. Clouds parted just enough for us to make out the hills and slopes awaiting us.

"Where to now?" I asked. Sanja scanned the terrain and did not look all that confident in what she saw.

"I am not certain," Sanja said. "We must find Berkovac. Then we will be on the right path. We have gone so far off our route it is hard to tell where we are. But Berkovac is not far, in that direction." She waved her left hand, which encompassed a whole lot of territory.

"What's there?" I asked.

"A place to sleep and a good trail to take in the morning," she said. "What more could one ask?"

Not much, so I followed as Sanja led us along the grassy heights. I hoped my horse wasn't as tired as I was. Half an hour later, Sanja reined in and pointed to a tiny pinprick of light in the valley below.

"Berkovac," she said. "A small village. It marks where we go northwest on a trail through the hills. To Virovac."

"Good," Big Mike said. "You know someone down there? Think we can find a warm bed?"

"Yes, I know some of the villagers. We have no fighters there," she said. "But I worry about that light. Farmers do not waste oil this late at night. Soldiers do. Germans, perhaps, searching for the escaped prisoners. So, no warm bed tonight. But there is another place."

Well, in the middle of the night in occupied Yugoslavia, with Nazis and other assorted cutthroats on every side, I was happy to hear there was another place to lay down our heads. Fifteen minutes later, I wasn't so sure.

"Kula Varna," Sanja declared. A dark form arose above us as we urged the horses up a steep slope, their hooves kicking up loose dirt that slid back down the hill. At the crest stood the remains of a stone tower and ancient walls that were well on their way to crumbling back into the earth itself. "It was once a mighty fortress. The Mongols destroyed it hundreds of years ago."

"Did a pretty good job of it too," Big Mike said.

We dismounted and unsaddled the horses. Sanja told us there was a spring on the other side of the hill, so we took them down the slight incline until we heard water bubbling out from between a cluster of rocks. Every fortress needs a water supply, and Kula Varna still boasted a nice one. We filled our canteens while the horses drank, then led them into shelter provided by the three stone walls that were still standing. We tethered them to the gnarled remains of a spruce and hunkered down opposite. I missed the hay. And the roof.

"Can we start a fire?" Big Mike asked. "Just a small one to heat the C rations."

"No fire," Sanja said. "At this height, any light will be seen for miles. Cold food is still food." We busied ourselves opening cans of frankfurters and beans and drinking fresh, freezing water.

"I need to explain about the playing card," I said, once we'd gotten a few mouthfuls down. "We told you about some of our investigations, but not about the guy who got away."

"It happened in Italy," Big Mike said. "Anzio."

"I have heard of Anzio. But why tell me this? The battle was almost a year ago."

"Because I think he's here," I said, and began the story of the Red Heart Killer.

I'd been sent to the Anzio bridgehead, south of Rome, last January. The job was to track down a killer who was targeting officers. First a lieutenant was found with the ten of hearts on his dead body, followed by a captain who sported the jack of hearts. The brass started getting nervous when they saw the pattern was headed to a general being graced with the ace of hearts. Before we got close to the murderer, he'd also knocked off his own lieutenant, a doctor, a captain, a major, a POW, and at least one sergeant from his own platoon.

My kid brother, Danny, had just arrived at Anzio as an

infantry replacement. As soon as the killer realized we were on to him, he took Danny hostage and made for the German lines. Danny ended up wounded, along with Big Mike. The killer got away, across a river where he could surrender to the Germans.

"When I saw the queen of hearts on that table, things started to fall into place," I said. "I remembered that Big Mike asked if I had any enemies in Yugoslavia. That was after the shooting that wounded Rudy. He was only joking, but there was something in what he said that bothered me."

"You think this killer is here?" Sanja asked.

"Yes. I believe he's mixed in with the aircrew waiting in Pranjani. I'm thinking he broke out of his POW camp and joined in with the aircrew heading here," I said. "He may even have been with the group that escaped with the man we're looking to rescue."

"Why is this a problem?" Sanja asked as she sniffed the cold C ration. "When we return, you kill him. Problem is solved, yes?"

"No. What I haven't had the chance to say is that he's following us. Just before we lit out of Planinica, I saw him through my binoculars. Or at least I saw an American in a leather flight jacket on that crest overlooking the village. He was atop the light gray horse we saw a Chetnik officer ride into Pranjani this morning, and he was unfolding a map. If it's the one you marked up for Rudy, he knows our route," I said.

"This is a seriously evil man," Big Mike said. "He doesn't care who he kills."

"I do not understand. Who is this man and how did he get here?" Sanja asked. She ate another forkful of franks and beans. "This is better than American spaghetti."

"Sergeant Amos Flint," I said. Flint was smart enough to know he couldn't wait in a POW camp to be liberated. He needed to get away before the army started processing prisoners for the trip home.

"Of your air force, yes?"

"No. He switched identities with another soldier before he fled, and I'm certain he's masquerading as someone else here," I said. "My bet is he planned to get back to Italy and simply disappear. But then he spotted me and couldn't risk being identified."

"You are certain of this?" Sanja asked.

"I wasn't certain until I saw the horseman on our trail," I said. "But before that, I didn't entirely buy the idea of a lone German terrorizing Pranjani. My hunch is that Flint was one of the airmen in on the fight at the bridge. We stopped in front of their camouflaged position where he would've had a clear look at me."

"Ripper," Big Mike said. "We never laid eyes on him, did we?"

"Never," I said. And then it hit me. "Shakey. There was no German. Flint murdered Shakey."

"Why?" Sanja asked. "If this is all true, why would Ripper, or Flint, or whatever you call him, kill his friend?"

"Ripper is supposedly a B-17 pilot, right? Only member of his crew to survive. Word was, he didn't like to talk about it, right? What if Flint got a hold of Ripper's ID and uniform? He's a smart one and could pull off an impersonation, especially if he fakes being so upset he doesn't want to speak about it."

"But Shakey was a flight engineer on a B-17," Big Mike said. "He'd know every detail of those birds. He might've gotten suspicious."

"Which means it was Flint who tossed the grenade into our trench," I said. "Then killed Shakey when he took him to hunt for the fake Kraut."

"I spoke to Lieutenant Ripper a few times," Sanja said. "He was very nice. Friendly."

"I'll bet he was friendly with Rudy too," I said. "Most likely asked about info on the next flights out of here." Sanja nodded.

"He sees us go, visits Rudy to get the dope on where we're

headed, and picks up the map as a bonus. Then steals one of the best horses in town," Big Mike said.

"He must know that he'll be one of the last men out since he was among the last to arrive," I said. "He can't allow us to return."

"And he's got to be back for that last ride outta here," Big Mike said.

"Well, that's something we have in common," I said. "Time is not on our side."

"Perhaps the Black Legion will take care of him for you," Sanja said. She pulled a blanket tight around her shoulders and lay back on the saddle. "Or the Germans. Now sleep. In the morning, we go to Virovac and find your Johnny Adler. Then this killer. I am not happy with men who shoot into my house."

I pulled the wool cap over my ears and rested my head on the leather saddle. Maybe Flint would get caught by the Ustaše, who were sure to make short work of him. If it was the Krauts, at least we'd know the name on the dog tags he was wearing. Not that he'd stay Lieutenant Ripper for long.

Then it hit me. Flint had information to trade. He knew about the airstrip at Pranjani and when the last flights were due in. He'd trade that for a new set of dog tags and a cushy spot in a POW camp in a heartbeat.

He wasn't just a danger to me. He was a threat to everyone waiting in Pranjani.

CHAPTER THIRTY-ONE

BETWEEN THE COLD and my worries about Flint, I should've had trouble sleeping. But the next thing I knew Big Mike was kicking my boots, telling me to wake up. The eastern sky was brightening, which was a considerable improvement over my mood.

Sanja reached into her bag and handed out the last three lepinja. "Feed the horses," she said. I saw Big Mike's face fall, but she had a point. The horses needed nourishment and snatched the meat pies from our hands. We led them to the stream for a drink, then saddled up. Big Mike opened a can of bread biscuits from his C ration stash, which served as our breakfast, washed down with cold water.

"Are we close to the route you mapped out?" I asked Sanja while she adjusted her saddle. "I know we went off course, but are we back on track?"

"Soon," Sanja said, and gave her horse one of her crackers. "We go on this ridge until we see Komanice, another small village. Then we are back on the path I showed Rudy. A road through the hills. It was made to take trees out of the forest."

"A logging road," I said. "Not paved or well-traveled?"

"Yes, a road for logs," Sanja said. "Dirt. Mud, perhaps. There is little fuel for tractors, so only farmers with horses go there to take out wood. Logs."

"You got something in mind, Billy?" Big Mike asked. Watching Sanja, he sighed as he gave his last biscuit to the horse nuzzling him.

"I'm worried that Flint will squeal to the Germans or their Ustaše pals if he gets caught," I said. "He'd sell out every soul in Pranjani to save his own life."

"This is a man without honor," Sanja said.

"From what a doctor told me, he wouldn't understand what the word *honor* meant," I said. Then I gave in as well, and fed my grateful horse a biscuit. "He's a psychopath. No understanding of human emotion. But great at disguising it and imitating what a normal human being would do."

"It is not only the Germans who would want to know about Pranjani," Sanja said. "The Partisans want to cut us off from Italy. They would destroy the airfield and the village."

"But they're on our side," Big Mike said.

"Do you think they would let the Chetniks show their value to the Allies? No, they would rather defeat us and place the blame at our feet if any of your airplanes were lost," she said. "And they would reward any man who brought them the location."

"Basically, Flint will turn anyone he meets to his advantage, by betraying everyone in Pranjani. We can't let that happen," I said.

"Let's not forget the part about him wanting to kill us," Big Mike said. "Kinda weighs on my mind."

"We must go," Sanja said, and put her foot in the stirrup. "This morning the three planes come. The day after tomorrow is the last plane. By then, we need to be back and with this man Flint dead."

"Or prisoner," I said.

"Dead," Sanja said. She clucked and moved out.

An hour passed. The sun began to rise and lit the orange tile roofs of Komanice as it came up on our right. From the ridgeline, I could see a cluster of houses in the valley below and a smattering of farms among the rolling hills. We left that view behind as the trail surmounted the ridge and descended steeply down the other side. We were on open ground, barely hidden in a grove of barren trees.

"Wait," Sanja said as she urged her horse forward. Straight ahead, the path crossed a wide road, and she cautiously looked both ways before waving us forward. We trotted across the paved road and into a thick forest. A clearing held logs stacked in long pyramids, and stripped bark carpeted the ground.

"Nothing fresh," Big Mike said. "Nobody's hauling timber."

"This path is safe," Sanja said. "As safe as anything in life."

"Safe from Flint?" I asked.

"I did not draw the exact route," Sanja said. "I only marked the villages along the way. He would not see this path coming from Planinica. I will show you the road he will take."

The horses clopped along as the trail wound through the forested hills. Every now and then, through a gap in the fir trees, Sanja pointed out a road below us that ran parallel to our course. An hour later, she called a halt and we dismounted. Rifle at the ready, she led us between thick-trunked trees on what was little more than a deer trail, until we came to the edge of the forest. We crouched behind the upended roots of a fallen pine, bleached gray by the sun and wind.

"Here, last year, we ambushed German trucks," she said. "See, the road is close."

"Real close," Big Mike said, and raised his eyebrows at me. It was a nice spot for an ambush. The road was wide and straight, but the hill we were on jutted out close to it, putting us no more than thirty yards away and under good cover. On the other side of the road, a few houses sat farther back, cleared fields in front of them. "Nowhere for the Krauts to run."

"Yes. The attack was good," Sanja said. "You should wait here, until Flint comes. Then kill him."

"It's not bad, Billy," Big Mike said. "He's gotta be behind us."

"If he isn't?"

"Then I will kill him, the moment I see him," she said. "It is not far to Virovac. You wait while I go to get Johnny Adler. I meet you back here, up on the trail. I will bring help."

"I'm not sure," I said, and took out the binoculars. I scanned the road as far as I could and saw nothing in either direction. "If he got to Virovac first, there's no telling what you could walk into."

"No. He needs daylight to travel. We went miles at night; I am sure we are ahead. Remember, too, he had to wait for the Ustaše to pass through Planinica before he could," Sanja said.

"Okay," I said. "I don't like to split up, but it makes sense. Maybe you should wait for us in Virovac, instead of heading back with Johnny, in case Flint slips by."

"No. That is not possible," she said. "I must take your horses. It is too dangerous to leave them. If they make a noise, it could be heard from the road. Or if a farmer comes to look for firewood, he would help himself. It would not be good."

"No," I said, even though I was having a hard time accepting the logic that would leave us out here alone. I suddenly realized how comforting it was having Sanja as our tour guide. "It would not be good."

"If Johnny Adler is in Virovac, I will be back well before dark," Sanja said. "Do not worry."

I told her I wasn't worried at all, and I almost believed it. Big Mike went off with her to grab some chow and came back with two C ration packs. We settled in behind the gnarled roots and kept an eye on the road. Our first customer was an old man in a horse-drawn cart, puffing on a pipe while he hauled a load of manure.

"Thrill a minute around here. Let's eat," Big Mike said. We tore open the cardboard boxes and Big Mike rolled his eyes. "Ham and lima beans."

"Me too," I said. It was just about the worst-tasting meal the army had to offer. But I went at it, ignoring the starchy, bitter taste of the beans.

Then I heard it.

Clip-clop.

The distant sound of hooves. Not a rapid pace, just a leisurely, slow trot. More than one horse, definitely.

"Company," I said, and tossed aside the grub. Through the binoculars, I spotted a small group of horsemen headed our way. The way to Virovac. As they came into focus, their black coats were the first thing I saw. Three of them. "Damn. Now we got the Ustaše Black Legion on horseback instead of in trucks."

"Just let 'em pass by," Big Mike said. "Sounds like there's plenty of Chetniks ahead to deal with them."

"Wait," I said as I worked at a better focus. In the middle of the three black uniforms, I saw a leather jacket. A brown flight jacket and an officer's service cap, and the guy who wore them was astride a light gray horse. I handed the binoculars to Big Mike. "Goddamn. It's Flint."

"What the hell? It looks like they're all pals," Big Mike said. "He must've spilled the beans already."

"There's only three," I said, and looked at Big Mike. "Plus Flint."

"I'll take Flint out," Big Mike said. "Once they get closer. Then you open up with the tommy gun on the other three."

"We've got no choice," I said. I didn't mind firing at the enemy from a good hiding place, but it felt strange to take down an American, even if it was Flint. However, he was a killer, not to mention an immediate danger to the Chetniks and his own countrymen in Pranjani. So I shifted left to give Big Mike the best firing position and settled in, ready to spray the unsuspecting Ustaše with as much hot lead as I could manage. Big Mike was a good shot, and I knew he wouldn't miss such an easy target.

"Once you take out Flint, I'll fire a full clip. Then reload and move in," I said. "They should be too surprised to react, especially if the horses start to rear. We need to get close and finish them."

"Right. We can't let any of them get away," Big Mike said. "Not after what they did to that village."

And for the damage they might do to Pranjani. I took one last look through the binoculars. The Ustaše were still tightly packed, and I could see them gesture to one another. One of them must've spoke English, because Flint kept turning and making gestures, like he was part of the conversation.

"Whenever you're ready," I whispered. I sighted down my Thompson and targeted the last man in the group. Flint was now slightly in front, maybe eighty yards away.

Big Mike fired his M1. I squeezed the trigger. I saw a black uniform go down as Big Mike fired again. One rider pulled on his reins to turn around, but I caught him with a long burst. I dropped the empty clip and ran another in, leaping out from behind the tree and to the road. Flint was down, and three other bodies lay in or near the road.

One horse was dead. I felt bad about that.

"We got 'em," Big Mike said as he jogged beside me.

"Check the bodies," I said as I made for Flint. He lay face down, the exit wound on his back marked where Big Mike had hit him dead center. I kicked him with my boot to make sure he wasn't still with us and felt nothing but inert flesh. I rolled his body over.

It wasn't Amos Flint.

CHAPTER THIRTY-TWO

"Check the other bodies! This isn't Flint," I shouted to Big Mike. The face that stared at me with vacant eyes was dark hued with a bushy beard. A Ustaše in Flint's clothing, right down to the boots.

I ran to the side of the road where Big Mike stood near two corpses and the dead horse. One horse pranced nervously, holding its head high as it backed away from the bodies in the blood-soaked street. I glanced at the two men. Neither was Flint.

"In there," Big Mike mouthed, pointing with his M1 to the trees. I looked up and down the lane, not wanting to be surprised by reinforcements. All I saw was a couple of men advancing across the fields on the other side of the road. They had shotguns.

While I watched for movement in the trees, I spotted drops of blood on the ground. I knew all four men had been hit, but this one had crawled away.

Flint.

I fired a burst high into the trees, mostly for the benefit of the two fellows bearing down on us with shotguns. Buckshot didn't count for much against .45 slugs, and they wisely halted.

"Come out!" I shouted. "Flint, I know it's you."

Nothing.

"Fine with me if he bleeds to death," Big Mike said in his booming voice.

"Toss in a grenade," I said. My eyes flitted between the gents in the field and where Flint hid in the trees. "Make it two."

"No! Wait, I'm hurt. Bad." It was Flint. He moaned from his hiding place behind the thick pine branches. I was tempted to put an end to him right then and there, but I needed to know if he'd blabbed about Pranjani to anyone who wasn't sprawled dead in the road.

"Come out," I shouted. "Hands up."

"I can't. They tied my hands, and I'm hit," Flint said. I heard the quiver in his voice. Was it a ruse, or was he bleeding to death?

"Stay where you are," I said. I looked to Big Mike and shot a glance at the men in the field. Another guy had joined them, and I wanted to be sure Big Mike was covering me and watching our backs.

"Be careful," he said, and nodded his understanding.

I stepped forward, suppressing a bitter laugh at the notion of being careful while surrounded by bloodthirsty fascists and going in to drag a homicidal killer out of his hiding place.

I moved slowly, following the blood trail. As I approached the first small trees, I saw scuff marks on the ground where he'd crawled to cover. Blood had pooled there, and I figured he must have stopped for a moment to gather his strength, if not his wits, then worked his way deeper into the trees. I squatted in front of the first large pine I came to and pushed aside a low-hanging branch with the snout of my Thompson. Flint's crawl was evident by the gouges his feet and knees had made in the carpet of fallen needles, but it was too dark and dense to see beyond a few feet.

I went in on my knees. As I pushed aside the drooping branches, I thought I might find Flint huddled underneath, but I was alone. I moved around the thick trunk and through the next layer of branches. One snapped as I held it back.

I froze. My eyes darted across the gloom in front of me.

Nothing. No moans, no cries for help. I pushed aside another branch and crawled out from under the tree, still on my knees. As I steadied myself with one hand on the ground, I strained to hear the rustle of movement ahead.

"He's got a knife!" Big Mike shouted.

I swiveled my head, searching for the threat. I felt my heart pound as I tried to stand, the thick branches snarled in my webbing.

A form flew from the trees, a blur of black with a blade aimed straight at me. I swung the butt of the Thompson, instinct taking over, and slammed the hands that held the knife. Hands bound with thick rope. Flint howled in pain and tumbled against me, both of us going down in a tangle of flailing limbs. He worked to get upright as I held the Thompson sideways in front of me, pressing against his wrists as he thrust at my face, the knife tightly clasped between his hands. His mouth was set in a grimace, a guttural growl stuck deep in his throat. He pulled the knife back to have a go at a different angle, but I thrust upward with both hands and rammed the gun's receiver against his jaw. His head snapped back, and his hands shook, which gave me a chance to swing the Thompson and whack him on the side of the head.

Flint collapsed. I pushed him to the side and grabbed the knife.

"You okay in there?" Big Mike yelled.

"Yeah," I gasped. "Hang on."

I patted Flint down. Carefully, in case he was playacting. Again. He was clean, and I dragged him through the trees by his bound hands, paying no special attention to sharp sticks and rocks.

"Is he dead?" Big Mike asked as I emerged from the woods and pulled Flint to the edge of the road.

"No. Thanks for the heads-up about the knife," I said, and

handed him the blade. As I looked around, I realized our crowd of onlookers had grown and moved closer.

"I saw the empty sheath on this guy's belt," he said. The nearest corpse wore a leather belt around his black coat, a pistol still in its holster. "I guess Flint only had time to grab the knife."

"It would've taken some time to cut through that rope, but he could've done it," I said. "I'd winged his arm, probably slowed him down. Any idea what the locals want?" There were now six men and two women, all stout and dressed in muddy clothes. Farmers, by the look of them.

"I'd guess the horses," Big Mike said. "But they don't seem angry, like they would be if they were fans of these Black Legion bums." The three mounts were huddled at the other side of the road, away from the bodies, nibbling at what little forage there was. I took the knife back from Big Mike and strolled over to the gathering, my Thompson slung. Just a friendly visit with the neighbors. I went face-to-face with an older woman, her gray hair sticking out from under her headscarf.

"Good day." I bowed to her, knowing the value of showing respect. "I am sorry to have made so much noise. But we had to stop these men. Ustaše," I said, and pointed to the three dead men. I knew they wouldn't understand the words, but I hoped they'd get the basic idea. Unless those were their cousins out there.

"Ustaše," the woman spat. She lifted both hands as if she were holding a rifle and made shooting sounds. *Tat-tat-tat-tat.* "Dobro."

"Good," I said. It was one of the few words I knew. "Dobro."

Everyone laughed, smiled, and agreed dead Ustaše was a good thing. Dobro. I handed the knife to the guy with the biggest beard, pointed to the dead horse, and beckoned them all to join us. With hand gestures I relayed that we needed the three horses, but that they were free to take whatever they could from the bodies as well as butcher the horse. Food on the table and feed for the pigs, if any were left after four years of war and occupation. No one seemed to disagree, and the old lady gave orders that sent two men hustling back to the nearest house.

"They're not fans of the Black Legion," I said to Big Mike. "I think they weren't too certain of us either, but now we're dobro. Flint showing any sign of life?"

"No, but he's probably faking," Big Mike said, his M1 pointed at Flint's prone body.

"I dunno, I gave him a good whack," I said. I took out my canteen, unscrewed the cap, and poured it onto his face. Flint's eyes opened and he surveyed the two of us calmly. He hadn't met Big Mike face-to-face back in Anzio, so he reserved his attentions all for me.

"Billy Boyle, I do believe," Flint said. He blinked away the water from his eyes and sat up, his hands around his knees as if we were about to catch up on old times. His sky-blue eyes were just as I remembered, along with his strong chin, now covered by a brown beard. "It's been a while."

"You mean since you tried to kill me a few minutes ago?"

"Oh, that? Come on, Lieutenant—no, it's Captain now, I see—that wasn't personal," Flint said. His smile was apologetic, the perfect imitation of a man truly sorry for his transgressions. "Tell me, how's Danny? Did he recover from that gunshot?"

I couldn't help but look at Big Mike. I'd never told anyone what really happened when I'd caught up to Flint, and as far as Big Mike or anyone else knew, it was a shrapnel wound that had put Private Danny Boyle on a hospital ship home. I looked away, but not before I saw the confusion on Big Mike's face.

"Oh. I didn't know," Flint said. "Sorry, Billy. You know I had no quarrel with your kid brother. He was the kind of guy I was trying to help."

"By killing officers," Big Mike said.

"Who gets more guys killed? The Germans or our own brass, huh? Some days it's hard to tell," Flint said. "You know I'm right. By the way, thanks for saving my life. Those Ustaše guys are real maniacs. Did you see what they did in that village? Now *that's* insanity. Any chance I could get some sulfa and a bandage on this? And maybe my flight jacket back? This black coat stinks."

"Your leather jacket has two big bloody holes in it," Big Mike said. "In and out. Just too bad you weren't wearing it when I pulled the trigger."

"Billy, your companion is extremely disagreeable. If we're going to hit the road together, we might as well have a civilized conversation while we head back to—well, you know where," Flint said, casting a suspicious glance at the folks busy butchering the horse's carcass. "Mind if I stand?"

"I do. Stay where you are," I said. I turned away and whispered to Big Mike, telling him to ignore Flint. He was a manipulator, and words were one of his weapons. Grim-faced, he nodded his understanding.

As I sought out the old lady, I spotted the two guys she'd sent packing on their way back. They each pushed a wheelbarrow and carried a large knife. One held hay and the other buckets of water. They dropped the hay in front of the horses and set a bucket near each one.

"Thank you," I said, and pointed to the horses. She nodded, said something that was probably *thank you*, and gestured to the dead Ustaše, now relieved of anything useful. I performed more pantomime and managed to communicate that I needed rope. She called out again to one of the men, who trotted off to do her bidding.

I tried to ask about sightings of more Ustaše in the area, but it was too much to get across in gestures and we gave up.

Meanwhile, the wheelbarrows began hauling cuts of horse-meat away, the guys with the big knives working expertly, ankle-deep in blood and gore. The old woman pointed to the meat, then us, and made an eating motion. I shook my head and crooked a thumb in the direction of Flint, then to the road south, telling her we had to go. But I did wonder what horse steaks would taste like. She patted my arm. Probably told me I didn't know what I was missing.

"Think we can get the horses back up on the trail?" I asked Big Mike, not telling him I'd turned down an invite to a barbeque.

"Yeah, we can lead them around the fallen tree," he said. "But we gotta hang on to Flint at the same time."

"We will. Now let's get him patched up and then we'll move out." I didn't care much about Flint being in pain, but I didn't want him passing out before we had a chance to interrogate him. And preferably not out in the open.

"Thanks, guys," Flint said when he saw me kneel and pull a medical kit out of my pack. He made it sound like we were squad mates and we'd come to his rescue. He held up his bound hands. "If you cut through this rope, I can get the coat off."

"No need," I said. I took the scissors and cut through the blood-soaked cloth and wool shirt underneath. A slug had grazed his upper arm, leaving a deep gouge that still dripped blood. I cut away more fabric and rinsed the wound with water to see how bad it was. Flint gasped and I almost said I was sorry. I sprinkled it with sulfa powder and pressed a dressing against it, then wrapped the arm with a gauze bandage. "That ought to stop the bleeding. Now get up."

Big Mike gave Flint an assist and grabbed his collar and hoisted him up. One of the farmers handed me a length of rope, and I tied a noose around Flint's neck, pulling it tight and resisting the temptation to play the hangman.

"Hey, I can hardly breath," he said.

"Relax and you'll be fine," I said, and pulled on the rope. I waved to the old woman as she cheerfully supervised the slaughtering. She gave me a gap-toothed grin and returned to the job. We led the horses off and headed back to our ambush site. Big Mike led two horses, and I fell in behind with the third horse, and Flint on a short leash in front of me. Folks waved at us, cursed the black-coated Flint, then quickly returned to their work. Bodies were dragged off, probably for a quick burial before any more Ustaše passed through.

The horses followed Big Mike around the fallen pine and up the hidden deer trail until we reached the logging road. I had to yank the rope on Flint a few times to keep him moving. I had no idea what he was planning, but I knew he had to be figuring the angles. A guy like Flint would never go meekly.

"Which way now?" Flint asked. "Up to Virovac or back to Pranjani? Those three planeloads must have made it out by now, right? Lucky stiffs."

"Where's the map?" I asked. I'd been so focused on capturing Flint and then getting out of there that I hadn't thought of Rudy's map. It was a trail of breadcrumbs leading back to the secret Chetnik airfield.

"Don't worry, Billy, it's safe. I wouldn't let those animals get their hands on it. I want to get to Italy too, remember," Flint answered. "It's in my back pocket."

Big Mike turned him around and pulled out the folded map, complete with Sanja's markings.

"Whaddya know, he was telling the truth," Big Mike said.

"Of course I did," Flint said. He straightened his shoulders as if upset by the insinuation. "Why wouldn't I?"

"Yeah you would, if it serves your interest," I said. "Now let's move. I don't like being this close to the road. Any one of those farmers could sell us out."

"It's been hardly a year since I last saw you, Billy. Look how cynical you've become," Flint said. He shook his head slowly, in mock sadness.

"It's been a tough year," I said. I looked to Big Mike and nodded in the direction of Virovac. "Let's walk and find a nice place to chat."

Our procession walked single file, me bringing up the rear again, as I held the reins to the light gray mare and the rope around Flint's neck. I had to figure a way to get the truth out of him and be sure he hadn't tipped his hand to the Ustaše. It didn't seem like he had, given that the map was still in his possession. But I wondered why they'd take him alive. A bounty paid by the Germans, perhaps?

Sanja and her friends might have the answer to that. So now all I wanted was a secluded spot to wait for her. And to interrogate Flint. But even he couldn't answer the two most pressing questions.

How many Germans, Partisans, and Ustaše were there between us and Pranjani, and would we make it back in time?

CHAPTER THIRTY-THREE

HALF A MILE on we found a clearing where cut logs waited to be pulled out of the forest. Big Mike tethered the horses, and I tied Flint's noose to a branch, then sat him on a log where I could keep my eye on him. I checked the saddlebags on the light gray mare and was rewarded with a loaf of brown bread and a bottle of slivovitz in one. The other held a change of clothes, courtesy of the Chetnik officer in Pranjani. The clothing he'd get back.

"Anything in those?" I asked when Big Mike finished with the bags on the Ustaše horses. He shook his head.

"Nothing but dirty drawers and extra ammo," Big Mike said. "Plus some light reading material, courtesy of the Krauts." He tossed a couple of booklets entitled *Islam und Judentum* on the ground. As if the Ustaše needed any assistance from propaganda when it came to hate. He emptied the rest of the contents onto the ground, collected the ammo, and left the clothing, including gray brimless felt caps with a skull and crossbones embroidered on the front. Charming.

I sat on a log across from Flint, tore off a piece of bread, and gave it to him. "Tell us what happened," I said.

"When?" he asked.

"When the Black Legion captured you," I said. I had other

questions as well, but they could wait. There were things I needed to know right now. "Just stick to the facts."

"I took my time at Planinica," he said. "I watched you two and Sanja almost get nabbed, and I didn't want to get surprised like that. After the truck convoy passed through a second time, I figured the coast was clear, so I headed down. The village was a mess, but you know that. I figured Sanja knew all the shortcuts and would stay off the main roads, but I didn't have a choice. I almost turned around and gave up outside Berkovac."

"Why didn't you?" I asked.

"Because I made a promise to you, Billy. Don't you remember? Didn't Danny tell you?"

"I'm hazy when it comes to Anzio. Remind me," I said. It wasn't a subject I wanted to get into, but I had to let Flint have his say or else we'd never move on.

"That there would be a joker waiting for you. Downriver," Flint said. "You're the wild card, Billy, and here we are. Down the river and not a paddle between us. This had to happen."

"But not exactly as you'd planned," I said. "I'm not dead and your cover's blown."

"It's all a matter of perspective," Flint said. He bit into the bread and chewed. "But you're right. I'm not dead, which is always a plus in my book. And tell me, when did you figure out it was me? You weren't surprised to see me, not one bit." Flint leaned forward, his eyes drilling into mine.

"Playing the rogue German was a little over-the-top," I said. "It was obvious who those shots at Sanja's house were meant for. Why would a single Kraut, separated from his unit, go after me?"

"No, Billy, I don't believe you. It was out here when I was hunting you, wasn't it? Did you spot me? That must have started the wheels turning," Flint said, and laughed with an almost childlike delight.

"It wasn't any one thing," I said. That was true enough. It was all the little things, starting with Big Mike's question about having an enemy out here and finding no shell casings. When I'd found the queen of hearts amid so much blood, something started percolating in my mind. Then when I'd spotted the guy following us, I subconsciously recognized his size and stature. That's when I knew. Maybe it was because I remembered what Flint had said about getting back at me downriver. Or maybe it was because Flint had never been far from my mind since I'd let him get away at Anzio.

"But who back at Pranjani knows, that's the question," Flint said. "I say no one. We're a long way from home, boys. Anything can happen."

"Like a bullet in the head," Big Mike said.

"You won't."

"How do you know?" Big Mike asked.

"Because you didn't," Flint answered. He popped the rest of the bread into his mouth and chewed slowly. He gulped and wiped his lips. "And because you still haven't."

"You're right," I said. "We haven't killed you yet. Let's go back to how the Black Legion boys got a hold of you." I felt Big Mike's anger, which was exactly what Flint was trying to brew up. An explosion that he could exploit. He'd done the same with me, sensing that no one back at the airfield knew he wasn't really Lieutenant Ripper.

Always play the percentages.

"Okay. I was trying to make good time and get to Virovac ahead of you. I gambled and took the main road. Bad luck to run into those three when I did," Flint said. "They were behind a farmhouse. One walked out, his rifle on me, while the other two rode and blocked the way. They pushed me around a bit, took my jacket, cap, and boots, and gave me this crap." He lifted one leg to show the sole half off a well-worn shoe.

"What did you tell them?" I asked.

"There wasn't anything to tell," he said. "None of them spoke English. But they kept saying *Nemci*, their word for *German*. I figured they were going to turn me in for a reward, since they were in high spirits and hadn't slit my throat. There was no other reason for them to let me live."

"You would have fit right in with those monsters," Big Mike said, his teeth gritted. I willed him to ease off. I didn't want to say anything that would give Flint the satisfaction of knowing he'd driven a wedge between us, no matter how small.

"With those animals?" Flint said, and pointed to the death's-head cap and German propaganda. His head reared back as if he were about to strike. Instead, he shuddered. "Indiscriminate killing never held any appeal for me. What meaning is there in butchering a village of women, children, and old men? Nothing but terror. Terror is easy. The Nazis do it, we do it when we burn cities, officers on both sides do it when they send men to their deaths. They all lack finesse." The word came off his lips like the hiss of a snake.

"I'll show you finesse," Big Mike said as he stood with his M1 leveled at Flint's chest.

"No, you want to show me *terror*," Flint said. A grin lit up his face as he leaned back to stare up at Big Mike. "You want me to beg and scream, just like the Ustaše made those villagers cry for mercy. Don't you?"

"Sit down," I said to Big Mike, my tone light and casual. "He's just flapping his gums. Anyway, it's not time for him to die. Not right now."

"Not right now," Big Mike agreed. He sat down heavily, his exhaustion showing. "Not right now." We sat quietly. I was waiting for Big Mike to calm down and focus. As I glanced his way, my eyes fell on the booklets and the Ustaše cap. I looked away quickly, not wanting to betray my rapidly forming thoughts.

"Here's the thing," I said to Flint. I tried to appear

disinterested in his baiting of Big Mike or what I'd just noticed. "We know you're an artist. We saw that at Anzio. The cards were inspired, and they sure got the brass all in a snit. So you must be smart, right?"

"Coming from you, Billy, I'll take that as a compliment. After all, you're the only one who came close to catching me."

"I *have* caught you," I clarified. "Last time was close, but you have to admit, I've literally got your neck in a noose."

"True enough," Flint said. He gave a shrug and graciously allowed me to continue.

"Here's what I don't understand, then. You've tried to convince us that you haven't spilled the beans about the airstrip to anyone. Doing a pretty good job of it too," I said.

"It's not hard, since it's the truth," Flint said. "And I kept the map safe, didn't I?"

"Yeah, the map. That clinches the deal, doesn't it? So, really, what do we need you for?" I said. For the first time, I thought I saw a flash of fear in Flint's eyes. I tore into the bread again and handed Big Mike his piece. He sat down and we ate. And I watched Flint.

"I thought you'd be glad," Flint said. "The secret of the airfield is safe, and you've got me hog-tied. What more could you want?"

"We'll get to that. First tell me why you killed Shakey," I said, mainly to give me more time to think. It was pretty obvious why Flint had done it.

"He talked too much," Flint said. "Always going on about his B-17 and his crew. He got on my nerves."

"You don't have nerves," I said.

"Ha! Yeah, I don't get nervous in the service, that's true. But I can smell a threat, and Shakey was asking too many questions," Flint said.

"Questions a B-17 pilot ought to be able to answer," I said.

"Exactly. That's when I decided the lone Kraut commando

was going to have his moment on stage. We all carried German potato mashers, so it was easy to sneak up on you during the fight and toss one in. You've got good reactions, Billy. No nerves yourself."

"Then you shot Shakey," I said.

"Yeah. That night. It was quick, he never knew it was coming," Flint said, as if this were a magnanimous gesture. "No reason for him to suffer." I repressed the natural desire to strike out at Flint with words or fists. But neither would accomplish anything.

"You know, these woods are lonely," I said. The gray sky was turning dark, the afternoon's gradual slide into night just beginning. "Cold. This would be a lousy place to die."

"What are you talking about?" Flint demanded. "Aren't we going to Virovac?"

"Why? What's there for you?" I stood and walked behind Flint, untying the rope from the tree. I set my foot on his back and pulled, then let go.

"Nothing, I just thought you were headed there," Flint said. "Take it easy, huh? It's marked on the map. Virovac, where you're meeting up with that Limey."

"How many Ustaše really picked you up?" I pulled the rope again and held it until I heard a choking sound. Flint was entirely too relaxed about this whole situation. He should have been worried, and it worried me that he wasn't. What worried me even more was that the map held two important pieces of information. The village of Pranjani, where we'd started, and Virovac, where we were headed to pick up Johnny Adler. I'd been so focused on the airstrip that I hadn't even considered our destination.

"What did you hear about the Limey?" I asked, and gave another sharp tug. "Tell me everything you know."

"Let me catch my breath," Flint gasped.

"No," I said, and pulled again. It was important to keep him off-balance. "Tell me right now."

"Okay, okay. He's special enough for you to come all the way from England to pick him up, for starters. Scuttlebutt is he's some kind of radar specialist," Flint said. "Just chatter. There's nothing to do but sit around and yammer, so everything gets gone over again and again. No secrets in Pranjani, that's for sure. And those Black Legion savages don't give a damn about radar."

"Who else picked you up!" I demanded. I knew Flint was too smart to give up the airstrip, not when there was a chance in hell of him getting out. But Johnny Adler at Virovac? That would buy him plenty with the Germans. "Ustaše? Or were they Krauts? Who did you tell about Virovac?"

Big Mike fired his M1, right between Flint's legs as he sat on the log. It scared the hell outta me, and it did the same for Flint.

"It was the SS," he gasped.

CHAPTER THIRTY-FOUR

HOOFBEATS THUNDERED DOWN the trail as Flint's confession hung in the air. Big Mike raised his M1, ready to meet the threat. I hurried to tie the rope to the branch, but Flint must've felt my grip loosen.

He bolted and leapt over the log where I'd been sitting. He darted into the woods as Big Mike and I knelt behind the log, weapons aimed at the trail. The thunder of galloping horses shook the ground, and, in seconds, Sanja burst into the clearing, pulled on the reins, and wheeled her mount to a halt. Two men, both with riderless horses in tow, followed. Guns were quickly drawn, and it took only a few words from Sanja to have them pointed away from us.

"Flint!" I shouted, and Mike and I took off into the woods, barely registering the look of surprise on Sanja's face. First she'd heard a gunshot, then came hell bent for leather to our rescue, only to find us here, unexpectedly, with three horses, then witness our sprint into the forest.

Big Mike was by my side, and I signaled him to go left, where ten yards away a stone cliff face dripped water. I knew Flint couldn't scamper straight up that, so I stayed close to the trail, figuring he'd veer out into the path to make better time. Bushwhacking is hard, worse than hard if your hands are bound. I thrust my way between trees, watching for what lay ahead while keeping an eye out for glimpses of the trail on my right.

Nothing. All I heard was Big Mike barreling through the pines and the sound of my own gasping breath. I jumped over a moss-encrusted log and skidded to a halt, listening for anything other than Big Mike's footfalls. I moved around a thick pine, slowly now, since Flint had only a few seconds on us.

A shadow passed before me, and something pressed against my neck as I was yanked backward. Roughness tightened around my neck, and I lost my grip on the Thompson.

Rope. My hands clawed at the figure behind me. I wanted to scream but all that came out was a choking gasp. I tried to dig my fingers under the rope, but it was impossible. I stomped my feet, aiming for Flint's shins, but he danced around my bootheels easily.

"Relax, Billy," he hissed into my ear. "Just float downriver, it's easy."

I had to get at him or the rope, and I didn't have long. His grip was strong. I tried to take a step, as if I were running away. His hands tightened as he leaned forward to pull me back.

Which was when I scuttled back and dug in my heels to put everything I had into it. Flint was a fraction off-balance, just enough to make him waggle his arms to regain his hold. But I continued to plow backward and forced him into the pine. The branches broke and snapped, making enough noise to catch Big Mike's attention.

I rammed Flint back into the tree trunk, heard him grunt, and felt the rope loosen. I tried to call out. My voice came out in a low rasp, a strained and nearly silent cry for help. I worked one finger under the rope and felt my lungs draw air, but Flint pulled harder. He was trying to get to my .45 automatic, and I had only a second before he reached it. I threw myself forward, and flipped Flint over my shoulder. With the rope still around my neck, I went down next to him and scrambled to draw my pistol.

It wasn't there. Flint didn't have it, but at the same moment we both looked at my Thompson, five yards away on the ground. I grabbed the rope, still loosely wound around my neck, and pulled. His noose was still tight, and I heard him gag as I loosened mine and crawled to my tommy gun.

"Billy?" Big Mike shouted. "Where are you?"

"Here," I gasped weakly, spinning around with the Thompson in hand.

Flint was gone.

"Here!" I tried again, and rose, working to sense which way Flint had gone. Big Mike shouldered his way through the pines, picked me up with one hand, and handed over my .45 with the other.

"Where's Flint?" he asked.

"The trail, maybe?" I said as I rubbed my throat. Then, the sound of hoofbeats. I followed Big Mike, worried that Flint might attack Sanja and steal her horse. He was adept at using whatever he had handy as a weapon. I heard the skitter of stones on the trail, a thump, and a high-pitched whinny. I feared the worst as I tumbled onto the path, Big Mike close behind.

"We ran into Ripper," Sanja said with a grin. She gave her mare's neck a pat and looked at the body on the trail. "Flint, I mean."

"Nice work," I said. "He almost got away."

"He is still breathing," Sanja pointed out. "Do you want him alive?"

"We need him alive," I said. "And we need to talk."

Big Mike roused Flint with a good kick to the ribs and got him vertical. We both checked the knots to be sure he hadn't tampered with them and then led him back up the trail to the clearing. Flint was quiet. Perhaps stunned, perhaps plotting.

"Where did you get the horses?" Sanja asked as she dismounted and eyed the light gray mare. "I know this one."

"First, you need to warn the people in Virovac," I said. "The Germans are headed their way, probably SS and some Black Legion Ustaše."

"You are sure of this?" she asked. I told her I was certain. She spoke quickly to one of the men. He jumped on his horse and rode out to give the warning. The other fellow made Flint sit on the ground and stood behind him, a pistol in one hand and the rope in another. Flint's eyes had a dull sheen, and he was strangely silent. Maybe he was biding his time, but I hoped the fight was out of him. For now.

We sat and I filled in Sanja on our ambush of the Ustaše horsemen, how one of them had been wearing Flint's clothes, and our friendly relations with the farmers from the other side of the road.

"They were happy to see the Ustaše dead and have a horse to butcher," I said. "Not to mention stripping the dead."

"A bounty in these bad times," she said. "Why did Flint tell you of the SS?"

"I knew he was holding something back," I said. "Big Mike put a round between his legs to loosen his tongue."

"Right there," Big Mike said, pointing to a bullet hole in the log where Flint had been sitting, his legs splayed wide. "He didn't need any further convincing."

"Well done," Sanja said, with a brief smile and a glance at Flint before inclining her head in the direction of one of the horsemen. "Gricko can use his knife instead of wasting a bullet if he needs more convincing. Now, tell me. How badly has he betrayed us?"

I told her I didn't think he'd said anything about Pranjani. It wasn't in his own self-interest. But he had told the Germans about someone important being picked up by Americans in Virovac. My guess was the SS wanted him alive to confirm his story and identify us, so they'd had the Ustaše mounted troops bring him close to the village while they organized an attack.

"We may have a little time," Sanja said. "The Germans patrol often, but not in large numbers. Not enough to attack the village if they believe our fighters are there."

"How long, if they picked up Flint earlier today?" I asked.

"Tonight, maybe. Or the morning. The Germans like to see what they kill," she said.

"Is Johnny Adler in Virovac?" I asked. It was time to focus on why we were here.

"Yes. He is safe. Another POW is with him," Sanja said. "They are both exhausted and hungry. I thought it best to allow them to rest tonight."

"Let's go," I said. "With any luck, we can get them out before the Germans surround the place."

"Is that all you care about? It is your fault the village is in danger. This man wished you harm, and now the people in Virovac will suffer," Sanja said as she cast a venomous glance at Flint. "If not for him, and you, there would be no danger."

"She's got a point, Billy," Big Mike said.

"Adler is important," I said. "For the war effort. We don't want the Germans to catch him, and we need information only he has."

"Virovac is important," Sanja said. "It is why we fight. To protect our people."

Both things were true. But if Sanja stayed to fight, we'd never get back to Pranjani on our own. We needed her.

"How many people in Virovac?" I asked. "Can they be evacuated?"

"Two hundred, I think. Some are old, others children. It would be very hard with so little time," she said. "We must go now."

"Let me go," Flint said.

"He is useless," Sanja said, without bothering to look at Flint. "Gricko can cut his throat and we will be done with him."

"Let me go," Flint repeated. He appeared livelier now, perhaps because he had a scheme to pitch. "I'll tell the Germans whatever you want. Like a column of Tito's Partisans hit us and I managed to escape. I've got the wound to prove it. And I'll say you two were with them, and you already had Adler in tow. That'll take the heat off Virovac, right?"

"Great story," Big Mike said. "Too bad you can't be trusted to deliver it."

Sanja drew a finger across her neck and held my gaze.

"Not yet," I said. I wouldn't have minded not having Flint to drag around, but dead, he was worth nothing. Alive, there was a chance he could serve a purpose. If not, Gricko looked ready and willing to solve that little problem. "Let's get to Virovac and lend a hand."

We mounted. Gricko tied the end of Flint's necktie around his wrist and rode beside him. Sanja led the way and Big Mike kept one eye on our rear. I glanced at Flint a few times and saw his eyes dart around, looking for any way out. He'd snapped out of whatever shock he'd endured from Sanja's horse barreling into him. If it hadn't been an act.

"How many fighters are at the village?" I asked Sanja as I brought my horse close to hers.

"Ten," she said. "But we have the radio and will call for more."

"I hope a lot more. We need to be back the day after tomorrow. Early, for the last flight out," I reminded her.

"If we live, we shall ride all night. There will be enough time," Sanja said.

If we lived. Not always a certainty, especially in these parts. Not if Flint, the SS, or the Black Legion had anything to say about it.

CHAPTER THIRTY-FIVE

THE TERRAIN GREW gradually steeper until we came out from the forest trail and onto a plateau overlooking gently sloping fields. It was strange being out in the open after being under the cover of the pines, and I kept swiveling my head, searching out potential threats. But soon the well-trodden path descended lower, and we didn't stand out for all to see as we had when we rode along the highest point.

"Here," Sanja said. She halted her horse and dismounted. Big Mike and I followed suit while Gricko kept Flint on his short leash. She took a few steps to the high ground and pointed to the village below. "Virovac."

In the fading light, I could see rooftops spread out in a narrow valley below. One road came in from the south, a narrow S-bend where a bridge led to what looked like a mill. At the north end of the valley, the road ascended a steep hill and disappeared into the woods. On the far side of the valley floor, a river churned over jumbled rocks.

"Not a bad defensive position," Big Mike said. "Narrow entry and exit points, and a river on the flank."

"Yes, and we have the high ground here," Sanja said. She pointed downhill from where we stood. "These are grazing lands. Open except for trees and stone walls. If the Germans mean to surprise us, they will come this way."

"Or if they have tanks, they come straight in down there," I said. The Chetniks didn't have much in the way of anti-tank weapons, but on the winding road any armored vehicle would be vulnerable.

"They could draw our attention down there," Big Mike said. "Distract us as they sneak over this ridge and hit us from behind."

"It would be a good plan," Sanja said. "If they have no tanks, they will send Ustaše to attack the mill crossing. Then the SS will come down from here while we are busy killing the Croats."

"It seems quiet," I said. Parts of the valley were already in deep shade as the sun dipped lower to the horizon. "Wouldn't we hear something if the Krauts were close?"

"Tanks we would hear. Men walking through the forest, no," Sanja said. As she shielded her eyes against the rays of the setting sun, I wondered who might be hidden in the trees below, watching us and waiting for darkness. "I told Tomas to radio for reinforcements. They may already be on their way."

"Looks like we beat the Krauts," Big Mike said.

"I hope so," she said. "And I hope our men get here soon. Now come meet your Johnny Adler."

About damn time. It was only a few days ago at St. Margaret's at Cliffe that Sally had told us that Johnny knew the secret behind the stolen equipment. It felt like months, and here, deep in Yugoslavia, the concept of electronic warfare seemed like something out of a *Buck Rogers* comic strip. Finding Johnny had never been a sure thing, and now that he was only minutes away, I was having a hard time grasping it was really going to happen.

We rode downhill through fields to the road that ran along the valley floor. There wasn't any center to this village, just houses with tile roofs and curling smoke rising from the chimneys dotting the landscape. We headed to one of the larger houses, close to the mill by the river. A sturdy barn stood to the rear, the lowing of cows telling me Virovac had avoided the worst of what had befallen other villages.

Men spilled out of the house, followed by two young boys and a girl who took the reins of our horses. I dismounted and looked for a guy in RAF flight clothes while Sanja spoke with one of Chetniks. As the kids led the mounts to the barn, I spotted him. Fleece-lined leather jacket, heavy sweater, blue wool pants, and sensible hiking shoes.

"Are you Flight Sergeant Johnny Adler?"

"That's me, Captain. You've come a long way, haven't you?" Adler spoke the King's English with only a faint hint of his childhood tongue. He had dark wavy hair, a scruffy beard, good looks, and a ready smile.

"All the way from RAF Hawkinge, Johnny," I said. "I'm Captain Billy Boyle and we've been through hell and high water looking for you. We need to talk."

"Talk is fine, Captain, but don't we need to get a move on?" Johnny asked. "The Nazis are headed our way. I hear you're my personal escort, so isn't it time to escort me the bloody hell out of here?"

"Our departure is delayed," Big Mike said. "Now let's chat inside. Got any grub around here?"

"I'm not moving until you explain yourself, sir," Johnny said, his eyes locked on mine. "What do you know about the base at Hawkinge?"

"Enough to know you have valuable information in that head of yours," I said. "About radios and thefts at the air base."

"All right," Johnny said. "You've got me curious enough. But let's put some miles between us and the Nazis first. You know what they say about curiosity and the cat."

"We've got Germans and Ustaše all over the place, Johnny," I told him. "We can't head out until the coast is clear. Sorry."

Johnny was clearly disappointed at the news but gestured for us to follow him into the house.

"I've got to check on Flint, I'll just be a minute," I said. Behind us, Flint complained loudly as Gricko, none too gently, pulled him out of the saddle.

"That's one of yours?" Johnny asked. "Why's he dressed up like a Ustaše?"

"He's in custody," I said. "The Black Legion grabbed him, swiped his uniform, and left him that getup. We're bringing him back to stand trial."

"You're busy chaps. I'm sure our Chetnik friends could circumvent the need for a trial," Johnny said. "I have to say, I was surprised to see anyone wearing that black jacket alive in this village, even tied up."

"The offer has been made," I said. "I'll join you in a few minutes."

Gricko hauled Flint into the barn, his grip tight on the rope. Flint grimaced and looked at me, as if I might care to intervene. I followed and found Sanja still engrossed in conversation with one of the fighters as the kids rubbed down the horses.

"Do you have a safe place to keep him?" I asked as Gricko led Flint up steep wooden steps.

"Yes. Tomas has a room for special guests," Sanja said, and introduced us.

"Good room," Tomas said. "No leave."

"You speak English? Very good," I said, then waited to see if there was more.

"I learn from British. They go. Now I learn from Americans. But they go too, yes?"

"We're here," I said, for what it was worth. "Can I see the room?"

"Come, come," Tomas said, eager to show off his special accommodations. We took the steps to a level high above the main floor. At the far end, bales of hay were stacked. Closer to the stairs, two doors stood open. The first room held old barrels, rusted tools, a wooden chest, and the usual dusty debris gathered over decades. In the next, bales of hay were stored up against the wall. Gricko was busy securing manacles on Flint's wrists. The iron handcuffs looked a couple of centuries old.

"Are you handing me over to these people?" Flint asked. I wasn't sure if that was what he wanted or not. I also wanted to remind him he'd just tried to kill me, and I might not be up for polite chatter. But I knew it would be meaningless.

"For temporary safekeeping," I said. Gricko moved a hay bale away from the wall and exposed a U-shaped iron bar with both ends bolted to the wood. He ran the chain through that, then connected the links to the cuffs. He pushed the bale back in place, shoved Flint down on it, and produced a knife from his belt. I enjoyed seeing Flint's eyes widen, even if all Gricko did was cut away the knotted cords around Flint's wrists. He loosened the noose and pulled the rope away from Flint's neck, quickly, leaving a line of torn, bleeding skin. Gricko laughed, and Flint spat in his face. Tomas spoke to Gricko sharply and pointed to the door.

"Room is good," Tomas said as Gricko left. "Hay for sleeping. Chains keep him. We lock door, guard outside."

"He will try to trick you," I said, and watched Tomas to be sure he understood. He nodded and Gricko returned with two buckets. One filled with water, the other empty. He set them down within reach of Flint and tossed a small loaf of bread on the floor.

"We'll leave tomorrow, after the Germans are dealt with," I said.

"I could still help," Flint said. "Remember that. I have a plan."

"The only plan you have is to remember which pot to piss in," I said, then turned to leave.

"I always have a plan, you ought to know that. And I had one beautiful plan, Billy. To watch you go downriver while I held you in my grasp," Flint said in a whisper. "We were almost there. The joker was in play."

I stopped, thinking of a hundred things to say. But Flint's warped mind wasn't a place I wanted to venture into, so I did the one thing I knew would disappoint him. I showed him my back.

"It is a very good room," I said to Tomas as he locked the door. "You don't use the other room for prisoners?"

"Prisoners, no. No prisoners," he said with a shrug of his shoulders. "We keep bad people here. Talk with them. You understand?" I did. The room was not a long-term accommodation. Tomas took me into the next room, opened the wooden chest, and removed an inset shelf holding moldy work clothes and moth-eaten blankets. He pulled out two burlap bags of grenades. "We need soon, yes?"

"Yes," I said, and wished there was a way to save the villagers from this battle. At the bottom of the chest were two German uniforms, neatly folded. One had SS runes on the collar tab while the other was regular Wehrmacht. There were even boots.

"Officers," Tomas said. "No longer need."

"Interesting," I said. "Do your men wear these?"

"Some speak German very good," he said. "Good enough to fool Ustaše, but not Nemci. You?"

"No, I don't speak German," I said, but I wondered if there was any way to use those Kraut duds. Order the Ustaše to retreat, maybe? I filed it away among all my other half-formed thoughts to let it simmer. I followed Tomas out into what was now full darkness, and we entered the farmhouse.

The main floor was one open room, allowing the warmth of the stove to spread farther. Three fighters were headed out, their rifles slung and curious eyes lingering on me. Did they all hold us responsible for the upcoming onslaught? Hard to blame them if they did.

"Come, eat," Sanja said. An older woman ladled something into a bowl and it looked hot. Big Mike was already digging in, seated next to Sanja. Johnny and another RAF man sat across from them. Tomas lit a cigarette and leaned against the counter.

"Flight Sergeant Nick Stanich," Johnny's pal said, extending his hand.

"Captain Billy Boyle," I said as we shook. "You made it out with Johnny?"

"All the way," Nick said. "As soon as those Mustangs hit the column, I looked at Johnny, and we both knew it was our chance."

"Nick speaks some Serbian, which came in handy," Johnny said. "When they moved us out of the camp, we decided to escape as soon as we could. Didn't fancy our chances in the Reich."

"And Johnny's German came in handy too," Nick said. "Once, we were hidden not ten feet from two Jerries, and I was ready to jump them. But Johnny heard them say they wanted to get back for their supper. Saved their lives, and probably ours too. It would've set off a manhunt."

I congratulated them both on their escape, then turned to Big Mike, who was scraping up the last dregs from his bowl.

"We need to talk with Johnny," I said, then succumbed to hunger and the aroma wafting through the kitchen. "After a few bites, I guess. What do we have?" I sat and smiled at the woman who placed a bowl in front of me and sprinkled a little cheese on top. She held the spoon above the bowl, her eyebrows raised, asking if I wanted more. I didn't know how much there was to go around, so I passed.

"Pura," Sanja said. "It is porridge, made with cornmeal. With feta cheese."

"It's good," Big Mike said as the woman patted his shoulder. His enjoyment of food pleased cooks everywhere. "Flint is secure?"

"Yeah, locked up tight with bread and water," I said, and dug into the pura. Just the thing after coming in from the cold. "So, are more fighters on the way?"

"Five more men came today, before we radioed," Sanja said. "From the south, around Planinica, there are too many German patrols. Perhaps they are among those coming this way. But from other groups, we will have fifty by morning."

"That's good," I said.

"Not if Jerry comes tonight," Johnny said.

"Maybe we should give ourselves up," Nick said. "There's fewer than twenty of us here. We can't defend the village. It'll be a bloodbath."

"We can't let Johnny fall into the hands of the SS," I said.

"Listen, I know he's from Germany, but they didn't punish him for that before," Nick said. I realized Johnny hadn't offered any information about his religion or his role in radar countermeasures. With good reason.

"New orders from Adolf," Big Mike said. "Any former German citizens who attempt to escape from the Fatherland a second time are to be shot." I was impressed with how fast Big Mike had come up with that story.

"Well all right, then," Nick said. "We can't let Johnny be put up against the wall. What's the plan?"

Sanja and Tomas exchanged a few quick words and then she laid out the plan. Two men with a machine gun were situated at the S-bend where the road curved on the way into the village. A second machine gun was set up in the mill, which was a stone structure, providing good cover. The road at the opposite end of the village was lightly defended. Since the river had flooded the road, it was barely passable for vehicles. Three men patrolled the high ground behind the village where we'd ridden in. The rest were held in reserve to respond where needed.

The reserve was us and eight Chetniks. If the Krauts hit us tonight, it would be a massacre.

"Okay," I said, and released a sigh while trying to sound upbeat. "We need to debrief Johnny. Then you, Nick. Procedure."

"There is a room," Tomas said, pointing to the stairs.

"I will show you," Sanja said as she pushed her chair away from the table. "A bedroom where you will sleep."

The door flew open and one of the kids burst in, shouting. Sanja shot her a question and then slammed her fist on the table.

"Flint. He's killed Gricko."

CHAPTER THIRTY-SIX

As I ran to the barn, I realized what must've happened. Flint hadn't spat at Gricko out of anger. It was a plan. He'd told me straight out—he always had a plan. He'd baited his captor, and Gricko had obliged. I drew my pistol and vaulted up the stairs. An anguished cry came from the room where Flint was held. It was one of the boys. The door was wide open, flickering lantern light illuminating the scene.

I moved along the hall, my back pressed against the wood railing. I could hear Flint mutter, almost plead, and as I moved into the open doorway I took in the scene, ready to fire.

Gricko, dead on the floor, blood pooled beneath him. Flint, one hand gripped the boy's wrist, the other held Gricko's knife.

"Welcome to the party, Billy," Flint said. "Take the key. The kid is useless."

"Let him go," I said. The boy held a key, and I could see by the design of the manacles that Flint couldn't reach the lock to free himself. It was set in the center of the iron bar that separated the two wrist shackles.

"You come get the key. Unlock the cuffs, then I let him go," Flint said. "Otherwise, it's all over for him, sad to say."

"Then I'll kill you," I said as I calculated the odds of taking my shot right now.

"And you'll live with the guilt of the kid's death," Flint said.

"For the rest of your days. Such a delicious thought. Just might be worth it. Now take the key. After you toss your weapon in the corner."

I did. There were plenty of guns right behind me, the light and noise in the hall told us both that much. One less wouldn't matter. I slid it to the far corner. I took the key from the boy's trembling hand and tried to ignore the noises from outside the room.

"Let him go," I whispered.

"Unlock the cuffs," Flint countered. The kid looked at me and I did my best imitation of a smile, but I don't know if I convinced either of us. I took hold of the iron bar.

"What does this gain you?" I asked, the key poised above the lock.

"You all spend your whole lives shackled," Flint said, his eyes boring into mine. "To each other, to your churches, to your ridiculous beliefs. You wouldn't understand what even ten seconds freed from these irons means to a man like me."

Flint tightened his grip on the kid and pulled him closer to the tip of the knife. I saw him glance at the pistol, calculating.

I put the key in the lock.

Turned it.

The lock opened, the chain clattered to the floor, and Flint let fly a backhanded slash at my face. I wheeled to the side and one hand grabbed the bar that loosely hung from the cuff on his wrist. I twisted it hard and heard the snap of bone and cartilage.

Flint howled, unleashing an ungodly, sharp shriek of pain. He kicked out, enraged, and sent me flying against the wall. With one arm dangling at an odd angle, he grabbed the cowering boy with his free hand and stumbled toward the door. He dragged him into the hallway where a half-dozen guns were trained on him, and the child as well.

Flint looked at me, his teeth gritted in pain and his eyes on fire with hatred and anger. It was only a split second, but I knew what he was going to do. Haunt me forever.

He ran at the railing and smashed through it, the kid still in his deadly grip. I launched myself, landing hard, and got a hand on the terrified boy's ankle. The railing had broken, but not fully. Flint had one foot in the air and the other braced on the floorboard as he held on to the boy with his good arm. People screamed, but all I heard was the crack of wood as it gave way. I tugged on the boy's leg as the railing broke, and his arm slithered free of Flint's grasp.

Flint fell thirty feet to the hardpack dirt floor. The sound was a cross between a wet thud and a bundle of sticks breaking.

I pulled the boy close. Hands reached out to take him away, to comfort him. I dragged myself by my elbows to the edge, where shattered banisters marked Flint's passage. Below me, Flint, my tormentor, lay on his back, arms and legs at odd angles, his dull eyes focused on nothing.

We were unshackled.

"You okay, Billy?" Big Mike asked as he picked me up.

"What's the kid's name?" I said. Big Mike moved me away from the precipice, and I asked again, catching Sanja's eye.

"Filip," she said. "He is not hurt. Frightened, yes. He told me he tried to help Gricko when he heard him yell."

"He's a brave lad," I said. I rubbed my face, as if it might banish the vision of Flint's last moments. Or erase his words.

"Billy, you sure you're all right?" Big Mike said.

"I'm not hurt," I said, even as I patted myself to be sure. I glanced at Flint again to be certain he was dead. "Let's go back and talk with Johnny. It's time to get what we came for."

We filed by Tomas and another man headed into the room with blankets, about to carry Gricko away. I should have been firmer with Tomas about warning Gricko, who'd underestimated Flint. Gricko's death was my fault. As we walked downstairs, I thought about what Flint had said. If he'd killed Filip, I would've felt the guilt forever. I stopped by his body and had to acknowledge how right he was. It would've shattered me to be responsible for Filip's death. But how different was that from the death and destruction we were about to bring down upon the entire village?

"Billy?" Big Mike said, the concern in his tone evident.

"I'm fine," I said as I held up a hand. "Just thinking."

"I will have the body taken away," Sanja said. By the look in her eye, she thought I was shell-shocked as well.

"Hang on," I said. "When we were back in Pranjani, talking about routes and coming here, did anyone mention Nick, or the two RAF men waiting here?"

"I am not sure," Sanja said. "I think it was all about Johnny Adler. You would not have come otherwise."

"Right. So that's what Flint would have picked up, and what he would have told the SS," I said as I tapped my finger against my lips and thought it through. "So let's give them what they want."

"My English is good, but I do not understand," Sanja said.

"I think I do," Big Mike said. "I'll get Johnny and Nick." He darted out, while Sanja and I stood by quietly as Tomas helped carry Gricko's body down the stairs. Sanja rubbed her jaw, looked at the body, and nodded to herself.

"I see," she said. "You dress him as RAF. This is Johnny Adler, as far as the Germans will know."

"Exactly. I haven't figured out how we'll deliver him yet, but there's got to be a way," I said.

"I understand you have some sort of scheme, Captain Boyle?" Johnny said as he entered.

"I do. I'd like to avoid unnecessary bloodshed," I said. "The scheme starts with one of you donating your uniform."

"What? Which one of us?" Nick demanded.

"Whichever is the better fit for the late Amos Flint," Big Mike said as he gestured to the corpse.

"Odds are the Germans only know about Johnny being here," I said. "Flint gave them what information he had when they nabbed him."

"He gave them a name? Johnny's name?" Nick asked, his eyebrows furrowed as he looked at his fellow escapee. "I'm beginning to think there's more to you than you let on, mate."

"Nothing I want the Nazis to know about, Nick. But it seems that this fellow may have dropped a hint or two. Right piece of work he was, I gather," Johnny said.

"You have no idea. But he is your size, Johnny, so strip," I said.

"Are you sure about this?" Johnny asked. "What am I going to wear?"

"I will get you clothes, do not worry," Sanja said.

"We'll need everything," I said. "Even your identity tags. We want the switch to hold up if the Germans get suspicious and check things out."

"Well, he's not getting my long johns, I'll tell you that much," Johnny said.

We hoisted Flint up and carried him to a workbench set under the stairway. Undressing and dressing a dead man is harder than you'd think, and having him at this height helped. First, we removed the dangling shackles. Then I unbuttoned the double-breasted black coat, and we began to divest Flint of his worldly garments.

"You said he was captured by the SS and told them about Johnny," Sanja said. I nodded. "It is possible the same SS officer will return here. He might recognize the man he spoke with."

"You're right," I said. I stopped to study Flint's features. His hair was long and his beard was catching up to it. "Shave and a haircut ought to do the trick."

We kept at the disrobing until Sanja returned. She'd decided against a clean shave since it would make sense for any escaped prisoner to have some beard growth. She snipped away at Flint's facial hair until it was a uniform length, more or less. Then a trim around the ears and some off the top. Johnny pulled his leather flying cap out of his pocket and fitted it on Flint's head.

"There. Different chap entirely," Nick said.

"And the cap's got my name written on the label, there's a plus," Johnny added as Filip entered the barn, his arms laden with garments. "Thanks, lad."

Filip smiled as he set down the clothing. His eyes avoided the spectacle of Flint's transformation.

"These are his brother's," Sanja said. "The Germans killed him. He is glad to help and says it will be like his brother striking back from the grave."

"Tell him I am honored," Johnny said, coming to attention and offering a salute. As Sanja spoke, Filip returned the salute, his lip quivering as he verged on a sob. He ran outside to do his crying in private.

"There is a sheet," Sanja said. She whirled her finger around. "To cover him."

"A shroud," I said, and she nodded.

"'Nothing in his life became him like the leaving it,'" Johnny said.

"Eh?" Nick said.

"*Macbeth*," Johnny said. "You know, Shakespeare. The bloke who also wrote 'the apparel oft proclaims the man.' Let's hope he knew what he was talking about."

Johnny removed the identity disks from around his neck and placed them on Flint, then stripped down to his long johns. We finished with Flint as Johnny dressed. He donned a wool jacket over a heavy sweater. Filip's big brother was a fair fit for Johnny, and the only problem was with Flint's shoes. The cracked leather was falling apart, but they looked like they'd last a couple more days.

I wound a length of rope around the shroud to keep everything in place.

Dead and hog-tied. Flint had never looked so good.

CHAPTER THIRTY-SEVEN

BACK IN THE house, Nick and Sanja sat at the kitchen table chatting in Serbian. Johnny stood there, looking at me as if I'd forgotten something.

"Ready, Billy?" Big Mike said. He gave me a thump on the back that was more energetic than it needed to be. But it did the trick.

"Right, right, let's go upstairs and have that chat, Johnny," I said. Lack of sleep, physical exertion, and the horrors of evil men were all catching up to me. My brain was foggy, and my legs felt like lead, but I knew we had to get at what was inside Johnny's head.

And then?

Sleep.

No. We had to double-cross the Krauts and palm off Flint as Johnny Adler. The plan had sounded so simple, but right now I couldn't figure it out. Never mind, I had another job to do first. Johnny showed us into the small bedroom he and Nick shared. One bed and a couple of straight-backed chairs completed the decor.

"Have the comfortable seat, Captain," Johnny said as he gestured to the bed. I declined, afraid I might keel over and fall asleep. Big Mike and I pulled up two chairs, and Johnny sat on the edge of the bed.

"I assume you're here because of 101 Squadron," Johnny said in barely a whisper.

"Partially," I said. "Do you know a Major Frederick Brockman?"

"Of course," Johnny said. "Yank. He's in charge of outfitting his aircraft with some of our special equipment. Why?" I could see Johnny's eyes narrow with concern as he tried to figure out what was up.

"Don't worry. We're not going to talk about what you do. Not here, anyway," I said. "But we do know some of that special equipment pulled a disappearing act. Major Brockman knew as well."

"You didn't come all this way to accuse me, did you?" Johnny asked, a laugh escaping his lips. "We were both concerned about it."

"We came all this way because you told Sally Miller you knew who was behind it," I said. "When she visited you in the men's barracks, the night before your last mission."

"My god. Sally. How is she?"

"She's fine. Squadron Officer Conan Doyle had to send her off to a small listening post down the coast. Apparently, Lieutenant Walters reported her for the crime of entering the men's barracks."

"That sot," Johnny spat out. "Full of himself and none too friendly when it comes to Jews. He once let slip a comment about people sticking to their own kind. He wasn't happy Sally and I were seeing each other."

"Back to the thefts," I said. "You told Sally you knew who it was."

"Yes," Johnny said. "It was the wiring diagram she brought me, the one for the H2S ground-mapping radar that tipped me off."

"Johnny, who is it?" Big Mike said.

"Bigs, the little rat," Johnny said. "I knew he was mad about electronics and radios, but I never had him figured for a thief. There's nowhere to sell that stuff. What's in it for him?"

"Wait. You're talking about Bigsby? Leading Aircraftman Roscoe Bigsby?" I said. "He's a kid."

"I began to get suspicious and asked around. He was always underfoot when something went missing," Johnny said. "He was always eager to learn and willing to lend a hand, so at first I didn't think much of it. But when Sally told me about finding that diagram, I knew it was Bigs."

"Why?" I asked.

"He'd been asking me about the ground radar and how it worked. At first, I was impressed with his interest and depth of knowledge. But when I told him I could only go so far explaining H2S without a wiring diagram, he stopped pestering me about it."

"You think he stole the diagram?" I asked.

"I know he did. It disappeared right after that. He must've figured he didn't need me if he got a hold of the diagram," Johnny said. "Bigs was the last of the ground crew in my Lanc. I watched him enter after the others were done and just chalked it up to a last-minute check. But I had my suspicions, so I followed him. He was in front of the H2S screen, fiddling with it, the diagram laid out on his lap."

"What did he say?"

"That if I told anyone, he'd kill me," Johnny said. "Then he claimed he was just curious about the mechanism, but he'd be ruined if anyone reported him. I said it was all very suspect what with the rumors of missing electronics, and he got very angry. I grabbed the diagram, and he threw a punch. We tussled about but it was too cramped to have a proper set-to. I pushed him away and said I'd be talking with Major Brockman after my mission."

"You took the diagram?" I asked.

"Thought I did. I'd stuffed it in my pocket, but it must've come out in the struggle. I guess Bigs didn't notice that either."

"But Sally found it. She must have seen Bigsby after you left," I said.

"Yes. I went to grab some sleep. When Sally showed me the diagram, she thought I had left it and wanted to save me from trouble with Walters. I was worried for her, so I told her not to say a thing. I was going to talk with Brockman after my mission. But right then, I needed sleep with my round trip to Berlin starting in a few hours. Guess I should have gone to the major instead."

"Brockman had a list of missing hardware," I said. "H2S was on it."

"Had to be Bigsby," Johnny said as he leaned back and rubbed his chin. "But that doesn't explain why you're here. You could've waited in Italy, or England, for that matter."

"It's not just about the thefts, Johnny," I said. "We got involved because Major Brockman was murdered. Do you see Bigsby as capable of murder?" There was more news to deliver, but I wanted Johnny thinking straight for as long as he could.

"I didn't think he'd be capable of theft, especially military hardware, so who's to say?" Johnny said. "What happened to Brockman?"

"He was bludgeoned and thrown off the Dover cliff outside Capel-le-Ferne," I said. "Smashed in the back of the head with something like a lead pipe."

"Bloody hell," Johnny said as he shook his head in disbelief. "I wouldn't have thought Bigsby a killer, but he was right single-minded about electronics. Had a hard time taking no for an answer when I had to end one of our talks for my kip."

"Even though he threatened to kill you?"

"I thought he was just running his mouth," Johnny said. "I knew he was mad, but not murderous."

"What else can you tell me about him?" I asked.

"He grew up in a rough part of London. Hackney. Gangs and bullies around every corner, that sort of thing. Told me once that he began fiddling with his father's shortwave radio after he died to keep off the streets and out of trouble. He became fascinated and decided that was how he was going to make his living," Johnny said.

"Right. We were told he was a voluntary interceptor with the Radio Security Service before he was old enough to enlist," I said.

"He mentioned it often," Johnny said. "And his desire for a job in electronics after the war so he could support his mum in her old age. She's in poor health and depends on what he sends her, which is little enough. Come to think of it, the only time he left base was to take the train up to see her."

"Father dead, his mother poorly and barely getting by. Fairly sad stuff," I said.

"So, yes, I could see him striking out if someone was going to threaten the things he cares about. Radios, electronics, plans for the future, and his mother. Prison would mean shame and failure. A murder might be worth it to him," Johnny said.

"If he was pushed around on the streets of Hackney, he might have a real fear of prison," Big Mike offered. "Did he look like a guy who could take care of himself?"

Johnny and I agreed he didn't. Slight of build, very focused mentally, but not strong enough physically to stand up to a tough guy. The more I thought about it, the more I could see how appealing a quick whack to the head would seem to him.

"You don't think he's selling this gear to the enemy, do you?" Johnny asked.

"I don't see how he could manage it," I said. "But I do wonder what he's doing with it."

"Selling it on the black market?" Big Mike said. He shifted

around in his chair, trying to get comfortable. Or stay awake. "Maybe to some Hackney gang?"

"This isn't the sort of thing you hook up to the radio receiver in your sitting room," Johnny said. "This is advanced gear. I imagine a lot of it will lead to improvements after the war, but right now it's fairly limited to finding the target and fooling the Luftwaffe."

"Then we have to consider it's being sold to the enemy," I said. "Through a neutral nation, perhaps. We should inform MI5."

"It won't be that easy," Johnny said. "The RAF keeps a tight lid on radar countermeasures. I doubt they'd share much with other intelligence services. You'd best work with Conan Doyle and have Bigsby isolated so he doesn't do any further harm."

"Okay," I said. I rose and stretched my stiffening back. "But he's already done further harm. You're friends with David Cohen, aren't you?"

"Oh no," Johnny said as his hand covered his mouth. "Not David too?"

"Yes, I'm sorry to say. Killed in his own Lancaster while it was being repaired. He took a blow to the head just like Brockman. Traces of machine oil were left behind in both cases," I said.

"Any idea why he would have been attacked?" Big Mike asked.

"I'd told him about the missing hardware," Johnny said. "We all expected things to be misplaced, that's normal in such a big operation. The ground crews work hard, and they take the job seriously. They get things done without a lot of regard for paperwork. David was angry when he heard it might be deliberate theft. After my kite went down, he may have taken up the cause."

"It's a helluva thing," I said. "To escape the Nazis and end up murdered by one of your own."

"One of their own? Not every Englishman thinks that, Captain. But when you've seen your father beaten in the streets of

Leipzig, a few stray words here and there don't seem all that serious," Johnny said.

"You don't think anti-Semitism played any role in these killings?" I asked. "Major Brockman was Jewish as well."

"I had no idea," Johnny said. "And no, I don't think so. The English are pretty wary of foreigners to begin with, so I tried not to take it too seriously. One fellow called us Yids and then said he didn't know it was a derogatory term. It's just what he'd always heard. For the most part, we special operators can deal with that kind of everyday ignorance. The actual bigots, I simply ignore."

"What about being called a Jonah?" I asked.

"That's the worst part," he said. "Because it's based on the truth. As far I know, the rest of my crew is dead. It was chaos up there, all fire and explosions, but once I bailed out, I was alone. Just like Jonah about to be swallowed by the whale."

CHAPTER THIRTY-EIGHT

DOWNSTAIRS, SANJA POURED three glasses of slivovitz. "Do you know what day it is?" she asked.

"Sunday?" I guessed. The days of the week were a blur to me.

"No. Tomorrow is the eve of the New Year," she said. "We may not be back in Pranjani in time to celebrate properly. So, a toast, while we can make one." She raised her glass. "Srećna Nova Godina."

"Happy New Year to you," Big Mike said. "Let's hope it's a better one."

"Home alive by '45," I said as we looked each other in the eye and drank. That was the phrase GIs had come up with to replace "Out the door in '44." I hoped we didn't need to come up with a rhyme for the next New Year.

Sanja tossed wood into the stove. All I wanted to do was curl up on the floor and let the warmth sink into my bones like an old dog. But first, I had to get a message out. The local radioman could contact Rudy, who'd relay the message to Bari. From there, Colonel Harding could take care of the rest.

Except for getting us out of harm's way. For that, we were on our own.

"Sanja, we need to contact Rudy," I said.

"You must wait," she said as she shut the door on the woodstove. "The radio team is hiding in the forest. They cannot be taken."

"How far away?" Big Mike asked. "We've got to get a message out now."

"No one knows. That is the plan," Sanja said. Of course. Anyone who was captured would ultimately reveal the truth after the pains of torture grew intolerable.

"We need to get that message out," I said, then made the mistake of sitting in a comfortable armchair.

"What's the plan, Billy?" I knew it was Big Mike, and I knew it was important to talk about, but all I wanted to do was close my eyes for a minute. I struggled to speak, tried to open my eyes, but gave up the fight and drifted away as the warmth from the woodstove enveloped me.

I jolted awake moments later. I glanced at the luminous dial on my wristwatch. Correction, hours later. It was dark, except for a flickering candle on the kitchen table. Sanja was asleep in a chair across from me, and Big Mike was curled up in a blanket on the floor. I knew I should rouse myself, but instead, I enjoyed the satisfaction of knowing Flint was no longer a threat: dead, dressed, and trussed, ready for his final curtain. And that we now knew who'd killed Major Brockman and Sergeant Cohen.

But all that was worthless unless we got out of here alive, soon, and got the lowdown on Bigsby to Colonel Harding.

How?

Flint was ready to play his part, costarring in this charade as Flight Sergeant Johnny Adler. What we needed was a big-name star to pull off the con job I had in mind.

A big name.

Hmm.

If Flint was playing Johnny Adler, then why couldn't Johnny take on the starring role?

"Sanja," I said. She woke in an instant, her hand producing a pistol from under the thin blanket wrapped around her shoulders. Big Mike rustled on the floor.

"What?" she gasped.

"Those officers' uniforms in the barn. Do you know the rank and unit for each man?"

"No. We can ask Tomas," she said, barely awake. "I think he has Soldbuchs for both." The Wehrmacht Soldbuch was the standard identity document in the German military. It allowed the owner to draw pay and identified his current and former units. It also included his rank and personal information.

"Let's do that now," I said. "Big Mike, wake up."

"Jeez, Billy, it's hardly three o'clock," Big Mike grumbled as he gave out a great yawn.

"Then we ought to have just enough time," I said.

Sanja woke up Tomas, and he went to grab the uniforms from the barn. She explained that this was his house, and his mother would put together breakfast while we discussed my plan. Big Mike got Johnny and Nick downstairs, and, within a few minutes, a bleary-eyed crowd was staring at the German uniforms laid out on the kitchen table.

"Just to make sure I'm not wasting everyone's time, am I right, Johnny, that your German is flawless? I know you were a child when you left."

"It has to be, in my job, remember?"

"Okay. This idea assumes two things," I said. "First, that the SS sends the Ustaše in along the mill road. To test our defenses and serve as a distraction as they hit us from the ridge above. It's a smart tactical approach, so I think the chances are good. Second, that one of these uniforms fits you, Johnny, well enough to be convincing."

"And that you're willing to do it, mate," Nick said.

"Do what, exactly?" Johnny said.

"Have you ever played poker?" I asked.

"No, but I have wanted to learn," he said.

"Well, knowing how to bluff is very important. This will be your first lesson," I said. "Now let's check these fancy duds."

The SS uniform was in excellent shape, except for some bloodstains on the collar. According to the Soldbuch, it once belonged to Sturmbannführer Alfred Hansen of the 21st Waffen SS division. That rank was equivalent to a major and would allow Johnny to throw some Teutonic weight around. The Wehrmacht uniform belonged to a lowly lieutenant, so it made sense to go with the SS uniform with the shiny boots.

Johnny traded his civilian clothes for the Sturmbannführer's uniform, and it was a fair fit, as long as the belt was cinched tight. Herr Hansen had a few pounds on his former countryman, but the folds of fabric weren't noticeable. With an extra pair of socks to fit into the oversize boots, Johnny looked ready to take the stage in his debut performance.

"You look good," Tomas said. "So good, I want to shoot you." He handed over a German greatcoat, which Johnny shrugged on, doing a turn to show off the fit. Tomas's mother came into the kitchen and pointed a knife in his direction, saying something that gave Tomas and Sanja a chuckle.

"I wouldn't take a walk in that getup," Nick said. "Your throat will be cut in no time."

"Nick raises a good point, Captain," Johnny said. "How do we proceed?"

"It's okay to call me Billy," I said. "Everybody does."

"I shall stick with *captain* for now. It gives me confidence that you actually know what you're doing, if you don't mind," Johnny said. "Now, what exactly *are* you doing?"

"To Nick's point, we need to clear all the fighters out of the village," I said. "It's easier than explaining our plan, and there's not enough men to defend the place anyway."

"We can do that," Sanja said, and gave Tomas a quick rundown in case he'd missed anything. "We agree it is wise."

"Okay," I said. "How about a truck? Something in decent shape, fit for a Sturmbannführer?"

"Yes," Sanja said, after consulting with Tomas. "We have a Fiat. Italian army. It is hidden in the woods. But there is not much fuel."

"That's not a problem. We won't be going far," I said.

We made our plans. First, the village had to be cleared of Chetnik fighters. Then we needed our own small force of Black Legion types. Tomas said both would be easy. He'd tell his men to scatter, except for four whom he could outfit with Ustaše caps and crests. Two of them spoke enough German to be understood. He'd be the boss, wearing Flint's black coat.

"Maybe instead of scattering, those guys stage a distraction," Big Mike said. "Somewhere south of here, they shoot off a few rounds. Could get the Krauts to investigate."

"Good idea," Sanja said. "Everyone has a part to play."

We went over timing as Tomas's mother served coffee made from acorns and a few other ingredients I didn't ask about. It was hot, and it helped wash down the dense bread she doled out.

The phony Ustaše would be positioned on the ridge overlooking the village. Not to repel the Germans, but to greet them with the news that an Englishman had been captured. Figuring that the attack along the mill road would happen first, Johnny would be there in the Fiat, with Flint's corpse in the truck bed. The real trick was to contact the enemy without getting shot up. Then convince them to take the body to their SS commander, with the Sturmbannführer's compliments.

"Hold on," Big Mike said as he chewed on the crusty bread. "Johnny's gonna need someone to translate, ain't he?"

"Serbian is not on my list of languages," Johnny said.

"Tomas?" I asked, since he could communicate with Johnny in English. Quietly, I hoped.

"Yes. I go," he said. "Is good. We fool Ustaše."

"I'll go with the chaps on the ridge," Nick said. "I'll keep my mouth shut, not that the Germans will be able to tell my Serbian isn't perfect."

"I will go too," Sanja said. "But there is a problem, I think."

"What?" Big Mike asked.

"We need another German. They do not travel alone. Two Germans with a driver, yes. One SS man with no companion, it is suspicious," she said.

"Guaranteed that Kraut uniform ain't gonna fit me," Big Mike said.

So that's how I found myself squeezing into a Wehrmacht lieutenant's uniform, hoping the buttons didn't pop at the wrong time. I completed the look with a camouflage smock that at least hid the fact I wasn't with the SS like my pal. It was a small detail, but the kind of thing that might arouse suspicion.

"Very good," Sanja declared, and left with Tomas to pass the word and get men in position.

"What about me?" Big Mike asked.

"There's high ground at the curve in that S-bend," I said. "If you can find a spot up there, you can cover us. We'll drive right out like we don't give a damn, but not too far."

"I'll take our packs and get a sack for your clothes and boots," Big Mike said. "If things go south and the Krauts search the joint, it'll be a bullet in the head for everyone if they find a couple of Yanks passed through."

"Good point. Once the truck is here and the guys on the ridge are in place, we'll bring Flint out and put him in the flatbed. Then it's lights, camera, action," I said.

"You make it sound exciting, Captain," Johnny said.

"That's how we're going to sell it, Johnny. An exciting opportunity for our Ustaše friends to serve their German masters," I said. "They'll eat it up."

Or have us for lunch, but I held back on that one.

CHAPTER THIRTY-NINE

I WATCHED BIG Mike disappear up the slope to the sniper's spot he'd picked out. It gave him a good view of the road and was the perfect location from which to cover us if things spun out of control.

"You'd just love that, wouldn't you?" I said to the corpse of Amos Flint, laid out on the flatbed. We'd removed the shroud but left the hands and legs bound for easier carrying. And to keep the broken bones from dangling in various directions. After a night in the cold barn, he didn't look all that bad. For a stiff.

"When do we go?" Johnny asked, his peaked cap set at a rakish angle.

"Almost time," I said. I glanced at the faint light beginning to show on the eastern horizon. "Tomas?"

"We wait longer, they come. Light will be good for shooting," Tomas said as he leaned forward in the driver's seat and checked the predawn sky.

"Okay," I said from my spot on the passenger-side running board. I held on to the Fiat, a Schmeisser submachine gun draped over my shoulder. "Let's go."

Tomas started the engine, giving it a few loud revs for effect. We drove past the mill house and halted just before the curve, where a low-lying fog made the boundary between road and river difficult to detect. There, Tomas turned on the headlights.

They cast a sickly yellow glow into the grayness, the illumination vanishing in an indeterminate mist.

"Now," I said. Tomas laid on the horn and flashed the lights on and off. We were still out of sight, but the sound and reflected light would certainly be noticed.

Tomas eased the truck forward, inched around the curve, then halted.

Next, he bellowed out the message not to shoot. Then Johnny did the same in German, along with a notification that he was a deutscher Offizier. More flashing of lights and honking followed, the idea being to let the Ustaše know we weren't a threat.

Or that we were the juiciest target to come down this road in a long time.

I rapped on the roof of the cab. Time to see what, if anything, we were up against. Tomas shifted into first and the Fiat lurched forward. He advanced past the stone outcropping that forced the bend in the road.

The headlights pierced the darkness and fought against the gloom to pick up anything in the featureless landscape. The road and the sloping bank of the river were heavy with mist, as was the thin stand of pines to our left.

Tomas gave out another yell and called for his Ustaše brothers to show themselves. He gave them the news that the village was secure. Johnny followed up with his own message about the reward for the Englishman and how it could be theirs.

Nothing.

He got out of the cab and slammed the door shut. He did a great job of imitating an officer impatient with soldiers slow on the uptake as he unleashed a stream of angry German that almost moved me to click my heels.

In the silence that followed, Tomas drummed his fingers on the steering wheel.

A shot spat out.

I looked at Johnny and Tomas. We were all in one piece. I gripped the Schmeisser and pointed it straight ahead.

"No," Tomas whispered. "Pistol. No hit."

He was right. Most importantly, that one shot wasn't followed by a fusillade. A signal, perhaps? Or just one shaky guy off in the woods?

"Komm hier," Johnny said, this time in a gentle voice, tinged with exasperation. Just perfect.

A figure rose from the gloom and stood not ten yards in front of us. The fog reached to his knees, having fully hidden him. Then two more behind him. Four along the riverbank. Three, four, five more from the roadway. Soon another dozen stood all around us.

Guns pointed our way. Tomas berated the men who had arisen like wraiths from the fog, gesturing to Johnny as he did, making a case for them to demonstrate respect, as we'd rehearsed. I made a show of lowering my weapon and letting it dangle from my shoulder. The gesture was easily visible in the gathering light, and tensions seemed to ease, just a bit.

One tall fellow holstered his pistol and advanced toward us. Johnny pointed to the weapon and asked a question. Tomas translated, and it ended with laughter all around. Then the tall guy walked around to Tomas, who stayed at his driver's post. We'd agreed it wouldn't be wise to allow our supposed allies a chance to snatch the vehicle, so Tomas sat with one hand on the wheel and the other holding a pistol.

"Nagrada?" Tall Man asked.

"Nagrada," Tomas answered, making the universal sign for money by rubbing his thumb against the tip of his fingers.

"Ja," Johnny said, and issued instructions to Tomas, who relayed them to the now growing and curious crowd of Ustaše. The story we'd concocted was that the Sturmbannführer had tracked down an important escaped prisoner with the help of the pro-German villagers. Perhaps the good men of the Ustaše had heard of the Royal Air Force Sergeant Adler? Heads nodded, yes, they had. The Sturmbannführer had urgent business elsewhere but trusted the Ustaše could deliver the proof of Adler's capture to his SS colleagues on the hill above the village. Yes, there would be a reward.

Nagrada.

Two men jumped on the flatbed and checked the body. When they saw the identity tag, they gave out a whoop that earned them a rebuke from Tall Man. He pulled a flare pistol from a sack slung over his shoulder and raised his arm. A green flare shot high into the sky, exploded, the remnants floating lazily to earth.

My hand went to my weapon at the same time Johnny unsnapped his holster. Tomas uttered calming words as Tall Man looked perplexed and shocked at our surprise. Johnny reacted quickly, nodded, and clapped the guy on his shoulder.

A green signal flare. Should have been obvious, but I hadn't considered it. Without a radio, it was the perfect way to communicate over short distances. I just hoped green meant everyone was happy and ready to go home.

All eyes watched the sky. Finally, an answering flare flew up from the ridge above the village. The bloom of matching green drew murmurs of approval loud enough to cover my sigh of relief.

Tall Man came to attention and offered Johnny a fascist straight-arm salute, which was returned with great fervor. With that, men swarmed the flatbed, hoisted Flint onto their shoulders, and carried him off and up into the wooded hill. In seconds, they all vanished into the trees, leaving us with wisps of fog swirling at our ankles as the sun struggled to rise.

"Bloody hell," Johnny gasped.

"Good, good," Tomas said. "Good Nacisti."

"What was that gunshot for?" I asked.

"Ustaše wanted to know if we shoot back," Tomas said as he held his hand like a pistol. It was a test, and we passed.

We drove back into the village, where Tomas dropped us off. He went off to hide the truck. Sanja and Nick were among the first to come down from the ridgeline, and in the faint light, I could see a gaggle of others not far behind.

Sanja spoke to Johnny in Serbian, her tone subservient. Nick called him Sturmbannführer and gave a Nazi salute with his right arm, while holding his left hand close to his chest and gesturing with his thumb.

Ten paces behind, unmistakable even in the early-morning gloom, an SS officer strode briskly our way trailed by a soldier toting a Schmeisser. This wasn't part of the show I had planned. Not at all.

"Sturmbannführer!" the SS man said, his arm jutted skyward. The only good news was that this guy was a junior grade, since he offered the salute. And that his escort, even as he checked the buildings and people in the area, didn't point his submachine gun anywhere.

Evidently our ruse had worked too well, since these two decided to drop by and Sieg Heil for a while. Johnny returned the salute with a lazy indifference while he framed a quick question that sounded like a rebuke. I had to hand it to him for coming up with anything but a stammer. I tried to remain calm, but as the soldier's gaze drifted over to me, I felt sweat break out in the small of my back and my heartbeat quicken.

The officer answered Johnny and then asked me a question. His tone was neutral, maybe even pleasant, but I had no idea what to do. I waited a beat for Johnny to step in, but he didn't, so I trotted out the one word I was sure of.

"Ja."

Gunfire broke out in the distance. Single shots, the *rat-a-tat-tat* of a machine gun, along with grenade bursts. Right on cue, our Chetniks created the distraction we'd planned, never realizing how important it would be.

The SS trooper wheeled around. He searched for a threat, but the firing wasn't close enough to be a danger. The officer spoke with Johnny, who replied in a roar worthy of Hitler giving one of his spittle-laced speeches.

"Nimm deine Truppen!" he shouted as he pointed to the ridge where the rest of the Germans were. "Jetzt!"

The SS supermen were so shocked by his vehement order that they gave a bare-minimum Nazi salute and hightailed it back up the hill. As we watched them go, the firing became more sporadic but didn't die down. I hoped our guys kept it up and led the Krauts on a long and tiring chase.

"What happened?" I asked Sanja.

"It went well," she said. "We called out in German, lit a lantern, and told them another German patrol had captured the Englishman. They wanted proof, but when they saw the green starburst, they were happy. We told them our Ustaše brothers were bringing the body, but the officer who led them wanted to meet the other Germans."

"We were outnumbered," Nick said. "We couldn't say no. But you sent him on his way, Johnny, like a rocket! What did you tell him?"

"To see to his troops, immediately," Johnny said. "But if you'll excuse me, right now I just want to get out of this disgusting uniform. It makes me sick to wear it."

CHAPTER FORTY

"Glad we didn't need your services," I said to Big Mike as he returned from his perch, laden with our packs and my uniform.

"I couldn't see where that pistol shot came from," he said as he handed me my gear. "When nothing happened, I figured it was a trick to flush out snipers. I never even saw the SS who followed Sanja down."

"It shook me up," I said as we entered the house. "We planned well, except for not planning for the unexpected."

Inside, there was laughter and backslapping, everyone glad at having avoided a pitched battle with the combined forces of the SS and Ustaše. Slivovitz was broken out, toasts were made, and it looked like it was shaping up into a party that would guarantee hangovers by noon.

"We need to go," I said to Sanja as she broke free from Tomas's mother, who was giving bear hugs all around. "We have twenty-four hours to get to Pranjani."

"Yes. If we leave now, we should get there before nightfall," she said. "Do you want to leave a message for the radio? They should return by ten o'clock."

"Yes," I said. "As soon as I get out of this uniform."

Johnny and I both changed, glad to be rid of our Nazi costumes. We carried them downstairs, and I thought about what the radio message needed to say. We didn't yet have proof of Bigsby's guilt, and I didn't want him to suspect we were on to him. If he were trading with the enemy, he could disappear into a neutral country, and we'd never hear of him again.

We stacked the clothing on the table, and I sat to compose my note to Colonel Harding, pencil stub in hand.

> *Suspect is Leading Aircraftsman Roscoe Bigsby. Further evidence needed. Do not detain or allow to leave base.*

Short and sweet. Kaz and Conan Doyle would figure something out. If we got back for the last flight out of Pranjani, it would be only a couple of days before we were back at RAF Hawkinge.

Big if.

Sanja wrote out the message in Serbian and gave it to Tomas, who'd just come back from concealing the truck. He promised to have it transmitted when the radio team came down from the hills. Their first task would be to contact the groups sending fighters to Virovac and have them recalled, or to harass the Germans and Ustaše who'd just been here. If the Chetniks could keep the enemy distracted and off-balance, they might not think about revisiting the village.

Tomas's mother gave us some lepinja and five apples from last year's harvest. My bet was they had damn few left, but I didn't want to hurt her feelings by refusing the offered food. I hugged her and thought of my own mother, who never let a soul leave the house hungry. Boston or Virovac, some things never change.

I grabbed my pack, then stopped to look at the German uniforms. I thought about how lucky I'd been not to have to utter more than one simple word, but also about how well Johnny had played the mad Prussian.

"Tomas, do you think we could take the SS uniform?" I asked.

"It is yours," Tomas said, and gave a firm nod. "We owe you much."

"What are you thinking, Billy?" Big Mike asked.

"It worked once," I said. "You never know. It might come in handy."

"Okay, but let's not tell Johnny unless we have to," he said.

Tomas stuffed the clothing and boots into a burlap sack, along with the Ustaše cap he'd worn, then tied it shut with a length of rope. Flint's rope. A souvenir of our time in Virovac. I carried it out with my gear to where Nick and Johnny were saying farewell to the folks who had protected them since their arrival.

Sanja asked me what was in the sack.

"The Sturmbannführer," I told her.

"What is the word for when people go to a party dressed as others?" she asked.

"A masquerade," I said.

"This is war," Sanja said, and slung her rifle. "Not a masquerade. Tricks are very well until they get you killed. Now we go."

Filip and his friends brought the horses out of the barn, and we mounted up. I hung the burlap bag from my pommel, hoping our SS friend wouldn't need to be recalled to duty. As Sanja led us to the hill where we'd ridden in, Filip ran alongside. When we reached the top, he stood at attention and saluted. We each returned it as we passed. Filip smiled as he watched Johnny, once again wearing his brother's clothes, sit tall in the saddle and snap off that British open-palmed salute.

We rode along the ridgeline. I felt exposed knowing that a short time ago SS troopers had been here, ready to attack. As we approached the forest, I let out a sigh of relief, grateful to get under the cover of trees.

Seconds later the *pop-pop-pop* of distant gunfire jolted me alert.

"Glad that's not aimed at us," Johnny said.

"It sounds pretty far away," I said. I strained to pick up direction and distance. After a few single shots, the firing ended. We entered the protective forest canopy.

"It could be miles away or over the next ridge," Sanja said from up ahead as she turned in the saddle. "Sound makes its own way. Listen, and make no loud noises."

"She's right," Big Mike said. He brought his horse close to mine and spoke in a low voice. "The Krauts are probably hunting the Chetniks from Virovac, plus the groups who are headed there. If they bring in reinforcements, it's going to be tough going."

"Slow going," Johnny said from behind us. "And I've got a plane to catch."

"We'll make it," I said. I damn well hoped so. I had a killer to put behind bars, and as much as I liked Sanja and her Chetnik crew, I wasn't excited at the prospect of waiting out the end of the war here. With the Allies cutting off aid to Mihailović, Pranjani was going to be a desperate place for anyone left behind.

As we descended, the horses' hooves kicked up rocks that clattered against each other as they rolled down the hill. The path finally evened out and we stopped to let the horses drink from a small stream that gurgled its way across our route. I hadn't realized how much noise we were making until we stopped, and the constant click-clack of stones ceased.

A buzzing sound, like an annoying insect, grew louder, or perhaps we were finally able to hear it.

"Me 109," Nick said as he identified the fighter with an airman's trained ear. He craned his neck to search what sky was visible between the branches.

"Do not look up," Sanja ordered. "Follow me."

She dismounted and led her horse away from the stream and off the trail, deeper into the trees. It was hard not to stare at the sky, but I knew how clearly an upturned face would stand out. The snarl of the plane's engine grew louder and more insistent. Sanja stood close to her horse, her face pressed against its neck. The forest was a mix of evergreen and bare branches, and we had to hope it was enough camouflage to keep us hidden. The opening where the stream cut across the path would've had us on full display.

The fighter flew lower and closer, then gained altitude. It sounded like it was flying in circles, searching. For what, exactly?

The chatter of a machine gun broke the silence. Not the Me 109's multiple guns, but a single weapon firing. And damn close. A volley of rifle fire answered only to be drowned out in the roar of the fighter coming in low, guns blazing. The machine cast a brief dark shadow as it swooped over us.

"Now," Sanja said, then mounted. We followed slowly, bent low in the saddle, as if that might hide us from the pilot overhead.

We plodded on, past the spot where we'd met Sanja as she returned with the horses from Virovac. More gunfire rippled ahead and the Me 109 continued to circle above us. I checked my wristwatch. Almost eleven o'clock. It would be dark in less than six hours. We'd be making the last leg of this journey in the pitch black.

At the site of the ambush where we'd taken out the Ustaše, not a soul from any of the farmhouses stirred. The sun was bright and the sky clear. A fine day even in winter, and the fact that no one was out doing chores told me they were playing it safe, waiting for the shooting to stop and the Kraut aircraft to cease its hunting.

We rode on and stopped at another stream, this time letting the horses have a good long drink. We did the same upstream, where clear water gurgled over jumbled stones before muddying our path. The German fighter was behind us now, and no shots had been fired for a half hour. It was almost peaceful. We divvied up the lepinja and ate quickly. Big Mike was about to bite into his apple when Sanja admonished him.

"Feed your horse," she said. "He deserves it."

"Aw, I was just gonna take a small bite," Big Mike said. He cut his apple and fed it to his mount, who gave out a neigh and shook her head. "I'm so hungry even the thought of K rations makes my mouth water. Wonder what they'll feed us in Pranjani tonight?"

As we got back on the horses, the topic remained food. Johnny and Nick looked forward to Italy and sampling what was on offer there. The aircraft's drone became a constant companion as it faded into a nondescript buzz on the horizon. It was no more than a faint nuisance, but then it changed course and drew closer, lower, and louder. We hurried off the trail into a thick stand of pines and dismounted.

"Who are they looking for?" Big Mike asked, more in frustration than expectation of an answer.

"Our people in Komanice were sending twelve fighters," Sanja said. That was one of the villages we'd passed on our way to Virovac. "They may have been sighted as they returned. Or it could be anyone, even Tito's Partisans."

"The pilot has to be in radio communication with someone," Johnny said as he patted his fidgeting horse. "If he spots us, the Jerries will know soon enough."

"The way ahead is too open," Sanja said. "We must wait."

"We're near Komanice, aren't we?" I asked. I recognized the terrain. It was close to where we'd spent the night in the ruins above the village. We had a long stretch of open ground to traverse.

"Yes. It is not far," Sanja said. She buried her face in her horse's mane as the Me 109 dove low and flew overhead, sending pine branches into a swirling back draft. We ducked instinctively, then heard the plane climb, the growling engine fading away.

"Maybe the bastard's low on fuel," Nick said.

"Or he's been vectored to another target," Johnny suggested.

"It does not matter," Sanja said. "We must go before the machine returns."

We led the horses out from under the trees and mounted them once we reached the trail. It was already past noon. The clock was ticking as the path took us uphill toward the ruins of Kula Varna. But at least we weren't being bothered by the constant threat of a fighter plane on the prowl.

The forest cloak gave way to open air as the trail followed another ridgeline. We passed above the small village of Komanice. Smoke curled from chimneys. Orange-tiled roofs stood out beneath the midday sun. No vehicles or uniformed men were visible on the roads through the village, and the sky was clear, so Sanja decided to make up some time. We went into a canter and crossed over the wide ridge in a few minutes.

"Is this really the fastest way to Pranjani?" Nick asked after we were back under the cover of the trees. The trail was narrow and rocky, forcing the horses to slow their pace.

"No. We came this way to avoid the main roads after we saw what the Ustaše had done to an entire village," I said. "It wasn't pretty. They were in trucks on the main road, so we took to a logging trail."

"That fighter could pick us off on the road and be back at his base sipping schnapps before our bodies cooled," Johnny said. "This route is fine with me, as long as we keep going."

"Kula Varna is just ahead. It's a good view from up there," I said. I told them about the tower and ruined walls where we'd spent the night. "We can see if there's any trouble headed our way. The trail gets easier too."

But here, the trail only grew steeper as we drew close to the ruins perched on the hilltop. We went on foot and led the horses over the uneven ground until we emerged from the woods into a clearing dotted with shrubs and boulders. Sanja ordered the others to halt and pointed to the crest of a hill.

"From that point, you can see Kula Varna," she said. "Go up with your binoculars and be sure no one is there. Be careful."

"That's my middle name," I said. The slope was thick with rocks and brush, which provided cover in case the Me 109 decided on a return engagement. I handed Sanja my Thompson, not wanting to be weighed down if I had to skedaddle. I scrambled up the hill on my hands and knees, alert for any sound of the enemy on the other side. I halted at the top, right at the edge, and slowly raised my head for a quick look.

The Kula Varna tower was about seventy yards away. There was no one close by. The path dipped before it rose again and climbed to the ruins sited on the highest point around.

I pulled my head down. Slowly, since quick movements attract the eye. I dug out the binoculars from my jacket, held them at the ready, and eased my head up. I scanned the ground near the ruins first, then took in the tower.

I froze.

Two figures stood at the top, their Wehrmacht helmets silhouetted against the sky. One man was speaking into a radio handset. As the other turned, I saw the binoculars in his hand.

He was looking straight at me.

CHAPTER FORTY-ONE

I DIDN'T MOVE, afraid that a sudden movement might catch his eye. As he turned away, I motioned for the others to stay put and scuttled my way back down the hill.

"Two Krauts in the tower," I gasped out. "They have a radio."

"You didn't see any others?" Big Mike asked.

"No, but they could be hunkered down in the ruins. No way to tell," I said.

"We need to turn around," Nick said. "It's getting late."

"No," Sanja said. "The ridge is too steep to go through the woods. To get to the main road we must go far. And then the airplane can see us if it returns."

"Which means?" Nick said.

"Which means we hope there is only two of them," I said. "If I can get close enough, I can take them out."

"What about the noise?" Nick said. "If that's a German observation post, that means other Germans must be close. They could be on us in minutes."

"The idea is to do it without noise, Nick," I said.

"Oh," he said. He looked a bit shocked. I guess when you do your killing from thirty thousand feet up in the dark of night, silent and stealthy doesn't spring to mind.

We decided on a plan. Big Mike, with his M1, would be at the top of the hill, ready to fire if more Fritzes showed up. Which would mean we were in a world of trouble. He settled into a firing position behind a rock. Then I told Johnny I needed him to help as well.

"I'm not putting on that bloody Nazi getup again, if that's what you're suggesting," he said.

"No, it isn't. All you need to do is yell out a few things," I said, and tapped his arm. "I'll show you where."

We got our eyeballs over the crest, and I pointed out the crumbling wall that jutted out from the tower. I told him I was going to the right of the wall so I could see into the ruins to determine whether there were more Germans at the base.

"And if there are?" Johnny asked.

"Then things don't go so quietly," I said. "I've got two grenades. But let's think positive, okay?"

"I'm positive you're daft, but go on."

"Okay. We'll go along that thicket," I said, and pointed to the jumble of wintering shrubs and spindly pines that ran at an angle to the base of the hill. "Once we get to the bottom, I'll go up along the stone wall. You make for that stand of trees to the left. See?"

"I see the trees," Johnny said as we both pulled our heads low again. "Won't the Jerries see us?"

"They can see straight across easily enough," I said. "But down there the angle is too steep. They can't see what's close to them. So don't worry. Just get behind some cover and say something convincing in German. That's your job, isn't it?" I tried to smile when I said it, but I think it was more of a grimace.

"Special operator, that's me. All right, then, let's go," Johnny said.

"All clear," Big Mike said as he searched the ridgetop with my binoculars. "Right now, they're facing away from us. Go."

"Stay low and right behind me," I said to Johnny. I ran at a crouch to the line of shrubs and stayed as close as I could while we made our way downhill. At the base, we got behind a jumble of rocks and caught our breath.

"When you get into those trees, wait three minutes," I said. "That'll give me time to check out the rest of the ruins. What are you going to say?"

"I'm going to tell them the field kitchen is sending up hot food," he said. "That ought to bring them running."

"Good," I said, and peeked out from around the rocks. "It's clear."

We both took off, and I jumped over what was left of the wall built for a war centuries ago. I knelt and listened for voices or footsteps.

Instead, I heard the drone of an approaching aircraft.

Damn.

I cocked my head to pick up the direction, but it was still some ways off. It wasn't the throaty snarl of a fighter plane, but more of a high-pitched whine. The only good news was that it might encourage the two Krauts to keep their eyes fixed on the sky.

I scrambled forward, my pistol at the ready. I passed the spring where water bubbled out from the rocks. Then I approached the spot where we'd camped out, keeping low against the wall. I took a deep breath to calm myself and rose up, my .45 pointed at nothing but air. The space held a couple of bedrolls and two knapsacks.

There were only two.

I stepped into the base of the tower, a round room where a few stone steps led to a rickety circular wooden staircase. I holstered my pistol and drew my knife, tossing a quick glance upward. Light filtered down from the opening at the top, and I moved to the door opposite, positioning myself against the outside wall. If Johnny's fake summons worked, I should be able to grab the guy who came down to investigate.

I hoped it would be only one. Two would be a problem. The

only solution would be two shots from my automatic, which would alert any nearby troops. The aircraft drew closer, the sound echoing from beyond the next ridge. I prayed the Krauts would look up.

I heard a shout from the thicket of small trees. Johnny let loose a stream of German that had a lighthearted, friendly sound to it. He even laughed at the end. An answer came back from atop the tower, followed by footsteps on the wooden stairs.

The aircraft surged above the ridge. It was a Fieseler Storch, a small spotter plane, the German equivalent of our Piper Cub.

Boots clomped down the stairs. From above, I heard one German speak into his radio and give what sounded like a call sign. Johnny said something from close by. The Storch flew overhead as I gripped my knife and waited. I pressed myself flat against the stone tower, close to the open archway.

Time slowed.

Part of me knew I was about to take a life while the rest focused on timing and stealth. It had to be quick. Better for everyone.

Bootheels hit the bottom stone steps. I exhaled and readied myself. It wasn't me who was doing this. It was simply part of the plan, a necessity of war.

He stepped out into the open.

My left hand shot out and grabbed him by the jaw as my knife hand drew the blade across his throat. There was a lot of blood but little noise as he slumped back, the heavy weight of death against my chest. I lowered him to the ground, taking in the SS runes on his collar, now soaked in crimson.

The Storch circled lazily above. The Kraut in the tower was still at it, repeating his call sign. I stepped carefully up the wooden steps, not trusting their age or condition. I neared the top, stopped, and listened. I couldn't tell where he was standing, but I didn't dare give him time to make contact.

I ran up the remaining few stairs and came face-to-face with the radioman, who had his transmitter in hand and was wearing a headset. I rushed him and made two quick stabs under the rib cage. His eyes went wide as he stumbled back against the chest-high wall, still holding the transmitter as if he wanted to send one last message. I yanked it and the headset away from him. He gasped and wheezed. One hand clawed at his holster as his brain grasped what was happening. Before he could draw the weapon, I grabbed his legs and lifted, tipping him over the parapet and down to the cold hard stones below.

"Johnny!" I hollered, and waved the all-clear sign to Big Mike. I watched the Storch bank, soar over the town below, and level out. It was coming straight at me. "Hurry! Get the bodies out of sight!"

I heard a tinny noise coming from the headset. I put it to my ear and heard a burst of static and a garble of German. The plane was coming closer. The radioman's helmet was next to his set, and I traded it for mine, hoping the pilot wouldn't notice my khaki-colored Mackinaw.

"Johnny? You there?" I shouted. I grinned and waved at the approaching plane. I held up the transmitter to show it wasn't working. Maybe it worked, or maybe the pilot didn't care, because he kept on course and vanished over the hills.

"Got them out of the way just in time. Nice work," Johnny said as he poked his head up from the stairs. "You think you fooled him with that tin pot?"

"I don't know. Why don't you ask?" I tossed the Kraut helmet aside and handed Johnny the transmitter and headset. "Somebody's trying to get through. Maybe you can work that special-operator magic of yours and spoof them."

"I may as well keep my hand in the game," he said as he donned the set.

I left him to it and went down to meet the others. While Sanja kept a lookout, Big Mike and Nick searched the backpacks for food and came up with a few tins and some hard sausage. I explained what Johnny was up to and went to wash my hands at the spring.

There was a lot of blood.

CHAPTER FORTY-TWO

"I PICKED UP the aircraft after a few minutes," Johnny told us as we mounted our horses. "I told them an Ustaše cavalry patrol was in the area and had spotted Chetniks to our north. That ought to keep them off our backs and searching in the wrong direction. Then I smashed the radio."

"Smart," Sanja said. "By the time the Germans send a patrol, we will be far away."

"Far enough?" I said. It was after two o'clock and the sun was thinking about settling into the horizon.

"To ride at night is no problem," Sanja said. "Every hour we are closer to Pranjani. Every hour I know the ground better." With that, she kicked her horse into a trot and moved out. We were in open country, and I hoped Johnny's ruse about an Ustaše cavalry unit would give us an edge if the Storch came back around.

"Things go okay in the tower?" Big Mike asked as we followed Sanja down the trail.

"Yeah. They never knew what hit them," I said. Which is how I preferred things when it came to killing up close. While I knew it was kill or be killed, and I knew the evil we were fighting, it was tough to watch life drain away from another human being, even an SS bastard. A guy like Flint wouldn't bat an eyelash, which was another reason I liked it to be over quickly. It meant I wasn't Flint.

"Good," Big Mike said. He nodded his understanding.

"I was glad they were SS," Johnny said from behind us. "The more fanatical Nazis who are killed, now, means the smaller the odds are they'll have another go at it."

"We're burning their cities to the ground, Johnny," Nick said. "You think they'd try again?"

"Fanatics will always find an excuse," Johnny said. "They are driven by hate. Hate for my people, hate for anyone who does not fit into their insane vision of the world. Mark my words, the fanatics will fight to the last and take the innocents with them."

From what I'd seen in this war, Johnny had a handle on things.

We kept on the trail until it turned into a narrow, overgrown path. This was the route we'd taken after the farmer had tried to turn us in. Which meant that there were Ustaše in the area. His daughter had run off and fetched them in no time at all. We left the cart path behind and moved quickly down the road, passing the farmer's house with the burnt barn. No one took notice of us, as far as I could tell.

The Fieseler Storch returned, flying low off to our right.

"I wonder if someone went to the radio post when they didn't check in," Big Mike said.

"It will be dark soon, and the machine will not be able to hunt us," Sanja said. For the first time, I sensed real worry in her usually upbeat voice.

We put a few miles between us and the barn and took a break where the trail crossed a stream at the bottom of a ravine. The Storch's motor was still buzzing around above but hadn't come close. We tied the horses to saplings at the edge of the stream where they could drink and arranged ourselves on a pile of rocks to divvy up the German rations. We'd need the energy to get through the night.

There were two tins of biscuits, plus one of a meat spread that resembled liverwurst, and another with cheese.

"Not bad," Big Mike said. He munched away, chewing on the hard biscuit for all he was worth.

"But not as good as American spaghetti in tomato sauce," Sanja said with a smile. "Of course."

The Storch flew closer, then banked and headed north. The drone of the small engine was replaced by a louder, more insistent *thrum* of aircraft at a much higher altitude.

"What the hell?" Big Mike uttered as he searched the bits of sky visible from between the branches.

"The horses!" Nick shouted, and moved toward them. Twenty yards away, they were in plain sight from above and clearly a target, which meant our cavalry ruse had failed.

"No! Stukas!" Sanja said. She leapt up as the screaming sirens on the Stukas' wings heralded their steep turn into a dive-bomb attack.

"Take cover now!" I yelled, and dove behind the jumble of rocks where we'd been seated. The shrill sirens whined and reached an earsplitting crescendo as they plummeted straight at us. The horses panicked, heads raised and ears held back. My mount reared and pulled her reins free, taking off as the two Stukas dropped their bombs. They pulled out of their dives and soared upward. I watched the bombs fall.

I ducked as Nick sprinted for cover. Multiple explosions erupted around us, raining debris and choking the forest clearing with smoke. I kept my head down, ears ringing from the blasts, until I heard a shriek of pain.

It was Nick. He writhed on the ground and clutched his leg. The incoming roar of engines meant the Stukas were coming back for a strafing run, a coup de grâce by machine gun. I vaulted over the rocks just as Big Mike did the same. He grabbed Nick by the shoulders, and I took hold of his feet, ignoring his screams of pain. We scrambled back over the rocks and went flat, as we covered Nick with our bodies.

The percussive chatter of machine guns hammered at us. Bullets zinged off the rocks and shredded branches, which cascaded from the treetops. Then they were gone, their deadly work done. Big Mike and I untangled ourselves and rolled off Nick, who groaned through gritted teeth. I shrugged off my rucksack and dug out the medical kit.

"You're going to be okay, Nick," I said as I pulled out the supplies. "Where are you hit?"

"Legs, I think," he gasped. "My arse too. Oh my god." He reached down to feel his privates, then breathed out a sigh that told me things were intact.

"Okay, we're going to roll you over," I said. Big Mike and I eased him onto his stomach, and I set to work cutting away his blood-soaked blue wool trousers.

"We'll look for the horse," Johnny said. He knelt by Nick and squeezed his arm. "It'll only be an improvement to your backside, mate. Be right back."

"How bad is it?" Nick asked. He was calmer now, likely because Johnny had made that joke. If it were really bad, he wouldn't have played it for a laugh.

"You caught some shrapnel," I said as I snipped off cloth around his left thigh and buttock. I splashed water to wash away the blood and see what I had to deal with. A jagged piece of metal protruded from his upper thigh, and I plucked it out with the forceps and sprinkled sulfa powder on it. I repeated the process up and down his left leg, which had taken the brunt of the hit. He'd lost blood, but there wasn't any serious damage I could see.

"I hit the dirt, soon as Sanja yelled," he said. "I was worried about the horses."

"Billy's broke free," Big Mike said as I wrapped gauze bandages around compresses as best I could. "As for the others, you would've been a dead man if you were anywhere near them."

For the first time, I looked over the rocks that had sheltered us. It was a bloody mess. The bombs had been right on target, leaving a mass of gore that even the swiftly flowing stream couldn't wash away.

"Jesus," I said. I returned to tying off bandages while I wondered what the hell we were going to do.

"What?" Nick asked.

"The horses. Four of them took a direct hit. Mine's missing."

"Nick, I gotta ask. Can you walk?" Big Mike said.

"Walk? Bloody hell, I'm not sure I can stand. Give me a minute," he said with a wince as he worked his leg.

"There may still be shrapnel in your leg," I said. "I took out what I could see, but for now you're patched up as best as I can manage."

"Listen, Nick," Big Mike said. "It's getting close to sunset. We only have one horse, and that's if Sanja and Johnny can find her. You need to walk or, hopefully, ride. Can you manage it?"

"You're a cheery fellow, aren't you? I've just had shrapnel pulled out of my rear end, and you want to know if I can ride a horse? Lend a hand, will you?"

Big Mike helped Nick stand. He was wobbly and complained of the cold, so I wrapped the rest of the gauze bandages around his leg to keep his trousers intact. Nick took a few tentative steps and asked if there was any morphine in my medical kit. I told him there was, but only for serious injuries. Big Mike walked with him while we checked for any further bleeding.

Johnny and Sanja returned, leading my horse by the bridle. She was unhurt but kept shaking her head, ears back and eyes wide open.

"We cannot take her past the other horses," Sanja said. "The smell of death frightens her. I will take her through the woods to the path beyond them."

"Good to see you up on two feet, Nick," Johnny said. "We need to move."

"What difference does it make?" Nick asked, his voice bitter and angry. "We'll never make it on foot."

"The difference is that those Stukas carry four bombs on their wings and a larger five-hundred-pounder under the fuselage," Johnny said. "They dropped the smaller hundred-pound bombs on us. If they come back, we won't be so lucky when they unleash the rest of their payload."

"Lucky?" Nick said. He winced as he took a few exploratory steps on his own. "Speak for yourself, mate."

CHAPTER FORTY-THREE

Big Mike cut a stout branch for Nick to use as a cane. We crossed the stream and skirted the disemboweled carcasses of the four horses. Two of the bombs had hit next to where they were tethered, which was more than enough to gut them. It looked like the second plane had missed entirely, according to the four bomb craters up the trail.

Sanja awaited us with my horse, keeping a tight grip on the reins as she stroked the mare's neck.

"She is calmer now," Sanja said. "Nick, you will ride."

"Johnny's the one you need to get on that plane," Nick said. "He's the bloke the Jerries are after."

"You forget, I'm dead," Johnny said. "Come on, I'll give you a boost."

"Hard to keep track," Nick said. "All right, help me get my foot in the stirrup, but then hands off. It hurts everywhere."

Johnny helped with the foot and Big Mike got on the other side of the horse and pulled Nick by the hand. He got onto the saddle with a groan and a wince.

"You okay, Nick?" I asked.

"Nothing a nice soft pillow wouldn't take care of," he said.

Johnny had cocked his head skyward. I heard it too. The Storch, coming back to make sure the job had been done.

"Let's go," Sanja said, and led the way. "Do not fall off the horse, Nick."

"It might hurt less than this," he said as he leaned against the horse's neck to take pressure off his hindquarters.

We trudged on as the light faded behind the high ridgelines. Big Mike cut up the hard sausage, the last of our food, and passed it around. We ate and walked, stumbling along the rocky path. The Storch made a few more passes and then gave up. I envied them their evening meal. And soft bed.

We walked silently for hours, too exhausted for words. In the light of the partial moon, the landscape looked familiar, but whenever I thought we were close to Pranjani, I spotted a landmark that told me we still had too damn many miles to go.

Nick was doing okay, holding tight to the reins while resting with his face buried in the horse's mane. His bandages were caked with blood, but there was no new bleeding. My biggest worry was an infection from any shrapnel left inside. He'd have to wait for Rudy to look, then a real doctor in Bari.

I glanced at my watch. I tried to focus my eyes, which were gritty from lack of sleep. I blinked until I could make out the luminous dial. Quarter after three in the morning.

"Happy New Year," I said, not feeling much joy about it.

"What time is sunrise?" Big Mike asked.

"Seven o'clock, or very close to," Sanja said. "You are thinking of the aircraft?"

"Yeah. They'll probably take off from Bari before dawn and cross the coastline just before first light to avoid detection," I said. "Then land at Pranjani the moment there's enough daylight."

"In four hours, then," Big Mike said. "They won't want to stay on the ground long. Maybe twenty minutes and they'll be gone. The last flight out of Pranjani."

"They know we're coming, right?" Johnny said. "Tomas would

have radioed the news, and your chaps in Pranjani are sure to wait."

"No, they're not," I said. I rubbed my eyes and tried to make out the rocks and roots in the trail ahead. "First, it's politics. Both the Brits and the Yanks have withdrawn their support for Mihailović. Churchill has eyes only for Tito, and this operation to rescue downed airmen is our last hurrah. Our OSS contact told us the flight this morning was the last one, to extract any stragglers."

"What's second?" Johnny asked.

"They probably think we're dead," I said. "There had to be a lot of radio communication between Tomas and other units. Rudy would've heard about the ambushes, spotter planes, and bombers. When we don't show up on time, it's the obvious conclusion."

"Maybe they'll be delayed by weather," Big Mike suggested. It was cold, but the stars were bright and the wind light.

"Mechanical failure," I said. "The whole thing's postponed until tomorrow."

"I'll buy that," Johnny said.

The trail smoothed out and, finally, the going was easier. Staying awake wasn't. I lost track of time until we halted on the outskirts of Planinica. It had taken about an hour and a half for us to ride here from Pranjani in daylight. On foot, it would take more than twice as long. I could see the first signs of predawn as a diffuse, reflected light in the east.

I explained to Nick and Johnny what had happened there, as Sanja and Big Mike went to scout things out.

"We don't know if the Ustaše have come back or if any villagers returned," I said. Johnny and I leaned against the horse, feeling the welcome warmth of its flanks. Just as I began to worry about how long they were taking, Sanja and Big Mike jogged back.

"Most bodies have been buried, where they lay. Not all," Sanja said. "Some houses are burnt."

"Everything's been looted," Big Mike said, and threw a blanket over Nick. "This was all I could find."

We moved out without a word. In the faint light, doors gaped. Roofs had fallen in where they'd burned through, and flares of soot framed the windows. It smelled of woodsmoke and decaying flesh. I looked straight ahead, my eyes fixed on nothing but taking the next step, and the next, and all the while I tried not to think of what had happened to that village with its neatly tended apple orchard.

It soon grew lighter but no warmer. We were now on the wooded trail we'd taken from Pranjani. Carpeted with leaves, it ran along a gurgling stream and rose steeply until it led us out from under the forest canopy and onto a main road. I was exhausted.

As we stood on the road, gasping, a C-47 Skytrain flew overhead, gained altitude, and banked on a westerly course to Italy.

The last flight from Pranjani.

CHAPTER FORTY-FOUR

VILLAGERS SURROUNDED US as we made our way into town. They embraced Sanja, patted us on the back, and commiserated with Nick over his injuries. I shuffled through the gathering crowd, the image of the departing C-47 burned into my mind. I didn't know what to do next except lie down and sleep for a day or two.

Rudy and Captain Dilas ran over and joined the throng, full of apologies and concerns. Rudy gave Sanja a hug and I told him to help Nick. He led the horse to the town hall, where a makeshift infirmary was set up. Nikola helped to ease Nick off the horse and carry him inside. I told Nick I'd figure something out, but that was just to cheer him up. He knew it too.

I untied the sack with the German uniform from around the pommel. I don't know why it mattered at this point, but maybe the OSS crew could use it.

Dilas said he'd have Rudy send a radio message to Colonel Harding at Bari, once he'd gotten Nick patched up. He said some other things, but they weren't about food, soap and water, or a warm bed, so I ignored him. I followed Sanja, who was being swept along by four older women who seemed to have taken charge of her.

At Sanja's place, a gray-haired lady was already at the stove stirring a pot. The smell and warmth hit me hard. I dumped my gear by the couch and collapsed. Big Mike and Johnny fell into chairs. We slept, but for how long, I had no idea. I awoke to the sound of a creaking pump and gushing water. I managed to get up to investigate, only to be shooed out of the kitchen by two women, but not before I caught a glimpse of Sanja at the far end of the kitchen, wrapped in a towel as she stepped out of a wooden tub.

At some point we were invited to remove our boots and wash our feet in the tub. Our coats and boots were taken away, and we wordlessly soaked our aching feet and cleaned our faces with the clear, cold water.

Rudy returned. He'd removed more shrapnel and stitched Nick up. He didn't think there were any other pieces, but only an X-ray could confirm it.

Then came the goulash. Lamb, I think. It warmed my stomach and soul, but I still felt lost, stranded behind enemy lines. We were alone, except for these good people who shared all they had. Sanja appeared, dressed in clean clothes, her hair still damp. She poured slivovitz and we drank.

"Now sleep," she said as she set her empty glass down with a thud. "Then we talk."

THE NEXT THING I knew, I awoke in bed to the sound of Big Mike's snoring. It was dark outside, my watch showed five o'clock. I didn't know if it was late afternoon or early morning. Groggy, I rolled out of bed and found my boots by the door. Cleaned and buffed, with my socks, stiff from being dried in front of a fire, draped over them.

I went downstairs and found Marty Dilas at the kitchen table. "Good afternoon," he said. That answered that.

"Which day?" I asked.

"Same day you arrived," Dilas said. "But you looked beat enough to have slept straight through."

"Where's Johnny?" I asked. I had a recollection of leaving him asleep on the couch.

"He and Sanja went to check on Nick," Dilas said. "He's doing okay, considering."

"Considering that we're stuck here," I said. "Do I smell coffee?"

"Yeah, I just made some," Dilas said. He got a cup and filled it. "Figured you might be up. They resupplied us this morning. Our orders are to wait here for orders."

"Sounds like the army," I said, and accepted the cup. I drank it and felt more awake than I had in days. Dilas looked like he had something to say, but I was in no mood to drag it out of him. "You got everyone else on the plane okay?"

"Yeah. Ten guys. They all left their boots," he said.

"So did I. The only difference is I'm still wearing them," I said, and took a sip of coffee.

"Listen, Billy, we had orders," Dilas said. "Ten minutes on the ground, no more. It was out of my hands."

"I know," I said. "No one's to blame. We would've made it, but things went wrong after we left Virovac."

"What went wrong is that you ran into a German anti-Partisan offensive," Dilas said. "Units were brought in from Belgrade to Sarajevo. You're lucky you made it at all."

"That explains the Luftwaffe," I said. "It seemed pretty heavy-handed just to track us down." I didn't have the energy to tell Dilas the story about how we met Flint. "Are they headed this way?"

"No, doesn't look like it," he said. "Sanja told me about the Black Legion at Planinica. That's as close as they came to us. Which raises an interesting possibility."

"If it doesn't include bombs and hiking in the dark, I'm ready to listen," I said.

"There's a large Allied base on the island of Vis in the

Adriatic," Dilas began. "It's about forty miles offshore, manned by British and Yugoslav troops. Tito's Partisans, to be exact. Nice little stronghold. There's an airstrip for fighters and a Motor Torpedo Boat Squadron as well."

"If there's an airstrip, why can't they fly us out?"

"It's a British operation in conjunction with Tito, that's why," Dilas said. "Plus the fact that the runway is too short for anything except single-seat fighters."

"I get it. Politics. So we've got an island bristling with guns thirty-five miles off the coast," I said. "What good does that do us?"

"How about I fix you up with a ride?" Dilas said with a grin. "I can arrange a rendezvous with a motor torpedo boat for tomorrow. At night, of course. The Germans have damn few warships of any size in the area, but as you know, they're not short of airpower. So it must be after dark. Then we get you to Vis and figure things out from there. There have to be ships supplying them from Italy."

"Sounds simple," I said. "What's the catch?"

"Well, mainly that it's about two hundred and twenty miles to the coast on bad roads, and we can't say for sure you won't run into trouble. Once you get near the coastline, your chance of running into a German or Ustaše patrol increases. Oh, and the truck has a tendency to break down."

"Okay, enough joking," I said. "Tell me the real plan."

"That's it, Billy," he said. "Unless you want to wait and see where the OSS sends us next and tag along."

"Helluva choice," I said, and gulped the coffee, which had long since gone cold. "Tell me more about the patrols."

"We know for sure the Krauts have pulled units northward for the anti-Partisan campaign. But they will still have some patrols along the coast to watch for landings. They obviously know about Vis and that we could launch a raid at any time," he said. "My bet is that they're light on the ground, and you can get through. I'll request a diversionary raid down the coast at Dubrovnik to draw their attention."

I refrained from reminding Marty he was betting on our lives. Big Mike came downstairs and announced himself with a yawn.

"I smell coffee," he said. "What's up?"

"Our number, maybe," I said. "Marty's got an idea." I went to the stove and poured a cup for Big Mike, then refilled my own as Dilas went over the plan again.

"They don't have Lysanders or any other plane large enough?" Big Mike asked. "They could do two trips in no time." The Lysander was a special-operations aircraft used to deliver agents behind enemy lines. It could take two passengers in a pinch.

"Like I explained to Billy, Vis is a British base, and they no longer support the Chetniks," Dilas said. "But I can call for an extraction involving you four. Two Yanks and two Brits are right up their alley."

"Just the four of us on this trip?" Big Mike asked.

"Right. I can't even send a guide. There's only enough fuel to get you there, and I won't strand one of the Chetniks in Ustaše territory," Dilas said. "I'll give you a map, don't worry."

"I'm not worried about a map," I said. "I'm worried about running into the Black Legion or the SS."

Sanja, Rudy, and Johnny walked in at that moment. Big Mike and I looked at each other, the same idea slowly dawning in our exhausted brains.

"What?" Johnny said, looking at the two of us.

"Captain Dilas has a plan," I said. "The good news is that it doesn't involve horses. But we do need to travel in the company of Sturmbannführer Alfred Hansen, 21st Waffen SS."

Dilas was confused, which of course he would be, not

knowing about the German uniform. I fetched the bag I'd carried in and displayed it for Dilas.

"Impressive," he said. "Even a Soldbuch."

"Disgusting," Johnny said. "But we need to get Nick back. He's running a fever. Tell me more."

We went over it again. This time, with the added touch of a German officer in the entourage. I'd wondered about Nick impersonating an Ustaše, but if he was in bad shape, that wasn't going to work. He could have driven, since a Sturmbannführer wouldn't be at the wheel.

Sanja mentioned that Nikola had a cousin in Brist, which was very close to Klek. If he volunteered to drive, he could seek refuge with him. Nick, Big Mike, and I would be in the back of the truck, prisoners being transported.

"To Dubrovnik," Dilas said. "It's a large town on the coast and garrisoned by the Krauts. I've got a German typewriter and I'll get something official-looking typed up. I'm sure it'll pass muster with the Ustaše, at least."

"There'd be a guard in the back," Big Mike said.

"I don't know if we can risk another man," Dilas said. "Nikola's cousin will shelter him, I'm sure. A second man might be too much to ask."

"Tie them up," Sanja said. "They are dangerous men, as we know."

"This gets better and better," Big Mike said. "No way for Nick to play the guard?"

"No," Rudy said. "I have his leg well wrapped and the fever might mean an infection. I've given him penicillin, which will help, but he'll have to lie flat."

"We'll all be patients, then," I said. "Bandage us so it looks like we couldn't make it ten paces."

"With pistols hidden in slings, that sort of thing," Big Mike said. "It'll be a breeze."

"Perfect!" Dilas said as he slapped the table. "Rudy, let's get a message coded and send it off."

"You sure you're up for this?" I asked Johnny after the two OSS men had gone off to radio the base at Vis.

"I'm sure," Johnny said. "As long as the breeze doesn't turn into a hurricane."

CHAPTER FORTY-FIVE

THAT NIGHT WE had a feast. Beef stew, courtesy of Uncle Sam. Served with bread, cheese, and wine, all sent unofficially by Colonel Harding himself to thank the Chetniks and the OSS for helping us. The food, mostly C rations, was given to the villagers. The case of wine stayed with Rudy, and when the first bottle was opened, I sent up a silent prayer I'd soon be able to compliment Harding on his good taste.

Dilas confirmed the Motor Torpedo Boat Squadron had received his message and agreed to both the pickup and the diversionary attack at Dubrovnik. The attack would kick off at 1800 hours and last thirty minutes. Our pickup was set for 1815 hours. Dilas gave me a map and pointed out a small inlet near the town of Klek. A bombed-out hotel with a concrete quay was our rendezvous. I'd use a flashlight with a red filter to signal the boat.

"I used your name and connection to SHAEF in the message. In code, of course," Dilas said. "I thought it might impress the Royal Navy."

"You should have mentioned Johnny and Nick of the Royal Air Force," Big Mike said. "Escaped from the Nazis and made it halfway across Yugoslavia."

"Živeli," Sanja said as she gave the Serbian toast. With her glass held high, her eyes searched out each of us. "To victory. And peace."

We all drank to that.

THE NEXT MORNING, we gathered at the town hall to begin our journey. Dilas had the Opel Blitz truck ready, an extra jerry can of gas stowed in the back. Nikola checked the engine and declared it dobro. Good thing.

Big Mike helped Nick into the truck. His fever was down, but he was still hurting. While Johnny paraded around in the SS uniform, Rudy bandaged Big Mike and me, wrapping cloth around our heads and legs. Then came the slings, each with a pistol hidden inside. Would it work? I hoped we wouldn't need to find out.

Nikola pulled the Ustaše cap on tight and declared us ready.

I shook hands with Rudy and Dilas.

Sanja gave me a hug and told me to return when her country was free.

"I hope that's soon," I said. Big Mike and I climbed in the back and made Nick as comfortable as we could with the few blankets available.

Nikola started the engine. Johnny tossed off "Auf wiedersehen" to everyone and it got a laugh. I prayed it wouldn't be our last.

We waved goodbye from the truck bed as Nikola pulled onto the road. We tied down the flapping canvas but left it loose enough to see through the gaps. Johnny slid the small back window open.

"Comfortable, gents?" he asked.

"Ask me in a couple of hours," I said. "Do you have the map?"

"Nikola said to leave it. He knows the way, and the Ustaše would be suspicious of a stranger who needed a map," Johnny told us.

"It's his backyard," Big Mike said, and closed his eyes.

It was a smooth ride for the next hour and a half. We saw no one, even as we drove through two small villages. Armed men on the road meant it was a good time to stay indoors. Then it began to rain. A light mist at first, then a steady downpour. The road was two lanes of hardpack dirt, the dips and depressions filled with water. Nikola had to slow down.

"He says not to worry about the rain," Johnny relayed to us. "If I understand him properly, the Ustaše are too weak and cowardly to get wet. And lazy, especially if they're doing Jerry's work for him."

"I'll buy that," I said. "Right, Nick?"

"Same here," Nick said. He sounded tired, but alert. "Chetniks have been saving my skin for days, no reason to think different now."

"Good man," Big Mike said. He glanced at his watch. "We're making good time, even with the rain."

The next twenty minutes were spent navigating a switchback route that took us to a higher elevation, where the rain turned to snow. That caused Nikola to drive even more slowly. Johnny explained that although Nikola had faith in the engine, the tires were another matter. The treads were worn down, and since Nikola didn't want to skid off the road and into a gully, we'd have to putter along at twenty miles an hour.

"I think horses would have been preferrable," Nick said.

Three more hours ticked by, and the landscape began to slope toward the sea. The snow turned to a mist, which gradually faded away. Nikola pulled off the road and filled the gas tank from the jerry can. Then after a brief break to eat bread and goat cheese, Nikola started up the truck and gained speed on the downhill.

"Dobro!" he said, and pointed to the horizon emerging from the low clouds.

"Dobro bloody well indeed," Johnny said. "The Adriatic, dead ahead."

Nikola drove on, the clear road and downward slope welcome after the long slog through filthy weather. The thin blue line of the Adriatic Sea was still far off, maybe thirty miles, but our luck held. No patrols, no roadblocks.

The road rose again and took us to the crest of a small hill. A sign pointed to the village of Hutovo. From here, the blue waters seemed very close. As we rounded a curve on the downhill run, the village came into view.

It was filled with Germans. Trucks drove across our path in the village center as Krauts unloaded a truck twenty yards ahead, blocking most of the road.

"Johnny, any ideas?" I said through the rear window. He shouted at me in German, which I hoped meant he was getting into character. He rolled down his window and tapped the horn for Nikola to give it a workout.

Johnny gestured with his arm as he leaned out the window enough for the startled soldiers to see his SS runes and rank on his collar tabs. Nikola laid on the horn and glared at the Fritzes scrambling to the side of the road. One of them, a Wehrmacht sergeant, gave Johnny a stiff-arm salute and then got his men out of the way. As the truck slowed, Johnny shouted at the noncom and pointed to the traffic cutting across our path. The guy jumped to it, probably happy to get this loudmouth SS officer on his way. He ran into the intersection and stopped traffic, windmilling his arm to signal Nikola to proceed. At which point I shut the rear window, lay back, and gratefully felt Nikola accelerate through the intersection.

It took another hour for us to get close to our destination. Nikola took a back road to skirt the village of Klek in case there were any Germans about, which suited Johnny just fine.

"My acting days are over," he said. "Give me a nice quiet bomb run over Berlin any day."

The sun was about to set as Nikola parked outside the

deserted hotel by the inlet. Bombed and burned, the three-story structure was blackened and shattered. But the squat concrete quay was intact, and we didn't have long to wait. We helped Nick out and discarded our white bandages as Nikola gave each of us a knuckle-crushing handshake. He and Nick spoke, then the big Chetnik drove off.

"What did he say?" Big Mike asked.

"That we should tell the generals in Italy not to forget the Chetniks," Nick said. "They want freedom from both Hitler and Stalin."

"Freedom. Ain't that what we're fighting for?" Big Mike asked.

"Tell it to the generals," Johnny said.

CHAPTER FORTY-SIX

IT HAD BEEN dark for two hours. The luminous dial on my watch read almost six, which was when the diversionary attack to our south would kick off. We were on the quay, trying to stave off the cold. Nick was wrapped in his blanket, and Johnny paced to keep his blood flowing. Big Mike scanned the dark horizon with the binoculars while I watched for the six o'clock fireworks.

Bursts of yellow and red lit the sky, miles down the coast. Tracers arced toward the shore as explosions boomed. Rapid machine-gun fire mixed with the blast of antiaircraft guns from the attacking motor torpedo boats.

"They're putting on one helluva show. All eyes will be on Dubrovnik," I said, then turned away from the display to retain what night vision I could.

"Keep your eyes peeled," Big Mike said. "They'll probably come in on muffled motors, and with all that racket we won't hear a thing."

I got my flashlight ready. The firing continued to light up the sky, creating strange flashes and sudden shadows. I thought I saw movement on the water and blinked my eyes to bring it into focus. Big Mike elbowed me and pointed.

"Movement at eleven o'clock."

"Got it," I said. I picked up a large object floating silently toward us. I flicked on my flashlight and gave the recognition signal. Three short and one long flash of red. It came back, one long and three short. "It's them."

The hundred-foot motor torpedo boat was thirty yards away before I heard the low rumble of its engines. It eased up gently to the quay, and two sailors leapt out with mooring lines.

"Four of you, right? Hop aboard," one of them said.

"Give us a hand," Big Mike said as he helped Nick limp over the gunwale. Arms reached out to haul him in.

"Someone keep a bead on the Jerry!" the sailor with the rope shouted, pointing at Johnny.

"That's Sturmbannführer to you, mate," Johnny said as he went aboard, one step ahead of me. "Let's get the bloody hell out of here."

"Aye-aye," the sailor responded with a surprised grin. In seconds, the boat was moving away from the quay. I made my way midships, past the twin Vickers machine guns, and looked up to the bridge where an officer stood at the helm.

"Thanks for the lift, Captain," I said.

"No problem, Billy," a familiar voice said. "Come on up."

"Harry? Is that you?" I said as I clambered up the ladder. Harry Dickinson of the Royal Navy Reserve. It wasn't my first time on a boat of his. "How long has it been? Since Sicily, right?"

"Half a year, half a lifetime, who knows?" Harry said. He offered his hand and we shook. He still had his rugged good looks beneath bright blond hair, and, as always, carried himself with a piratical air. But now he looked tired, with lines around his eyes and a furrowed brow. I'd been on a few runs with him. Once he slugged me over a mission that had gotten some of his crew killed. But that was all water under the bow by now, or at least I hoped it was.

"Good to see you, Harry. What are the chances you'd be the one to pick us up?" I said, genuinely glad to see him. Even with our past differences, I'd never forget the debt I owed him. He'd saved Diana's life back in Algiers.

"Chances were very good once I saw your name on the orders," he said. "I was curious what you were up to and wanted to handle the pickup myself. Something interesting I'd say, based on your pal in the German uniform. Hope things worked out inland."

"Thanks, Harry. That means a lot," I said. "We got stranded after the last flight for Bari left with a load of downed airmen. Johnny—the guy in the uniform—is important, let's just say. We needed to get him out."

"Yeah, we heard that the Chetniks sheltered fliers," he said. "Seems like Winston has taken a liking to Tito, so we've been told 'hands off.'"

"Well, there's no Chetniks here, so you don't have to worry. You have any trouble on the way over?" I asked.

"No. Unless we get spotted by a shore battery, we're safe at night," he said. He called down to his radioman and told him to give the signal for the other vessels attacking Dubrovnik to disengage. Then he opened the throttle, and the motor roared to life. "Hang on."

I had to. It was cold, but the rush of movement was exhilarating. As we sped out into open water, Big Mike came up onto the bridge.

"Billy's told me a lot about you," Big Mike said after I introduced them.

"Did he mention how I usually end up wounded when he's around? Shot in the leg, shrapnel in the arm, that sort of thing?" Harry said.

"No, but it sounds familiar," Big Mike said. Big Mike had joined our crew in Sicily, but after I'd last encountered Harry. A lot had happened since then, so I caught Harry up on Diana and Kaz as we raced along.

"We need to get to Bari pronto," Big Mike said. "Any chance of hitching a ride over there?"

"We've made the trip several times," Harry said. "On a calm, sunny day with air cover, it's delightful. But we've got an operation coming up, so the long-range taxi service is out. But there is a destroyer bringing supplies next week. You could return with them."

"Can't wait," I said. "We heard the runway at Vis is short, suitable only for single-engine fighter planes. Is that right?"

"Basically," Harry said. He spun the wheel to starboard as he took the boat around one of the offshore islands. "The runway's only twenty-two hundred feet and bombers need five thousand. Impossible to land anything larger than a fighter. Except for the guy who just did it in a four-engine heavy bomber."

"That's a fellow I'd like to meet," I said. "How'd he manage it?"

"Guts and skill, I'd wager. Wouldn't have believed it if I hadn't seen it myself," Harry said. He slowed the boat as he eyed the horizon. "Last week a B-24 came in with one engine dead and the other on fire. It was trailing thick black smoke, and I thought it was going to hit hard and explode. There are several wrecks of bombers that have tried it alongside the runway. Not very inspiring to see, but he had no alternative. He needed every inch of that runway, but he did it, with the help of a couple of parachutes."

"What?" I said, thinking I'd misheard him.

"Yes, parachutes. He had his crew lash two chutes to the stanchion holding the ball turret. As the plane touched down, they pulled the rip cords and tossed the chutes out the waist gun windows. Helped slow down the bomber. Brilliant maneuver."

"He's still here?" Big Mike asked.

"Indeed, but not for long. They've been repairing the engines, and I hear they're set to fly out tomorrow morning," Harry said. "Everyone wants to watch, of course. Thinking of tagging along?"

"If he'll have us," I said.

"And if he isn't a maniac," Big Mike added.

"Ha! Wise to be cautious, my friend. I'll give you an introduction and you can decide Now, get out of the wind and help yourselves to a ration of rum belowdecks," Harry said.

MY BELLY WAS warmed with rum by the time we docked at Vis. Johnny had divested himself of the SS uniform in favor of Royal Navy blue, which, as a fashion statement, suited him much better. We stood on the deck as we entered the harbor packed with small craft, from fishing trawlers to motor torpedo boats. Near the dock, an ambulance waited to take Nick to the base hospital. I'd told him about our chance to fly out tomorrow, and he wisely suggested a few days of hospital care might be better for him. Hard to disagree.

We shook hands and promised to visit Nick in the morning if the flight didn't pan out. Which meant we reserved the right to chicken out. Harry told his executive officer to secure the motor torpedo boat and took us to his jeep parked next to an antiaircraft emplacement.

"Seeing as you're light on luggage, I'll take you right to George," Harry said. "Splendid fellow, by the way. One of your all-American types."

Big Mike and I piled in back with our rucksacks, and Johnny took the passenger seat. Harry drove on land as he did at sea. Slow at first, then fast and faster.

He pulled onto the runway and sped past rows of fighter planes and finally braked close to a big B-24. They called them flying boxcars, and it was evident why. They didn't have the smooth angles of a B-17, but they got the job done and carried more bombs to boot.

Work lights set up around the aircraft illuminated the engines. Crewmen stood on ladders, tools in hand. An officer in a leather flight jacket held a clipboard and talked through a checklist with a mechanic.

"George, how are things?" Harry said as soon as they were done.

"Fine, Harry," he said. "We're as ready as can be. You coming to wave goodbye in the morning?" George was square-faced with a strong jaw and a clear Midwestern accent.

"Wouldn't miss it," Harry said, and introduced the three of us. "Lieutenant George McGovern."

"Lieutenant McGovern, we'd like to fly out with you, if that's all right," I said. "It's critical that Flight Sergeant Adler get back to England."

"What are you boys doing here?" McGovern asked. "I didn't think there were any American troops on Vis."

"Big Mike and I have just come from Yugoslavia, courtesy of Harry and his crew. Johnny escaped from a POW column and has been on the run for days. I can't say more, but it is vital that we get back," I said. I filled him in on the Chetnik rescue of aircrew and how we'd missed the final flight.

"Okay," McGovern said. "One second and you'll have your answer." He shouted to the copilot and told him to start up number three. The propellor turned, the engine coughed, belched gray smoke, then caught. The prop spun into a blur and the turbocharged piston engine's growl turned into a purr. McGovern made a cutoff motion and the copilot shut number three down. "You're welcome to join us first thing in the morning, Captain. The Dakota Queen is ready."

CHAPTER FORTY-SEVEN

I'D RADIOED COLONEL Harding. He'd confirmed that he'd be waiting at the Bari airfield with a C-47, ready for immediate takeoff. We cleaned up, got a change of uniform, and enjoyed a hot meal. Harry regaled us with tales of smuggling agents and arms into Greece and Yugoslavia. Lieutenant McGovern talked about how the thick flak they flew through was worse than any image of hell he'd ever imagined.

"But you know what really frightens me?" McGovern said. "My wife is going to have our first baby in a couple of months. The thought I might never see my first child keeps me up at night." His voice trailed off and his gaze rested on the far wall, decorated with the Union Jack.

"Let's hope we're making the world a better place," Big Mike said. "Otherwise, what are we doing here?" The question was left unanswered, and McGovern once again warned us he couldn't guarantee success in the morning. He'd offered his crew the chance to stay behind and wait for a ship, but they said they'd stick with him, which I figured counted for a lot.

That's how I ended up, an hour after dawn, aboard the Dakota Queen, hunkered down aft of the waist gunners' positions with Big Mike and Johnny, sitting on equipment boxes. With no bombload and enough fuel for only the hundred-mile jaunt to Bari, the B-24 was as lightweight as a forty-thousand-pound four-engine bomber could be. It sat at the far end of the runway. A drop-off at the other end of the airstrip led directly to crashing waves on a rocky spit of land.

"Hang on," one of the waist gunners told us as the first engine turned over. "The skipper's going to bring all four engines to full throttle before he releases the brake. Things'll be shaky as all hell." From our makeshift seats, we held on to the bulkhead as the powerful engines roared into life.

The fuselage rattled and shivered as the throttle increased. The engines snarled and the noise reached a high pitch that threatened to pierce my skull. The waist gunner braced himself and shouted, but his words were lost in the vibrating metal. Outside the gunner's window, I saw the wing flaps go up, and I felt the aircraft straining to leap forward and take to the sky. I wondered how much strength it took to keep the brakes on, when, suddenly, the howling engines reached a crescendo and the bomber shot down the runway. The force hurtled us back, which, thankfully, made it impossible to spot the wreckage of bombers that had been bulldozed off the runway.

I braced myself for impact. Instead of heading into a grinding crash, I felt the slightest lift as the wheels left the ground. McGovern pulled the aircraft into a steep ascent, sending us tumbling once again. The hydraulic whine of the retractable landing gear meant we'd passed the point of no return. I made my way to the window as the plane continued its sharp climb, and was rewarded with the sight of the dark blue Adriatic waters beneath our wings.

"The man can fly," Johnny said as he pulled himself upright. The engines had been throttled down but were still loud as the B-24 settled into a more leisurely climb.

"The skipper put us down on that rock," the waist gunner said. "That was the hard part. I knew he'd get the Dakota Queen back in the air."

"Fighters," Big Mike said, and pointed to circling planes high above us. Two of them rolled into a dive and headed straight for us.

"Don't worry," the gunner said as two silver P-51 Mustang fighters swooped down over us. "It's our escort. They'll take us into Bari."

"Red Tails," the other gunner said. "Best in the business." The tails of the Mustangs were painted a deep red, easily recognizable even at high speeds.

"What makes them so good?" Big Mike asked. He squinted into the sunlight and followed the arcing path of the fighters.

"They stick close to us," the gunner said. "Other squadrons take off as soon as they see Kraut fighters and engage. It's what flyboys do, but that leaves us holding the bag. By the time they return, we're fighting off the next wave by ourselves."

"They're a great outfit," the other gunner said. "I breathe easier whenever I see the Red Tails."

"The 332nd Fighter Group, right?" Johnny said. "Negro pilots, aren't they?"

"Yeah. Some of us wondered about how good they'd be, but now there's damn few of us who wouldn't buy a round of drinks for those guys," the gunner said. The plane leveled off and the gunners took their positions and kept an eye out for the enemy.

"You know, my father fought in the Great War," Johnny said as he sat down. "For the Kaiser, and he was proud to do so. Quite odd to think that if there had been no Nazis, I might have fought for Germany myself. Much like those chaps. Not fully accepted, and prone to be abused, but still willing to fight and die for the nation of their birth."

"You're fighting for a good cause, Johnny," I said.

"True enough. But even so, I do feel unmoored at times," he said as he rubbed his hand over the wool of his heavy blue RAF jacket. I guessed this was one of those times.

■ ■ ■

AN HOUR LATER we touched down at Bari on a nice long runway. No parachutes were needed to slow the ship. McGovern cut the engines and we all piled out. Colonel Harding awaited Big Mike, Johnny, and me in a jeep, and two other vehicles were ready to pick up the Dakota Queen's crew.

"Thanks for the ride, Lieutenant," I said as we shook hands. "I don't think I'll ever forget that takeoff."

"You're not the only one, Captain," McGovern said with a grin. "Good luck getting Sergeant Adler back to England. You've still got a lot of flying to do. Take care, fellas."

We said so long and hustled over to where the colonel sat in his jeep, and snapped off our salutes.

"Colonel Harding, this is Flight Sergeant Johnny Adler," I said as we clambered aboard.

"Congratulations on a magnificent escape, Sergeant," Harding said. "You covered a lot of ground."

"Thank you, sir. I was highly motivated to avoid any further hospitality courtesy of the Third Reich," Johnny said. "But I couldn't have done it without the Chetniks."

"A lot of our men are telling the same story," Harding said as he accelerated. "Now, tell me, do you have the goods on Roscoe Bigsby?"

"Not hard evidence, Colonel," I said. "Johnny suspected Bigsby of stealing equipment and was planning on speaking to Major Brockman after his next mission, but then his Lanc went down."

"Several pieces of equipment had already gone missing, but Bigsby was very interested in the H2S ground-mapping radar," Johnny said. He had to lean forward from the back seat and hold on to his hat as Harding sped down the runway. "Then the wiring diagram for it vanished, and Sally found it in my Lanc after following Bigsby. She was returning it to me when she got nabbed for entering the men's barracks."

"The H2S radar was on Brockman's list of missing parts," Big Mike added.

"It sounds like you can link Bigsby to the stolen diagram, if you're lucky," Harding said, slowing as he approached a waiting C-47.

"We can put pressure on him to reveal his accomplices," I said. "He's got to be selling this stuff to someone."

"Unless we've totally missed a German spy ring, there isn't a single enemy agent left in Great Britain," Harding said as he braked to a halt. "At least none that haven't been turned by us. The black market is more likely."

"Colonel, there's no value for this hardware on the black market. No one would know what to do with any of it," Johnny said. "It's too advanced to be of practical use."

"It's up to you and Boyle to put the screws to this guy and find out what he's up to. We need to know who's gotten their hands on this hardware," Harding said.

"And why two people had to die," Johnny said. He lifted his face to the sun. The feeble winter warmth washed over him as he closed his eyes.

"Because they were close," I said. "There must be evidence that Bigsby is desperate to cover up. That's what we need to find."

"Any news from Kaz?" Big Mike asked.

"Yes. They shut down the base. Said it was due to an influenza outbreak," Harding said. "No one in or out. They're watching Bigsby from a distance, just to make sure he doesn't get suspicious and lam it. The local doctor and a Lieutenant Walters of the RAF Regiment are in on it, but Conan Doyle says they're trustworthy."

"Walters is a prig, but I guess he can be trusted," Johnny said. "Doc Yates is a good man, no worries there."

"Okay, Boyle, get Sergeant Adler up to RAF Hawkinge," Harding said. He looked up to the cockpit and waved, and the pilot turned the engines over. "Lieutenant Kazimierz has your ETA. Big Mike and I will be in Paris at SHAEF in a couple of days. Get this straightened out and meet us there."

"I'll do my best, Colonel," I said as I got out of the jeep and grabbed my pack. "Big Mike can fill you in on our encounter with Amos Flint."

"Flint? From Anzio?" Harding said. "What did you do with him?"

"We pulled a helluva switcheroo, Sam. I'll tell you all about it over coffee and donuts," Big Mike said.

"Just focus on this case," Harding said to me as we headed to the C-47. "No more trips down memory lane. That's all I ask."

CHAPTER FORTY-EIGHT

WE FLEW ALL day and touched down at RAF Hawkinge long after dark. It was cold, and the ground covered in puddles of water. Johnny and I exited the hatch as Kaz pulled up in a staff car. Brockman's staff car, which I'd appropriated. It looked like the army hadn't come looking for it yet.

"Welcome back," Kaz said as he got out and opened the trunk. Johnny stood at attention and saluted. Kaz returned it quickly and told him that was enough of that. We tossed in our gear and got in the car, which was a lot warmer than the airplane had been.

"What's the plan?" I asked.

"You are both to join me at Elham House," Kaz said. "We decided it would be best for Johnny to keep a low profile."

"Right, so I don't get my head bashed in while I sleep," Johnny said. "I like the way you think, Lieutenant. When do we have a go at Bigsby?"

"First thing in the morning," Kaz said as we pulled up to Elham House. "Right now, dinner is being prepared. We shall catch up with each other and review our plans with Squadron Officer Conan Doyle. Angelika and Diana will join us as well."

"Angelika is still here with you?" I'd filled in Johnny on who was who, but I'd figured Angelika would be back at Seaton Manor by now.

"Oh yes, indeed," Kaz said. He switched off the ignition and we grabbed our bags. He led us to the top floor, which ended in a narrow hallway with several small rooms. One was for Kaz and I to share, and, across the hall, Johnny had what amounted to a large closet. Kaz told us to clean up and come downstairs to the dining room next to Conan Doyle's office.

Twenty minutes later, washed and wearing a fresh uniform, I went down with Johnny. The door was open, and I spotted Diana right away, her sandy-colored hair gleaming in the light. She was in conversation with a WAAF who faced away from me, but as Conan Doyle entered from a rear door, the corporal turned around.

"Angelika!" I said, stunned. She wore the blue-gray Women's Auxiliary Air Force uniform with corporal's stripes on her sleeves.

"Corporal Kazimierz, if you please," she said. A smile lit up her face. I gave her a hug and then took a step back and tried not to be too unmilitary.

"Angelika is our newest Y Service operator," Conan Doyle said. "Her language skills are quite excellent, and we're glad to have her."

"I decided to join officially after seeing the work that goes on here," Angelika said. "It all happened so quickly, but I am thrilled."

"We all are, Angelika," Diana said as she gave my hand a discrete squeeze.

"But first and foremost, welcome back, Flight Sergeant Adler," Conan Doyle said as she stepped forward to shake Johnny's hand. "We are so glad to see you, for many reasons."

"Thank you, ma'am," Johnny said. "It's good to be back. I appreciate everyone's efforts to get me here. I just hope I can help bring the guilty party to justice."

"We'll talk more about that later," Conan Doyle said as Kaz

entered with two bottles of wine. "Right now, we want to celebrate your extraordinary escape. You are the guest of honor, Sergeant. Take your seat."

Kaz opened the wine and poured. We toasted Johnny and then Angelika, who'd been sworn in two days before, after a few strings had been pulled. I could see how pleased Kaz was, given the relative safety of Angelika's post. Safe compared to being with the Polish Home Army, but still a high-pressure job.

We drank and talked. The burden of the last days fell away in this room filled with people I cared deeply about. The dangers and long distances traveled faded as I held Diana's gaze, watched Kaz's pride and relief at his sister's new role, and witnessed how far Angelika had come from her time at the hands of the Nazis. I gave an involuntary sigh, amazed that we were still alive, survivors of a war that had killed so many. It wasn't over, but here we were, Diana and I, her clear eyes softening with welling tears. I wanted to ask what was wrong, but I didn't have to. It was the joy of love mixed with the fear of losing life now that it had become so precious. Kaz and Diana had both been careless with their lives in the first years of the war, but now every heartbeat marked the moments until the end of it. We all wanted to be there to drink in the peace to come, and now each bullet or bomb that came our way was out to steal that moment away.

I wanted to embrace Diana, but instead I sat quietly and drank in the sounds of laughter and clinking glasses. My eyes stayed with her, and it was enough.

But once the glasses were cleared away, it was time to move on and consider our next steps. Johnny went over what had happened with Bigsby and the H2S ground-radar diagram, along with his suspicions about other items that had gone missing.

"Bigsby had access to every missing piece of hardware on Brockman's list," Diana said. "We've continued questioning people but made it a point not to mention Bigsby as a suspect."

"I spoke to Bigsby as well," Kaz said. "We didn't want him to grow suspicious about being left off the list of potential witnesses. I see no reason for him to think we are on to him."

"Which is another reason I had you brought here, Sergeant Adler," Conan Doyle said. "You must stay at Elham House until this affair is settled. Bigsby would undoubtedly do a runner if he knew you had returned."

"Oh, he'd have good reason to worry," Johnny said. "I said I'd report him as soon as I got back. Never thought it would take so long."

"Good. Stay out of sight until things are resolved," Conan Doyle said. "Elham House personnel know you are here but are under orders not to mention it to anyone."

"Understood, ma'am," Johnny said. "I certainly don't want Bigsby to bolt, but isn't the base locked down?"

"We had to give up that charade as of this morning," Diana said. "It worked well enough until people noticed no one had fallen ill."

"We declared victory in the fight against influenza," Kaz said with a rueful laugh. "But no passes are being issued for another forty-eight hours."

"Which begs the question, how best to use that time?" Conan Doyle said. She drank the last of her wine and set the glass down. "Interrogate Bigsby and confront him with Sergeant Adler?"

"That could work," I said. "But if he denies the accusation and sticks to his guns, we've got nothing to fall back on. Nothing else turned up when you questioned other ground crew?" I glanced at Kaz and Diana.

"Nothing, other than a certain defensiveness about electronics being misplaced," Diana said. "Apparently it was taken for granted that a detailed inventory was not worth the time it took to maintain. Parts were moved about to wherever they were needed most."

"It's certainly an area we need to address," Conan Doyle said. "Sadly, the chaos of daily operations gave good cover to the theft of electronics over time. Some of the components are rather small and easily transported."

"The casings are often large, but those could be easily obtained anywhere," Kaz said.

"By whom? We need to know more about Bigsby's connections," I said.

"I received the distinct impression that he has no close friends on base," Kaz said. "Everyone I spoke to said he worked hard and helped wherever he could. Friendly enough, but more interested in electronics than football, according to one of his fellow crewmen."

"He seems to have been keen on radios from an early age," Conan Doyle said. "His file says he joined the Voluntary Interceptors at the age of fourteen. He had a radio he'd built himself."

"He visits his mother often," Diana said. "In Hackney, a rather depressed area in East London. We don't know much else about his family other than his father died nine years ago."

"No one's talked with his mother?" Angelika asked. She'd been quiet up until now but looked at us like we'd all missed a clue. "A mother knows when her child is in trouble, doesn't she? Even if she doesn't know what that trouble is, exactly. Don't you think?"

"Well, dear, I think we should have made you a sergeant straightaway," Conan Doyle said. "Excellent observation. Although it is unlikely Mrs. Bigsby is a partner in crime with her son, she may be able to lead us to an acquaintance who knows more."

"We'll have time if we drive there in the morning," I said. "We can interrogate Bigsby when we return. Even if we don't come up with any hard evidence, it could knock him off his stride to learn we've been nosing around his home."

"All right," Conan Doyle said. "You and Lieutenant Kazimierz go in the morning and see what you can find out." She stood, dismissing us.

"Could Captain Seaton accompany us?" I asked. "It may be helpful to have a woman present."

"Impossible," Conan Doyle said. "We have work here that overrides it, but bringing a woman along is a good idea."

"I could go," Angelika said. She looked eagerly from Kaz to Conan Doyle and then to me. "The squadron officer gave me leave to go to Seaton Manor and retrieve some of my belongings, since this recruitment was so unexpected. You could give me a ride to London and then I'll take the train to Norfolk. Simple. And Mrs. Bigsby might find a younger person easier to confide in."

Kaz's eyes flitted to mine, and I gave a slight nod. London was no more dangerous than RAF Hawkinge with a killer on the prowl. Conan Doyle, who knew of Angelika's recent past and the injuries to her leg, waited a beat as she studied Kaz.

"Very well," she said, with a firm nod to Kaz. "Another smart suggestion. I'll notify Lieutenant Walters to escort you to the main gate in the morning."

"To override the no-pass restriction," Diana explained. Of course.

"Sergeant Adler, Corporal Kazimierz, it has been a pleasure," Conan Doyle said. "Please excuse us as I need to speak with the others for a moment."

Kaz, Diana, and I followed Conan Doyle into her office.

"This won't take long," she said, once the door was shut. "But the Air Ministry has decided that it would be a breach of security to bring charges against the guilty party for crimes committed on the base."

"Murder and theft, you mean?" I said.

"I am afraid that is exactly what *they* mean," she answered. "Their thought is that if the suspect is arrested for the murder of Major Brockman, which happened off the base, there would be no need to mention anything about radio countermeasures. And the result would be just as final."

"Death by hanging," Diana said.

"Which would avoid any hint of scandal," I said.

"Always a desirable outcome for the high and mighty," Conan Doyle said. "And just for the record, a WAAF squadron officer is not privy to those exalted ranks."

"I didn't think it sounded like your style, ma'am," I said.

"It isn't, but I could only protest so much. I dare not risk putting our work here in jeopardy," she said. "When some men are crossed, their reaction can be all out of proportion."

"Especially when it comes to a woman who is in command," Diana said. "Of anything."

"We accept the challenge," Kaz said as he slapped his hand on the back of a chair and brought us back to the problem at hand. "Major Brockman was the first victim, so let us deal with his killer and be done with this."

"Agreed," I said. "It sounds to me like this needs to be treated as a civil, not military, matter. You know what that means."

"It means Detective Sergeant Henry Ruxton," Diana said. "Now I am even more angry at the Air Ministry."

Conan Doyle offered Diana the use of her telephone to make the arrangements with the Kent County Constabulary and bade us goodnight. As Diana contacted the switchboard, I told Kaz about our encounter with Amos Flint.

"He was a slippery character," Kaz said. "I am not surprised he took advantage of the attack on the convoy to escape, as Johnny did. He must have been worried about being liberated and then being found out."

"Right. He probably killed the guy whose name tags he wore. Knowing Flint, he wanted to find some out-of-the-way place to hide and then melt away in the confusion when the war ended," I said.

"I've left a message," Diana said as she rose from behind the desk. "We will meet Ruxton at eight o'clock at the Capel-le-Ferne police station. I say we are done for the day, wouldn't you?"

"I shall say goodnight," Kaz said. He smiled and slipped out the door.

"Would you like to see my room, Billy?" Diana asked. A sly smile graced her face. She slipped her arm into mine as we walked out into the hallway.

"And risk being exiled to St. Margaret's at Cliffe, on that lonely windswept coast?" I said.

"We can dream, can't we?"

CHAPTER FORTY-NINE

"Good morning, Sergeant Halfpenny," I said as I descended the stairs. The lobby was empty except for Halfpenny at her usual post.

"It promises to be," she said, with a glance out the large windows. Clouds moved across the sky, chased by a line of blue and early-morning sunlight. "Good to see you back, Captain. And Johnny as well." The last bit came out as a whisper.

"Johnny who?" I said, and shot her a wink just as we heard voices raised in argument out front.

"*That* Johnny," Halfpenny said as she jabbed her pen in the direction of the entrance. "He came downstairs and got upset when he saw Lieutenant Walters outside. I told him not to go but he was fuming."

Damn. I sprang for the door and threw it open. Walters stood next to his BSA motorcycle while Johnny berated him for a multitude of offensives, most involving Sally. Walters unbuttoned his long dispatch rider's jacket as if he were getting ready for a fistfight.

"Johnny, get the hell inside," I said, and grabbed him by the arm. "Now."

"I will, now that I've had my say!" He stomped inside just as Kaz came out.

"Do we have a problem?" Kaz asked. He checked the road for anyone who may have witnessed the argument.

"Adler will, if he tries that again," Walters said. "I could have him up on charges of insubordination."

"See how well that works," I said. "Johnny's one of the few POWs who's made a home run. I doubt your superiors would look kindly upon a chicken-shit charge like that his first day back."

"A home run is like hitting for six in cricket, Walters," Kaz said from behind me. "As for chicken shit, I believe you know what that means."

"We'll all be in the shit if you don't keep Adler confined," Walters said as he climbed on his BSA and pulled down his goggles. "I'll wait at the gate." He kick-started the motorcycle and drove off.

"He does have a point," I said. "I haven't had a chance to speak with you much. Safe to say you're happy with Angelika's decision to join up?"

"Quite. She was truly fascinated by the work here, and it is very good for her to keep her mind occupied. She continues to heal and will have regular checkups when we visit Sir Richard at Seaton Manor."

"He had a role in this?"

"Only to expedite the paperwork," Kaz said. "Conan Doyle is very supportive and is glad to have Angelika's language skills at her disposal. Plus, I believe she is smart enough to know that Sir Richard is a good man to have on one's side."

"Good," I said. "I'm glad. It's nice to see Angelika happy."

"She just mentioned the same about you and Diana," Kaz said. Now it was his turn to wink.

I turned up the collar on my trench coat to hide the blush on my cheeks and the smile on my face as I left to get the staff car. The sky had begun to clear, and contrails streamed toward Germany. How much longer were the Germans going to take that sort of around-the-clock punishment? Adolf and his pals had nothing to lose, since a hangman's noose was the best they could expect. But the everyday people under that reign of steel, what was their breaking point?

"Shouldn't I drive?" Angelika said as she came down the stairs and joined Kaz. "You two are officers and deserve a corporal as your driver."

"When did you learn to drive?" Kaz said as he opened the rear door and gestured for her to enter.

"In Poland. I once stole a German truck," she said as she slid into the back seat.

"Thanks for the offer, but we can't have a car thief driving a US Army vehicle," I said.

"Which you have stolen, if I'm not mistaken," she said.

"Was she like this growing up?" I asked Kaz.

"Worse," he said. "Hardly housebroken."

Angelika laughed as we approached the gate. Walters stood by the side of the road with a sour look on his face. He ordered the gate up and pointedly turned his back as we drove through.

"An unpleasant man," Angelika said.

"He thinks the war has passed him by," I said as I took the turn to Capel-le-Ferne.

"Millions wish it had. He doesn't understand his good fortune," Kaz said.

Who does? I wondered. What had driven Roscoe Bigsby to commit murder? Didn't he understand his good fortune in having a safe job working with electronics, the only thing he seemed to care about? What topped that?

I parked in front of the police station and noticed Ruxton's vehicle was nowhere in sight. We went inside and found Constable Sallow at his desk.

"Good morning, Constable," I said. "We're expecting Detective Sergeant Ruxton."

"Captain, you can expect much from the man, but showing

up today is not one of them," Sallow said. He rose as Angelika entered. "He directed me to accompany you and report back to him. In his words, he declined to go along with 'that woman's foolishness.'"

"We shall be delighted to have you along, Constable Sallow," Kaz said, and introduced Angelika.

"From what I understand, it will be a much more pleasant ride than we had anticipated," Angelika said. Sallow beamed, and I began to think Angelika might be right about her putting Mrs. Bigsby at ease. She did have a way about her.

As we drove on to London, we gave Sallow an update, sanitized of any reference to missing radio gear, which meant it wasn't really all that informative. Kaz focused on a witness we'd brought in, and how we needed more background information before proceeding with an interrogation.

"Aye, it makes sense," he said. "Maybe we'll get lucky, and his mum will tell all. Then won't Ruxton be sorry he didn't take this wee ride today."

"Anything new on your end, Constable?" I asked.

"No, sad to say. A killing on Christmas morning doesn't make for many witnesses," Sallow said. "I'm thinking that was the idea."

"One of Brockman's ground crew said he heard the major talk about taking a hike to see the White Cliffs," Kaz said. "He'd apparently flown over but never walked along the top."

"I'd guess your killer picked up on that," Sallow said. "What else do you have on this fellow?" As I drove, Kaz admitted it wasn't much.

We crossed the Thames at Tower Bridge. With Kaz giving directions, we made it to Sutton Place, where Mrs. Bigsby hung her hat.

"We just passed Hackney Central," Kaz said. "It is a short walk to Sutton Place from the train station."

"Not the most pleasant spot," I said as I pulled the car over to park close to the house number we'd been given. Most of the structures on this street were two to three stories, built with red brick, now blackened with soot. Some buildings were damaged, standing but empty. A few lots were bare except for stacked bricks piled up neatly and awaiting new construction. A handful of ground-floor shops were open, but it was mainly a residential street that curved into a dead end.

We surveyed Mrs. Bigsby's house. It had a tall, slanted roof with chimneys on either end. To the left, a narrow alleyway connected with another street, and on the other side, a two-story brickwork building was boarded up, a gaping hole in its roof.

"What are we going to say to her?" Angelika asked.

"We're doing a routine security check," I suggested. "Because Roscoe is engaged in vital work, we want to be sure no one has been asking about what he does. How does that sound?"

"It sounds fine," Sallow said. "Except why would you have a copper along? Four of us going into those small rooms might be a bit much."

"You're right," Kaz said as he cast his eyes up to the narrow windows. "Perhaps you should wait here."

"Good idea. And we don't want anyone stealing the car while we're in there," I said.

"I'll lay on the horn if there's trouble," Sallow said, and moved to the front seat. As the three of us crossed the street, I spotted curtains drawn back as the neighborhood took stock of the new visitors.

The door opened to a small foyer with mailboxes on the wall. Mrs. Bigsby was on the top floor, so we began to make our way upstairs. On the second floor landing a door creaked open as we passed and was shut quickly at the sight of our uniforms. The stairs were worn from generations of footsteps. Dust and cobwebs gathered in the corners, and, on the third floor, the hallway light was out.

"Spooky," I said, and stepped forward to knock.

"No, let me," Angelika said, and rapped lightly on the door. Chips of peeling paint fell at her feet.

"Yes?" The voice was faint from behind the door.

"Mrs. Bigsby? This is Corporal Kazimierz. From RAF Hawkinge, where Roscoe is based. May we come in?"

"Is Roscoe there?" The door still didn't open.

"No, he isn't. But he sends his regards. We need to speak with you for a moment."

I heard the door unlatch and it opened a crack. A short woman with graying curly hair peered out at us. She wore an apron over a heavy sweater and eyed us fearfully.

"What do you want?"

Angelika spun the tale of a routine security check like an expert liar. A necessary skill to survive in occupied Poland.

"You know Roscoe, you say?" Mrs. Bigsby opened the door wider, but only to stare at us with increasing suspicion.

"Of course, he's a popular young man," Angelika said. "And he's told me all about you and how much he enjoys visiting. We only need a few minutes of your time, I promise."

"I suppose," Mrs. Bigsby said, and opened the door. "Wipe your feet first, I keep a clean house."

She did. The sitting room was small, with shelves full of carefully dusted knickknacks. Two armchairs were arranged close to a large radio. A table held a wedding picture of a far younger Mrs. Bigsby and her deceased husband.

Angelika introduced herself and the two of us. Mrs. Bigsby didn't acknowledge us at all but talked with Angelika as she walked to the kitchen, which was separated from the sitting room by a half wall.

"I have to finish my dishes, you know," she said. "Can't stand a mess." She began drying and putting away a few plates and a cup on a drying board. I glanced at Kaz, who gave a small shrug.

"I can see you keep the place well-scrubbed," Angelika said.

She leaned against the counter so she could study the woman in profile. "I imagine Roscoe must appreciate that."

"Oh, he does, just as his father did. Please remind me what it is you want?" Mrs. Bigsby put the last plate away and faced Angelika. She twisted the dishrag in her hand. Her forehead wrinkled, and her eyes betrayed confusion. "And what are these men doing in my house?"

"We are from RAF Hawkinge, where Roscoe is stationed," Kaz said in his most soothing tone as he stepped into the kitchen. "Your son's work is so vital that we need to be certain no one has come around asking about it. I'm sure he's told you that it is quite top secret."

"Shall we sit, Mrs. Bigsby?" Angelika said. She nodded toward the chairs by the radio.

"Oh no. I haven't enough seats. No one comes calling. Please just get on with it." She gripped the dishrag even tighter, her eyes darting between Angelika and the two of us. "I don't like strangers much."

"I understand," Angelika said as she flicked her eyes in our direction, a clear signal for us to back off. "Let's just get a few questions out of the way, and we'll be gone. Is that all right?"

"Yes, dear, you go right ahead, but I don't know how I can help you," she said. Kaz and I backed up a few paces into the sitting room as Mrs. Bigsby put her dishrag to work scrubbing the already clean counter.

"Have any of Roscoe's friends from the neighborhood come calling?" Angelika asked. Mrs. Bigsby looked perplexed. "School chums, that sort of thing?"

"Roscoe didn't hang about with the boys on the street. No, no," she said as she shook her head at the very thought. "Bullies, the lot of them."

"What about anyone from the Voluntary Interceptors?" Angelika tried. "He joined at any early age, didn't he?"

"Oh, that was all hush-hush," she said. "It wasn't to be mentioned, not to anyone. And yes, he was only fourteen, I think. Built his own radio two years before that. He got an early start on his trade, just like his father. Couldn't have done that running around with those hooligans."

"What about your friends? Do any of them ask about Roscoe and his work?" Angelika said. Mrs. Bigsby rinsed the dishrag, wrung it out, and proceeded to scrub the small kitchen table.

"I knew a nice lady next door," she said. "Bombed out in the Blitz. I don't have much company these days. Some thought us stuck-up, you see, since we kept to ourselves. But that's the way Roscoe liked it."

Angelika gave me a look. It didn't seem like we were going to get much out of Mrs. Bigsby. Her life seemed contained within these small rooms. I decided to try one last approach and stepped into the kitchen.

"We're done, Mrs. Bigsby," I said. "Except for a check of Roscoe's Voluntary Interceptor radio. We need to confirm it's still here. Then we'll be out of your hair."

"I suppose that's all right," she said. "It's still here. I'll show you to the attic. It's a bit cramped." Angelika offered to stay and wandered to the window. I hoped she'd use the time to snoop around a bit.

Kaz and I followed Mrs. Bigsby down a hallway to a narrow, steep staircase that led to the attic. She went up ahead of us and gripped the banister to pull herself along. She unlocked the door and stepped inside. A single bare bulb lit the small room, along with a dormer window that let in daylight. A workbench against the wall held a radio, headphones, and an array of forms scattered about. Above the radio was a painted sign that read BIGSBY & SON. The space was barely ten feet by ten feet, and we were crammed in side by side.

"That was his father's shop. He repaired radios and whatnot.

That's where Roscoe got his interest in all things electrical," Mrs. Bigsby said. "He wanted that sign very much. Said one day he'd open a new shop and pass it on to his son. My Roscoe's a good lad."

"You must be proud," I said as I looked at the paperwork. Empty forms with headings like SIGNALS HEARD, CONTROL, ANSWER, and other terms that meant little to me. I wondered about what messages young Roscoe had picked up. All in code, of course. Groups of letters that would later be decoded. Was there any way he could have contacted a sender? Not without a transmitter, and even with my limited knowledge, I knew this was a receiver only.

The muted growl of a motorcycle rose up from the street.

A horn blasted, again and again.

"Excuse me," I said, and moved Mrs. Bigsby aside so I could get out the door. With Kaz right behind me, I went down as fast as the steep staircase allowed.

A gunshot boomed.

"Angelika!" Kaz shouted, and pushed past me at the bottom step. I unbuttoned my trench coat and unholstered my automatic.

The kitchen and the sitting room were empty.

"Get back, old man!" A shout came from the stairway and the smell of gun smoke hung in the air. It was Bigsby. How the hell had he gotten here?

"Angelika!" Kaz shouted again. We stood on either side of the open apartment door, weapons drawn, and waited to get some sense of what we faced.

"Piotr," she responded.

"Where's Adler?" Bigsby shouted, and I motioned for Kaz to stay put as I eased myself out onto the landing.

"He's not here, Roscoe," I said. He was three steps down, one arm around Angelika's neck and the other holding a revolver. On the next flight, Constable Sallow leaned against the wall, his hand held over a wound on his arm.

"Are you hurt, Angelika?" Kaz said as he moved into the doorway.

"No," she said. I saw her lip quiver. "Please don't hurt me, Roscoe. We only wanted to visit your mother."

"Bring Adler out," Bigsby demanded. "I know he's here."

"Did Walters tell you that?" I said. Walters had seen Adler with us and had avoided looking at the occupants of the staff car as we drove out. Then I noticed Bigsby wore the dispatch rider's long coat I'd seen on Walters this morning. "Did you take his bike out the main gate, disguised in his coat and goggles?"

"He's not dead, if that's what you're asking," Bigsby said. "But I want Adler out here now."

"Give yourself up, lad," Sallow cried out from below, his face twisted in a grimace of pain.

"Shut up!" Bigsby yelled. He swung his pistol in Sallow's direction while he held Angelika as a shield. We didn't have a shot.

"Please," Angelika said in a more plaintive voice. "Don't hurt me."

"You shut your mouth," Bigsby said, and gave her a sharp rap with the barrel of his revolver before he turned back to Sallow. Angelika reached into her overcoat pocket, and I caught a flash of steel.

The gravity knife.

I watched Bigsby's face contort into a scream as Angelika jammed the knife into the only flesh she could reach—his thigh, right above the kneecap. She pulled up savagely. He dropped the pistol and tried to stem the flow of blood from the gash Angelika had opened. He staggered down the steps, lost his balance, and tumbled head over heels to the landing below. He didn't move. Sallow bent down and pressed two fingers against his neck.

"Dead," he said.

Kaz took Angelika in his arms and guided her back up the

stairs. Mrs. Bigsby stood in the doorway. Angelika discretely released the blade into the handle and dropped the gravity knife into her pocket.

"I am so sorry, Mrs. Bigsby," Angelika said. She kept her bloodstained hand behind her back.

"Are you?" Mrs. Bigsby said. She took a step and peered down the stairs. "Can't say as I am."

CHAPTER FIFTY

"It's a cruel thing for a mother to say, but I've been treated terribly for years by Roscoe. He got that from his father, along with his fixation with radios," Mrs. Bigsby said. We'd settled her into a chair while Angelika washed Sallow's wound over the kitchen sink. Roscoe's shot had grazed him, but it wasn't serious.

"What did he do?" I asked.

"Kept me here, for the most part," she said. "He wanted no visitors snooping around, as he put it. He'd come up from the base without notice to check on me. Everyone thought he was such a doting son, but he was just making sure. Of me."

"Why?" I asked. I had a hunch I knew.

"Because of what's upstairs," she said. "There's another room. He'd bring things from the base when he came home. It's all up there, not that I've ever seen it. I don't have a key, you see. I wasn't allowed. Roscoe always said it was his fortune for after the war, and I was to protect his secret while he was gone. If I knew what was good for me."

"Was he violent with you?" Angelika asked, as she wound a bandage tight around Sallow's arm.

"I lied before about bullies in the street," she said. "It wasn't the lads in the neighborhood. It was Roscoe. People were afraid of him. As I was, with good reason." She cast her eyes down and shook her head. A police siren wailed in the street below. "He pushed me down those attic stairs once. Broke my ribs."

"We are very sorry, Mrs. Bigsby," Kaz said.

"Just one question before the police arrive," I said. "Was Roscoe here Christmas morning?"

"Yes. He'd come up the night before. He left early, took the first train back," she said.

"Did he say anything, or act strangely?"

"Looking back on it, he was nervous. In a hurry, it seemed. Roscoe wasn't one to be worried about much, so I took note. Trod carefully, you understand."

I did.

I told Mrs. Bigsby not to relate any of this to the police.

We spent the next hour or so going through statements, telling our stories, and keeping them straight. We stuck to the murder investigation involving RAF Hawkinge and the Kent County Constabulary. One of the coppers remembered Roscoe from his younger days and said he wasn't surprised things had ended badly for him. I showed the detective in charge my orders and gave him Conan Doyle's telephone number if there were questions. The presence of a constable, even one from another jurisdiction, helped move things along quickly.

As soon as the body was taken away and the police left, Kaz and I went back to the attic. The radio room faced the front of the house, but the attic was obviously much longer than this small space. I knocked on the wall and was rewarded with a hollow sound. Kaz pressed his hand around the edges until something clicked and a section on hinges opened, revealing an actual door. A locked door.

Kaz gestured for me to have a go at it. I backed up and rammed it with my shoulder. Nothing. Then I reared back and kicked one of the panels underneath the lock. Four booted kicks later, it cracked into pieces. I reached in and unlocked it from the other side.

I pushed the door open and grabbed at a pull chain in front of my face. The ceiling light illuminated three plywood tables strewn with electronics that looked right out of a Flash Gordon film. I didn't remember everything on Major Brockman's list, but this sure as hell looked like it covered the bases.

"The future," Kaz said. "Of course. After the war, there are certain to be commercial applications."

"Roscoe's fortune." I looked at a cathode-ray tube and wondered what potential he saw in that. "He could probably have made a good living just repairing this stuff."

"Think about commercial airlines," Kaz said. "If ground-mapping radar is important for the military, I imagine it would be profitable for airlines to help locate airfields and avoid mountains. Roscoe was certainly a killer, but that doesn't mean he wasn't intelligent. He might have seen a way to produce such electronics for general use."

"Yeah, and he had all this to jump-start his civilian enterprise. Bigsby and Son."

"Greed and a wish to honor his father. A potent blend of motives," Kaz said.

"Let's get out of here," I said.

We had a lot to do. Angelika's trip to Seaton Manor was tabled. We needed to get a truck from the air base to haul away all this gear. Kaz went out to find a telephone box to ring Conan Doyle with that request and to inform her of what had happened.

Now that Mrs. Bigsby wasn't in fear of Roscoe turning up, she made a pot of tea and fussed over Constable Sallow, making him comfortable in one of the easy chairs.

"I'm sorry to bring more people in, but once they haul the equipment out, they'll be gone," I said to her.

"Will you be all right, Mrs. Bigsby?" Angelika asked. "Is there anyone we can contact for you?"

"I will be fine once all that is out of my house," she said, her finger aimed at the ceiling. "I shall enjoy going to the shops and not worrying about who I might find when I get home. I can stay out as long as I like, can't I? It's quite a feeling."

"She's been terrorized, the poor thing," Angelika said in a low voice. "I wonder if she's in shock." We stood by the window and watched for Kaz to return. Sallow dozed in the armchair, his arm in a makeshift sling.

"It sounds to me as if she's been in a state of shock for years," I said. "First with Bigsby's father, then the son."

"Look, there's Piotr," she said. "What's he carrying?"

"A truck will be here shortly," Kaz said as he entered the room. "Conan Doyle dispatched one from a nearby airfield. We shall follow them to Hawkinge."

"What's in the bag?" I asked.

"Oh, just a few things for Mrs. Bigsby," he said. "Bread, cheese, jam, chocolate, and a small ham."

"How did you come by all that?" Angelika asked. "You don't have a ration book."

"This is Hackney, my dear," he said. "Where the market is as black as a moonless night."

ONCE OUR SMALL convoy passed through the gates, my first stop was to drop Constable Sallow off at the base hospital to have his arm taken care of. I said I'd drive him back to Capel-le-Ferne as soon as the medics were done.

"I promise to send a report on our joint apprehension of a dangerous killer to Detective Sergeant Ruxton first thing tomorrow," I said.

"Well, lad, it'll be worth the bullet just to see the look on his face when he reads it," Sallow said. "Make sure you mention the role Captain Seaton played. A sharp one, that lass."

"I'll tell her you said so, Constable," I said. "I hope this doesn't cause you any trouble with his nibs."

"Oh, it'll be well worth it," Sallow said as a medic began to unwrap his bandages. "Especially when he sees Captain Seaton's name and realizes what he missed out on."

I left Sallow chuckling to himself and went to Conan Doyle's office, where she and Diana embraced Angelika and asked half a dozen times if she was okay. Johnny Adler was there as well, finishing his briefing with the squadron officer. A bottle of whiskey materialized, and we drank a toast to the case being solved.

"How is Lieutenant Walters?" I asked.

"He took a blow to the head, but it wasn't fatal," Diana said. "Evidently Bigsby believed Johnny had gone off with you."

"Meaning he must have spotted Johnny this morning," I said.

"Sorry about that," Johnny said. "Lost my temper."

"Yes, although it did set off a chain of events that led to a successful conclusion," Kaz said.

"Yes. Bigsby confronted Walters, who told him where you were headed. Bigsby then knocked Walters out, put on his coat, goggles, and helmet, and took off on his motorcycle," Conan Doyle said. "The guards had just seen Walters on his machine, so they simply opened the gate and off Bigsby went."

"Walters told me Bigsby was enraged, almost insane," Diana said. "To see Johnny after he'd thought himself safe may have pushed him over the edge. He threatened to kill Walters if he didn't reveal where you were headed."

"Lieutenant Walters said the boy looked shattered when he heard you were headed to his mother's," Conan Doyle said.

"He must have known he was about to be discovered," Angelika said. "And blamed Johnny for it."

We filled them in on Mrs. Bigsby and her sad life. We went over the details of the case, which was helpful since I needed to write a report in the morning on much, though not all, of what had happened.

"Tell me how Bigsby set up the meeting with Brockman on the cliffs," Conan Doyle said.

"I think Brockman was giving Bigsby a chance to return the parts he suspected him of taking," I said. "Everyone agrees that Bigsby was helpful, and that Brockman liked him."

"And that the major did want to see the cliffs up close. Christmas morning was quiet on the base, and he must have mentioned it to Bigsby," Kaz said.

"Didn't you find a return railroad ticket at the murder scene?" Conan Doyle asked.

"Yes. I believe Bigsby planted it there. He could have easily purchased it on his way back from London. He picked up his bicycle at the train station, pedaled to the cliffs, and killed Brockman. He placed the ticket in the shrubs where it wouldn't blow away. Then took Brockman's car with the bicycle in the back, parked it at the train station, and biked to the base."

"It was a clever ruse to cast suspicion on someone who traveled back to London on Christmas," Kaz said.

"Bigby was clever," I said. "No one suspected that his devotion to his mother was a cover for transporting stolen parts to his attic workshop. He was in a perfect position to declare electronics like the Mandrel unit inoperable, then pilfer them once a replacement came in."

"And it must have been Bigsby who attacked you in the hangar, Billy," Diana said. "Harker confirmed they'd let Bigsby off at the mess hall. It was a short run back to where you were. In the darkness, no one noticed."

"It's sad that people had to suffer for Bigsby's vision of his future," Angelika said. "So many lives are already lost and ruined. Why add to that?"

"'It's a wicked world, and when a clever man turns his brain to crime, it is the worst of all,'" Conan Doyle said. "Or so my father had Sherlock Holmes say. One more thing, Sergeant

Adler. I've decided to recall Sergeant Miller from her exile at St. Margaret's, since it appears she had good reason to invade the men's barracks."

"That's excellent news, ma'am," Johnny said.

"Perhaps you'd like to tell Sally yourself," Diana said as she produced an envelope. "Here are her orders, and a forty-eight-hour pass for each of you."

"Thank you," Johnny said, his voice choked with emotion. "Sally will love to be back, I'm sure."

"Well, you go bring her back, but take your time about it," Conan Doyle said. "There's a staff car parked out front. You'd best be on your way."

"Is that my staff car?" I asked Diana after Johnny scurried off.

"You've heard of Lend-Lease, haven't you?" Diana said. Angelika held a hand across her mouth to stifle a laugh.

"Enough about stolen automobiles," Conan Doyle said. "We should let Angelika change into something less bloodstained and get back to work. There's much to do."

"I need to check on Constable Sallow and drive him back into town," I said to Diana as Angelika took her leave. "I'll see you later."

"For how long?" she asked.

"Harding said to meet him at SHAEF in Paris," I said. "But not tonight."

"Then we have tonight, which is all the time in the world," Diana said, and brushed my arm as she walked by.

"I shall drive Constable Sallow," Kaz said. "He may enjoy a turn in the Aston Martin, and you, after all, have kindly given your purloined vehicle to the cause of true love."

"And a damn good cause it is," I said as we stepped outside. I stopped to breathe in the cold air, letting it fill my lungs. We stood at each other's side and watched the settling sun send long shadows across the runways. Engines started up along the hangars. It was a clear night, promising punishment to steel, stone, and flesh in the hours ahead.

"It must've been tough seeing Angelika in danger," I said. "Not what we expected."

"No. Quite a surprise," he said as he took a step toward the sports car. Then he stopped and turned to me. "But what really bothered me was to hear her plead with Bigsby."

"You can't hold that against her," I said. "She must have been frightened."

"That never concerned me. No, it was because I understood she did it to lull him into a false sense of security," Kaz said. "It was a calculated plan, and I knew she would unleash certain violence upon the man. The knife was my gift to her, remember."

"She may have saved Sallow's life, if not her own," I said.

"Yes. The constable benefited from her quick thinking. But, Billy, what bothers me is that my sweet little sister has become a killer. She had to be, to survive in Poland. To save others. She's endured terrible brutalities and still overcame what the war did to her. But who will she be after the killing is over, and how will she survive the peace?"

"How will any of us?" I said.

Kaz held my eyes, then gave the slightest shrug. How could anyone know?

He climbed into the Aston Martin, started the engine, and drove into the night.

HISTORICAL NOTE

THE FULL HISTORY of electronic warfare during the Second World War is a fascinating story filled with breakthrough scientific developments, top secret hardware, and human ingenuity mixed with a hefty dose of deceptive guile. Radar jamming and the spoofing of German ground-to-air communications were all part of the life-and-death struggle for dominance in the skies above Europe. Mandrel, Dina, Airborne Cigar, Jostle, Jackal, and H2S were code names for the actual devices used in radio countermeasures work.

In researching this topic, I was surprised to learn of the extensive role played by German-speaking Jewish refugees. As my previous novel *Proud Sorrows* detailed the US Army's use of German speakers for interrogation purposes, this story shows how the British used the native-language skills of young refugees against the Nazis in the air war.

The RAF special operators aboard aircraft and the WAAF wireless telegraphy operators on the ground consisted of many former refugees as well as volunteers from all over the world who brought to bear their fluency in languages and their desire to play a role in defeating the enemy.

The character of Johnny Adler is based on Reuben (later "Ron") Herscovitz, a special operator who brought civilian shoes on each raid. When asked why, he replied, "My friend, if you are shot down, you will either be killed or taken to a proper prison camp under the control of the Geneva Convention. I am a Jew, and as the Herrenvolk would like to liquidate my race, I aim to get away from the wreckage as soon as possible. How can I possibly do that in heavy fur-lined flying boots?"

As there are stories of Jewish special operators being tortured upon capture, or in one case committing suicide after parachuting, Reuben's caution was well warranted.

As I researched radio countermeasures during the war, I stumbled across the fact that Jean Conan Doyle, fifth child of Sir Arthur Conan Doyle, was an intelligence officer with the RAF. I simply could not resist having her play a role in this story, given she is only two degrees of separation from Sherlock Holmes himself. Squadron Officer Conan Doyle administered the Y (Wireless Interception) Service facility at RAF Kingsdown outside of London, conducting work much as described in this novel. I did take the liberty of shifting her location to RAF Hawkinge, to take advantage of the proximity to the White Cliffs of Dover. Jean Conan Doyle served for thirty years in the Royal Air Force.

The war in Yugoslavia was a confusing mix of German and Italian occupation troops, local fascist allies, monarchists, Communists, and Chetniks. The mainly Serbian Chetniks under Draža Mihailović conducted significant guerrilla operations against the Germans early in the war, but heavy civilian reprisals led them to pull back and await a hoped-for Allied invasion. They were allied at one time with Josip Broz Tito's Partisan Army, but the alliance did not hold. Tito's Partisans were aligned with Stalin and the Soviet Union, and atrocities on all sides were common.

The Western Allies soon diverted all support to Tito, abandoning the Chetniks even as they worked to rescue downed airmen and shelter them at great risk. The Office of Strategic

Services organized operations based at Pranjani to bring in C-47s to an improvised airstrip.

Ultimately 417 Allied airmen were airlifted from Chetnik territory, of which 343 were Americans.

After the war, Draža Mihailović was arrested by Tito's newly established government. Despite support from Americans who had been saved by the Chetniks, Mihailović was found guilty of high treason in what was regarded as an unfair show trial. He was executed on July 17, 1946. His last words were: "I wanted much; I began much; but the gale of the world carried away me and my work."

George McGovern, three-term senator from South Dakota and the Democratic nominee in the 1972 presidential election, was a B-24 pilot during the Second World War. In December 1944 he did make the dangerous landing on the island of Vis, as described in this story. Coming in with one dead engine and another on fire, he safely landed on an airfield half the length normally required for a heavy bomber and saved his crew. For that feat he was awarded the Distinguished Flying Cross.

McGovern never publicized his heroism for political purposes. He did cooperate with author Stephen E. Ambrose, who wrote about McGovern's service in his book *The Wild Blue*. McGovern's understanding was that the book was about the air war in general, but when he saw how prominently he was featured, he declined to participate in any publicity events, shunning the spotlight. He was a man from another time.

ACKNOWLEDGMENTS

As always, I owe a debt of thanks to my wife, Deborah Mandel, who has listened to every line of this book read aloud. She also has done a diligent job of reading and commenting on the first draft with a precise editor's touch. As have first readers Liza Mandel and Michael Gordon, who provided important feedback and found those pesky, elusive typos.

I am very lucky to work with the highly professional and hardworking staff at Soho Press. They excel at everything from editing, book design, cover art, and publicity, and they all are a pleasure to work with.

My agents, Paula Munier and Gina Panettieri of Talcott Notch Literary Services, are the best guides I could ask for to navigate the world of publishing.

I owe so much to the dedicated booksellers at independent bookstores across the country. So much of the success of this series is due to their efforts. I also owe a debt of thanks to the many librarians who keep their shelves stocked with the Billy Boyle novels, making these stories accessible to so many people.

The same also goes for you, the reader, especially those who have been at Billy's side throughout this journey. You're why he's still here, and why there are more stories to be told.